Praise for the w

Just One Reason

I had a lot of fun reading *Just One Reason*. I enjoy diving into a traditional romance where I know exactly what I'm going to get, and then being delighted with a host of clever details that make the story feel fresh and brand new. This book checked all the boxes on my list of what I want in a good book.

-The Lesbian Review

I don't want to spoil things, but I was cheering this couple on and I wasn't disappointed. Communication happens and it is beautiful and sweet, but not without a splash of angst. This book gave me all of the feels and really hit a home run with thoughtful, meaningful dialogue.

-Digby M., NetGalley

This is the third installment of the Paradise Romance series. I have gotten so much entertainment out of these books. I love the characters and friend group. That while each story focuses on a new budding relationship, the same characters pop in and we see that they continue to progress in their respective partnerships. There is always so much more depth and satisfaction when the writer can put people through the ringer so that they come out on the other side shiny and happy. Overall, this is another great addition to the Paradise Romance series.

-Bookvark, NetGalley

All the Reasons I Need

One of the reasons I love *Three Reasons to Say Yes* so much is that Clevenger wrote such strong secondary characters in Kate and Mo. I fell for them almost as much as the main characters, so to have them get their own book I was excited. This is a story about two best friends since college that have a ton of chemistry but have never done anything about it. …If you are looking for a well written, angsty romance, look no further. This is an easy romance for me to recommend. I think with this series, Clevenger is at the top of her writing game and I can't wait to see what she puts out next.

-Lex Kent's Reviews, goodreads

This book is the second installment in Clevenger's Paradise Romance series. It's not necessary to read the first book, *Three Reasons to Say Yes*, to enjoy Kate and Mo's story… *All the Reasons I Need* is a thoughtful summer romance full of emotion. It let me imagine myself on a tropical beach, napping in a hammock, and sipping an exotic drink with a little umbrella in it. There's just something about beautiful sunsets and waves crashing on the beach that make falling in love seem easy.

-The Lesbian Review

Three Reasons to Say Yes

This is without a doubt my new favourite Jaime Clevenger novel. Honestly I couldn't put it down from the first chapter. …All in all this book has the potential to be my book of the year. Truly, books like this don't come around often that suit my reading tastes to a tee.

-Les Rêveur

…this one was totally my cup of tea with its charming relationship and family dynamics, great chemistry between two likable protagonists, a very convincing romance, some angst, drama and tension to the right extent and in all the right moments, and some very nice secondary characters. On top of that, the writing is technically very good, with all elements done properly. Sincerely recommended.

-Pin's Reviews, goodreads

This was a really easy story to get into. I sank right in and wanted to stay there, because reading about other people on vacation is kind of like taking a mini vacation from the world! It's sweet and lovely, and while it has some angst, it's not going to hurt you. Instead, it's going to take you away from it all so you can come back with a smile on your face.

Party Favors

This book has one of the best characters ever. Me. Or rather you. It's quite a strange and startling experience at first to be in a book, especially one with as many hot, sexy, beautiful women in it who, incidentally, all seem to want you. But believe me, you'll soon get used to it. ...In a word, this book was FUN. It made me smile, and laugh, and tease my wife. I definitely recommend it to everyone, with the caveat that if you don't like erotica you should probably give it a pass. But not only read it, enjoy it, experience it, also find a friend, or a spouse, or even a book buddy online to talk to about it. Because you'll want to, it's that great.

-The Lesbian Review

I've read this book a few times and each time changed my decisions to find new and inviting destinations each time. This is a book you can read time and time again with a different journey. If you're looking for a fun Saturday night read that's sexy and hot as hell then this book is 100% for you! Go buy it now. 5 Stars.

-Les Rêveur

The story is told in the second person, present tense, which is ambitious in itself—it takes great skill to make that work and for the reader, who is now the narrator, to really connect to the thoughts and actions that are being attributed to them.

Not all of the scenes will turn everyone on, as we all have different tastes, but I am pretty sure there is something for everyone in here. And if you do as you're told and follow the structure the author uses, you can dip into this book as much or as little as you wish. An interesting read with some pretty hot interactions.

-Rainbow Book Reviews

One Weekend In Aspen

Other Bella Books by Jaime Clevenger

Call Shotgun
A Fugitive's Kiss
All the Reasons I Need
Just One Reason
Moonstone
Party Favors
Sign on the Line
Sweet, Sweet Wine
Three Reasons to Say Yes
The Unknown Mile
Waiting for a Love Song
Whiskey and Oak Leaves

Spinsters Ink

All Bets Off

About the Author

Jaime Clevenger lives in Colorado with her wife, two kids, two cats and one golden retriever. She works as a veterinarian and is occasionally guilty of bringing cute furry projects home. On days off, her favorite thing to do is write but she also enjoys swimming, hiking, teaching karate, and reading. She loves to hear a good story—especially a love story—and is always ready to listen.

One Weekend In Aspen

JAIME CLEVENGER

BELLA
BOOKS
2021

Bella Books, Inc.
P.O. Box 10543
Tallahassee, FL 32302

Printed in the United States of America on acid-free paper.

First Bella Books Edition 2021

Editor: Heather Flournoy
Cover Designer: Kayla Mancuso

ISBN: 978-1-64247-227-1

Acknowledgments

Some stories get more TLC than others and this one got a lot of snuggles in its journey from idea to finished book. Thank you, Corina, for your patience when I complained, for your hugs when I needed them, and especially thank you for reading this story that one last time—and liking it. Knowing you're in my corner makes all the difference.

Thank you to my writer friends and beta readers for your encouragement, advice, and most of all friendship. Each of you helped me in so many ways: Laina, thank you for teaching me the importance of sticking with a story; Aurora, thank you for convincing me to go for the romance; Sandy, thank you for wanting this story and giving me a kick in the butt when I needed it; Rach, thank you for knowing what the story needed at just the right moment; Alix, thank you for putting yourself in the character's shoes and reminding me to think of how they would feel; Shawn Marie, thank you for being so positive throughout and for turning me on to a cool editor.

As for that cool editor…Thank you, Heather, for the push and for believing in this story. It was a pleasure working with you. Thanks also to everyone at Bella. I appreciate all that you do to get our stories out to readers. Lastly, thank you to the folks who read this story. I hope you enjoy it.

CHAPTER ONE

Emily Brookstone read the invitation again, then carefully folded the embossed paper and slid it back in the envelope. Of course Katherine had used expensive cardstock. The woman had class, that was for sure. It also came as no surprise that she'd included plane tickets. She'd taken care of all the details. All Emily had to do was say yes.

"You do realize you can't say no," Gianna said. "These Aspen weekends are legendary. You basically have to win the lesbian lottery to get an invite." The invitation had been delivered by courier that afternoon, and Gianna had paced around the apartment until Emily had finally opened it. She'd leaned over Emily's shoulder and read every word aloud with little shrieks of excitement. "God, I wish I worked for Katherine."

"No, you don't." Emily flipped the envelope facedown. "She's a tyrant. I do my best to stay out of her way."

"But she's a sexy tyrant. Who hosts sex parties." Gianna pursed her lips. "Are you honestly thinking of turning her down?"

Of course she'd decline. *Right?* "Going on that dinner cruise with her and her friends was one thing. But a trip to Aspen? And this isn't an offer to go skiing."

"No, this is an opportunity to have your fantasies fulfilled. Did you read that part? Come on, Em, you know this would be good for you. Eight women, one weekend, and all you need to do is come up with a little fantasy."

"Yeah, that's not intimidating at all."

"You have to go. Please?" Gianna gave Emily a pleading look. "I need minute-by-minute tweets on the whole thing."

"No."

"You haven't even considered it. Okay, forget about how much I want the scoop on this. You know it would be good for you."

Would it be good for her? Technically there was nothing to stop her from going. She had the time off—Katherine had made sure of that by booking her in advance for that particular weekend, then canceling but promising to pay in full. Logistics, however, were beside the point. She was not someone who went to sex parties. Just thinking about it made her lightheaded. And a little shaky. The fact that her client was the host made it even more absurd to consider, especially considering Katherine wasn't simply another client.

While she might be difficult to work for, Katherine had done wonders for Emily's business. She was ridiculously rich and well connected, and her lucrative referrals were the reason Emily could keep a limited client list. Besides that, she was beautiful and charismatic. Katherine had countless admirers, and Emily had been drawn to her, too, the first time they'd met. But she'd carefully kept things professional. The dinner cruise invite had caught her off guard. *And now this.*

"Katherine's never come on to me, but do you think…" Emily's voice trailed as she wondered if she wanted to finish the sentence.

"Emily, she's not inviting you to try and seduce you. This is about having sex with a bunch of other people. Ooh, I bet there's an orgy."

"An orgy?" How had she been invited to a party where an orgy was even a possibility? "Maybe you could go instead of me."

"Sure. Katherine won't notice the difference." Gianna stuck out her tongue. After a moment, she took a breath and her tone softened. "Em, you need this. I mean, I need it too—let's be real—but you need it more. This is a chance for you to put yourself out there and meet people."

"Maybe I could join a hiking club."

Gianna's eyebrows bunched together. "Since when do you hike?"

"My point is, I'm still getting used to thinking of myself as single. I haven't even kissed someone since Cass."

"Which is why you need to go to Aspen."

Emily shook her head. "I need to start slow. It's only been two months."

"Two months since you moved out, yeah, but how long has it been since you got lucky?"

"Too long." Emily didn't want to admit exactly how long. The lack of sex in her marriage hadn't been a secret, but seven years was flat-out embarrassing. "I can't jump back in the saddle at a sex party."

"You never told me you had a thing for cowgirls." Gianna's brown eyes sparkled mischievously. She picked up the envelope and rubbed it like a magic lamp. "One fantasy fulfilled. What should I wish for?"

"Don't look at me. With my luck, I'd wish for a cowgirl and end up with a pony."

Gianna laughed, playfully swatting Emily with the envelope. "So you do have a thing for cowgirls!"

"At this point I wouldn't turn one down. Leather chaps are hot."

"Mmm…So are nice tight jeans and a cowboy hat."

"Don't forget the rope," Emily added.

"How could I?" Gianna held the envelope up to her lips and kissed it. "I'll take a cowgirl, too, Genie. And make sure she's kinky." She looked back at Emily. "Now if only you could sneak me along in your luggage. Do you think this is at a lodge? Or is Katherine renting a house?"

"I'm not sure. She's mentioned she owns a ski cabin in Aspen—and a villa in Nice."

"Must be hard. San Francisco, Aspen, Nice. How do you pick? I think I'll take my sex weekend in Nice. Croissants and sex? Oui, oui."

Emily smiled. Despite their joking, her anxiety about the whole idea of a sex weekend hadn't gone away. "I still don't get why she invited me. I'm not like her—or any of her friends. I'm not some socialite. I don't have any connections. And at the moment, my life is such a mess that I'm sleeping on my best friend's couch."

Gianna tilted her head. "And loving every minute of it."

"Every minute. I really am grateful. *And* I promise I'll be out of your hair as soon as I can afford my own place."

"I'm only teasing. I like you here. Besides, you pay your share." Gianna paused. "I do worry about you, though. Cass did a number on your head, and even if you don't want to talk about it, we both know you're not over that mess. Aspen could be exactly what you need."

"Or it could be a total disaster."

"But think of the stories you'll be able to tell me after. All those sexy women. Bow-chicka-bow-wow."

Gianna jiggled her chest and Emily couldn't help laughing. She eyed the envelope again. "This is ridiculous…a sex fantasy weekend. Who does that?"

"Katherine." Gianna pushed the envelope closer to Emily. "It might be ridiculous, but I wasn't joking when I said it'd be good for you."

Emily slid the letter out and scanned the first paragraph again. The flutter of excitement she'd felt when she'd first read the invite zipped through her once more. But when she got to the second paragraph where it spelled out requirements for STD testing prior to the weekend as well as a statement on consent, she wondered who she was kidding.

"It's been seven years since I've had sex, Gi. What if I've forgotten how? And Katherine's friends are always these perfect women—beautiful, rich, confident. There's no chance they'll be bad at sex. Meanwhile, I'm...well...I'm me."

"You're beautiful too, and you know it." Gianna nudged Emily's chin up. "Maybe you're not like Katherine's other friends, but maybe that's the point. You're like the girl next door."

"I'm not just the girl next door. I'm the broke-ass girl next door. Which means, basically, I'm a charity case. Hey, at least I've got that going for me."

"What I meant, Miss Sarcasm, was that you're sweet. Sometimes you're even funny. And you're real. But I doubt any of that's why Katherine invited you."

"Why'd she do it then?"

"Are you kidding? You're gorgeous. Katherine probably looks at you and drools."

"That's gross." And Katherine definitely didn't drool. In fact, she was often so cool and distant it was hard to tell if she even liked her at all. "You really don't think this is charity?"

"Hell, no."

"But she knows I've been down since Cass and I broke up."

"Do you honestly think Katherine has sympathy sex? No. Way. In. Hell." Gianna punctuated each word with a jab at the letter. "This, sweetheart, isn't charity. This is the lesbian lottery. And the Emily I knew ten years ago would have taken one look at that invitation and circled yes. Then gone shopping for lingerie."

"You're right. Ten years ago I'd have jumped at any excuse to wear lingerie. But now—"

"You'd still look hot in lingerie. Probably more so. You've got bigger boobs." Gianna smirked, then added, "Want to talk about what happened to the only woman I know who could rock a lacy corset?"

Emily knew Gianna wasn't simply joking about lingerie. She'd changed after Cass, and maybe not for the better. But she didn't want to rehash all the ways she'd screwed up the past decade. Sure, Cass had been the one who didn't want sex after their first couple of years together, but she'd been the one who'd stayed long after it was clear the relationship was only platonic. "Can we say I got older and wiser? Lacy lingerie isn't that comfortable."

"Comfort isn't the reason we wear it. And you're not that much wiser."

"Thanks, Gi. I love you too."

"If you really loved me, you'd say yes. And then you'd tell Katherine to invite me next year." Gianna picked up the reply card and held it out. "You know you want to go."

CHAPTER TWO

Alex Murphy dropped into her seat in first class, sunglasses still on. She was not, despite the curious looks she got from the other passengers, anyone famous. The only thing she was trying to hide from was the glaring sun. She leaned across the empty seat next to hers and tugged down the shade. After a twenty-four-hour layover in San Francisco and too much partying at Katherine's house last night, jet lag had officially caught up to her. She stifled another yawn and closed her eyes.

No matter how many trips she took between Tokyo and the States, she couldn't get used to the time change. Fortunately, with the Sunito deal in the bag she had a week off to relax—a week in Aspen, at that. With luck, she'd spend most of that time either skiing or sleeping. Unfortunately, she'd been unsuccessful at getting uninvited from Katherine's annual sex weekend. At least she'd have the rest of the week to herself.

She could almost hear the crunch of snow underfoot and longed to be transported directly to the front door of her little cabin. Then she'd climb the stairs and tumble right into bed.

"Can I squeeze by you? I've got the window."

"Oh, sure." Alex straightened up. She'd slouched in her seat and stretched out her legs, taking up more than her fair share of space as she'd drowsily entertained the idea of sleeping through the flight. But one look at the woman passing inches in front of her and she felt like she'd had a shot of caffeine. She took off her sunglasses and ran her hand through her short hair, wishing she'd taken the time to glance at her reflection before hurrying from the shower to the waiting taxi.

The woman was beautiful. Not in a done-up sort of way, but in a natural way that caught Alex's attention all the more. Her outfit was simple—a cream-colored sweater, navy leggings, and leather boots. The sweater dipped low enough to hint at cleavage, and the leggings outlined her curvy hips while the boots hugged her calves.

It wasn't polite to stare, a distant voice reminded her. But a moment later she was drawn back and eyeing her as surreptitiously as she dared.

The woman's dark brown hair had a soft a wave to it, caught up by a clip at the low of her neck. Brown eyes were framed by long eyelashes. She didn't need mascara, and lip gloss seemed to be the only makeup she used. She'd sat down with her purse on her lap and was currently attempting to push her carry-on under the seat.

The case was clearly too large to fit, but she scrunched up her face and gave it a firm kick anyway. When it didn't budge after a second shove, Alex stood. "Can I put it up top for you? These little planes don't have as much space."

"Um, no. I can do it."

"Okay, but I'm already standing."

The woman bit her lip. After a moment's hesitation, she handed Alex her case. "Thanks. I think I overpacked."

"Better than underpacking." Alex swung the carry-on into the overhead bin and then dropped back into her seat. "It's a bummer to get where you're going and realize you don't have underwear."

The woman sucked in a breath. "I knew there was something."

"Seriously?"

"No. Not seriously." A smiled tugged at the corner of her lips. "I'm trying to joke so I don't freak out."

"Scared of flying?" Alex had been on more than one terrible flight into Aspen and didn't like the turbulence that came with flying low over the Rocky Mountains. She didn't blame anyone for taking sedatives or even drinking in the morning to take the edge off.

"I wish it were that." The woman buckled her seat belt and leaned back. She took a deep breath and let it out slowly as if she were indeed trying to calm her nerves.

"What is it?" Alex immediately regretted the question. Since when had she become the prying seatmate? "I'm sorry. Totally not my business."

"You're fine. I'm nervous about the trip itself, not the flying part."

"I get that. Is it a work thing?" Alex noticed the woman hesitate again and gave herself a mental kick. She held up her hand. "Sorry again. I'll stop being nosy."

"I don't mind. Really. But it's a little early in the morning…"

Alex glanced at her watch. "So should I ask you in an hour?"

The woman smiled. This time it was a full smile, and she was truly breathtaking. "I'm Emily." She stretched out her hand.

"Alex."

Although she wanted an excuse for more contact, Alex let go of Emily's hand after a brief clasp. Emily pointed to the ski magazine half sticking out of the seat back in front of Alex and asked, "Going to Aspen to ski?"

"I'm hoping to get some runs in, yeah, but mostly I'm going because I have a week off and I need to recharge. I've got a place there." No way was she going to fess up to her other plans. Admitting she was also going to a sex party would certainly end their conversation. "I'm guessing this isn't a ski trip for you."

"I don't ski. Give me a swimsuit over snow pants any day."

Alex imagined Emily would fill out a swimsuit in the best of ways and yet she'd still like to run into her on the slopes. Or at least the lodge afterward. "You could ski in a bikini. No one would judge."

"Maybe no one would judge, but I'm pretty sure my nipples would freeze off."

"I don't think that's possible." Alex's gaze involuntarily dropped to Emily's cleavage, but she quickly corrected the mistake. "Maybe you'd like spring skiing. Some days it's hot enough to be T-shirt weather when the sun's out."

"I'll keep that in mind."

Alex drummed her fingers on her knee. She'd promised not to be nosy, but now she was curious. Based on Emily's earlier response, she didn't think it was a business trip. If she wasn't coming to ski, the next likely option would be that Emily was meeting someone. But if that was the case, wouldn't she be happy about it?

"You're still trying to figure out why I'm going to Aspen, aren't you?"

"Maybe." Alex grinned. Emily's tone encouraged her. "People go for lots of reasons. Like to get a tattoo."

"Strike one. Try again."

"Or to attend their cousin's wedding."

"Strike two."

The first two guesses were only to break the ice. And from the way Emily was looking at her, it had worked. But now she wanted to take a real guess. "You could be going to see someone you met online. Maybe this is the first time you'll see him, or her, and you're nervous about it 'cause you don't know how it'll go."

"Is that your final guess?"

Alex couldn't tell if she was even close. Emily had a good poker face. Whether she went for women or not was still up for debate as well, unfortunately. "I think I'm going to wait and see if you drop any more clues before we land. Whatever you're doing, I hope you enjoy it."

"Me too."

Alex wanted an excuse to chat more, but when Emily reached for a magazine, she took the hint and found her headphones. The nature sounds deafened the noise of the engines and the chatter of other passengers but didn't stop her from thinking about Emily. She adjusted the cushioned headrest and closed her eyes, already anticipating a good daydream.

A moment later, Alex startled at a light touch on her thigh. She tugged off her headphones, suddenly hot under the collar and acutely aware of the exact location where Emily's hand had been. Fortunately, Emily seemed to have no idea how well reality had coincided with her imagination.

"Your seat belt." Emily motioned to Alex's waist. "I didn't want you to fall asleep and then have the flight attendant wake you."

"Oh, right. Thanks." How had she forgotten to buckle her seat belt anyway? She'd logged more miles than anyone else in her company, but apparently a beautiful woman was enough to distract her from the basics.

"Also…it's totally okay that you asked about my plans. It's a normal question. And I'm feeling a little silly being secretive about it."

"Don't worry. The secretive thing makes you seem that much cooler."

Emily shook her head. "I'm definitely not cool."

"We could argue that, but I'd need to know more personal information. Probably starting with what you're doing in Aspen this weekend."

Emily's smirk was perfect. Alex smiled back, holding her gaze and quite sure she could lose herself in those brown eyes. Katherine would call them bedroom eyes. She had a thing for women with dark eyes, and Alex didn't blame her one bit. *Seductive* was the word that came to mind…

In fact, Emily was exactly Katherine's type. Well, one of them, anyway. Alex considered the possibility that Katherine had recruited Emily for the weekend. She couldn't exactly ask if her secret plans involved a sex party, although that would certainly be a good reason for discretion.

"To tell you the truth, I don't think I should be going to Aspen." Emily glanced down at her purse. "But it's a little late to get off the plane."

"Can I try my last guess?"

"Go ahead. There's no way you'll get it right."

As much as Alex wanted to ask about Katherine's sex party, if it wasn't Emily's plan, she'd have a lot of explaining to do. Besides, what were the chances? Better to keep making Emily laugh rather than make her uncomfortable.

"You're on a top-secret mission to steal the world's best hot cocoa recipe. Everyone knows you have to go to Aspen for that."

"Strike three." Emily's eyes creased with her smile.

"But was it a good guess?"

"Not even close."

The tension had all but gone from Emily, and Alex counted it as a win. She didn't care if she'd made herself seem completely uncool. "Hot cocoa's not the only reason to come to Aspen, of course."

"Some people probably even come to ski." Emily's tone carried on the joke, and Alex was certain now they were in flirting territory.

"I'm sure someone's done that once or twice. They're missing out, of course."

"So where do you get the world's best hot cocoa?"

Alex opened her mouth and then promptly clamped it shut.

"Oh, right. It's a secret."

"It's not that. Well, it is, but…" Alex shook her head. "I was going to say my house, but now that sounds like a creepy way to ask someone out."

"I wouldn't say creepy. More like dorky."

Alex laughed. "I'll take dorky. Is this your first trip to Aspen?"

"Still trying to get clues?" Emily arched an eyebrow.

"Maybe. It's a fun town even if you don't ski. After you steal my secret hot cocoa recipe, there's a lot of places I can recommend you check out."

"How long have you lived there?"

"Technically, I don't live in Aspen. I've owned a cabin there for two years now, but most of the time it's rented out."

"Where do you live?"

"At the moment, Tokyo. But work moves me all over. My plan is to retire in Aspen."

"Already thinking about retirement?"

"If all goes well, I'm hoping to retire in five years."

Emily's eyes widened. "Either you make really good money or you're a lot older than you look."

"I'm thirty-nine. I won't make you tell me how old I look, though. Haven't slept in a while."

"Don't worry, you look great." Emily's cheeks reddened with a hint of a blush. "I think it's definitely the money thing and not some fountain of youth face lotion."

Alex laughed. "I do make good money. Not sure it's worth it in the grand scheme of things, though."

Emily pursed her lips, and Alex rethought her words. "Only people with plenty of money say things like money doesn't matter, right? That was a dumb thing to say."

"I can't talk. I'm in first class too. Though I didn't pay for my ticket." Emily looked down at her hands, clearly uncomfortable. Alex wondered if the unease was due to embarrassment, defensiveness, or something else entirely. She hadn't landed on an answer when Emily looked up and met her eyes. Whatever emotion had passed through her was carefully masked now. "Sounds like you have an exciting life. And I'm sure you work hard. Do you like it?"

"If you'd asked me when I started, I'd have said that I loved it. Now?" Alex shrugged. "Moving to a different city every year gets exhausting. I've lived in nine countries in the last seven years. I'm ready to paint the walls in a house I can live in for longer than a year. I know, not very exciting ambitions."

"But honest. There's gotta be parts you still like, though, right?"

"Plenty. I love learning new things. Every day there's something…A new way to get lost. New words to pick up. New people to meet. It's interesting for sure, but sometimes I want a box of Lucky Charms and no plans for the weekend."

"Lucky Charms and hot cocoa? You've got a sweet tooth."

"Would you trust someone's hot cocoa recipe if they didn't?"

Emily shook her head. "Do you want to know something funny? I'm actually a chef, and you've hyped this cocoa up so much that now I really do want the recipe." She held her hand up in the air. "But I solemnly swear I'm not in Aspen to steal your secret formula."

"Not sure I believe you. You might have to tell me what you're really doing this weekend."

"Nice try, but still no." Emily sighed. "It'll probably be a big bust anyway and I'll wish I'd come for hot cocoa instead."

"Would it be weird if I gave you my number?" Alex knew she was taking a chance, but what did she have to lose?

"In case I want the hot cocoa after all?"

"Okay, you're right. Too weird."

"Actually, it isn't…" Emily bit her lip. After a moment of deliberation, she reached for her purse. She took out a pen and a receipt from a parking garage and handed both to Alex. "Don't take it personally if I don't call you. I'm not sure what will happen this weekend. And I'm not usually brave enough to be the one who calls first."

Alex jotted down her number. She knew the likelihood of a phone call or even a text was slim, but her heart was partying in her chest all the same. She handed back the receipt and made a silent wish something would come of it. For all the women she'd asked out, this felt different. She wouldn't admit it aloud—she'd already made a fool of herself with the hot cocoa—but even if their weekend plans didn't align, their meeting felt fated.

Emily pointed to Alex's chest pocket, a smile playing on her lips. "Did you mean to steal my pen?"

"Oh, shit. Sorry." Alex reached for the pen. She stopped midway before handing it back, noticing Emily's name and number. "Emily's Catering and Personal Chef Services?"

Emily held out her hand. "Yes. I really am a chef."

"I swear I'm not usually a pen stealer, but this could come in handy."

"For when you need a personal chef?" Emily's look was skeptical.

"Or a caterer."

Emily dropped her hand and laughed. "All right, pen stealer. Keep it. But I'm not in Aspen often."

"Maybe that will change." Alex couldn't help but hope.

CHAPTER THREE

The turbulence over the mountains was no joke. Emily closed her eyes, but between the jolt she got every time the plane lurched and the conversation with Alex replaying in her mind, she had no chance of sleeping. When was the last time she'd flirted with a total stranger and then exchanged numbers?

Arguably, she hadn't planned on giving Alex her number. Yet it sent a thrill through her all the same to know her pen was in Alex's pocket. Their whole exchange felt like a warm-up to the coming weekend. Except Alex would probably be nothing like the women Katherine invited. She was easy; comfortable, even. A flirt, but not in an intimidating way despite how attractive she was.

Emily snuck another peek in her direction. It was impressive how fast she'd nodded off and slept soundly through even the worst of the turbulence. Clearly she was exhausted, but Emily wished she'd wake up so they could talk more. Not that anything would come of it. They were only sharing airspace for the rest of the flight, and then they'd never see each other again. Thinking about what-ifs was silly.

Forcing her attention back to the magazine she'd brought, Emily tried again to read the article. The problem was that Alex was everything she liked: masculine leaning, confident, funny… and good-looking. In other words, trouble. Again, Emily's eyes strayed. She could almost imagine running her hand through Alex's short, tousled brown hair. And that wasn't where her mind stopped.

Alex had a long, lean athletic build; a handsome, angular face; and gorgeous hazel eyes. To top it off, she was sharply dressed. She seemed to have come straight out of a business meeting in polished black shoes, charcoal slacks, and a lighter gray button-down shirt. No doubt she'd look good in gym clothes, too. *Or in nothing at all.*

A flush rushed up Emily's neck. One second she was admiring Alex's wardrobe and the next she was imagining what it would feel like to wrap her legs around Alex's naked waist. Conjuring up a sex fantasy about a perfect stranger was out of the ordinary to say the least. But, Emily reminded herself, that was exactly what the weekend was supposed to be about.

She thought of the way Alex's eyes had lingered on her and the moment when she'd realized that Alex was openly checking her out. Circuits in her body she'd given up for lost had switched on. When a pulse started in her nether regions, she almost laughed at how eager her body was. Eager, yes, but a little off course. After years not riding a bike, she needed something that came with training wheels, not a racing edition like Alex.

Still, her body's response was somewhat comforting. At the very least, it confirmed that she did in fact want to have sex again. She hadn't realized how much she'd missed the sensation of being wanted—and of wanting someone else.

When she'd been with Cass, she hadn't let herself even think about other women. After the breakup, she'd had no emotional energy left to even consider dating. But she had no reason to not let her mind fantasize about Alex now. Maybe Gianna was right. Maybe she needed this weekend more than she realized.

Alex rustled awake when the plane took a big dip. She straightened up in her seat and rubbed her eyes. A moment later the plane lurched again.

"There's that turbulence," Alex murmured. She looked over at Emily. "Welcome to the Rockies."

"Is it always like this?"

"Whenever there's a storm," Alex said. "I'm thinking there's gonna be a few more hiccups."

Right on cue, the plane dipped again. Emily wasn't sure if she should be relieved by Alex's anticipation of the turbulence or worried about a possible storm. She pushed open the window shade, and the sight of total whiteout made her breath catch. Mild uneasiness was replaced with actual fear.

"How can the pilot even see through this?"

Before Alex could answer, the plane abruptly tilted upward and then turned hard to the left. The pilot's voice came on over the speakers a moment later.

"Folks, we've got a little weather pattern up here that we didn't anticipate. The good news is, if you were coming to Aspen to ski, looks like you're going to have plenty of fresh powder." The pilot chuckled. "We're going to circle around and try a second approach. The seat belt sign is going to be on for the duration of the flight. I wouldn't try to stand up if I were you. Face-planting never makes anyone look good."

When the intercom switched off, Alex looked over at Emily. "Gotta love a pilot with a sense of humor."

"I think in this case I'd take smart and serious."

"Don't worry. This happens all the time."

"You sure?"

"Completely."

"Okay." Emily turned her gaze back to the magazine she'd been pretending to read for the past hour. Staring out the window and fretting about a plane crash wouldn't do her mounting anxiety any good. The turbulence had eased now that the pilot had taken them higher, but Emily knew they'd have to go through it all over again once they'd finished circling back.

"It doesn't feel right that it's morning again," Alex said, setting her watch.

Not many people wore a watch anymore—unless you counted those little wrist computers—but Alex's had an old-fashioned look of something that had been passed down and needed to be wound every day. Rather than make her seem low tech, it only made her seem more dashing.

"Where are you flying in from?"

"Tokyo. But I spent last night at a friend's house in San Francisco and my time zones are completely whacked." Alex nodded at Emily's magazine. "So, how *do* you have the world's best orgasm?"

"I'm sorry, what?"

Alex pointed at the headline of the article and Emily felt her cheeks flush. She snapped the magazine closed. "I honestly wasn't reading that article."

"You get the magazines for the pictures?"

Emily rolled her eyes, but her cheeks still burned. "It's not that kind of magazine. I'm sure it says something about exercise and drinking plenty of water. And Kegels. Doesn't that pretty much cure everything?" She smiled, hoping she could pull off pretending to be cool despite being mortified.

"Kegels?" Alex laughed. "I guess I should give that a try. You know, you don't have to close the magazine on my account."

"I was closing it on my account," Emily said.

"So you're not going to read it?"

"No." *Especially not with you looking over my shoulder.*

"But what if there's some secret that neither of us know? Aren't you curious?"

"I'm curious about a lot of things." Emily rolled the magazine into a tube and pushed it into the seat pocket.

"You have better restraint than I do," Alex joked.

Emily didn't know how to answer. She couldn't remember the last time she'd been that embarrassed. While being turned on.

Static crackled on the intercom and the pilot's voice came through the speakers once more. "Well, folks, apparently the storm is getting worse down there. Air traffic control is advising against another attempt at landing. I hate to say it, but we're being diverted to Denver."

A collective groan went through the cabin. Alex made a clicking sound with her tongue but didn't seem all that surprised.

Maybe for her it wasn't a big deal, but Emily had no idea how she was going to get to Aspen now. If it was a proper storm, she doubted there'd be any chance at another flight that day and she couldn't afford to rent a car to drive from Denver to Aspen. Maybe she could pay for a rideshare, but it occurred to her that she didn't even know Katherine's Aspen address. The itinerary only included a note about a driver picking her up at the airport and a number to call when she arrived.

She glanced over at Alex, all of her questions tumbling through her mind at once. "You don't look all that shocked."

"Been through this before. Is this going to mess up your weekend plans?"

"I don't know. Maybe." Emily had half a thought to finally admit everything. "Wonder how long the storm will last."

"The forecast yesterday mentioned a quick-moving cold front, but you never know." Alex leaned back in her seat. "Can't do anything about it now."

Within minutes of Alex's eyes closing, she was asleep. Emily doubted it at first, considering the noise in the cabin of everyone talking and the flight attendant's announcement after the pilot's, but the muscles of her face were completely relaxed and she was in fact softly snoring. Probably that was for the best. If Alex had stayed awake, Emily might have confessed her weekend plans.

* * *

Alex didn't rouse from her slumber until the wheels hit the tarmac. The moment she opened her eyes, the memory of her seat companion, the storm, and the change in airports hit her along with chagrin that she'd nodded off. Again. Only sheer exhaustion gave her that superpower. She glanced over at Emily, wondering if it would be weird to apologize for any possible drooling, but she was scrolling through her phone. The airlines icon was at the top of her screen and Alex guessed she was trying to find a flight from Denver to Aspen.

Whenever a freak storm came up, the chances of finding an open flight were virtually nil but telling Emily as much might be overstepping. She pulled out her own phone and quickly tapped the app for a car rental service. One of the perks of a job with travel was that she rarely had any trouble securing a rental car—even at the last minute. In a few clicks, she had an SUV with snow tires reserved.

The stewardess spoke over the intercom, giving information for rerouting to Aspen and connecting flights and baggage claim. When Alex looked over at Emily, it was clear she wasn't happy. Her jaw was clenched and she was scrolling through flights with an expression that bordered on a glare. If suggesting she abandon hope for a flight into Aspen in the next forty-eight hours was overstepping, then proposing they share the drive most certainly crossed a line.

As soon as the plane rumbled to a halt at the gate, the other passengers in first class stood up. Alex eyed Emily again. It was ridiculous to consider driving over four hours in a snowstorm with someone who was basically a stranger. Still, the idea nudged her again.

"It was nice meeting you," Alex said, standing up.

"You too. Maybe we'll see each other again sometime." Emily shook her head. "Actually, I guess that's probably unlikely."

"You never know. I travel a lot. We could randomly have seats next to each other again. I also have your number." Alex tapped the pocket where she'd put Emily's pen. "Who knows when I'll need a caterer?"

The almost-smirk on Emily's face buoyed Alex's spirits. Nearly enough to ask about sharing the drive. She got up to open the overhead bin and pulled out Emily's carry-on, then set it on the seat she'd vacated.

"You didn't have to get that down, but thank you."

"You're welcome." Alex eyed the short line filing toward the door. She had no reason not to step into the queue, but she hesitated and glanced at Emily again. "I may have accidentally noticed you were looking up flights. Did you find one?"

"There's nothing until Sunday night. I don't get what they expect everyone on this flight to do. Wait here until then? Take a bus? Actually, I can't even find a bus. Tried that already." Emily exhaled. "Can't find a rideshare either—at least not for under three hundred. I'm not sure what I'm going to do. Anyway, I'll figure it out." She smiled, but it was clearly forced. "What's a little more adventure, right?"

The other first-class passengers had exited and now everyone in economy was squeezing past. Alex stepped out of the way and back into their row, leaning somewhat awkwardly over Emily's suitcase.

"This is probably crazy, but do you want to share a ride with me? I've already got a rental car lined up."

Emily looked from her phone to Alex and then to her luggage. "That's generous, but…"

"We're both going to Aspen anyway." Alex tried not to sound too hopeful. A long car ride in crappy driving conditions wasn't exactly a promise of fun times. But still. She wanted Emily to say yes.

"You sure you don't mind?"

"Not at all."

"I can pay for gas or split the rental fee."

"Or you can keep me awake." Alex gave her a wry smile. "I'm sorry about dozing off earlier. Hope I didn't drool."

"No drooling. You did snore, but it was kind of cute."

Snoring was most definitely not cute, but the fact that Emily had dropped the word made Alex even happier they had an excuse for more time together.

"I was impressed by how fast you fell asleep. You didn't even wake up when we went through that second cloud bank."

"I barely slept last night," Alex admitted. "I really could use company to keep me awake on the drive to Aspen."

"How long is the drive?" Emily held up her phone. "I'm going to try sending another text to the person I was supposed to meet at the airport to let them know I'll be late."

"Four hours if we're lucky." As soon as Alex said it, she wondered if Emily would back out of their arrangement. A four-hour drive was typical in good weather, but with the snow it could certainly be longer. "But first we have to get out of the airport and into the rental. Denver's always a zoo when there's a storm. I'm guessing it'll be late afternoon when we get to Aspen."

"You sure you're okay being stuck with me that long?" Emily asked.

"It'll give me time to try and figure out what secret thing you're doing in Aspen."

A smile edged Emily's lips. "I appreciate the ride. A lot. And I'm still not telling you."

CHAPTER FOUR

Maybe it was the altitude. Or the company. Whatever it was, Emily had finally stopped worrying about the sex party. All her usual concerns had slipped away for the moment too. She felt strangely free. And like she was exactly where she was supposed to be—which was odd, considering stuck in traffic in a snowstorm had not been on her list of weekend expectations.

"We're going to lose this station pretty soon," Alex said, plugging her phone into the car's USB outlet. "Want to find some music for us?"

"Sure." Emily scrolled through the list of artists thinking Alex's tastes weren't so different from hers, then wondered which was her favorite. Over the past hour she'd come up with plenty of questions but had stopped short of asking each time. She didn't want to distract Alex from the road, and all of her questions seemed to be ones she'd ask someone she was on a date with.

When the local Denver station crackled out, she pressed the button on the dash switching from the radio to Alex's phone and pulled up the playlist entitled "Favorites." That was one way to get her question answered.

The first song was a hit by The Pretenders that Emily had loved in high school. As soon as the first chord played, Alex looked over at Emily. "Of all the music on my phone, you picked this one?"

"It's your playlist. If you're trying to keep your identity as a cheesy romantic a secret, you shouldn't make a favorites list that headlines this song." Emily laughed when Alex shot her a pained look.

"I'm not secretly a cheesy romantic."

"You sure about that? Even in my darkest hour, you wouldn't stand by me?" Emily winked when Alex looked her way and then held her hand over her heart and sang the rest.

"Okay, maybe I'm a little bit cheesy."

"A little?"

"Hey, you know the words to this song, too," Alex pointed out.

"Don't tell anyone." Once upon a time Emily may have been a cheesy romantic. Then she'd been introduced to reality. Still, the song was good. She started singing again and her heart skipped a beat when Alex joined in. Not only did Alex know how to harmonize, she had a gorgeous warm alto.

"You're a good singer," Emily said.

"Even better in the shower when I really belt it out," Alex joked. "So are you."

"My high school glee club was serious business."

"You were in glee club?"

Emily laughed. "That's by far the most enthusiastic response I've ever gotten to admitting I was a glee club nerd."

"Oh, I don't believe for one minute that you were a nerd."

"Jazz hands?" Emily waved her hands in the air.

Alex shook her head. "Still not a nerd."

The Cure's "Friday I'm In Love" came on next. "I love this song. Haven't heard it in ages."

"Apparently you need to hang out with cheesy romantics more often."

"Maybe." Emily heard the flirty tone in her voice but didn't care. She started singing, pushing herself to go for each note. Now that she'd admitted she'd been in a high school show choir there was no reason to hold back, especially when Alex joined in for the chorus.

The song ended, and Alex looked over at her and smiled. "We sound pretty good together."

"Yeah, not too shabby. But don't start doing jazz hands."

"Why not?" Alex's fingers danced on the steering wheel playfully.

Emily shook her head. She shouldn't be considering what else Alex's hands could do, but she was considering it all the same.

"You're thinking I should leave jazz hands to the professionals, aren't you?"

"Maybe I am, but I wouldn't say it." At least she could still banter. But she didn't chance another look at Alex in case her blush showed. Fortunately, there was no way Alex could know she'd been fantasizing about how her hands would feel.

Who was she kidding, thinking she was ready for a weekend with eight other women? She got embarrassed and hot thinking about Alex's hands touching her when sex wasn't even on the table.

The next song on the playlist wasn't as familiar to Emily, but Alex seemed to know all the words and bopped in her seat as she sang.

"Who is this?"

"Alicia Keys."

"I like it," Emily said.

Alex grinned and started singing again. As soon as the song ended, Emily clapped and Alex pretended to bow. "You should've been in glee club."

"I wouldn't go that far. But I do love singing."

"Me too. I miss it." Emily sighed. "I haven't sung much since high school."

"Why not?"

"Life gets in the way, you know? I'm not a real singer anyway. I only joined glee club because my parents insisted I do some after-school activity and I hated running. I figured no one would make me run the track in glee club."

"Seriously?"

Emily nodded. "Fortunately I fell in love with glee club."

"What about it did you love?"

"The dancing...the singing...being up on stage. All of it. Now I can't imagine doing anything like that." It wasn't only the being on stage part. Aside from busting moves solo in the kitchen while she cooked, she hadn't danced for almost as long as she hadn't sung. The two were definitely linked.

"Why can't you imagine it? You're really good."

"Well, there's not exactly adult glee clubs."

"You could join a choir. Or sing in a band."

Emily shook her head. In fact, she had been in a band in college, but all of that was years ago and they'd never been good enough to do more than practice in the garage of the guy with the drum set. She'd joined a community choir, too, but quit a few months in because Cass liked to spend evenings together.

"You've got a look on your face like maybe I said the wrong thing..."

"I was thinking about things I should do more often."

"Any chance eating pie is on that list?"

"Pie?" Emily narrowed her eyes at Alex. "Has anyone ever told you that you're a little quirky?"

"No. Never. Weird, yes. But I prefer different."

"Well, you are different." That was an understatement but actually more accurate.

"There's a little café about a half hour up the road with amazing pies. I was thinking maybe we could take a lunch break there? The café is right before we cut off the main highway. When we get on the mountain roads, there won't be many chances to pee."

"Sounds perfect."

"Good. It's hard to get pie in Japan. I called this bakery one time to see if they'd ship to Tokyo."

"They said no?"

"Yeah, can you believe it?"

Emily smiled at Alex's mock indignation. She stopped herself from saying Alex should call her next time she had the craving. It was ridiculous to entertain the idea of someday making her a pie considering they'd have to say goodbye as soon as they got to Aspen, but she wanted to anyway. And she was confident enough in her pies to promise she wouldn't disappoint. "What's your favorite pie?"

"Apple. Pecan's a close second. Then strawberry rhubarb." Alex clicked her tongue. "And now I really want pie."

"I make a damn good strawberry rhubarb pie," Emily said. "In fact, I won a blue ribbon at the state fair when I was fourteen for that particular pie."

"I've got it." Alex smacked the steering wheel. "You're coming to Aspen for a pie contest."

Emily laughed. "Keep guessing."

* * *

The bell over the door chimed as they entered the little café. An older woman with a gray bun and a red apron tied at her waist looked up from her book. She waved them in. "Have a seat anywhere you like. The storm's kept most sane people home."

"Good thing we're not sane," Alex murmured.

The woman heard and laughed. "Good thing indeed. Coffee?"

Alex glanced at Emily, and when she nodded, said, "Yes, please. Two."

"Two coffees coming up."

They settled into a booth with a window view out to the parking lot. Aside from their rental, only two other cars were in the lot and both had windshields covered in snow. Fortunately, most of the snow falling on the roads was melting fast.

Emily picked up one of the menus. "I'm not sure if I should order breakfast or lunch."

"I'm going with pie," Alex said.

"That's all?"

"And an order of fries."

"No fries in Tokyo either?"

"Oh, you can find them, but they aren't home fries like you get here." Maybe a chef wouldn't be impressed with the food, but Alex's mouth was already watering.

"Home fries and apple pie do sound good…but that's a lot of time in the gym."

"Calories drop right off at this elevation," Alex promised.

"I don't believe you."

"You shouldn't." Alex winked. "But come to the dark side with me anyway?"

Emily shook her head but set the menu back in the holder. "I'll worry about calories on Tuesday. After this, do you want me to drive for a while?"

"This is only the beginning. There's gonna be a lot more snow up ahead. And when the temperatures drop it'll be sticking to the road more."

"I'm good at driving in snow."

Before Alex could ask how Emily had gotten that experience, the waitress arrived with their coffees. She took the order for a shared plate of fries and two slices of apple pie, then convinced them to add a scoop of vanilla ice cream. Alex's taste buds salivated the moment she promised to warm up the pie.

"I'm guessing you're not originally from San Francisco," Alex said. "Not if you're good at driving in snow."

"Not originally, no."

"Where'd you grow up?"

"Northern Minnesooota, don't-cha-know."

The sudden Minnesota accent was adorable. "Can you keep talking that way?"

Emily laughed. "Not on your life."

"Minnesota's a long way from San Francisco."

"In a lot of ways." Emily bit her lip. She was quiet for a moment, and Alex wondered what she'd left behind.

After a moment, Emily continued. "I figured out I was gay in high school. That didn't go over so well in my little town and I knew I couldn't stay. Fortunately, I got a scholarship to a college in California."

"I bet there's a lot more to that story."

"There is. But that's all I'm up for talking about." Emily sipped her coffee, then kept her hands wrapped around the mug as she looked over it at Alex. "Where'd you grow up?"

"Right here. Or close enough." Alex took a sip of her coffee, then mirrored Emily's over-the-mug stare. "Any other questions?"

"Several." Emily's eyes narrowed. "I'm deciding which ones to ask based on what I want to answer in return. I don't think you'll let me off only asking you."

"You're entirely right. Choose wisely."

Alex wondered if Emily could sense how much she loved a challenge. It had been a long time since she'd met someone who turned on her head as much as the rest of her, but the likelihood of anything happening between them was practically nonexistent. She had to keep a handle on her libido.

Forcing her body to focus on something other than what Emily's lips would feel like against hers, she took a slow sip of her coffee. "While you think of your questions, I'll answer your earlier one. Yes, you can drive for a bit. I could probably use a break—I'm still on Tokyo time. But mountain roads can be tricky."

"There aren't many mountains in Minnesota," Emily said, apparently not taking any offense at Alex's warning. "If I get nervous, I'll let you take back over. I know when to say I need someone else to be in charge."

Emily's tone wasn't suggestive, but the look in her eyes struck a chord that reverberated. Arousal jetted through Alex's body. She swallowed, reminding her body that this wasn't a hookup. *Time to scale back the flirting.* "Hopefully I'll be as good a DJ as you were."

"I have no doubt you'll be perfect."

Was there a hidden innuendo in Emily's words? While Alex was debating a response, the fries came, perfectly crisp and still hot from the oil. Then came the pie—warm as promised and with vanilla ice cream melting on the golden crust.

"Oh, this smells amazing," Emily said.

Alex unrolled her silverware from the paper napkin. "Just wait. It's gonna taste even better." She forked a bite into her mouth, then closed her eyes and moaned. The cool smoothness of the vanilla ice cream warred with the flaky buttery crust, and the warm cinnamon apple filling tied everything together.

"That good, huh?" Emily smiled. She took a bite herself and made a very similar sound. "Okay, you're right." She took another bite. "I make good pies, but this might be better than mine."

"I wouldn't mind judging that contest."

Emily's eyes sparkled. She seemed about to say something in response, but the waitress reappeared at their table.

"Anything else I can get for you two lovebirds?"

Emily's mouth dropped open. Alex scrambled for what to say. "Uh, no. Thanks. We're good."

The waitress looked from Alex to Emily. After a too-long beat, she said, "I'm so sorry. I'm usually good at knowing who's coming in as a couple, but…"

"It's fine," Alex said quickly.

"Completely fine," Emily agreed.

The waitress clicked her tongue, murmuring another apology as she set the bill on the table. "If you need anything else, holler. I'll be in the back cleaning up."

As soon as she'd gone, Alex said, "Sorry. That was awkward."

"Why are you apologizing?"

"Well, I get read as gay all the time. And obviously I am. So if a woman's with me, I mean, not that you are *with* me with me, but maybe she can tell I like y—" Alex clamped her mouth shut. *Shit.* If she'd been trying to make the situation more awkward, she was succeeding. Royally. "What I was trying to say is I'm not sure you're used to people assuming that you are, and if you're not—"

"Okay, stop." Emily reached across the table and touched the back of Alex's hand. The contact sent a warm current through Alex's body.

Emily's lips turned up in a little smile. "You're cute when you're nervous."

Alex's heart raced. She barely resisted turning her palm up to clasp Emily's hand and had to remind herself to breathe.

"I may not be as obvious as you," Emily continued, "but I'd rather be misread as your date than misread as straight."

Emily pulled her hand back, breaking the contact and leaving Alex unsteady. Emily's words repeated in her head: *"You're cute when you're nervous."* Sure, they'd been flirting, but plenty of people flirted only for the game of it—even if they weren't available. But now, after that comment, at least she could be reasonably sure that Emily was into her.

"Are you single?"

Emily touched her left ring finger as if in the habit of checking that her ring was still on. The move was quick, maybe even unconscious, but when Alex's gaze followed her move, she seemed to realize what she'd done. "I just broke up with someone."

"Someone whose ring you used to wear?"

Emily nodded.

"I'm sorry."

"Don't be. It was my decision."

Alex hesitated, realizing how little she knew about Emily. She'd been either married or engaged and had broken things off. But what had happened? And how recent had it been?

"Sometimes being the one to end things makes the breakup even harder."

Emily again touched her ring finger. "You're right. There's more guilt, anyway. Most of my friends congratulated me when I told them, like they were impressed I'd finally done something they knew should have happened ages ago. It only made me feel worse."

"How'd your ex take the breakup?"

"Well, when I first told her I was done, she started screaming that I was making the biggest mistake of my life. Then the next day she asked me to apologize. Everything was turned upside down, and I did feel terrible, so I said sorry. Which she took to mean we weren't breaking up. So then I had to do it all over again a week later. She kicked me out of the house, froze our bank accounts, and *then* called everyone we knew to tell them I'd broken her heart."

"Sounds like she took it well."

Emily tilted her head as if unsure whether Alex was being sarcastic. Then a smile edged her lips. "Exactly. It was total mess."

"Total fucking mess."

"That too." Emily laughed, and the sound seemed to be half release, half nervous tension. "Honestly, I figured she'd be happy about ending things. We'd grown apart in so many ways." She shook her head and then held up her hands. "Anyway. Now I'm here. I probably shouldn't have told you all that, but...oh well."

"It's good to talk about things. We hold too much in trying to seem perfect. And I really am sorry. No one deserves to go through that."

"Thanks." Emily took another deep breath followed by an even longer exhale. She reached for a fry and wagged it at Alex. "Your turn to not be perfect. Clearly you know how it feels to break up with someone. What's your worst breakup story?"

Alex instantly thought of Rhonda. She was embarrassed to fess up to her part in their breakup, particularly considering how things had imploded, but she knew she needed to return the favor of honest admissions. "So, this story isn't going to make me look good, but I'm going to tell you anyway."

Alex swallowed and forged ahead. "I was dating this woman for a while who had a lot of trust issues. Like, she wanted a key to my place after our first date. She liked to show up randomly. Said it was to surprise me, but I knew she was checking up on me...She'd come to my work for spontaneous lunch dates. Even asked for my passcode for my phone. I'm pretty open, so I didn't think about it at first, but my friends kept saying it wasn't right.

"Anyway, we had other problems and the relationship wasn't going so well. I knew I needed to break up with her, but I didn't want to hurt her feelings. Tried dropping hints, not returning phone calls, that sort of thing."

"Uh-oh. I'm getting nervous."

"Yeah. I should have seen it coming." If the sex hadn't rocked her world at the time she probably would have, but she'd only been twenty-three. Not old enough to know she could have sex that good with women who were also sane. Of course, she didn't need to tell Emily that part. "Anyway, I finally told her it wasn't working for me. She didn't respond for a few days and then she showed up at my house with this box."

"Do I want to know what's inside?"

Alex wasn't entirely sure she wanted to tell Emily, but she'd gotten this far in the story. "Turns out, she was convinced I'd been cheating. So…she'd collected all of my sex toys and taken them to get DNA swabbed."

"You can do DNA tests on sex toys?"

"I don't know, honestly, but she said she did. And she had plenty of money. Could've paid someone for anything she wanted. Mostly I was pissed that she hadn't asked me. She'd scoured my place while I was at work for every little bottle of lube, every dildo, every vibrator."

"This lady was off her rocker."

"Right, but I didn't know it until that moment." Admittedly, there had been plenty of red flags and she'd chosen to ignore them. "Anyway, when she confronted me, I told her I hadn't cheated but it was over. She lost it. Yanked open the sliding glass door on my balcony and started throwing sex toys."

"No way!"

"Yes way."

Emily started to laugh. "I'm sorry, I shouldn't laugh."

"It's fine. Honestly, it was so weird it was funny. I lived on the third floor, and about a minute after she'd emptied the box, my downstairs neighbor started singing 'It's Raining Men!' I went out onto the balcony and looked down and there's this rainbow array of dildos in the parking lot."

Emily clapped her hand over her mouth as she laughed. She shook her head, then fell back against the cushions of the booth laughing harder.

"I know. Right?" Alex chuckled too. "I swear I didn't cheat."

"Oh, I believe you. Besides, the evidence cleared you on that one." Emily wiped tears from her eyes. "I do question your judgment on picking that particular girlfriend."

"Hey, yours froze your bank accounts. Mine only went after the dildos."

Emily laughed again. "Okay, maybe we both have terrible judgment." She sighed, then said, "I needed that laugh. So do you think we learned our lesson?"

"If not, there's always apple pie."

Emily held Alex's gaze, a smile still playing on her lips. "Thank you. For listening. And for having a story that makes me feel better about my disaster."

"No problem."

"I'm glad we met."

"Me too." Alex scooped up the last of the pie on her plate. "And I'm glad we had pie." She smiled, then popped the bite into her mouth. She savored it, trying to hold the apple and cinnamon flavor as long as she could. She wanted to do the same with the whole day.

CHAPTER FIVE

After their stop at the café, the drive was quiet. Not because Emily didn't have a hundred things tumbling round in her head but because the roads were worse than she'd expected.

It had been a long time since she'd driven in snow, and hairpin turns on steep roads were a different thing altogether. She had to focus nearly all her attention on simply following the track the cars ahead of them had left—nearly all her attention, since it was impossible to not think about Alex. Or how good it had felt to touch her hand.

For the most part, Alex kept quiet. She sang occasionally but softer now, as if she didn't want to disturb Emily's focus on the road. If only she knew it was too late for that. The stop at the café had triggered a whole rampage of thoughts. And feelings.

Emily had more questions than ever for Alex. What foods did she like as much as pie? Had she grown up skiing? What was it like to be a queer kid in Colorado? What was her family like? And how long had she been single? As good-looking as she was and as much as she flirted, Alex couldn't have gone long without a girlfriend. Unless she liked being single…

"How are you doing?"

"This is harder than I remember," Emily admitted.

"Want me to take a turn?"

Emily considered turning down the offer, but a semi sprayed the windshield with icy muck at the same moment. The wipers took a second to clear the sludge and she sucked in a breath. "Actually, that'd be great."

They came to a summit marker and she pulled off to the side. Ahead, the road curved downhill. They'd been climbing in elevation for so long Emily was surprised by the change, and even more surprised that the snowfall seemed lighter.

"How is the storm better up here?" The clouds even seemed to be clearing, and peeks of sunlight shone in the sky with splotches of crystal blue. On either side of the highway, the snow glittered.

"It's probably a lot colder," Alex said. "Ready for this?"

As soon as Alex opened the door the icy wind blasted inside. They hurried to switch sides, Emily wondering why she thought Aspen in February would be fun in the first place. When they were settled back in the car, Alex tapped the dash. "It's a balmy three degrees out there."

"In other words, too cold for snow."

Alex nodded. "But this storm's supposed to move through quick. It might not even be snowing in Aspen anymore."

* * *

Alex was right. By the time they rolled into town there was no sign of the storm save several feet of pristine snow. Fluffy white frosting covered every car, every rooftop, and every tree, but the afternoon sun cast enough light to make everything sparkle.

"As much as I don't miss snowy winters, this is kind of beautiful."

"Kind of?" Alex pointed to the mountain ahead of them.

With the blue sky above and the pines dotting the sides, the snow-covered peak was truly breathtaking. "And it's three degrees."

"It was at the summit. Now it's warmed up to fifteen. You brought a good coat, right?"

"I'll be fine. I'm not here to ski." Emily didn't want to admit that she no longer had a "good" winter coat. Once she'd left Minnesota, she hadn't had an excuse for anything that would keep her warm in subzero temperatures.

"Is it a salsa dance competition?"

"No. But good guess." Alex had clearly given up trying to figure out what she was actually doing for the weekend. Now she was only giving ridiculous guesses to put Emily at ease, which made it as sweet as it was funny.

"Really? Am I close?"

"Not at all."

Considering how many hours they'd been in the car, they seemed to get to the Aspen airport too fast once they passed through town. The truth was she wanted an excuse not to leave Alex's company. She didn't have one.

"Thanks for the ride. You sure I can't chip in for gas at least?"

"I'm definitely sure. You bought lunch. And you kept me company."

Convincing Alex to let her pay for the lunch hadn't been easy, but she'd managed that and decided not to push for more. "Well, thank you, again. I know this probably sounds crazy, but I'm glad there was a storm."

"Me too."

Alex parked at the curb and then got out to grab Emily's luggage. Emily considered hugging her, then decided that would be awkward, so instead extended her hand. Alex clasped it, a quirky smile on her face.

"Is shaking hands weird at this point?" Actually, it felt weird to Emily as well.

"A little. But I like weird."

"I like weird too." They both let go at the same time, and Emily felt a flush hit her cheeks. She could almost imagine stepping forward and kissing Alex. How much she wanted to do exactly that rocked her.

"I feel bad that I stole your pen." Alex looked down at her feet. "Should I give it back?"

"I want you to have it."

"Does that mean I can call you sometime?"

"I'd like that," Emily said without hesitation. She didn't know what, if anything, would come from Alex calling her, but she knew she wanted to hear from her again. She didn't want this to be goodbye forever. "Or maybe I'll call you first. Actually, I'd probably text. I'm better at texting."

"I'll take texting."

"Maybe I'll even text you tomorrow. Don't want to leave town without stealing that hot cocoa recipe of yours."

"I knew you were after the hot cocoa." Alex chuckled, looked back at the rental car and then back at Emily, clearly not wanting to leave. "I know I already said this, but I'm glad I met you."

"Same." And she didn't mind hearing Alex say it again.

Alex opened her mouth as if about to say something, but Emily's phone rang, interrupting her before she could. They both looked at her purse. The location of the loud ringing was easy to pick out.

"That's probably the person you're supposed to meet here. The hula dancer for that hula dancing competition you're doing this weekend."

"Probably." Emily's heart settled in her throat. What if Alex was the person she was supposed to meet this weekend?

"Anyway. See ya around." Alex raised her hand and a moment later was heading for the black SUV. As much as Emily wanted to stop her, she didn't say anything. What could she say?

Alex got in and started the engine but didn't rush to pull away from the curb. When she looked back at Emily, everything around them seemed to go quiet. Emily held Alex's gaze, wondering what would happen next if she simply got back in the car and asked Alex to take her wherever she was going.

The phone rang again, and Emily finally looked away to answer it. She needed to let Alex go. They were strangers who'd spent a day together. Nothing would come from wishing for more.

* * *

As hard as it was leaving Emily at the airport, it was even harder pulling into the empty garage. Alex sat in the car for a minute, eyeing the empty passenger seat. Emily had been an unexpected burst of brightness, but now that she was gone, reality invaded.

In a week, she'd be back in Tokyo. Starting anything didn't make sense. She wanted to call Emily right now, but the most they could have together was what they'd already had—a random connection with a stranger. She'd had too many of those to count. Their day hadn't been the start of something that would last. Nothing ever did.

Besides, Alex was nearly certain that Emily was in Aspen to meet someone. Probably a new girlfriend. Someone she'd met online maybe. Given her recent breakup, that made the most sense, as would her being a little embarrassed by it and not wanting to admit it to a stranger.

Alex grabbed her suitcase and let herself in. Thanks to the property manager who looked after the house, the heat had been turned up and the whole place smelled like freshly baked cookies.

Waiting on the counter was a plate of snickerdoodles wrapped in cellophane with a note taped to the top. *"I could be free tonight if you want to meet for a drink—or more. Happy to have you back in town. ~ Jorie."*

Jorie was the property manager, and there was no doubt she was interested in the "or more" part. They'd slept together once and had exchanged texts back and forth a handful of times since. Another short-term connection that wasn't going anywhere.

When they'd first met, Jorie had mentioned a boyfriend, but after only one drink she'd practically climbed into Alex's lap. Either she'd broken things off with the guy or they had some agreement now. All told, it had been a fun romp, and as nice as a repeat might be, Alex wasn't in the mood. Her thoughts were too caught up on Emily despite how she rationalized why she needed to forget about her.

With one last look at Jorie's note, Alex picked out a snickerdoodle and headed upstairs. The bedsheets were turned down and a nudge of guilt settled in at the sight of a heart-shaped chocolate Jorie had placed on her pillow. Alex took off her shirt and tossed it in the hamper, thinking of the last time she'd been in Aspen. She hadn't been with Jorie then. Or even in her own bed. She'd spent all her time at Katherine's.

When was it? *Late August.* Katherine had complained about having to wear clothes. Aside from that, Alex didn't remember anything else—other than the sex. They'd fucked like bunny rabbits who didn't really like each other but had too much damn chemistry to ignore. As usual.

Their problem was never sex. It was everything else. Alex had tried to start a conversation about exactly that last night. But Katherine had sidetracked her. She'd stroked her toe up the inside of Alex's leg and interrupted midsentence to say she was in need of a good fuck, and could they talk after?

Of course, they both fell asleep after, and then Alex had to leave before Katherine woke because of the early flight. Katherine had scheduled the flight and even bought her the ticket, but she'd arranged to fly out later herself with her girlfriend. Madison didn't care who Katherine slept with. If she did, it would make things easier.

Still, Alex was resolved to have the conversation about ending things with Katherine. The problem was that she got thrown off track whenever Katherine was right in front of her. All the reasons they shouldn't have sex, or even kiss, flew from her mind. But the reasons were there all the same.

She took off her pants and Emily's pen tumbled from her pocket. When she leaned down to pick it up, the imprint caught her eye. She read the number thinking how easy it would be to call.

Emily was exactly the type of woman she wanted to meet. Someday. If only today had been that day. She climbed into bed and shivered until the down comforter held in enough of her body heat for her to relax, longing for someone to be snuggled up against. That was the one problem with sleeping in her own room. Whenever she spent long in the house she actually owned, she felt lonely.

Most of the time she didn't think about being alone. It wasn't hard finding company when she wanted it. But all the one-night stands in the world didn't fill the hole that was a lack of an emergency contact. Maybe finding someone who wanted to build a life together was too much to hope for, but sex with women who didn't want more had begun to feel like a waste of time. *Great time to decide that.* She closed her eyes and nestled deeper into her bed. *Right before you go to a sex fantasy weekend, you realize meaningless sex makes you feel hollow. Nice one, Alex.*

CHAPTER SIX

The black SUV that pulled up to the curb was not Alex's. The fact that Emily wished it were was a problem. But not one she wanted to deal with at the moment.

She waved to the driver—recognizing him from the picture Katherine had texted—then picked up her carry-on and rolled her suitcase outside. The reality of what she'd signed up for, and all the nervous energy that went with it, had returned within minutes of Alex leaving. Arguably, it was different now. Yes, she was nervous, but it was more of a nervous excitement at the possibility that she'd actually go through with something as crazy as sex with a perfect stranger.

Alex had reset something in her body. Things she would have thought impossible only yesterday seemed like good options at the moment. *Like having sex with someone you met that morning and drove through a snowstorm with*. If only Alex was going to the party.

Katherine had sent a text a few minutes after Alex had dropped her off with info on her driver and a note about someone named Shay who'd be at the house. The storm had thrown a wrench in everything. All the flights that hadn't been rerouted were delayed. Katherine was stuck at SFO, still hoping to get to Aspen that night, but she'd sent a group email pushing the start of the weekend back to Saturday night. Emily, admittedly, was relieved. All she wanted to do was settle into her room and relax. *And think about Alex.*

"You here to ski?" the driver asked.

Emily shook her head. He didn't seem to notice her answer, promptly launching into a description of the ski conditions as they pulled away from the airport. He'd apparently memorized the weekend's expected weather, and without missing a beat asked if she needed a recommendation for a ski rental. Because it didn't matter, Emily nodded, and he began a rundown of all the local ski shops.

After they left the tiny airport behind, the dark green pines gave way to vistas of snow-covered mountains, along with a dusky blue sky. Emily snapped a picture and texted it to Gianna along with a message: *Maybe I've died. This could be the road to Heaven.*

Gianna immediately texted back: *I've always thought Heaven would be a big sex party.*

Emily laughed out loud and the driver glanced at her in the rearview mirror. Not wanting to explain, she shook her head then texted back: *How was your day?*

Gianna's response brought another smile: *Girl, I know how to have fun—spilled half a bottle of olive oil. Been mopping for the last hour. Now spill the deets on the sex party. Any hot women?*

Emily tapped her phone case, deliberating whether she should tell Gianna about Alex. Finally, she typed: *Long story short, it's been a heck of a day here too. Haven't gotten to the party yet. Had to fly to Denver first. Then had a five-hour drive in a snowstorm.*

Gianna: *Oh honey that's awful. Maybe you'll meet someone who makes it worth it.* A string of little fire emojis followed.

Emily felt a pang of guilt not mentioning Alex. Nothing about the day had been awful. In fact, the whole trip felt worth it already. Even if the weekend was a bust, she had Alex to fantasize about.

The driver pulled off the main road onto a snowy side street. They slowed to a crawl over the unplowed sections and then crossed a short bridge, slowing even further. Below them a river snaked through patches of ice, snow heaped on either side of its banks. For all Emily said about not liking the cold, the sight did bring an unexpected wave of nostalgia for Northern Minnesota.

The SUV pulled into a driveway on the other side of the bridge. An iron gate and an impressive rock wall blocked the entrance to a huge house right next to the river. Not a house, a mansion, Emily corrected. She took a deep breath, wondering again what the hell she'd gotten herself into.

The driver didn't waste time getting her suitcase unloaded. She tipped him with the wind whipping away her words of thanks, and then pulled her coat up to her throat.

Before the car had even pulled away, the front door opened and a twenty-something dyke with a mop of blue hair that cascaded over one side of her face gave her a wide smile. "Welcome to the illicit sex den. I'm Shay. I'm guessing you're Emily?"

Emily nodded. At least the welcome was warm. Shay hurried out to help with her suitcase and then ushered them inside.

"Katherine told me to not to scare you off. She also told me not to call her house an 'illicit sex den.'" Another big smile.

"Not scared off yet." Emily smiled back in earnest.

The warmth of the house enveloped her. She took a minute to get her bearings, shaking off her coat. Vaulted ceilings in the foyer boasted several skylights and natural light filled the space. On one end, a wide spiral staircase led up to the open second floor, and on the other a short hallway led to a living room with a huge fireplace complete with a crackling fire. Two closed doors led off from the foyer to what Emily could only imagine. *Secret sex rooms?*

Despite the cold outside, Shay was in a T-shirt and shorts. "Did you get the email? Katherine and Madison's flight got delayed. So did Ava's. All three of them are getting in late tonight. Nicola's flight is still on schedule last I heard—she should be here in a half hour or so—but otherwise it's only me and Lara here. We both got in yesterday before the storm. Lara came early to ski. I just came early. That sounds like a sex joke, but it isn't." Shay grinned. "I hate snow, so I told Katherine to make me the official greeter. Do you ski?"

"No. I was worried I'd be the only one." That wasn't all she was worried about, but Shay's youthful excitement made her wonder if she was silly for being nervous about the other part.

"We're possibly the only two in all of Aspen who don't ski. Or snowboard. By the way, I use they pronouns."

"Cool. I use she/her."

"Want me to show you to your room? This place is kind of a maze." Shay picked up Emily's bag and started for the stairs. "I told Katherine she needed to give us maps, and she told me it was a good thing I was cute." They looked over their shoulder and gave Emily a wry grin. "So how do you know Katherine?"

Emily should have anticipated the question would come up and she wished she'd prepared an answer. Knowing Katherine's friends, it was unlikely any of them "worked" for someone else. Usually they were entrepreneurs or CEOs or, even more commonly, philanthropists.

Shay stopped at the top of the stairs waiting for her. Emily had paused midway right in front of a stained-glass mosaic of two naked women, their limbs entwined. For the moment it was a good excuse to admire the artistry, but tracing the lines with her eyes did more to distract her than help focus on an answer to Shay's question.

She could simply say that she'd met Katherine at a gala for the symphony. That much was true. She'd gone to the gala with Cass back when they were still pretending they were happily married. Cass was used to hobnobbing with the likes of Katherine and had gushed about her afterward. She'd pushed Emily to send Katherine a note about her personal chef services. One week later, Emily had landed the job of cooking for Katherine three nights a week. But only saying they'd met at the symphony rang false. The truth was probably better.

"I work for her. I'm a personal chef."

"Really?" Shay tilted their head. "You're Katherine's chef? What's that like? I bet she's hard to please."

Emily doubted Shay had much experience being anyone's employee—or anyone's employer. One look and she guessed Shay was a trust fund kid which landed them in the philanthropist category of Katherine's friends. Mostly it was because they seemed too carefree. Even their flip-flops looked pricey.

"Katherine and I don't interact much, honestly. I try to do all the food prep and cooking when she's out of the house so I'm not in her way. Then I stock up her freezer with meals for the week and leave dinner on the table. That's my usual for all of my clients."

"That sounds perfect. Bet your clients love you."

"They do. And I love my job." That's what made the work worthwhile. She loved to cook for people who loved her food. Of course, it was also a job and she needed the money more than ever. She sometimes felt guilty for the prices she charged, but she had so many requests she had to choose her jobs somehow. Having all of her assets frozen by Cass had made her especially thankful for clients who could pay top dollar.

Admittedly, Katherine was one of her most difficult clients, and there were definitely times she didn't love working for her. But she wasn't about to tell Shay that.

"I'd love my own personal chef. So you live in San Francisco?"

"I used to. I moved in with a friend a few months ago, so I'm across the bay now. In Oakland." Emily wondered how different her world was from Shay's. Could they even fathom worrying about the monthly expense of bridge tolls?

She caught up with Shay as they started down a corridor. After passing a handful of closed doors, Shay stopped. "I think this one's yours." They looked across the hall at a different door and gave a decisive nod. "At least pretty sure."

"I wonder what it's like having a house with so many rooms. I'd probably forget which one I'm sleeping in."

"I'm sure Katherine's slept in all of the beds at one point or another. If you have a houseful of sexy guests, why not? Wonder who she picks first…"

Emily felt all her earlier uncertainties return. She was definitely not ready to sleep with Katherine. "We get some say in that, right?"

"Oh yeah. Nothing happens here if you don't want it to. Guess it would be awkward with you and Katherine since she's kind of your boss, right?"

"She's more of a client. I'm an independent contractor."

"Well, there'll be plenty of other people, so don't worry."

Unfortunately, her mind was stuck on one stranger. Emily walked past Shay and into the room, thankful the curtains were drawn and the light was muted. She pulled back the shade and glanced out at the gathering darkness. She couldn't help wondering what Alex was doing tonight.

She let go of the curtain and eyed the rest of the room. Whoever had furnished the place had travelers in mind. Along with a luggage rack there was a nondescript dresser, a writing desk and chair, and a king-size bed. A hotel room had about the same amount of personality, but maybe that was for the best. Maybe she could pretend to be someone else in a space where nothing was familiar or even notable. She'd forget the room, maybe even forget herself.

She glanced again at the bed and envisioned pushing the covers back to welcome a lover. The thought of making the mattress bounce promptly made her feel ridiculous. One thing was certain—if she had any sex at all this weekend, it was going to be awkward at first. Hopefully she'd get over the awkward part and have fun too.

Shay hefted Emily's suitcase onto the luggage rack. "Did you get the email with the revised schedule?"

"I did. I'm still getting used to the idea of a schedule for a sex weekend." Emily pictured a line of women conferring over their phones about their rendezvous points.

"You know Katherine. She's a planner. The first fantasy weekend I went to was at her place in Nice. Everything was timed down to the hour. Everything." Shay grinned. "But there's only nine of us this time. We'll have dinner together tomorrow and you'll meet everyone. The hat thing's after dessert. You know about the hat thing, right?"

Shay hesitated for about a second and then continued. "It's my favorite part. You write your fantasy down and put it in the hat. Then Katherine picks which fantasies happen, and you get paired off. Unless you want a threesome, of course."

"And the sex part happens right away?"

"Well, you have until Monday night, but most people don't want to wait. If there's planning involved or you want costumes, you might have to set up a different time." Shay paused. "You look worried."

"Maybe a little." Or a lot.

"It's your first time. That's normal. But I promise you'll have a blast. Everyone here is amazing. In bed and out."

That was definitely part of the problem. Everyone was probably a pro where sex was concerned. At least Shay wasn't intimidating. They looked like they were in their mid-twenties but even so likely had several years' more experience than Emily where sex was concerned.

"Any rules I should know about? Since it's my first time, I don't want to step on any toes."

"Not really. Well, the big rule is consent. Especially if you end up in Katherine's room."

"Why?"

"Think floggers and spreader bars. Spanking boxes. You know."

Emily definitely did not know, but she nodded anyway.

"Course not everyone's into that sort of stuff, but if you like kink, definitely check it out. There's also a room down in the basement that has all that and more—everyone calls it the private room but anyone can use it. By the way, Katherine's meticulous about cleaning the toys. She's got a whole system, so make sure you put everything back in the right place when you're done." At Emily's questioning look, Shay quickly added, "The system's easy to figure out. You'll see the signs. And, I should also say, if you get into a situation and need a way out, don't be shy about speaking up. Like I said, consent is huge around here."

About a hundred thoughts popped into Emily's mind all at once. She didn't want to seem like a total novice, but her experience with BDSM was limited to books. As much as it turned her on to think of trying some of things she'd read about, real life was different.

"What sort of fantasies do people usually put into the hat?"

"I wouldn't say there's anything usual. That's what makes it fun. There's always a little kink but plenty of other stuff too. I'm into role-play. Give me costumes and props any day."

"What sort of role-play?"

"Last time I went for pirates. Swashbuckling, you know?" Shay made a slash with a pretend sword and grinned. "I wanted costumes to make it more real, so I met with Nicola—she's the one who volunteered to do it with me—and we talked about that part beforehand. We sorted out what we were going to wear and the scene that morning over coffee."

"That sounds fun." Even if Emily couldn't see herself having sex in a costume, it sounded less intimidating than a spreader bar.

"Right? Nicola totally got into the role. The sex was hot, but you can't take yourself too seriously when you're shouting 'Arrr!' all the time." Shay laughed. Their phone buzzed and they quickly glanced at the screen. "And look who's here."

Shay held up their phone with the image of Katherine's front porch. An attractive black woman with big sunglasses and a puffy pink parka raised her hand to knock on the door. "Meet Nicola. Not only is she hot as hell, she's got an amazing British accent."

Shay pressed a button and spoke into their phone. "Hey, Nicola. I'm on my way." They looked up at Emily. "Since dinner tonight's canceled, I'm thinking of having pizza and salad delivered for the four of us who made it. Sound good to you?"

Emily nodded. Perfect, in fact. A pizza party with three strangers—two of whom liked to dress up as pirates and have silly sex games—sounded way less daunting than what sprang to mind at the mention of floggers and spanking boxes. Maybe she wasn't completely out of her league.

CHAPTER SEVEN

Twelve hours after promising to lie down for only a minute, Alex woke to her phone buzzing on the nightstand. She pushed back the covers, fumbling for the phone as a blast of cold air assaulted her chest.

After unsuccessfully trying to turn off the alarm, she realized the buzzing was from a text. A series of texts, in fact. All from Katherine. She squinted at the words and then gave up, deciding she needed water first. Her mouth felt like she'd been chewing on cotton balls all night.

Once she'd downed a glass of water and brushed her teeth, her belly grumbled, reminding her that last night's dinner had only been a cookie. Considering that she'd had pie and fries for lunch, yesterday's whole food day was a bit of a loss. She rubbed her eyes, grimaced at her reflection, and then went back to bed to read Katherine's texts.

Most of the texts had actually been sent the night before but she'd slept through all of those. This morning's text was simple: *Skiing today?*

Alex ran her hand through her hair and settled back on the pillows. Among the texts from last night was an invitation for Alex to join a foursome in progress in Katherine's room, then a rundown of who was there and what was happening. She yawned, wondering if something was wrong with her that she didn't regret missing the foursome, then went back to the last text and typed a reply. Skiing she'd always say yes to, and after yesterday she needed some exercise.

Hopefully the sunshine would kick the fog of jetlag, and even if moving anywhere fast sounded like a bad idea now, she knew she'd thank herself later. She added that she'd meet Katherine at the ski lodge, and then ran through all of her missed texts one last time.

She hoped that somewhere between all the notes from Katherine she'd find a text from Emily, but in her gut she knew Emily wouldn't be reaching out to her. Still, she'd hold out hope for the rest of the day. Emily had said she was only in town for a few days, so if by the evening she hadn't sent any note, Alex would take that as her answer. Chances were good she was already enjoying the company of whoever she'd come to Aspen to meet. As much as Alex wanted to send a text anyway, she didn't want to be pushy and she definitely didn't want to mess anything up for Emily.

* * *

Emily roused herself awake. Light filtered in through the blinds, and from the sound of voices in the hall, she knew others were awake. As much as she wanted to spend another hour in bed, she pushed herself to get up. Being sociable was the least she could do.

After dinner last night, she'd opted out of dessert and drinks and gone to bed early. It wasn't because she didn't like the company. Nicola, Lara, and Shay were all perfectly sociable and welcoming, but the day had caught up with her and she wanted some time alone to decide whether or not she'd try texting Alex. The what-ifs that might follow said text consumed more of her thoughts than worries about the sex party.

Once she'd showered and dressed, she stepped out of her room. Across the hall from her, one of the bedroom doors was open. She noticed an overturned suitcase and clothes spread out across the room, but the bed itself was still carefully made. She guessed that whoever's room it was had slept somewhere else, then wondered how much she'd missed going to bed early.

She headed downstairs, thinking of coffee. Shay had mentioned a well-stocked kitchen but she hadn't actually seen it last night. In fact, she hadn't seen much of the house aside from her room and the dining area where she'd been with the others.

From the foyer, the house split in two directions. On one side was a living room, a bar, and a rec room with a pool table. On the other side was the den, the formal dining area, and, she'd been told, the kitchen. She started down that direction and then paused at the entrance to the den. French doors led out to a courtyard. Someone had shoveled a path through the snow to a hot tub sheltered by a handful of snowy evergreens.

"The hot tub's clothing optional," Nicola said, coming up behind Emily. "I tested the temperature first thing this morning. Quite nice." She smiled. "But I recommend sandals for the path. It's nippy out there. And, good morning."

"Morning." Emily smiled back.

Nicola was slender and tall like a model. And entirely stunning. Her accent made her seem like royalty, but she'd said last night that she was a CFO or CEO—Emily couldn't recall which—of some corporation in London. How Emily had landed at the same party as someone like her was a mystery.

"Want to join me for breakfast? We're the only two home at the moment. Shay went to pick up Ava from the airport and the others are all skiing."

"I'd love to."

They passed through the dining room and Nicola continued. "Ava's also a virgin. A sex party virgin," she quickly corrected. "Katherine makes sure there's at least two of you."

Emily was relieved to know that she wouldn't be the only one who was new, even if the others were going to refer to them as virgins. Shay had dropped the word last night, and Emily had cringed but tried not to show it.

As soon as they reached the kitchen, Emily stopped in her tracks. With the skylights overhead and the bank of windows, the space managed to feel both warm and inviting but also airy and light. It was the view, however, that took the cake. A circle of snow, probably covering a lawn area, was surrounded with bare-branched aspen, and beyond this the yard sloped down toward the river. Snow-covered mountains towered in the near distance.

"Wow."

Nicola looked back at her. "Lovely, isn't it?"

"I think I'll move in. I'm sure it's in my price range," Emily joked. She was used to nice kitchens. Despite the fact that none of her clients liked to cook, they all had gorgeous kitchens. But this view was over the top.

A brown shape moved between the aspen trees, and a moment later she realized it was an elk. Nicola noticed it too, and they both watched as the huge animal ambled its way down to the river. When it lowered its head for a drink, two little brown birds jetted out of a nearby brush. The elk didn't pay the birds any attention, calmly taking its fill from the icy brink. The elk looked back at the house as if it knew it had an audience, then flicked its short tail.

"I had my doubts, but I have to admit Aspen is beautiful." Especially if you're rich and can afford a place like this, Emily added silently. She turned back to survey the rest of the kitchen. "I could spend all day right here."

"I don't blame you and I don't even cook. Katherine mentioned you're a chef."

"I am, though I'm happy to have a break from cooking this weekend. But with a kitchen like this I might have trouble completely holding back."

"No one will mind if you break down and bake something. Especially if there's chocolate involved."

"I'll keep that in mind." Maybe if she didn't meet anyone she wanted to have sex with, she'd drown her sorrows here. In a pan of brownies. It didn't sound awful.

"How do you feel about a spa date?" Nicola asked. "I thought all of us who aren't skiing might go for massages and pedicures. Shay's talking to Ava about it too."

"Shay's getting a pedicure?"

"I can be persuasive."

Emily didn't doubt Nicola's persuasive abilities one bit. "That sounds really nice." *But probably way too expensive.* She hesitated, then decided she couldn't hold back from everything. She had saved up some money for the trip, and other than yesterday's lunch with Alex, she hadn't spent anything yet. "I'd love to. Maybe afterward I'll whip up some brownies."

"Careful. Katherine might convince you to move in," Nicola teased.

"With this kitchen, I might say yes."

"I'm sure she'd happily let you stay in exchange for cooking. Among other things." Nicola raised her eyebrows, a smile dancing on her lips. "Katherine doesn't offer anything without conditions, as I'm sure you know."

Nicola's tone continued the joke, but Emily couldn't ignore her subtle warning. Shay's comment about Katherine sleeping in everyone's bed was still on her mind as well. By accepting the invitation to Aspen, had she unintentionally agreed to an unspoken quid pro quo? Emily dismissed the question as soon as it occurred to her. Worrying about an expectation that she'd have sex with Katherine was ridiculous. Considering the number of women she'd seen come through Katherine's house, there was no shortage of volunteers eager to satisfy her. She didn't need to manipulate anyone, or any situation, to get laid.

"This house is beautiful, and so is Aspen. But I like being an independent contractor."

"I don't like to be tied down either. Literally or figuratively." Nicola seemed to consider her words and then added, "Although depending on who's holding the rope…"

Emily laughed. She liked Nicola's directness and considered admitting to her that she'd never been tied up herself. Then again, there was a lot she hadn't done.

"It's been a while since I've had sex." Emily regretted speaking up almost as soon as the words were out of her mouth but forced herself to push on. "I'm not sure if I'll be any good at regular sex, let alone…" Her voice trailed off as she searched for what to say that wouldn't make her seem even more naïve.

"Let alone kink?" Nicola guessed.

"That. Yes." Emily paused, gathering courage. She wished she didn't feel nervous talking about sex. "I want to try new things but I'm not sure what I'll like, and it's probably silly but I'm worried I'm not good enough at the basics to be here at all."

"Definitely silly. But I understand." Nicola opened a cupboard and got out two coffee mugs. "You want to find someone you feel comfortable with. Then only do what feels right. Don't push yourself too far the first time."

First time. As if sex parties were going to be a regular thing. "Thanks for the advice. I might have more questions later."

"Give me a minute to get our tea, and you can ask away."

CHAPTER EIGHT

Alex slid off the lift then angled around a clump of snowboarders. Madison and Katherine hadn't waited for her, but she thought she might be able to catch up to them anyway. If she didn't, they'd already planned to meet at the lodge after the last run of the day and she'd see them there. She'd considered asking them for advice on whether or not she should call Emily.

Over breakfast at the lodge that morning, she'd mentioned that she'd met someone the day before. Despite Madison's eager questions and even Katherine's "Do tell," she'd only shared an abbreviated version, promising a full rundown later. They'd wanted to get an early start on the mountain and the line for the gondola had been long. But aside from the twenty minutes they'd shared that morning, she'd been alone with her thoughts. And throughout all the day's runs, one question had stubbornly bounced back and forth in her mind: Was everything with Emily only a chance meeting that she should let go of? Or was the universe trying to tell her something?

If only she knew what Emily was doing in Aspen. Whether or not she was meeting someone here would change everything. Alex would give up thinking about her if she knew that much at least. Otherwise, as impossible as any relationship seemed— even only a friendship—she couldn't let go of wanting it.

She balanced her skis at the crest of the slope, then squinted into the sunlight glistening off the snow. Above the mountains, the sky was a deep, clear blue—the shade of blue only a Colorado sky could be. She'd missed it more than she'd realized and took a long moment to let the view sink in.

Halfway down the slope, she spotted Katherine's neon green ski jacket and Madison's bright pink beanie. Thanks to the fresh powder and the long holiday weekend, the trail below was packed, but with a little racing and some fun carving she knew she could catch up. She tugged her goggles into place, then leaned forward and pushed off with her poles.

Crisp air braced her cheeks as her skis flew over the snow. The whistling sound helped to quiet her mind for a moment. Other than speeding toward the neon green and pink markers and a few jumps to challenge gravity's pull, she didn't think at all. Katherine had once joked that skiing was merely a graceful way of falling down a possible avalanche. Alex had argued there was a lot more involved—technique, power, speed—and yet she wondered if Katherine's simple description didn't have more merit.

Ahead of her, a snowboarder lost his balance trying to angle around a tree. Alex watched him tumble, slowing her own speed to avoid hitting him. Another skier whipped around her side. Clearly not paying attention, he slammed right into the snowboarder. Alex slid to a stop.

"You two okay?" she hollered.

The snowboarder took a minute to sit up on his butt, cussed, and then raised a hand, middle finger up. The skier let out a string of curse words but quickly righted himself too. Alex shook her head. They'd be fine. She wasn't going to hang around to referee two grumpy guys.

"Sounds like you're both good, then. See ya at the bottom." She jetted off, hoping she still had a chance of catching Katherine and Madison.

* * *

"There you are," Madison said. She'd already taken off her skis and now promptly stepped forward to kiss Alex.

Alex smiled. "What's that for?"

"We thought we'd lost you."

"And we weren't even trying." Katherine's blue eyes sparkled. She'd come up behind Madison and was also out of her skis. Katherine slipped an arm around Madison's waist. "We didn't see you after Powderhorn. What happened?"

"I took a break for lunch. Got my ass whipped on all those turns and then took a fall in Garrets Gulch."

"You had lunch alone? Oh, honey, why didn't you text one of us?"

Madison's concern was sweet but completely unnecessary. "Turns out I can eat alone," Alex said.

"Next time, you send me a text. I'll find you some company even if it isn't me."

"Thanks?"

Madison patted Alex's cheek. "Oh, you'd thank me." At thirty-one, Madison still had a baby face, but she swore it was her dimples that got her carded. Her strawberry blond curls and the fact that she often dressed like a teenager probably didn't help. But she was plenty mature. In fact, she was often the one putting Katherine in her place. Along with the angelic look and the sweet Southern accent, she had a playful little devil on her shoulder.

"Alex is naturally a loner." Katherine met Alex's gaze and added, "Unless she has a girlfriend. But that's always temporary. Any word from that woman you met yesterday?"

Alex shook her head. She knew from Katherine's tone that she was curious about the rest of the story. Despite the fact that Katherine was always in open relationships, she had a jealous streak that she admitted herself. This, however, seemed like innocent interest. Alex unclipped her skis from her boots. "Are we still having drinks at the lodge?"

"That's not even up for discussion. It's the best part of skiing." Madison led the way and Alex fell in behind Katherine.

"So did you decide if you're coming to dinner tonight?" Katherine asked as she held the door. "You're not on the email list but I pushed back the hat fun. Too many flights got delayed yesterday with the storm."

"Please come," Madison said, looking back over her shoulder. "It's never as much fun without you." She led the way through the crowded entryway and back toward the bar.

"And if you don't come, she won't stop talking about all the things she'd like you to do to her," Katherine added.

Madison stopped walking. She turned to Katherine and gave her a look that Alex interpreted as irritation, but then went straight in for a deep kiss. When she pulled back, she had a gleam in her eye. "You know you like me best when I'm naughty."

Katherine rocked her head. "Arguable."

Madison turned to Alex. "Please come. I want to be naughty."

"That's very hard to say no to. You should tell me more."

Madison waggled her eyebrows at Katherine and then latched on to Alex's arm. Of all the women that had come and gone from Katherine's world, Madison had lasted the longest. Their relationship was going on three years, though they hadn't lived in the same house for any of that time, and of course both slept with other women. Regardless, they did seem happy.

"I may have found your rope in Katherine's room last night," Madison said. She found them a table with two stools and Alex pulled over a third.

Alex sat down. "Hold up, is this a fantasy for the hat?"

Madison pursed her lips. "I'd rather it not be a hat thing."

"So something that happens before the party? Or after?"

"Before."

"She's hoping she'll hook you and you won't be able to leave," Katherine said.

Alex couldn't tell if she was joking or serious. With Katherine, it was a fine line. She looked back at Madison. "Where are we doing this?"

"The private room." Madison hesitated. "Is that a yes?" At Alex's nod, she clapped her hands together and cheered.

Alex chuckled as more than one pair of eyes turned to their table. If only those onlookers knew what was being discussed.

"She's been scheming a threesome with you for months." Katherine's blue eyes lit on Alex. "I told her you wouldn't turn down an opportunity to show off your skills with rope."

"I do love an excuse to tie someone up."

"Oh, I want you to do more than tie me up," Madison said. "That's only the beginning of what I need."

"Before she tells you the rest of her plans, I want to hear about the woman you met yesterday," Katherine said. "From the way you talked this morning, she definitely caught your attention."

"She did. But I don't think anything will come of it."

"Why not? Is she straight?"

Alex had fallen for more than one straight girl, and each time Katherine had been the one to say "I told you so" when things soured. "Not straight."

"Do I need to call her up and tell her what she's missing?" Katherine arched an eyebrow.

"Definitely no." In fact, Alex could imagine Katherine doing exactly that. Without permission. "The problem is the timing. I'm in Tokyo for another two months. At least. And she's getting over a fresh breakup. I don't think she's ready to start something new."

"Sounds like the perfect timing for a little fling."

"She doesn't seem like the fling type." Alex didn't want that either. Not with someone like Emily where so much more seemed possible. She wanted to do things the right way—hold hands on the first date, kiss on the second…

"You never know. Call her up and invite her over for a little rope fun and you'll find out." Madison's eyes sparkled. "Threesomes are nice, but foursomes are even better."

No way could she do that. A fling was one thing. Kink was another. "She didn't give me the vibe that she'd down with that."

"Then maybe she's not for you," Katherine said.

Alex wanted to argue but suddenly she worried Katherine was right. What were the chances Emily would want to date someone who regularly was a part of threesomes? Or someone who had been to way too many sex parties? Maybe it didn't matter. Emily hadn't texted her all day. If she did now, Alex couldn't exactly invite her to join a party where she was tying up someone else's naked girlfriend. Probably the best thing for both of them was to forget they'd ever met.

CHAPTER NINE

The sheets were pure luxury and the bed felt like an enormous pillow. Even now that she was awake, Emily didn't want to move. Taking a nap was a pleasure she rarely enjoyed and almost as decadent as the massage and pedicure that afternoon.

She rolled on her side and patted the bedcovers for her phone. No missed calls, no texts. As much as she didn't want to be let down, she'd been hoping for a text from Alex all day. And yet the way they'd left things, she knew the ball was in her court. The problem was, she didn't feel ready to go out on a date—not with someone as perfect as Alex. She needed her first foray back to the world of sex to be purely physical, with no potential for more. Sleeping with someone she could see herself caring about would defeat the whole purpose of coming to Aspen.

That aside, she'd started writing several texts in her head. The top contender so far: *"I'm at a sex party and wishing you were here."* Of course she couldn't send that, but it made her smile to imagine doing it all the same. After Alex's story about her ex-girlfriend and the sex toys, she didn't think Alex would be completely turned off, yet saying she was at a sex party felt like false advertising.

Her phone beeped and she tried not to feel let down when Gianna's name flashed on the screen. *Any sex yet?*

Nope. But I'm thinking of going to check out a room full of sex toys that everyone keeps talking about.

Gianna's response was immediate: *Yes please. Take pictures.*

Emily sat up in bed and checked the time. Two hours until dinner. Plenty of time for a little surveillance mission.

That afternoon while they'd waited for their pedicures, Nicola and Shay had both talked up the "private room." It was in the basement and not only filled with an assortment of sex toys, but boasted a big Jacuzzi tub, a fireplace, and more than one bed. Shay had promised it would be well used that evening, but Emily figured no one would be there before the party. Taking a picture of it was the least she could do for Gianna.

After a quick shower, she opened her suitcase and took stock of the outfits she'd brought. She'd tried to plan everything out but had no way of knowing how dressed up or down the rest of Katherine's guests would be. Katherine always looked as if she'd stepped out of a fashion magazine. Emily had no way to meet that standard. She did, however, have one fancy dress that she'd rented in case she needed it.

She brushed her hand over the silver satin. The formfitting spaghetti-strap dress with the slit up the thigh was over the top for any occasion she'd ever attended, not to mention completely out of her budget, but Gianna had convinced her to rent it. Now she wondered if she'd even be brave enough to wear it. She had two alternatives—a black sweaterdress or her favorite silk blouse with a pencil skirt. Neither option seemed exactly right, but she decided on the sweaterdress. It hugged her curves but still felt modest.

Once she was dressed, she eyed her reflection in the mirror. She'd probably be the only one in an outfit suitable for a schoolmarm, but she thought she looked good in it regardless.

"One schoolmarm ready for a wild night," Emily said aloud, hoping the faked confidence in her voice would convince her reluctant mind. It didn't work, but at least it got a smile on her lips.

She stepped out of her room and walked right into Nicola. "Oh gosh, I'm sorry. I wasn't looking where I was going."

"Gosh?" Nicola smiled.

Nicola was more stunning than ever, seemingly casual but undeniably sexy in a blouse with sheer sleeves and a cream camisole underneath. Ava was at her side, looking gorgeous in a short teal cocktail dress with a neckline that accentuated her ample breasts.

Like Nicola, charisma and confidence practically oozed from Ava's pores. She had curves in all the right places, long wavy brown hair, a perfect smile, and a smooth olive complexion. Her accent made Emily guess that her first language was Spanish, and she'd mentioned L.A. was home. Aside from that, the only other detail Emily knew was that she was a film producer.

Ava hooked her arm through Emily's. "We're on our way to check out that private room. I told Nicola I wanted a peek before dinner. Want to join us?"

"Sure." Emily wondered if she should admit that had been her plan too. Unfortunately, taking a picture for Gianna was now out of the question.

"Drinks first," Nicola said. "No getting dehydrated at this altitude."

"I definitely plan on drinking tonight," Emily said.

"I knew I liked you." Ava laughed, tightening her grip on Emily as they headed down the stairs. "Did you hear that Katherine reads our fantasies aloud? To the whole group?"

"What did you think would happen?" Nicola asked.

"I hadn't really thought about it. I guess I thought we'd pick a partner and whisper what we wanted." Ava glanced at Emily. "Did you know?"

"Shay warned me yesterday. And I probably should have thought of a fantasy then."

"Oh good, I'm not the only one! We'll have to think of one together."

Emily couldn't help but like Ava. She probably had a lot more experience when it came to sex, but tonight they were both newbies.

They entered the den and Nicola went over to the bar. "Wine or cocktails?"

"I'll take Chardonnay," Ava said.

When Nicola held up a bottle, Ava nodded. Emily recognized the winery only because she'd seen the labels in Katherine's kitchen. No way could she afford even a glass of it.

"And for you, Emily?"

She hesitated a moment but then reminded herself there wouldn't be a bill to pay later. "I'll have the same."

"Good choice," Ava said. "It's one of my favorites."

"Katherine knows her wine." Nicola poured and then raised her glass. "To my favorite two virgins yet."

Ava turned to clink Emily's glass. "To being virgins together."

Emily smiled despite a sudden wave of anxiety. She liked both Ava and Nicola, and although she'd felt comfortable at the spa, chatting away and feeling like she'd met two people who could be long-term friends, now it didn't make sense that she was at a party with either of them. A sex party, no less. She simply wasn't in their same league. Despite what Gianna said, she still had a feeling she was a charity case.

"You two ready to see the private room?"

"Can't wait," Ava murmured.

Emily fell into step behind Ava, reminding herself to breathe. Maybe she could simply enjoy a fancy dinner and go to bed early. Seeing the private room would be enough excitement for the evening.

"By the way, I love your dress," Ava said. She'd paused at the start of a staircase leading down to the basement and waited for Emily to catch up.

"Thanks." Emily would have normally admitted she'd gotten it on clearance at Macy's, but she stopped herself. "I was admiring yours earlier. Teal is one of my favorite colors, and you do it justice."

"Why, thank you." Ava flashed a smile.

"And your heels are fabulous."

Ava stretched out her leg, accentuating her calf muscle and showing off her heels. "My mom always used to say, 'If you feel like you have nothing to wear, buy new shoes.' I've found it to be some of her best advice."

"Did I lose you two?" Nicola called from the bottom of the stairs.

"I distracted Emily with my legs," Ava said, throwing a playful smile back at Emily. "We're coming now."

Emily caught her breath. Ava was flirting with her. It shouldn't be a surprise, and yet it was. She thought back on the afternoon and recalled all the times Ava had casually touched or brushed against her. She hadn't thought anything of it then, but now she realized how clueless she'd been.

Could she sleep with Ava? It certainly wasn't a terrible idea, but more than a little intimidating. She swallowed a fortifying gulp of wine, reminding herself that she was here for a good time. The least she could do was loosen up.

Emily paused at the bottom of the stairs. The basement was not a typical basement at all. In fact, it was more like a welcoming lobby at a fancy ski resort. Double the size of Gianna's apartment, the open central space was filled with several leather couches all situated on a plush cream rug in front of a big stone hearth. A crackling fire added to the cozy warmth.

"What's that little room for?" Ava asked, pointing to an alcove at the far end of the space.

"For when you want to pretend you have privacy but don't mind being filmed," Nicola replied.

Emily nearly choked on the sip of wine she'd taken. *Filmed?* She moved to get a better view of the alcove. On one wall there was what looked like a massage table, but a big screen was on the opposite wall. No chairs, no sofas.

"I'd like to avoid cameras," Ava said.

"Honestly, me too," Emily said. Although probably for different reasons. Cameras intimidated her, and tonight she definitely didn't need anything making it harder to relax. Still, a fantasy sprang to mind of a woman stretched out on the table getting a *very* thorough massage…

"Then maybe you two would prefer the private room. No cameras." Nicola started toward a closed door at the opposite end of the room.

Emily told herself it was only a room full of sex toys, but still her heart raced. Once upon a time, she'd been into toys. Her experience, however, had not included spreader bars or spanking boxes or anything like what Shay had mentioned. Vibrators were the extent of what she'd tried, and over the years Cass's scorn for anything more than a non-phallic vibrator had made her question her own desires.

"Shay mentioned there are rules," Ava was saying.

"Yes." Nicola stopped in front of the closed door. "For one, the door's always locked if someone's using the space. Whoever's in the room can decide whether or not they want to let anyone else in—and if you'll participate or only watch."

"Shall we see if it's locked?" Without waiting for anyone to answer, Ava stepped past Nicola to reach for the door handle. She gave it a turn. "We're in luck."

As soon as the door swung open, Emily felt heat shoot up from her neck to her cheeks. She registered her blush and her loud gasp in the same moment. Alex—the same Alex she'd eaten pie with—was stripped down to a pair of black boxers and standing in front of a woman tied up on a chair.

"Emily?"

Emily opened and closed her mouth. She couldn't form any words. Her pulse whooshed in her ears and her legs felt shaky. She glanced from Alex back to the woman in the chair. Aside from a bright red rope that laced between her breasts in an intricate pattern, she was otherwise naked. Her ample breasts moved up and down as she panted, and the expression of bliss on her face left no doubt that she was enjoying the afterglow of a climax. It took a moment for Emily to recognize the woman. *Madison.* She'd seen her a handful of times at Katherine's and thought maybe Madison was Katherine's girlfriend for a time—there were always so many women coming and going.

Alex stepped forward. Probably her intention was to shield Madison but the move also called more attention to herself. It didn't hurt, of course, that she was also half naked. Toned muscles outlined her arms and legs, and her sculpted shoulders begged to be touched. But Emily's gaze was drawn to her boxers and the obvious bulge. No doubt about it, Alex was packing. *Okay. No big deal. This is probably totally normal. For other people.* They were at a sex party, after all.

The sound of someone clearing their throat yanked Emily back to reality. Only then did she realize there was a third person in the room. *Katherine.*

This was getting worse by the second. Katherine, with her signature long golden locks and willowy build, stared right at Emily. She was standing off to the side and fully dressed—unlike the others. In black leggings and a tight white tank top accentuating her breasts, she could have been on her way to a Pilates class except she held something resembling a riding crop in her hand, and her expression told Emily not to ask what it was for unless she wanted to be on the receiving end.

"Sorry about the interruption," Ava said. "Carry on."

Ava stepped back from the doorway, but in the same moment Emily reached forward to push the door closed. They bumped into each other and Emily's wineglass slipped from her grip.

Time slowed as the glass tipped end over end, wine spraying the door and the plush cream rug before shattering as it struck the wall. Emily's mind slowed too, stumbling over the words *this shouldn't be happening*. She wasn't a klutz. She didn't do things like drop wineglasses at parties. But the door shouldn't have been unlocked, and Alex—her Alex—shouldn't be at this party at all. Alex belonged in her fantasies, not in her very real but at the moment completely bizarre world.

"Good thing we went for the Chardonnay," Nicola said dryly.

"I'm so sorry." Emily bent down to pick up the pieces closest to her, wishing her voice hadn't sounded shaky.

"It's fine. People drop glasses all the time," Alex said.

"Yeah, and this whole scenario of walking in on a threesome is completely normal too," Emily said. "Happens all the time to me, in fact."

Suddenly, everyone was laughing. Alex included.

Alex carefully picked her way up to the doorway. "Is it bad timing to say I'm happy to see you here?"

Emily knew she couldn't simply stare at Alex's bare feet. But her cheeks were still burning with a blush that would only get worse if she had another look at Alex's midsection. And her damn heart wouldn't stop tap dancing. Finally, she lifted her eyes and met Alex's gaze. "It's not the best timing, actually."

Before Alex could respond, Nicola intervened. "You two can reconnect later. Perhaps with more clothes on, Alex." In one swift move, Nicola reached forward and swung the door closed.

CHAPTER TEN

"Where the hell you been?" TJ asked. "And how is it that the party hasn't even started but you've already managed to royally piss off Katherine? And Nicola too. That takes talent."

"Hey, man, it's good to see you, but I'm looking for—"

"We're going outside to talk. Here, hold these." TJ handed Alex two bottles of beer and then took a coat from the rack. "Do you know how much trouble you're in?"

"I can guess." Which is why she didn't have time to talk. She had to find Emily and check in on her. "I want to catch up, but I need to find someone before dinner."

"Let me guess—the new girl? I've been here for all of an hour and I've already heard all about it." TJ held out her hand for one of the bottles of beer, then pointed to the back door. "Grab your coat."

"It's like ten below." Alex reluctantly reached for her coat anyway. She knew better than to try to change TJ's mind when she was set on something.

"Actually, it's a balmy fourteen. I checked my phone." TJ wrapped a yellow scarf around her neck. "You look good, by the way. Missed you."

"I missed you too," Alex said, letting TJ pull her into a hug. In fact, until that moment she hadn't realized how much she was in need of a friend. If she had to talk to anyone except Emily right now, she wanted it to be TJ. Maybe TJ would tell her it was all going to blow over. She stepped back and adjusted TJ's scarf. "How is it you get more handsome every time I see you?"

"Good genes."

"So it's not all the facials?"

TJ laughed. "That too." She did look even more handsome than the last time they'd met up. Not that it was hard for TJ to look good. Where most tried and failed, TJ truly pulled off being a suave stud. She always dressed to the nines—today she had on trim black slacks, a black button-down, and a pinstriped vest—but it was more than that. Everything from her sharp features to her smooth light brown skin and closely shaved dark black hair was meticulously perfect.

They stepped outside and Alex wished she'd grabbed a scarf too. And a hat. "Damn, it's cold out here."

"Says the person from Colorado."

"Yeah, but I live in Tokyo now. I'm not used to this." Maybe she should have stayed in Tokyo. Meeting Emily had made everything seem worth it, but now she worried she'd screwed up any chance they ever had. "It feels like it's been forever since we last saw each other. When was it?"

"August. London."

"Oh. Right. London."

"Your memory coming back about that disaster?" TJ shook her head but chuckled. "At least we have fun when we get in trouble."

First Madison and Katherine had gotten into an argument, then somehow TJ and Nicola landed on opposite sides of said argument. Alex had tried to stay out of the yelling match until the hotel manager showed up threatening to kick all of them out. "What was that fight even about?"

"Who knows. Something really important at the time. So I hear you walked out with Madison tied up. Katherine's pissed. Given how you blasted Lara for that time she left a sub, you better have a damn good excuse to get yourself out of this one."

"I didn't leave Madison alone. Katherine was there." Alex heard the defensive tone in her voice. She did feel bad for the scene getting interrupted and for leaving early, but it was nothing like what Lara had done.

TJ rocked her head side to side. "You know Katherine gets protective of a sub."

"I did what they asked me to do. I tied Madison up and gave her what she wanted." Fortunately, Madison had already climaxed by the time the door opened. Alex even had a second to make sure the cock was tucked away. Not that it had been that discreet. She thought again of how Emily had stared right at her crotch.

The wind came up, shaking settled snow off the trees and sending little biting crystals of ice at her face. She shivered and tugged up the zipper, closing the gap at her neck. "Can we go back inside now?"

"You haven't told me why you bolted."

"I didn't bolt." That was definitely an exaggeration and probably Katherine's words.

TJ tipped back one of the chairs, tossing off the piled snow, and then sat down. "How is it you always manage to get yourself in some kind of drama at these parties? You're one of the least dramatic people I know."

Alex eyed the bottle TJ had given her. "You bring an opener or we just holding these things?"

"I should make you sit there holding it for all the shit I had to listen to. You know how Nicola gets. Makes Katherine seem tame." TJ pulled an opener out of her pocket. She popped the lid off her IPA and then handed it to Alex.

Katherine clearly had her reasons, but why was Nicola upset? Maybe she blamed her for the door being left unlocked. "Who told you what happened? Nicola?"

"Nicola, then Katherine. Madison tried to tell me, but she busted up laughing."

Alex exhaled. "At least one person isn't mad at me."

"Madison's never mad at anyone. Actually, from what I hear, you made her very happy."

"Yeah, but Katherine's right. It wasn't cool leaving when I did. I should apologize." Alex had fulfilled two of Madison's requests at least, but after seeing Emily she hadn't been able to get back into the scene. She'd tried for Madison's sake but couldn't focus. Finally she'd begged out, hoping she could catch Emily and talk before the evening got started. By the time she'd taken a shower and gotten dressed, Emily was nowhere to be found. She'd considered texting Emily, or calling her, but talking to her in person seemed like the better option.

"For the record, I'm not the only one in trouble," Alex said. "Nicola sent me a text this morning saying she thought she might leave before you got here. What'd you do?"

TJ took a long sip from her beer and then settled back in her chair. "I told her the truth."

"Which truth is that?"

"That it's not working for me—her and I trying to be in a relationship. She's pissed because I brought it up now. Right before we get to spend the weekend together. And her response is to threaten to leave?" TJ shook her head. "Women."

"It was kind of crap timing for you to bring that up now."

"You think I don't know that?" TJ kicked at the snow near her chair. "We see each other three, maybe four times a year. I need more. She thinks it's about the sex, that I only want more of that, and told me it wasn't a problem if I slept with someone else. I don't want someone else. I want her.

"I want to come home to the person I'm with. I want to go grocery shopping together, maybe a movie, maybe pick up tacos. It doesn't matter what it is we do, but I need more of her. I'm tired of constantly missing the person I'm in love with."

"I don't blame you." Coming home to someone was what Alex wanted as well. It didn't sound like too big of a request. Except TJ lived in Oakland and Nicola lived in London. "What are you going to do?"

"Ask her to move to California. Again."

Alex didn't want to bring up the conversation she'd had with Nicola when they were in France, but it weighed on her—especially Nicola's admission that she loved TJ but no relationship was enough for her to sacrifice her career. "What about you moving to London?"

TJ shook her head. "You know I've got my dad to take care of."

"He could move too."

TJ didn't respond. She'd missed the last sex party in Nice because her dad had gotten sick. She'd stayed home to take care of him and fortunately he'd gotten better, but Alex knew she'd always put his needs before her own. And Nicola couldn't understand the choices TJ made.

"I feel like I've been chasing Nicola for five years. Ever since you convinced me to go to that sex party Katherine had at her house in San Francisco." TJ's jaw clenched. "She knows this isn't enough for me. If it's all she wants, then I gotta move on."

Alex puffed a breath, feeling the heaviness of TJ's decision weigh in the air around them. Her breath steamed in the icy air and then vanished a moment later. The temperature had dropped when the sun set and low clouds had moved in, threatening more snow. "I think it's getting colder out here."

"Yeah, what are we doing outside?"

Alex gave her a look and TJ laughed. She took another sip of her beer and then tugged on the label. "Can you believe we're still doing these parties?"

"This is it for me," Alex said. After the drama of the past hour, she was more certain than ever.

"I'll believe it when you break up with Katherine."

Alex cocked her head. "I'm not dating Katherine."

"That's what you say." TJ took another long drink and then smacked her lips when she set the bottle in the snow.

"I'm not."

"Sure."

Alex didn't feel like arguing. Not with TJ. She wouldn't win anyway. She'd known TJ long enough not to try. They'd met when they were both working at Cisco. They'd been assigned to the same team troubleshooting a huge network problem, and the month they'd spent working together had bonded them for life. Alex hopped to a new job after the project finished but TJ stayed on. She'd only changed companies once in the past decade and hadn't left the Bay Area. Meanwhile, Alex had lost track of the number of jobs she'd held and she'd done enough traveling to last a lifetime. Still, they were both in the same place now, wanting more from life and wanting someone to love, but stumbling on the "how to" part.

"So why exactly did you leave with Madison still tied up? Nicola says the new girl knows you from somewhere?"

"Is that why Nicola's upset? Because she thinks I knew Emily and didn't say anything? I didn't know her before yesterday." Alex took a deep breath. "You want the whole story or the punch line?"

TJ gave a half shrug and Alex decided she might as well tell her everything, starting with how she'd felt like Emily was the one she'd been looking for—even though she knew how ridiculous it sounded. By the time she got to the part of the door opening and Emily standing there, jaw dropped, TJ's expression made Alex think that she was as screwed as she'd feared. "The door should have been locked but it wasn't."

"But you were done fucking Madison, right? I mean she didn't actually see that part."

"No. But I think she guessed." Alex was too cold to be drinking ice-cold beer but she took another sip anyway.

"Knowing the way you flirt with a woman you like, I'm guessing this Emily chick was imagining the rest of her life with you after one day together."

"I don't know what she was thinking, but I was imagining it," Alex admitted. "Honestly, she's one of those women that's too good to be true. Sweet, smart, funny…"

"And hot?"

"So damn beautiful. I literally had to remind myself to breathe when I first saw her on the plane. But that's not why I like her."

"Sure."

"Not the only reason, anyway," Alex continued, ignoring TJ's smug look. "I think she's the one."

"Since when did you believe in that?" TJ laughed.

"I'm serious. We had this instant connection, and when we were at that café eating pie I had this feeling like I could eat pie with her for the rest of my life."

"Is pie a euphemism for something I don't know about?"

"What I meant was, everything felt exactly right. Like it was all meant to be. Fate or whatever. But then I screwed everything up."

"Maybe not everything, Alex. She is here for a fantasy weekend after all. Maybe seeing you like that turned her on."

"She gave my boxers a good long look, but I think it was mostly to avoid looking anywhere else. Honestly, I think she was more shocked than turned on."

"New girl had to expect threesomes. Probably all that's going on is she was surprised to see you."

Alex wanted TJ to be right. In some ways, Emily being at the party was the best thing she could have hoped for. What were the chances that they would have seen each other again otherwise?

"You know, I'd have been shocked too," TJ continued. "You meet someone on a plane, share a ride with them but figure you'll never see them again, and then, boom—you open a door and there they are. Pants down and a girl tied up in front of them."

"Is that supposed to make me feel better?"

"Yes. Because it's no big deal."

If TJ was right, maybe she still had a chance. But even as she risked hoping, she knew Emily's look of shock was about more than simply seeing someone she hadn't expected. Or walking in on a threesome.

"If I'd known she was gonna be here, I wouldn't have said yes to Katherine and Madison. And I would have done everything I could to not make that kind of impression."

"Too late. Anyway, that's part of who you are. She either likes that or she doesn't."

"In other words, there's nothing I can do to fix this?"

TJ shook her head.

Alex recalled the moment she'd seen Emily in the doorway and the stream of emotions that had passed through her. Regret at not locking the door didn't come until much later. "Katherine was the last one in," Alex said, realizing it only then. "I thought it was me and that I'd been the one who forgot to lock the door, but I had my hands full with the ropes and she came in after."

"You thinking Katherine intentionally left the door unlocked?"

"Maybe?" *But why?*

"Did Katherine buy your plane ticket?"

Alex nodded. "I told her I had free miles, but you know Katherine."

"Bet she bought new girl's ticket too. Probably set you two up."

Alex considered that possibility. There was no way Katherine could have foreseen the storm or the plane getting rerouted, nor the decision to rent a car and drive together. But it seemed likely she'd intentionally gotten them seats next to each other. It was exactly the type of thing she'd do. Had she also set Alex up for getting caught by Emily literally with her pants down?

TJ picked up her bottle from the snow and clinked it against Alex's. "Cheers. Why is beer a Colorado thing? It's too damn cold to even drink it here."

"But it stays nice and cold."

TJ looked unconvinced by Alex's logic. "Katherine should get some of those big heaters out here."

"You suggest it and Katherine will have them installed by tomorrow night."

TJ raised an eyebrow. "I think you mean if *you* suggest it, she'll have it by tomorrow night. We both know who Katherine bends over for."

Alex met TJ's gaze. "For the record, I did talk to her about boundaries."

"And let me guess, you woke up in her bed the next morning?"

TJ knew her too well. "I know we're not good for each other."

They could never have a serious relationship. Not one that made them both happy, anyway. Alex needed someone who could open up enough to fall in love, someone who wanted to share a life together. Katherine didn't have any interest in sharing more than a bed, and her affections only went so far. She'd never give herself completely to anyone, and all of her relationships revolved around sex.

Alex needed more of a connection. In fact, sex was becoming less and less important when she thought of the type of relationship she wanted. *Yet here I am at a damn sex party.*

"At some point, you're going to have to cut Katherine off," TJ said. "You know that. If you think this new girl—this Emily—has potential, maybe now's the time."

"After everything, I don't think Emily's even gonna look at me."

"See, that's your problem. You give up too easy on the women who are worth fighting for and you go back to the ones who aren't good for you." TJ stood. "What would happen if you tried?"

Alex was certain of one thing: Emily was the kind of woman who only came along once in a lifetime. It was no surprise why Katherine had latched on to her. She was beautiful but she also had a soft innocence about her, and a sweetness, and that made her exactly the type of sex party virgin Katherine loved to claim.

Guessing Katherine's intentions only made Alex feel more protective of Emily, enough so that she wanted to offer her a ride back to the airport. She was so obviously unprepared for the weekend. Unprepared for Katherine especially. No one understood exactly how good Katherine was at manipulating a situation until they were in the middle of it—Alex knew that all too well.

If Emily got caught up in Katherine's web, she'd feel personally responsible, at least for not trying to keep her clear. Yet she didn't actually want Emily to leave. And maybe her reasons for wanting Emily to stay, even if they were different than Katherine's, were equally problematic.

CHAPTER ELEVEN

"There you are." Nicola poked her head in the den. "Ava thought you might have gone up to your room."

"I did for a bit," Emily admitted. After cleaning up the broken glass, she'd needed a minute alone to think. Unfortunately, there was only so long she could hide out.

"Is the altitude bothering you?" At Emily's half shrug, Nicola pointed to her glass and added, "Good call on the water."

It wasn't the altitude. It was all Alex. And the fact that somehow they were at the same sex party. Emily had first considered a shot of vodka, but her stomach was a knot of anxiety, and mineral water seemed a safer option.

"When I couldn't find you, I assumed you were avoiding someone." Nicola went over to the bar and poured herself a glass of wine, Shiraz this time. "If so, I completely understand."

"Are you avoiding someone too?"

Nicola rocked her head side to side. "I wouldn't say I'm avoiding, exactly. I'm preparing. In fact, we already crossed paths, but I was upset at Alex and since the individual in question is good friends with Alex, I naturally blamed her too. She, of course, had nothing to do with it. The good news is that I didn't immediately jump her, which is progress."

Emily smiled, relieved for the moment to have something to think about besides her own worries. "Who is this? And why were you mad at Alex?"

"TJ. You'll meet her at dinner." Nicola sipped her wine. "And you can guess, I think, why I'm mad at Alex."

"Because the door was unlocked?" Emily didn't think that was enough reason—they were the ones poking around, after all—and how could Nicola be certain Alex was at fault?

"No. Because clearly Alex knew you and didn't tell anyone about a connection. Katherine has rules about that. We were sent your name and Ava's as well. If anyone has any previous association with a virgin they have to say so, mainly so you could be warned before you arrived. Alex, however, never reads Katherine's emails. Or texts, for that matter."

"She didn't know me before yesterday."

Nicola tilted her head. "You met yesterday?"

"We spent the day together. Kind of on accident." And by Alex's response to seeing her now, Emily didn't think she had any idea she was coming to the party. Probably Nicola was right and she hadn't read any email or didn't make the connection to her name. If she did, she'd hidden it well. "With the storm, our flight got rerouted to Denver. She gave me a ride here. Well, not here, exactly, she gave me a ride from one airport to the other."

"And neither of you knew the other would be at this party?"

"No. She asked what I was doing in Aspen, but I evaded the question."

Nicola nodded slowly. After a moment she said, "It doesn't take long to fall for Alex."

"I didn't fall for her. I…" Emily searched for words. The longer she took finishing her sentence the more she revealed. So much for pretending she could keep any secrets to herself. "We only spent one day together. More like half a day."

"Alex is very good at being exactly what you've been waiting for." Nicola met Emily's gaze. "Please don't misinterpret that. I'm not suggesting it's an act. It's simply Alex. Not even Katherine's immune."

"Are Katherine and Alex together?" Emily could easily picture Alex with someone like Katherine. It made a lot more sense than Alex going for someone like her. But what about Madison? "I've seen Madison at Katherine's house in San Francisco and thought they might be dating."

"They are. Madison and Katherine have been together for several years now."

"Then how does Alex fit in?"

"That's where things get complicated." Nicola sat down on the sofa. "It's no secret that Katherine likes Alex. She's the only one Katherine has ever really wanted but couldn't have."

"Because she's with Madison?"

"Katherine and Madison have an open relationship. They both regularly sleep with other people."

That explained all the other women Katherine entertained. "But not Alex?"

Nicola hesitated, seeming to debate her answer. "Alex doesn't want to be caught."

So Alex *was* a player. And not even Katherine could tie her down. Emily felt even more like a fool for falling for her now. She should have guessed as much from Alex's confidence and charm. But somehow she'd let herself get swept up in the idea that they actually had a connection. Something real.

"I only say this because it's fair you know what the rest of us know."

"I appreciate that. Maybe now I can try not to say or do anything dumb before dinner."

Nicola raised an eyebrow. "Anything more, you mean?"

"Thanks for that." Emily liked Nicola's dry sense of humor. In a way, she reminded Emily of Gianna. A very proper Gianna with an English accent. Their penchant for sarcasm would be well matched.

"I want to apologize," Nicola said. "I had no idea anyone was using the private room. That door is supposed to be locked, but I should have insisted Ava knock first. Katherine and the others must have come in through the garage or one of the back doors."

"You don't need to apologize. I wasn't expecting something like that, but I can handle it. Honestly, it was hot. Until I dropped the wineglass."

"At least you made an impression." Nicola patted Emily's knee. Her teasing actually helped some. "Truly don't worry. Everyone will have something else on their mind by the time dessert's served."

"What?"

Nicola laughed. "Did you forget you're at a sex party?"

"Right. That." Getting through dinner would be a small miracle. She didn't think she could handle more. Maybe she could use the altitude excuse and beg out. "I need to come up with a fantasy."

"Am I interrupting?"

Emily glanced up at the voice. Lara. Over the pizza dinner last night, she'd come to a few quick conclusions. Lara was an even bigger flirt than Alex but shared three things in common: attractive, butch, and cocky. The ABCs of everything she was drawn to but definitely didn't need.

"Come on in, Lara," Nicola said smoothly. "Emily needs help picking out a fantasy."

"Music to my ears." Lara headed over to the bar, but instead of picking out a beer as Emily would have guessed, she poured herself a Sprite and dropped a cherry in with the ice. "What are your ideas?"

The problem wasn't simply being embarrassed about her fantasy in front of strangers. Now, Alex would be there on top of everything. Before she had to admit she didn't have any ideas, Lara said, "You can put in more than one if you're wavering on two."

Emily wondered if it ever happened that someone didn't have a fantasy.

"Everyone loves virgins," Lara continued. "You'll be snatched up quick no matter what."

"Lara's right," Nicola agreed. "But it is best to think of something before the hat comes out."

Emily glanced from Lara to Nicola. She'd had a hard enough time talking about sex back when she was having sex regularly. She thought of all the times she'd agonized over bringing up the conversation with Cass. Why had she thought a sex party would be a good idea? "I appreciate the advice. I'm not sure what I want is—"

"Oh, don't worry if it seems over the top," Lara interrupted. "Chances are, no matter how crazy you think it might be, one of us has done it. And even if we haven't, no one's going to judge. Trying something new is what this weekend's all about."

Emily stopped herself from telling Lara she'd misunderstood. What she wanted was plain vanilla sex. But she knew it was too simple. Too boring.

"If you are interested in BDSM," Nicola said, picking up where Lara left off. "Lara and Alex are the pros. And I'm not only saying that because Lara's here. I recommend both of them. Experience is important and, the truth is, they're excellent. Katherine's good as well, but she doesn't have as much patience."

Lara didn't blush. She smiled, flashing perfect teeth, and said, "Can I get a written reference, Nicola?"

Nicola ignored Lara and added, "Alex is the one to pick if you want to be tied up—she has all the Shibari magic up her sleeve—but Lara will do for everything else."

"Will do?" Lara laughed. "Thanks for that."

Nicola arched an eyebrow. "You know I tease only because I love you."

Shibari. Emily had heard the word before but hadn't thought of it when she saw Madison bound on the chair. Between the mix of shock and arousal, she hadn't considered who had tied Madison up. Now she recalled the intricate rope pattern lacing between Madison's breasts, knots binding her hands and her legs, and the beauty of it all struck her. *Alex had done all of that.* A flush that had nothing to do with embarrassment burned through her.

"Whatever fantasy you come up with will be fine, Emily," Lara said. "I promise. Don't stress about it. This night is all about having a good time." She took a sip of her Sprite and headed for the door. "By the way, I think dinner is about to be served. You don't want to be late and get on Katherine's bad side this early in the game."

"We'll be there in a minute." Nicola waited until Lara had left to say, "You know, your fantasy doesn't have to be kink. I wasn't going to say as much while Lara was here, but..."

"You guessed?"

"You're a bit of an open book."

"Can I ask you one more thing?" She waited for Nicola's nod and then took a deep breath. "If Katherine's with Madison but wants Alex, why was Alex...well, you know..."

"Fucking Madison?" Nicola smiled. "I'm sure Madison begged Katherine for that whole scene. She loves threesomes. And being the one in the middle."

"So, she doesn't mind that Katherine wants Alex?"

"Everyone who dates Katherine understands that Alex is part of the equation. But I don't think Madison has any doubts about Katherine's affection. She loves them both, in her way. Though Katherine can be more territorial when it comes to Alex."

"Figures I'd like the one person I shouldn't."

Nicola's look was full of understanding. "You can like her and even have sex with her. The trick is keeping your heart out of it." She stood and extended her hand to Emily. "Shall we brave dinner?"

Facing Alex again was daunting, everything considered. But she was done playing the damsel in distress. She intended to enjoy the evening. All she had to do was keep her heart from making any decisions.

CHAPTER TWELVE

The dinner table had a seating arrangement and Alex was certain Katherine had placed Madison next to her on purpose. Emily, however, was only across the table, and maybe that was intentional too. Ava, the other new arrival, was skillfully entertaining both Madison and Emily. From her perfectly coiffed hair to her manicured nails and the stylish cocktail dress that fit her like a glove, there were no flaws to be found with Ava. She was beautiful, as nearly all of Katherine's acquaintances were, as well as confident and flirty.

Alex couldn't help wondering if Ava was Emily's type. What she wondered even more was how Emily felt about her. Before dinner, she'd bumped into Nicola and Emily coming out of the den. She'd tried to intercept, hoping to apologize, but she'd been not so subtly dismissed before she got the words out. In a cheerful tone, Emily had said, "Oh, hi. Fancy meeting you here," and then gone to the dining room without another look.

"I hear you're a famous chef, Emily," Lara said. "What's it like cooking for Katherine?"

Alex glanced up from her salad and studied Emily.

"Katherine's my favorite client," Emily answered. "But I'm definitely not a famous chef."

"Your favorite?" Katherine looked over her wineglass at Emily. "Why?"

"I like a challenge."

Lara chuckled. "Is anyone surprised Katherine's a challenge?"

Katherine kept her gaze trained on Emily, purposefully ignoring Lara. "How am I a challenge?"

"Well, your appetite for one."

Lara chuckled again, and Alex wanted to throw something at her.

Emily immediately blushed and added, "I didn't mean that you eat a lot. You don't. What I meant was that you don't like any meal to be repeated. And you like trying new ingredients. That keeps me searching out new recipes."

"Is that all?"

"You also like the meal to be healthy, so I can't simply add more cream to a dish to get better flavor. I have to play around with the spices and try other tricks."

"I sound like a pain in the ass," Katherine returned evenly.

"I wouldn't say that."

"Madison might." Lara coughed, pretending to cover as she spoke. Madison laughed, as did Shay. Even Katherine's lips twitched.

Lara was only poking fun at Katherine, but Emily didn't know that. Alex could tell she was nervous. She wanted to jump in and save her but had a feeling that would only make things worse.

When the others stopped laughing, Emily said, "You are a challenge. That's different, though, than being a pain in the ass. I wouldn't want to impress a pain in the ass."

"Nicely played," Lara murmured. She was seated on the other side of Emily, and not surprisingly had been vying for both Emily's and Ava's attention.

Lara loved anything shiny and new—her words—so it came as no surprise whenever she went after one of the virgins. Once upon a time, Alex had been as close to Lara as she was to TJ, but they'd grown apart after a few disagreements that turned into proper fights.

The last straw came when Lara callously walked away from a crying sub during a play scene that she'd taken too far. Alex had watched the whole thing, and while Lara might have meant the walking away to be part of the power dynamic, she'd overplayed her hand and the woman was a mess after. Eventually Lara did go back to soothe her sub, but only after Alex and Katherine had stepped in. By then, everyone had seen Lara's true colors. Alex had argued against Katherine inviting her back, but she'd lost that fight two years in a row.

"Emily, did you have any trouble with your flight yesterday?" Ava asked, clearly sensing when a change in subject was needed. Before Emily could answer, Ava continued. "I hear the airport is going to be a mess for the next week with all the flights that were rescheduled."

"My flight got rerouted to Denver, but I found a rideshare." Emily glanced at Alex. It almost seemed involuntary, or at least on accident, because she quickly looked away. "Wasn't a big deal."

"I never even think of rideshares," Ava said. "That's smart. I'm always trying to charm one of the agents to get me on another flight."

Alex returned to her salad, wondering if Emily would be open to talking after dinner. She wanted to at least figure out why Emily was upset. Was it because she hadn't told her about going to the sex party? Or was it what she'd seen in the private room?

Maybe she should give up hoping Emily might like her. If she was keeping her distance now, what more was there to say?

"Butter?"

Alex glanced at the butter dish that Madison was holding out, for a moment completely thrown. "No, thank you."

"I'll take it," TJ said, holding up her hand.

Alex passed the butter. TJ was sitting next to Nicola, and Alex hoped for her sake that the weekend would turn things around for them. If TJ wasn't able to convince Nicola to change her mind and consider moving to America, in TJ's mind that meant

Nicola didn't love her enough. But Nicola wouldn't accept that TJ asked her for a sacrifice she wasn't willing to make herself. Unless they came to a resolution, Alex guessed it would be the last party with both of them together.

"These rolls are amazing," TJ said between bites. "Even better than sourdough, and you all know how I feel about sourdough."

Nicola shook her head. "You need to try fresh Parisian rolls. In Paris."

"Sounds like an invitation," Lara said. "Does it apply to the rest of us?"

"Anytime. You know that." Nicola didn't look at Lara, however. Her eyes were on TJ instead.

TJ stopped chewing. She set the half-eaten roll on her plate and reached for her napkin. Then she took a sip of wine, all the while holding Nicola's gaze. There had to be a middle ground, but they were both too strong to back down.

"Do you not like bread?" Emily asked. "Or is it a new health craze to eat pie for lunch and save everything healthy for dinner?"

At the word *pie*, Alex looked at Emily. She hadn't realized the question was directed at her until too late, and now that Emily was staring right at her, waiting on her answer, Alex had no idea what she'd asked. *Something about pie.* "Sorry, what?"

"I know you aren't gluten intolerant."

"No."

"But you didn't take a roll."

"A roll? No." Alex glanced at the breadbasket. She'd passed on the rolls because her thoughts had been on dessert. And what would come after dessert. But she couldn't exactly say all of that. "I tolerate gluten fine. Maybe a little too fine."

Emily cocked her head and smiled. The expression was so endearing that Alex wished they were talking about anything besides gluten. It occurred to her that since Emily was a chef, of course she'd ask about food, but maybe she was also looking for an opening. Alex quickly sized up everything on Emily's plate. No bread for her either.

"I would have taken a roll, but I saw the dessert trays in the kitchen," Alex admitted.

"Planning your meal with dessert in mind? I like that. So are you thinking the chocolate mousse with the dark chocolate glaze and the raspberry liqueur? My mouth started watering as soon as I spotted it."

"I love chocolate. And raspberry liqueur. But what I really want is one of those little lemon tarts."

Emily picked up her wineglass and took a sip. "Somehow, I'm not surprised you'd go for the tart."

"I bet a chef can guess a lot about a person by what they like to eat."

"No comment."

Alex felt a flash of hope at Emily's subtle smile. She knew they were on shaky ground, but Emily wasn't ignoring her, and she'd take that as a success for the moment.

Madison and Katherine were chatting about the chance of fresh snow overnight, Nicola was telling TJ about a nightclub in London that her friend owned, and Shay was being Shay, entertaining Ava and Lara with a story about a girl they'd met in airport security and then had sex with twenty minutes later in a somewhat secluded spot behind a vending machine. All of that meant that no one seemed to pay any attention to Emily and Alex.

"It's nice to meet someone else who thinks about dessert before dinner," Alex said, wishing they could be talking about what was really on her mind. Finally, she decided that she might as well go for it. The worst that could happen was that Emily would shut her down. "I'm sorry I didn't tell you that I was coming here. Honestly, I wasn't sure that I would."

"I didn't tell you I was coming either."

"Yes, but you didn't lie. You let me try and guess. I told you I was only here to relax and ski."

"Lies of omission." Emily glanced at the others, still distracted with their own conversations, and added, "Maybe I should admit my own lie of omission. I like bread as much as dessert."

"Then why didn't you take a roll?"

"I'm a chef. I love to cook for other people, but I also love to eat. And high cholesterol runs in my family. The good news is that big boobs go along with that."

Alex couldn't help laughing. "Would it work if you skipped the butter?"

"Skip the butter?" Emily's mouth dropped open.

"Right. What am I thinking?" Alex grinned. Emily's honesty was refreshing. It was as if she hadn't read the memo about how you were supposed to impress everyone at dinner parties with an unrealistic version of yourself. Alex thought again of how Emily had gasped when she'd seen her earlier. She hadn't tried to hide her emotions then either. Maybe she was always real. If so, that only added to how perfect she was. Alex wanted to ask if she still had a chance with her. As crazy as it sounded, she thought Emily would tell her the truth.

"What if you only ate half a roll? Then you'd only need half as much butter and you'd still have room for dessert."

"And leave half a roll on my plate?"

"Well, that's clearly out of the question. I don't have that much self-control either. But we could share a roll. I'll even let you pick top or bottom."

Emily opened her mouth as if to answer and then abruptly closed it. Her gaze didn't leave the rolls, but she seemed truly tongue-tied, and Alex wondered what she'd said wrong. Then it hit her. *Top or bottom. Shit.* After what Emily had seen, she had to be thinking that there was some hidden message in her words.

"I didn't mean anything by that," Alex said quickly. "It wasn't code for anything, I promise." *Dammit.*

Emily shook her head but didn't say anything.

"I feel like whatever I say next will be the wrong thing." Alex wondered if she could simply admit the truth. What did she have to lose? "The thing is I like you and—"

"Yeah, that's the wrong thing to say."

"Wait, you didn't let me finish."

Emily continued. "You hardly know me. You can't know if you really like me or not. I think we should forget about yesterday and start over from here. Two strangers at a sex party."

"Is that the start of a joke?" Shay asked.

Alex hadn't noticed when the other conversations had dropped off, but she felt the table listening now.

Shay pressed on. "Two strangers walk into a sex party. One turns to the other and says, 'Come here often?'"

Madison and Ava laughed, but Emily only waited for Alex's response.

Alex took a deep breath. She had a feeling she only had one chance to set things right. "I don't want to forget what happened yesterday. And I know I like everything about you—at least everything I know so far. I'd like to get to know you more. But you're right. There's a lot I don't know."

"She wants to know how you look horizontally," Lara said.

More laughter. Alex ignored everyone, focusing only on Emily. She didn't care that the others were listening now. Not if Emily didn't mind.

"Aside from liking dessert before dinner, we probably have nothing in common," Emily said.

"Well, we also both like to sing in the car."

"How often do you have a conversation with a woman when you're not trying to get into their pants?" Emily reached for her wineglass and took a sip. "We're both here for sex, Alex. You don't need to pretend it's about anything more."

Alex felt her cheeks get hot. It had been a long time since she'd blushed from straight-up embarrassment, but she couldn't beat it back.

"Looks like Katherine invited someone to put Alex in her place," Lara said, chuckling.

Alex continued to hold Emily's gaze. "I was trying to get to know you yesterday. Not get into your pants. But if that's how you felt, maybe I need to learn how to have a conversation with a beautiful woman without flirting."

"That's not happening." Lara snorted. "Al, you're too old a dog to learn a new trick."

Alex didn't like Lara's nickname for her. She'd never liked being Al, and at the moment it pissed her off more than it should. Lara knew what she was doing. But Alex wasn't about to engage. She didn't care what Lara said or thought about her. She only cared about what Emily thought. And now her expression was impossible to read.

Did Emily believe her? After what she'd seen, why should she?

"So, who's hitting the slopes tomorrow?" Madison asked. Under the table she gave Alex's thigh a light squeeze. Madison might seem like the playgirl of the group, but she had a knack for knowing when to intercede.

Alex exhaled. She'd officially messed up her chances with Emily. That, on top of lingering guilt from walking out on Madison earlier, made her think she should call it a night and leave the party now.

As the conversations around the table picked back up, Alex tapped Madison's wineglass. "Hey. I'm sorry about earlier. After Nicola and the others opened the door, I couldn't get my head back in the right space."

"Katherine took over where you left off. Don't worry." Madison's voice was as quiet as Alex's. "And since you gave me one of the best orgasms I've had in a *very* long time, you have nothing to apologize for." She cleared her throat and jumped into the conversation about skiing.

Alex didn't feel totally off the hook despite Madison's words. But nothing about the day had gone right. Alex eyed Emily. She was chatting with Ava and laughing about something. If only she'd called her earlier… She hadn't wanted the pang of rejection, but Emily thinking she was someone she wasn't had turned out to be much worse.

I'm an idiot. Alex sighed and picked up her fork, stabbing the lettuce leaves on her plate. She chewed the food and swallowed without tasting it.

"Want to split this with me?" Emily held out a roll she'd cut in half, a tentative smile on her lips. "Really, you'd be helping me out."

"I feel like I should be the one making a peace offering."

Emily shook her head. "I shouldn't have jumped on you like that. The truth is, I don't want to forget about yesterday either."

Alex took the roll and then the butter dish when Emily handed that to her next.

"I have to ask one thing, though. Did you know on the plane that I was coming to this party?"

Alex considered her answer. Emily deserved the truth even if she didn't want to admit it. "I thought maybe, but I didn't know for sure. You said you were only coming for the weekend, and you seemed like someone Katherine would invite. But the more I got to know you, the more I didn't think this would be your scene."

Emily nodded slowly. "Thanks for telling me."

Alex wanted to say more, but the set expression on Emily's face made her wonder if she'd already said too much. Had she said all the wrong things? Or did she still have a chance?

CHAPTER THIRTEEN

Emily locked the bathroom door and then paced between the shower stall and the sink. Finally, she sat down on the toilet, lid still closed because she didn't actually need to pee. After talking with Nicola, she'd convinced herself she could stay cool and detached around Alex. Cool and detached had quickly gone out the window.

Alex was a force she couldn't resist. Even when she'd tried to focus on the others, tried to keep up with dinner conversation, tried to feel some attraction to anyone else, Alex's eyes pulled her back. She'd spent half the meal wondering what Alex was thinking. The other half she'd spent wondering how it would feel to kiss her. How it would feel to have Alex's arms wrap around her body…

She pulled up Gianna's number and tried to slow her breathing as she listened to the ringing.

"Having fun yet?"

"No. I'm freaking out." She got off the toilet and walked into the shower stall. The whole stall was made out of quartz rock, and it took her a moment to even figure out where the faucet handles were hidden. "Gi, I'm not cut out for sex parties. What the hell am I doing here?"

"Oh, sweetie."

Hearing Gianna's comforting voice made Emily long to be sitting with her on the saggy couch in the living room. "I don't think I'm ready to have sex."

"Is there no one there you're interested in?"

"That's not it. Everyone here is perfect. Sexy. Confident. Gorgeous. I'd be lucky to have sex with any of them." *Especially one person in particular.* She closed her eyes, remembering the look Alex had given her as she handed her the dinner roll. She'd hardly been able to swallow, let alone think.

A damn dinner roll and Alex had thrown her brain on a roller coaster. She still wasn't sure why she'd gone off on her. Alex triggered some need for her to prove herself—as if she could to someone like that.

"They can't all be perfect," Gianna said. "Maybe pick the one who seems the least intimidating? Tell me about who you like the most."

That was a terrible plan, but she couldn't resist. "That'd be Alex. I can't even think around her. She's so damn hot." She wanted to go on in detail, but she didn't need more reason to be fixated on Alex. With a sigh, she added, "She even smells good."

Gianna laughed. "Only you would say that. Tell me you snapped a picture of this hottie."

"What? No." Emily blushed.

"Well, now you have homework. So, wait, why are you freaking out? Sounds like you found the person for your fantasy."

"I can't have sex with her."

"Why not?"

Because Alex was a player? Actually, that made her ideal considering Emily only wanted drama-free sex. But Alex didn't seem like a player, and that part bothered her more. And yet it wasn't about Alex at all. It was her. No way would Alex be interested in vanilla sex. And, even if she was, Emily worried she'd be a disappointment at that as well.

"What if I can't remember how to do the basic stuff? Like what if I'm not good at going down on someone? It's been so long."

"Sweetie, it's a bike. You get on and pedal." Gianna paused. "Em, I know you're still thinking you're not good enough for this party. But that's all because of what Cass told you. It's not true. I've seen Katherine's friends. You're as sexy as any of them."

"You haven't seen this group. I swear most of them could be models. And they're way more experienced."

"Are you whining?"

"Maybe?" Emily pressed her hand over her eyes.

"And why do you sound like you're in a tunnel? Where are you, anyway?"

"The bathroom. Technically, the shower. Do you think anyone would notice if I left the party?"

"You're not leaving. No way. No. Absolutely not. That isn't even up for discussion. Wait, why are you taking a shower? Aren't you supposed to be at the dinner?"

"The dinner already happened. I'm standing in the shower. In my dress."

"Why?"

"I needed to think." Emily tugged on the hem of the sweaterdress. The outfit had ended up being a fine choice. Everyone was dressed nicely but not extravagantly. And given the way Alex had checked her out, she knew she looked good. Unfortunately, looking good wasn't enough. She stared at her heels and at the quartz sparkling under her feet. "This is a nice shower. Someday I'd like to have a house with a shower like this."

"You're so weird sometimes. What fantasy did you decide on?"

At the thought of that unfinished business, Emily did have to pee. She stepped out of the shower and lifted the toilet lid. "Gi, I'm going to pee with you."

"You know I can't see you, right? You're not peeing in the shower, are you?"

"I'm not that weird. In fact, after what I've seen, I'm starting to think I'm more normal than I thought."

"What do you mean, 'after what you've seen'? Have people already started to have sex?"

Emily wished she could simply be excited like Gianna. "Yes, and I promise I'll tell you everything. But not now. Right now, I need a fantasy."

"You haven't come up with your fantasy yet? Em, what have you been doing?"

"Freaking out. I told you." In truth, she'd come up with several fantasies in the past eight hours but didn't want to admit any aloud, let alone write them down. Every single one involved Alex.

"Can you give me a fantasy? I'll use anything."

Gianna gave an exasperated groan. "Group sex."

"No. Not that. Give me another one." Now that she was sitting on the toilet, she couldn't actually pee. Even her bladder was nervous.

"Group sex is a good one. Why not that?"

"Something different." Emily's mind spun to whom she'd have sex with if an orgy actually occurred. Her traitorous libido went right to the image of Alex, of course. But the thought of having sex with Alex while others were watching was too much. "I'm not ready to have sex with more than one person."

"Okay. How about something tame like sex in the shower? Apparently, you really like showers."

Emily laughed. "I do like showers, but everyone's had sex in the shower. It needs to be more exciting than that."

"Okay…Sex in a hot tub? Or what about sex in a car?"

"It's below freezing. I don't think I could pull down my underwear in a car right now." But sex in a hot tub wouldn't be bad. Nicola had assured her that no matter what she wrote, she'd have someone interested simply because she was the newbie—but that meant she'd have to go through with whatever she decided on. "Gi, I don't know if I'm ready to have sex at all. Maybe it's too soon. It's only been two months since Cass and I separated."

"We've been through this." Gianna gave an exaggerated sigh. "You have to get back on this horse at some point."

"I thought it was a bike."

"I'm being serious. You want to have sex sometime, right? Like sometime in the next decade?"

"Yes, but…These people are into whips and tying each other up."

"Damn, that's hot."

"Yeah, it is, and I'm not ready for anything like that." Which was not the same as not wanting it. But after years of no sex, she wasn't ready to jump in at the deep end.

Gianna was quiet for a moment, and Emily said, "I did have one idea, but maybe it's terrible. What do you think people would say if my fantasy was watching other people have sex?"

"Like voyeurism? That's perfect. Do you think you'll get off watching them?"

"No. I mean, I don't know. Maybe?"

The image of Madison naked and tied up popped in her head. Walking in on anyone having sex would have been unsettling, but she'd really been thrown when she'd recognized Alex and realized she was packing. That Katherine had a crop she seemed about to use on someone only put everything over the top.

It didn't seem possible that something like that could happen in real life, something right from her fantasies. And yet as intimidated as she'd been, she'd also been turned on. Maybe if she wasn't ready to participate, she could watch.

"You really think it works as a fantasy?"

"Definitely."

"Gianna, I owe you. Thanks for picking up. I'm going to pee now."

"Good luck, sweetie. And call me later. I want to hear everything."

CHAPTER FOURTEEN

After dessert, the party moved downstairs to the bonus room and Emily rejoined the others there. No one seemed to notice she'd been gone, but as soon as she returned Katherine immediately cleared her throat and asked everyone to take a seat.

Emily spotted a black fedora on one of the coffee tables and guessed it was the infamous hat. Next to it was a notepad and several pens.

"Ready for this?" Shay asked. They rubbed their hands together. "It's almost as good as Christmas."

Emily sat down on the same sofa Shay had picked. Nicola sat next to her and, once everyone was settled, said, "I look forward to this more than Christmas."

"Me too," TJ seconded. She'd picked the sofa directly opposite them and Alex sat down next to her.

Between their almost argument at dinner and her anxiety over picking a fantasy, she wasn't ready for the rush of arousal that came when Alex's gaze settled on her. If only she could turn her attraction to someone else—ideally someone Katherine wasn't in love with.

Emily scanned the room. There was Ava, of course, but she'd pulled Emily aside right after dinner and whispered she'd decided on a fantasy involving either Katherine or Lara. TJ was certainly as hot as Alex but seemed to only have eyes for Nicola. And, Emily had come to think of Nicola as too much of a confidante. Madison was beautiful and flirty, but her connection to Katherine, and Alex as well, made things too complicated there. Lara was a possibility, but Emily was still annoyed with her for the conversation over dinner. She'd realized the ribbing was more for Katherine, but she hadn't appreciated being a part of it. The only other option was Shay, but Emily wasn't up for a role-play fantasy. Well, technically there was one other option. *Katherine.*

What would happen if she went for Katherine? She shook her head before her mind ran with the idea. It wasn't going to happen. Yes, Katherine was hot. But she worked for her. She couldn't have sex with her and pretend everything was normal after. And that wasn't the only problem. If she did anything with Katherine, she'd think of Alex.

Once Madison and Lara claimed the third sofa, Katherine picked up the notebook. "For most of you, this isn't your first time," she started. "You know all the rules." She tore off several sheets of paper and handed them to Shay to pass out along with pens. "But we do have two virgins."

Lara let out a whoop and started clapping. Emily knew her cheeks had gone scarlet, but Ava was smiling like she'd won an Oscar. When she stood and curtsied, all the attention was on her. *Thank God for Ava.*

Shay handed her one of the notebook pages and grinned. "Didn't realize you'd be the main attraction?"

Emily didn't get a chance to respond before Katherine was tapping her wineglass.

"As I was saying…" Katherine raised an eyebrow at Lara, who only laughed like she enjoyed the reprimand. "We do have rules we agree to follow. You've all been tested and sent me your results. Thank you for that. As you know, anything goes as long as it's consensual. That means everyone picks a safe word. You can start with writing that word down now."

Emily picked up her pen. She hadn't anticipated needing a safe word, but one instantly came to mind. *Raisins.* Even the word looked unappetizing. So far, so good.

"Under your safe word, please write down your fantasy—"

"Or fantasies," Lara interrupted.

Katherine narrowed her eyes at Lara and said, "As Lara likes to point out each time, more than one fantasy is fine, but I'm only going to read one. Once you're finished, put your name on the back of the paper and drop it in the hat."

"And, Shay, don't write someone else's name on your paper." Lara chuckled.

"I was the virgin then," Shay said. "I didn't understand the rules. How many fantasies you got this time, Lara?"

"Three. But I'm thinking of adding a fourth because I do love me some pirates."

When Shay sat down, Emily leaned over and whispered, "Why'd you write someone else's name?"

Shay lifted a shoulder. "I thought we were supposed to write down who we wanted to have the fantasy with. Lara was the person I wanted to tie up. It didn't go that way." They laughed. "But it was a lot of fun."

Emily stared at her paper. Everyone else was busy writing, but suddenly she had more questions. Once her fantasy went into the hat, what exactly happened next? How did they pick who to have sex with—or in her case, who she would watch? Would Katherine decide all that?

Her heart hammered when she stood up. She'd apparently finished first but didn't want to hold on to the paper for appearance's sake. She folded the sheet in half and then in half again before dropping the little rectangle into the hat.

Katherine immediately followed—apparently as quick with her writing or maybe as brief. Everyone else was still writing, and as Emily scanned the room, the only one who caught her eye was Katherine. Emily remembered the first moment she'd met Katherine. She'd been enamored with her then, though she'd fiercely kept that secret and tried not to let any attraction show. Now, as Katherine held her gaze, she wondered if she'd known all along.

Emily broke away, deciding her black polished heels were safer to stare at. Jazz music played in the background. A horn solo blended with the sound of the crackling fire and pens scratching paper. At least her fantasy wasn't a terrible one and she wouldn't be laughed out of the room. She took a steadying breath, then looked up from her heels to the one person her thoughts stubbornly kept returning to.

In her defense, it was hard to not look at Alex. They were sitting directly opposite each other, exactly like at dinner. Still, the flood of longing surprised her all over again. Why did she have to have it so bad for the one person who made everything more complicated?

Alex's brow furrowed as she squinted at her paper. Emily couldn't see what she'd written, but she told herself that it didn't matter. She didn't need to know Alex's fantasy. She certainly wouldn't be playing any part in it.

The door to the private room was closed, but Emily's eyes strayed to it. Was Alex thinking of tying someone up again? But she'd already done that... Maybe when you'd done so many things it was harder to come up with a fantasy.

Alex was the last to finish, and Emily decided that alone answered her question. Been there, done that. Probably nothing was all that exciting when you'd tried everything.

* * *

Alex had never liked this part, but she knew how much the others did. Mostly it was the rules and the feeling that they were all at a middle school dance waiting to pick partners. Tonight was worse than ever. Her eyes were drawn back to Emily again and again, and each time she saw only coolness reflected. No way was Emily going to pick her.

"Now for the fun part," Katherine said, reaching for the hat. She gave the hat a shake and then pulled out the first slip of paper. After she'd scanned both sides, she said, "Safe word is, 'Corvette.'"

"That's Madison, right?" Shay said.

Katherine gave Shay a piercing look, but before she could reprimand them, Madison tossed a pillow at Shay's head. "You're not supposed to know whose fantasy it is based on the safe word!"

"Well, you should've changed your word."

"It's not like a password with a reset button." Madison threw her arms in the air. "If I use a different one each time, what happens when I forget?"

Alex couldn't help laughing along with the others. Shay was sweet, although at times clueless.

"Oh." Shay scratched their head. "I change my safe word every time. I never thought about what would happen if I forgot the word."

"Relax, Shay, we all love you," TJ said. "Although every time you do mess this hat thing up somehow."

"Yeah, but if it's not Shay getting in trouble, it'd be one of us," Alex said, elbowing TJ.

"And Shay's too cute to stay mad at for long," Madison added. She stuck out her tongue at Shay, making it clear she wasn't truly upset.

"Since apparently some of us have memorized all of our safe words, I'll read those after we've picked partners for the fantasies." Katherine eyed the paper again and read, "'I'd liked to be spanked—'"

"Who wouldn't?" Shay interrupted.

A round of laughs followed.

Katherine arched an eyebrow. "I'm not finished. Since we all know who this belongs to anyway, Madison would like to be spanked by a teacher who secretly has the hots for her. Who's up for role-playing?"

Shay's hand shot up in the air, followed by Lara's. Katherine looked at Madison. "Would you like to pick, or shall I?"

"I'll take both."

"You only need one for this fantasy," Katherine said. "Unless this is happening in the teachers' lounge and you want someone to catch you in the act."

"Ooh, I like that. Then definitely both. Shay and I have some things to settle, so they can be the one to catch me sucking off Lara."

Lara whistled. "Hot damn."

Shay narrowed their eyes at Lara but said, "Wait, so am I the teacher who gets to spank you?"

"You can try," Madison returned evenly. "You're the teacher who walks in while Lara's schooling me on how to get her off. And you're jealous. You say you're gonna turn us both in and then I change your mind."

Katherine reached into the hat again. "Big D, little s. In the sex dungeon. Ahem. Since there's no *sex dungeon*, I'm assuming whoever wrote this was referring to the private room."

"Otherwise known as the sex dungeon," Lara said.

Alex caught Emily looking her direction. Was she into D/s play? How much experience did she have with kink?

"Anything the Dom wants?" Shay asked, looking right at Lara.

"Anything the submissive wants," Lara said.

Shay and Madison both raised their hands. Ava tentatively wiggled her fingers in the air. "Is there an option for a possibly interested but nervous first-timer?"

"Always." Lara smiled. "Everyone's welcome in the dungeon."

Shay said something to Emily that Alex couldn't hear. She hoped Shay wasn't encouraging Emily to join. Not that she could stop her—and she didn't want to if that's what Emily wanted. But if only they had a moment alone... It seemed like they'd come to an understanding at dinner, and Alex's hopes had buoyed, yet by the time dessert was served, Emily's mood had cooled again.

"Open invite? I might have to make an appearance myself," Katherine said.

"The more the merrier," Lara said. "You joining as a D?"

Katherine narrowed her eyes. "When have you known me to be submissive?"

TJ bumped Alex's shoulder and subtly winked. The only person Katherine ever switched for was Alex. Lara knew that as well as everyone else. Well, the newbies wouldn't know. Alex glanced at Emily again, wondering if she was thinking of what she'd seen in the private room earlier. That had been tame compared to what would go down with Lara and Katherine running a dungeon.

"We doing this tonight?" Shay asked.

Lara eyed Katherine for a moment and then nodded. "I'll need some setup time, but I wouldn't want to keep anyone waiting. Especially not you, Shay."

Shay laughed. "So thoughtful. I'm not going to be able to stand later, am I?"

Katherine reached into the hat again and read, "A massage that turns dirty. Well, that leaves plenty to the imagination." She flipped the paper over and read the back to herself, then added, "Whoever takes this one is in for a good time."

Alex knew the fantasy belonged to TJ, but Emily's eyes zipped right to hers. Did Emily think it was hers? Would she volunteer for it? If Alex could have picked anyone for Emily—other than herself, of course—it would have been TJ. Katherine looked Emily's direction as well, and Alex wondered if she was thinking the same thing. Was that why she'd made the extra recommendation? Before Katherine could ask for volunteers, Nicola raised her hand.

Shay whispered loudly, "Is that one TJ's?"

"I'd bet money on it," Nicola said, not bothering to whisper.

"And you'd be right." Katherine smiled. "You two look ready to devour each other. Try and leave a little for the rest of us, will you?"

TJ grinned. "I'll try."

"I won't," Nicola smoothly answered back.

As the others laughed, Katherine picked the next slip of paper. She scanned it and said, "Hmm. Okay. This person would like to watch. Considering how many of you are exhibitionists, I don't think a voyeur will be any trouble at all. Anyone have any issues with an audience?"

Alex instinctively looked at Emily. Her blush gave her away. A voyeur didn't exactly fit what she thought she knew about Emily, but clearly she had more to learn. Everyone in the room was shaking their head—no one minded being watched. Katherine didn't single Emily out, which Alex was thankful for, and she wouldn't bet that the others knew whose fantasy it was. The only problem was that Alex couldn't exactly volunteer.

"I'll leave it up to the person whose safe word is 'raisins' to decide who they'd like to watch." Without waiting for Emily to say one way or the other, Katherine reached into the hat for another fantasy.

* * *

All that stress and it was over that fast? Emily could hardly believe it. She also had more questions. Was she allowed to simply walk around and watch everyone? Even in the private room? And what about Alex? Could she watch her have sex with someone?

As soon as Katherine had read her fantasy, she'd felt Alex's gaze on her. Somehow, she'd known it was hers though no one else seemed to. And was it disappointment on her face? Emily thought it might be. Did that mean Alex had been waiting to volunteer for her fantasy and was disappointed that she couldn't? Emily felt a pang of regret. Maybe she should have simply written what she really wanted.

"Well, I guess I can still be surprised," Katherine said, breaking into Emily's train of thought. "This person would like to have sex on the floor in front of a fire."

A murmuring went round the room. Apparently, no one was exactly certain who had written the fantasy.

"Any takers?" Katherine looked right at Emily as she asked the question.

Emily swallowed. It was a perfect fantasy. Exactly what she wanted, in fact. But with Katherine eyeing her, she couldn't bring herself to raise her hand. What exactly would she be signing up for? There had to be a catch.

"Is that one yours?" Shay whispered.

Emily shook her head. It didn't seem likely that it was Katherine's fantasy either, given how she seemed truly surprised as she'd read it. Maybe it was Nicola's or Ava's? Maybe Katherine wanted to set her up with one of the two of them. She might have noticed that they'd already become friends. But Katherine hadn't read Alex's fantasy yet either.

"Can you give us a hint on the safe word?" Shay asked.

Katherine looked over at Alex and said, "Kiwi."

So much for a hint.

TJ slapped Alex on the shoulder. "Of all the crazy mofo things you've done, you're telling me you haven't had sex in front of a goddamn fireplace?"

"Well...no."

Lara turned to say something to Madison, Shay and Nicola started joking about sex on hot coals, and Katherine simply stared right at Alex. "Sometimes you skip over a few things," Alex said over the noise.

"You like to keep us guessing," Katherine said. "I'll repeat, any takers?"

Ava's, Madison's, and Nicola's hands went up. Shay's went up a moment later. Emily looked over at Shay and mouthed, *You too?*

Shay shrugged and murmured, "Alex is worth it."

Alex quickly said, "I wouldn't mind all of you. One at a time. That'd be hot."

"Because it'd be in front of a fire?" TJ shook her head. "I can't believe I said that out loud. Alex, your bad jokes are wearing off on me."

"My jokes aren't bad." When TJ raised her eyebrows, Alex playfully pushed her shoulder.

"To be clear, is this going to be an orgy?" Katherine asked. "Or would you rather I pick for you?"

"She's waiting for someone else to raise her hand," Lara said. She might have meant to say the words under her breath, but everyone heard, and the bite in her tone made Emily wonder what she was missing.

"We all know who Alex wants." Lara looked right at Emily when she spoke this time, and everyone else seemed to as well.

Before Emily could figure out what to say, Alex turned and immediately cussed Lara out. The tension in the room seemed to shoot up by about a hundred notches when Lara spat back a string of her own choice words.

Shay murmured, "Shit's getting real," and then added something about an old disagreement. When Emily looked again at Alex, her jaw was clenched, as were her fists.

"Al, if you want to fight, bring it. We both know this isn't really about—"

"I don't want to fight," Alex said, cutting her off. "It's not cool to pressure anyone and you know it."

"I was helping you out."

"Yeah, well, I don't need your help." Alex looked right at Emily and said, "I'm sorry. Whatever you do, don't raise your hand."

"What if I want to?" Emily couldn't believe she'd spoken the words aloud. Her voice sounded so even and calm. *Thank god.* But her hands were shaking, and her heart pounded as if trying to break out of her chest.

Alex held her gaze and then shook her head.

"Would you not pick me now?" Emily asked.

"No. I wouldn't. Because I wouldn't know if you wanted to do it in the first place or if you were only doing it because you felt pressured."

Emily raised her hand.

"Put your hand down."

Emily only raised it higher.

No one spoke for a long moment. Finally, Katherine cleared her throat and said, "Shall we go back to the beginning? Sex in front of the fire. Any takers?"

Everyone else had lowered their hand when the argument between Lara and Alex started, and no one seemed ready to get in the middle of it now. Besides, Alex was only looking at her.

"You sure about this?" Alex asked.

Emily nodded. She could hardly swallow but knew it wasn't a mistake. She'd signed up to have sex with the one person who intimidated her the most, but also the only one she was drawn to. Maybe fighting it had been pointless all along.

"Then I pick you," Alex said.

"What a surprise," Lara said flatly.

A beat passed, then another. Alex didn't look at Lara, but her anger was palpable.

"We have a few more fantasies to read," Katherine said, shaking the hat.

Shay leaned over and whispered, "Don't worry about Lara. You're gonna have a blast with Alex. And don't be surprised if Katherine wants to watch. You know Alex is her favorite, right? She thinks you two are hot together."

Emily forced a smile even as her mind spun with questions. What had she gotten herself into? Was Katherine part of the deal because of Alex?

"Finally, a proper request for an orgy," Katherine said, holding up the slip of paper she'd pulled out.

"From Shay?" Lara guessed.

TJ shook her head. "Nicola."

Nicola held up her hands. "Guilty."

"Everyone likes a group activity," Katherine said.

It was quickly settled that Nicola's request would be fulfilled on Monday as the culmination of the long weekend. Emily wondered if she'd make it till then. With an orgy she could at least hang in the background and watch the others. But now she'd agreed to have sex with Alex, and there'd be no chance of simply watching.

Katherine held the next slip of paper she'd picked for a moment before reading it aloud: "Katherine."

"Wow. No beating around the bush." Shay's mouth was open in awe. "Wait, was that you, Ava?"

Ava hesitated. "Depends on the answer."

Katherine met her gaze. "My room, my rules."

"Tell me when and I'll be there," Ava said without hesitation.

Shay shook their head. "I can't believe you went right for it."

"Gotta go for what you want in life."

"On that note," Katherine said. "Who wants to be Queen Guinevere?"

"That one's definitely Shay's," TJ said. "We all know how much Shay likes princesses."

"For the record, I also put in for an alien abduction."

"But that one didn't get picked," Katherine said. "I like this one better, Sir Lancelot."

"Does that mean you're volunteering to be Queen Guinevere?"

Katherine cocked her head, eyes locked on Shay's. "Maybe I am."

Shay clapped their hand to their hip. "I need a sword."

"When you find a sword, come find me," Katherine said.

The others laughed as Shay fell back on the sofa cushions in a mock-swoon.

"As for my fantasy," Katherine said, holding up the last slip of paper. "You'll know what I want when I give this to you."

"Ooh, I like that," Nicola murmured. "A little mystery."

Several others echoed Nicola's sentiment, and then the next minute everyone was standing up and talking at once. TJ and Nicola met in the middle of the room. Shay went to join Katherine and Madison. Ava and Lara had paired up and were already laughing. Before Emily had time to decide which group to join, Alex was heading her direction.

CHAPTER FIFTEEN

"Hey," Alex said. "Is it okay if we talk for a minute?"

"Considering what we're going to do later, I hope so." Emily tried to sound flirty, but she knew it didn't quite meet the mark.

"About that, I don't feel great about how things went down. I kind of lost my temper with Lara and I'm sorry you got dragged into it. If you want to back out—"

"You regretting your choice?"

"No. Not at all."

"Good. Me neither. Glad we got that settled. Shall we go fuck?"

Alex opened and closed her mouth. After a moment, she said, "I was hoping we could hang out first and get to know each other better. Maybe go to my place?"

Emily had tried for a more assertive tone, trying like she'd done earlier to act more confident than she felt. But going to Alex's to hang out sounded a lot less intimidating than jumping right to the sex. Plus, she wouldn't have to worry about Katherine being around to watch. Losing her nerve and not having sex at all was still a real possibility.

As Emily was debating an answer, Alex said, "We've got all weekend, you know. Nothing needs to happen tonight." She offered a half smile and added, "Unless you're worried you won't like me once you know me better."

Emily told herself to relax and play along. "That could happen."

"If it makes a difference, the hot cocoa offer still stands."

"I almost forgot about my secret mission to steal your recipe." So much had happened since the flight. It didn't seem possible that the Alex standing in front of her—the one more than half the party wanted to have sex with—was the same person who had made herself seem like a dork just to get Emily to smile.

"So, is that a yes to my place?"

Admittedly, she was curious about what Alex's house might be like. Would it be a mansion like Katherine's? That didn't seem to fit her, but clearly she had money. And clearly, she was out of Emily's league. For one night, though, none of that mattered.

"How else am I getting that recipe?"

"Good…Also, I don't really want to bring this up, but if you want to talk at all about what you walked in on earlier, I'll answer any questions. I know you didn't expect to see me here, especially like that. It was a little awkward for both of us."

"A little." Emily could see the tension in Alex's face and she suddenly wanted to ease it. "I thought you were interesting when I first met you. Turns out I completely underestimated *how* interesting."

"Interesting? I'll take that." Alex chuckled. "So, no questions?"

"I don't think so." In fact, she had lots of questions. Could she actually relax enough to have sex with Alex? Was she playing into some plan of Katherine's? And, if so, was a threesome the next step? Although she'd briefly entertained that fantasy, she didn't really want Katherine. She only wanted Alex.

"If anything comes up, just ask. I know it can be hard coming in as the new person. A lot of the drama has been going on for years. It's a lot to walk into."

Emily wasn't sure if Alex was referencing her fight with Lara and how she'd gotten pulled into that, or the threesome she'd walked in on. She didn't care about Lara, but keeping Katherine happy was an issue. Nicola's comment about Katherine being territorial regarding Alex replayed in her head.

"Well, one question. Katherine won't mind us leaving the party, right? I don't want to seem rude ditching."

"I doubt she'll even notice. She's got plenty of others to entertain her tonight."

"Maybe, but I've heard from more than one person that you're her favorite." Emily had tried to keep her tone playful, but as soon as she saw Alex's expression, she immediately regretted her words. Unfortunately, once it was out there she couldn't simply pretend it wasn't an issue. "I don't want to steal you away and get in the middle of anything."

"I'm not dating Katherine. And I'm not sure what you heard, but I definitely don't belong to her. Madison and Katherine are a couple. Considering what you saw, I could see how you might think I was with them, but I'm not. That was...well...a favor." Alex shook her head. "That sounds bad, doesn't it?"

"You getting called in for sex favors? It doesn't sound bad. More like intimidating." Emily sighed. In a way, though, it felt good to get everything out in the open. "It's none of my business if you're with Katherine or not, but I work for her and I don't want to do anything that will piss her off. Again, that doesn't make what you do with her, or with Madison, any of my business, but—"

"You need to know what you're getting yourself into. That's completely fair." Alex took a deep breath. "Madison and Katherine have an open relationship. They both sleep with other people, and, yes, sometimes I'm one of those people. They also have threesomes and sometimes I'm the third." Alex met Emily's gaze. "If any of that makes you change your mind about me, I get it. Or, if it's better that we stay here, that's fine too."

Emily wished she hadn't brought any of it up. She didn't want Alex to feel like she had to explain herself. After all, she was the one who only wanted tonight to be about sex. Now she'd made that more complicated. "I still want to go to your house, but maybe we should skip to the sex. I think I mess things up when we talk."

"I like talking to you."

"That might be all you like," Emily said, half joking, half serious. "It's been a while for me. Even if I hadn't complicated everything bringing up Katherine, you'd probably be happier with someone who—"

"Stop." Alex reached out and caught Emily's hand.

The unexpected warmth of Alex's hand gripping hers instantly triggered a shock of desire. Emily didn't have time to get her bearings before Alex let go.

"Sorry. I shouldn't have grabbed your hand. Or interrupted."

Emily held her breath. She was still too thrown by the feel of Alex's hand, and by her body's response, to think of what to say.

"The truth is, Lara was right, even if she's an asshole. You're the only one I wanted."

Emily could feel the heat between her and Alex build as the seconds passed. She held herself back from stepping into a kiss, but it was suddenly all that she wanted.

Alex continued. "I wasn't sure coming to this party was a good idea. I've had a lot of meaningless sex and I'm kind of over it. But I kept thinking I'd meet someone one of these weekends. Someone I connected with. And this time it actually happened. And I know you're gonna say that I don't know you well enough to know if we really connect, but I've never wanted to get to know someone more."

A long moment passed, and Alex's brow furrowed. "Now you're not talking. Did I say the wrong thing again?"

"Maybe." Or too much of the right thing. Nicola's words passed through her thoughts like another warning: *Alex is very good at being exactly what you've been waiting for.*

"What can I do?" Alex's concern was obvious.

"This is my first time with sex parties, obviously, but do you always do a lot of talking first?"

"No. Usually if I know someone's interested, I pretty much go right to that." Alex gestured to the couch across from where they stood. TJ and Nicola were lip-locked and already undressing each other.

Emily was more surprised that she hadn't noticed when they'd started than that it was happening. But TJ and Nicola weren't the only ones. Madison and Shay were half naked as well, and Ava seemed intent on doing more than watching. Lara and Katherine were MIA, and Emily realized they were probably setting up the dungeon.

"We don't have to talk at all, but *just sex* isn't my thing anymore."

"You do realize you're at a sex party, right?" Emily had to point out the obvious logical flaw, but she wished she could simply enjoy the fact that Alex wanted her for more than just sex. "I'm not saying it's a bad line to use to pick up dates most of the time, but in this case…"

"You don't have to believe me. The fact that platypuses lay eggs seems pretty unbelievable, but that's true too."

"Platypuses?"

Alex shook her head. "That sounded better in my head. I'm a little nervous around you."

"You're nervous?" Emily nearly laughed, but the look on Alex's face stopped her. She was serious, which only made her more endearing. Endearing Alex wasn't, however, what she needed. She needed confident, horny Alex. "Why are you nervous?"

"I don't want to screw anything up with you. Well, not more than I've already done, anyway." Alex exhaled. "Look, things are complicated with me and Katherine. I'm not gonna lie. But we aren't dating because we don't want the same things."

"What do you want?"

Alex dropped her chin. "To be in love with the person I have sex with. Katherine's convinced the two things are mutually exclusive."

"Sex and love?" Emily thought of telling Alex what Nicola had said—that Katherine did love Alex. Maybe Alex didn't know. But it wasn't her place to say it. "Well, they can be."

"Right. But I want both."

"So you go to a sex party to find someone you can fall in love with? Someone Katherine's invited. Someone who's probably only come to have sex." Emily gave Alex a skeptical look.

"When you put it that way—"

"Alex, I'm completely out of my league here. But I'm not looking for love or any kind of relationship. I'm here for that meaningless sex you mentioned. If that's a problem, maybe we shouldn't go to your house."

Alex was quiet for a long minute. When she spoke again, her tone had changed. "Turns out I like sex." A little distant, and almost professional. "You should grab a coat. It's cold outside. I'll meet you by the back door."

"You sure about this?"

"Until we sleep together, I won't be able to think about anyone else."

Emily nodded, refusing to let her tumble of emotions show. For better or worse, they'd set the groundwork. No expectations. Only sex. If she was a disappointment, it wouldn't matter. Alex would move on to someone else.

CHAPTER SIXTEEN

"Are you at least going to thank me?" Katherine sidled between Alex and the coatrack.

"For what?"

"For the candy I picked out for you."

Alex reached for her coat, evading Katherine's attempt at a kiss as she did. "Jealous, huh?"

"I'm not jealous."

"No?" Alex pulled on the winter parka. The heavyweight down seemed overkill for the two-minute walk from Katherine's back door to her front door, but the wind had picked up and it looked like a blizzard outside. "If you're not jealous, what are you?"

"Pleased that you like my present. I knew Emily would like you, but I didn't anticipate how much you'd like her. You haven't ever taken anyone home."

"I'm only getting her out of here for a bit. She's nervous."

Katherine adjusted Alex's collar. She caressed Alex's cheek and murmured, "And you're the one to help relax her. Smooth."

Alex tried to pull back, but she was between the coatrack and the door. She straightened up and leveled her gaze on Katherine. "Speaking of smooth, we need to talk."

"That's what you said on Thursday. Right before you had me against my bedroom door, as I recall." Katherine glanced down the hall at the sound of voices. She hesitated a moment, then looked back at Alex and added, "Isn't that how our conversations always go?"

"I'm serious this time."

"I can tell." Katherine slipped her hand behind Alex's neck and pulled her in for a deep kiss.

The kiss was an obvious power play on Katherine's part—annoying given the timing and not even a little bit of a turn-on. Alex pushed Katherine back, but before she could say anything Katherine smiled and said, "Go have your fun. We'll talk later."

Alex clenched her jaw. As much as she wanted to, she couldn't put the blame entirely on Katherine. Not only had she slept with her in San Francisco—after saying she wanted to stop—then she'd agreed to the threesome with Madison. It was no surprise Katherine believed they were back at their old game. And now she was about to have sex with someone who only wanted her for that. Why would Katherine think she'd changed at all?

Emily appeared in the hall right as Katherine rounded the corner. If Emily had spotted Katherine leaving, her face hid the clues.

"This place is a maze," Emily said. "Sorry for taking so long."

"Is that your only coat?"

Emily nodded. The jacket she had on might be enough for February in San Francisco, but it wouldn't cut it here.

"You said your place was close."

"Not that close." Alex took off her coat and held it out. "Here. Take mine. You'll freeze in that."

"You'll freeze without a coat at all."

Alex held the coat out an inch higher. "Take it and we can pretend you think I'm chivalrous."

Emily rolled her eyes but reached for the coat anyway. "What would I do without someone to take care of me?"

"Nice sarcasm. And here I was about to say it's nice to know that you can do as you're told." Alex enjoyed Emily's feigned glare. After their earlier conversation, she wasn't certain what the vibe would be between them. Playful teasing felt exactly right. "But I won't. Unless you're into that."

"I'm not saying one way or the other."

Emily's glare turned into a coy look that brought a lot of questions to Alex's mind. Questions for later.

Alex shuffled through the coats on the rack until she found a fluorescent pink ski parka with a fake fur trim. It belonged to Katherine and was completely not her style—in addition to being too tight—but she pulled it on anyway and flipped up the hood. "Ready?"

"You look ridiculous."

"I know. And you feel more comfortable with me looking silly."

Emily narrowed her eyes. "You're right."

"Gotta watch out for the smart ones." Alex tapped her temple and then opened the back door. "After you."

Emily stepped past, yelping as the wind blasted her with a flurry of snow. She turned around to face Alex and quickly zipped the coat. Snowflakes dotted her dark hair and tipped her eyelashes.

"Holy hell! It's too cold to even breathe out here. Why do people live in places like this?"

"It's a real struggle living in Aspen," Alex joked.

"Seriously, why freeze?"

"Because it's also beautiful." *Almost as beautiful as you*, Alex silently added. She knew that comment would only come across as cheesy, but it was true. Too damn true. Pushing away the wish that tonight could be a date, she pointed at two trees covered in snow. "Path's right through those pines. I don't recommend talking much. The ice goes right to your chest as soon as you open your mouth."

Emily squinted and then shook her head. "I can't see any path. We're stuck in the middle of a snow globe."

Alex stepped in front of her and stomped her feet to pack down the snow. "Follow me."

The wind gusted again, and Emily reached for Alex's hand. "Don't lose me." When Alex glanced over her shoulder, Emily only tightened her grip. "Dying of frostbite the first time I go to a sex party would be a real bummer."

Before Alex came up with something witty to say in response, another gust sent more snow swirling. She trained her gaze back to the pine trees that marked the boundary between her property and Katherine's and marched ahead. Focusing on the trees and the path did not, however, stop her from thinking about Emily's hand and how good it felt nestled in hers. Her heart had lodged in her throat the moment Emily had reached for her, and it seemed intent on setting up residence there. Emily hadn't meant anything romantic by saying, *Don't lose me.* And yet Alex couldn't help wanting to believe the words were about more than a walk through a snowstorm.

When they reached her front door, she reluctantly let go of Emily's hand to find her keys. Despite the cold, she wished the walk had been longer. Or that she had some excuse to go back to holding hands.

They shook off snow and then hurried into the warm foyer. Alex hung their coats in the otherwise empty closet, making a mental note to return Katherine's old parka. When she turned around, Emily was rubbing her hands together and blowing on her fingers.

"I'll get a fire going," Alex said. "We'll warm up quick. And then hot cocoa?"

"That's why I'm here."

The flight and the offer for cocoa seemed like a week ago. It wasn't the date she'd imagined, but she was happy Emily was here all the same and she intended to make the best of it. A little part of her still hoped that by the end of it, Emily would want more than one night.

Emily walked into the living room and looked around. "This place fits you."

"How so?"

"It's nice, but not lavish. And not a mansion like Katherine's. More comfortable. More you, I guess."

"I like comfortable." Alex liked even more that Emily felt that way. "Wouldn't want to be a mansion."

"You're not a mansion. I mean, if someone described you to me, I'd probably think that you were fancy enough to be one. But you're..." Emily seemed to search for a word as she walked from the living room through the dining area to the kitchen and then circled back, stopping at the couch. "You're oddly cozy. Like a ski cabin."

Alex laughed. "Never got that compliment before."

"You're welcome." Emily ran her hand over the back of the leather couch. "I'm sure this place still cost a bazillion dollars."

"Not quite a bazillion, but close. It is Aspen, after all." Alex felt a little sheepish for how much she'd spent, but the prices had gone up in the area even more since she'd bought and she didn't regret the decision. "I had my eye on this cabin for years. Finally made an offer to the family who owned it. It wasn't on the market, but I knew they were thinking of selling."

Emily nodded at the fireplace and the rug in front of it. "And the rug seriously hasn't seen any action? After what I saw in Katherine's private room, that surprises me."

"No action. I swear." More than ever Alex wished she could turn back the clock on the day and say no to Katherine and Madison. But like TJ had said, Emily might as well know the truth going in. "I don't usually bring anyone here. Actually, you're the first."

Emily's look was one part surprise and one part something Alex couldn't quite place. Was she pleased to know she was an exception, or did she not believe Alex?

"I appreciate that you offered your place this time. Especially now that I know it's not your usual."

She was still nervous, clearly, and Alex had to stop herself from again suggesting that they didn't have to have sex. Emily had made it clear that was all she wanted, but Alex also knew they needed to take baby steps regardless. "I wanted you to feel like you could relax and have a good time."

"I believe you. In fact, I'm starting to think the chivalry thing isn't only an act."

"Don't let the secret out." Alex joked again, but the note of trust in Emily's voice was more than she'd hoped for.

"I have to give you props, too, for being dorky on my behalf. That fluorescent pink jacket with the fake fur collar is so not you."

"Being dorky on your behalf?" Alex held out her arms. "This is me all the time."

Emily laughed and the warm sound filled Alex's chest. The wide smile on her face, the first real smile Alex had seen all night, made her all the more gorgeous. Resisting her was going to be hard. But Alex wanted to resist—for a while, at least. They couldn't only have sex. She'd regret it too much if that was all that happened.

After all the highs she'd gotten from pleasuring women who simply wanted to be cherished for one night, she wondered why she needed more this time. Why did she want Emily to actually be into her as a person? Was it only her own ego saying that sex wasn't enough for her anymore?

Alex pointed to the record player in the living room. "If you want to pick out some music, go for it. You can tease me later about the number of Journey albums I own. I'll grab some wood and get the fire started."

It didn't take long to get the wood—Jorie had left a good stock in the garage—but she came back to find Emily sitting cross-legged on the rug with the box of records spilling out all around her. "Find anything you like?"

"Are these all yours?"

"Most of them are. A few belonged to my dad. He gave me some of his favorites after he went digital."

Emily held up Bob Dylan's *Blonde on Blonde*. "I listened to this album in middle school. Every day for months."

"That's from the sixties, isn't it?"

"And it's a great album," Emily said. "I take it this is one of your dad's?"

Alex nodded.

"Can we play it?"

"Knock yourself out. I'm still trying to wrap my head around you being a Dylan fan."

"He's an amazing songwriter."

"Yeah, maybe, but his voice—"

"Nope. Don't even go there. Not if you want to get laid tonight."

Alex laughed. "Fair enough. I'll stick to making a fire."

Once the fire was going, Alex left Emily sorting through the rest of the records and went to the kitchen to start the hot cocoa. With Dylan playing in the background, she couldn't help but think of her dad. He was a big Dylan fan, although as far as she could tell, that's where the similarities between Emily and her father ended. She missed him suddenly and resolved to give him a call. He wasn't the only one she needed to catch up with, and she felt a wave of guilt realizing how bad she was at keeping in touch with her family. Maybe if she paid more attention to the people who already loved her, she wouldn't feel like she needed anyone else to love.

CHAPTER SEVENTEEN

Quieting the worries in her head didn't seem possible, but Dylan had magic powers. Emily couldn't remember the last time she'd simply sat and listened to a record, and it had been even longer since Dylan was her musician of choice.

The fire warmed the room, crackling as if in testament to Alex's butch capabilities and giving her something to focus on besides alphabetizing the records. She finished her sorting and placed all the records back in the box, in order now, and moved from the floor to the couch. The smooth leather caressed her skin and made her wonder if Alex's tastes were always expensive. Then she remembered French fries and pie. Alex seemed to have two sides: one with tailored suits and polished pickup lines, the other unapologetically dorky and sincere.

Emily shook her head. It didn't matter how much she was drawn to Alex, even to the quirks of her personality. It didn't matter how much she wanted Alex to be someone she could know in real life. Alex was a fantasy. One night in her cabin and then the fantasy would be over.

"Here's your cocoa. Careful, it's hot."

Alex handed her the mug and then settled in on the sofa leaving at least a foot between them. She stared at the fire for a moment, holding her dark blue mug close to her chin but not drinking yet. Emily wondered what she was thinking. She hesitated asking what might seem too personal, but Alex was the one who wanted to talk. And maybe it would help her relax too.

"What are you thinking about?"

"That I don't do this enough." Alex sighed softly and brought the cocoa up to her lips.

"Have sex with random women you meet at a sex party?" Emily teased. "I don't buy it."

"You shouldn't." Alex chuckled. "What I meant was sit in front of a fire with no other agenda."

"Why not?"

"I don't slow down a lot to enjoy the little things." Alex took another sip of her cocoa and then shifted back on the sofa. "I know you didn't want to talk, but would it be a problem if we sit together for a while?"

"This is your fantasy. I'm here for whatever you want to do." Emily immediately regretted her words. She felt the heat of a blush start racing up her neck as she added, "Well, maybe not *whatever* you want."

"Noted." Alex nodded at Emily's mug. "Nervous about trying my cocoa?"

"More distracted than nervous." Emily raised the mug and breathed in the steam. "It smells delicious."

"Tastes even better."

"Is that what you say to all the women?" Emily laughed when Alex rolled her eyes.

"Go on, try it. You're killing me over here making me wait this long to find out if you like it."

"I'm killing you? You're the one who's making me wait for sex in front of a fire." Emily loved the way Alex was looking at her with a mix of desire and playful frustration. She wanted to prolong the moment, but the cocoa did smell good and her taste buds were getting impatient. She took the smallest of sips, letting only a little of the warm chocolate roll over her tongue. Closing her eyes, she savored the rich chocolate blending with a hint of Kahlua.

"So?"

Emily opened her eyes and met Alex's gaze. "Earlier I was wondering what you would taste like, but now I'm thinking you're going to have a hard time living up to this." She took another sip, enjoying the smile she'd put on Alex's face. "Kahlua and a little whipping cream?"

"You think I'm gonna give out my secrets that easy?"

Emily took a bigger sip, knowing she'd guessed at least partly right. "If I tell you this is the best cocoa I've ever had in my entire life, what do I get?"

"Keep stroking my ego and we'll see."

Emily felt a buzz that had nothing to do with the sugar—or the Kahlua. She knew she'd missed sex, but she realized now that it was foreplay she'd missed even more. The flirting that had an ulterior motive. The getting to know the someone who would later undress her. Someone whose desires openly matched hers. She gave her mug a swirl, sending the white foam on the top of the deep brown into a spin, then took another sip.

"Where do you hide the recipe?"

"You could search me for it. I wouldn't stop you."

Alex's tone suggested she was only joking, but the thought of a strip search made Emily feel hot all over. She couldn't imagine being brave enough to even unbutton Alex's shirt. But what if she went for it?

"Are we listening to this dude all night?"

"This dude?" Emily tilted her head. "You got a problem with Dylan?"

Alex laughed. "Apparently not."

"Good. Because, as I said, he's an amazing songwriter and his music is classic."

"And here I thought you liked his sexy voice."

"Maybe I like that too."

Alex cleared her throat and lowered her voice. "Hey. Wanna hang out with me?" She'd added a gravelly sound that was completely ridiculous, but the arched eyebrow topped the act.

Emily burst out laughing.

"So, I should keep talking like this?"

"How much do I have to pay you to stop?"

"A lot," Alex said, still in the fake Dylan voice. She fell back on the couch cushions, laughing too.

"I may have to move some nonexistent money from my savings account into checking, but it'll be worth it. How much?"

Alex stopped laughing but her smile didn't fade. She met Emily's gaze. "I like you."

"So you've said. And I appreciate how honest and open you are with your…hmm…are they feelings or cravings?"

"Feelings," Alex said. A moment later, she added, "And cravings."

"Whatever it is, it's good for me. It's been a while since someone has looked at me the way you do."

Alex seemed about to ask Emily to explain, but she only held her gaze. "Thank you for volunteering."

"You're welcome. Did you pick this fantasy because you thought I'd say yes?"

"Yes," Alex said. "Well, I hoped you'd say yes. After dinner, I didn't know about my chances with you. You're a bit of a puzzle. One minute I think you want to jump my bones, and the next I think you hate me."

"Pretty much, yeah."

Alex shook her head. "What am I going to do with you?"

"I could give you some suggestions, but I think you'll have even better ideas than I could come up with."

"Is that so? Hmm. Maybe later we should compare notes."

Emily smiled at the thought. She leaned back and took another sip of her cocoa. It hardly seemed possible, but she felt relaxed now. Sitting and talking with Alex was more than nice. Her desire hadn't changed—in fact her clit pulsed impatiently whenever she looked at Alex for long—but she was also okay waiting for what she knew would come soon. Besides, once they had sex, the fantasy would be over.

Hopefully she wouldn't freeze up. Or be terrible. God, it had been so long since she'd gone down on a woman. She slid her tongue over her lips. The longing for that salty musky taste mixed with a plain old-fashioned fear of failure.

"Since you asked me, I'm gonna put you on the spot too. What are you thinking?"

"Right now?" Emily stalled.

Alex nodded. "I dare you not to lie."

"I'm worried that I'm not going to be good. I'd like to knock your socks off, not because I think I'll have any chance at being memorable, but…" She swallowed against the sudden lump in her throat. "I need a good memory to fall back on in case I'm celibate for another seven years. Vibrators only get you so far."

Alex didn't laugh at the joke. She set her mug down on the coffee table and turned sideways on the couch to face Emily. "Your music choice alone would make you memorable."

"Great. Now I'll be the Bob Dylan Girl, won't I?" Emily joked again but she couldn't believe Alex was unfazed by her comment about it being seven years since she'd had sex. Did she miss that part?

Alex continued. "You already knocked my socks off yesterday at the café. I'll admit at first I was only thinking about how good-looking you were. You have a gorgeous smile and…other gorgeous things."

Emily laughed. "Maybe I won't ask what things you mean so we can keep pretending you're chivalrous."

"My point is there's a lot more to you than the fact that you're beautiful. You're smart and you're funny but you don't tolerate bullshit. The way you put me in my place is so damn hot. At dinner and then when you volunteered even after I told you not to…" Alex hesitated like she wasn't sure how to finish the sentence. After a moment, she said, "You make me want to earn taking you all the way. I'm the one who should be worrying about being memorable. I can already tell you're not easy to impress."

Emily felt shaky and hot all at the same time. She was turned on more than ever with Alex's eyes holding hers, and the tension only seemed to build between them. If only Alex would kiss her. She needed her to make the first move. But Alex didn't shift any closer and didn't seem in a hurry to stop talking.

"Did I say too much again?"

Emily shook her head.

"I'd like to kiss you," Alex said.

Thank god. Emily held her breath.

"But I want to take things slow. I know what's going to happen after we kiss, and I'm not sure I'm ready."

"You're not ready?" Emily would have laughed, but Alex seemed completely serious. "Do you mean we?"

"No. I mean me. It's no secret I want more, but if one night is all I get, I want to take my time. There's so many things we could do."

Emily's breath caught. She wanted to ask Alex what things she was thinking of but couldn't bring herself to say the words. All the things she'd wanted to try over the years…not only the toys that Cass had made her embarrassed to even think about, but the rest of it too. Desires she couldn't hold back. Suddenly she wanted to admit everything. What would it feel like to let Alex tie her up? To give herself over? And, what would it feel like to be the one in control? To reach across the sofa and unbuckle Alex's belt? She wanted all those things, yet she couldn't quite get past the seven-year boulder that blocked her path to all of that.

"I'm not sure if you caught what I said earlier." Emily heard the tremor in her own voice but pushed on. "I haven't had sex in seven years."

"I caught that. I figured you had your reasons. If you want to tell me, I'd like to know, but I won't press." Alex waited, but when Emily didn't speak up, she continued. "What happened in the past isn't as important to me as what you want to happen next."

"I might be terrible."

"Okay." Alex grinned. "I won't be."

"So cocky." She laughed, and the knot in her stomach loosened. With Alex knowing the truth, she felt lighter. Like she had nothing left to hide. "Seven years is long enough to forget a few things."

"I get that. We'll take it slow. Did I mention slow's my favorite way to fuck?"

Something about the soft way Alex said the word *fuck* made it more sexy than crass. God, she wanted to kiss her. The way Alex looked at her left no question of her desire.

"And, between me and you, it's a huge turn-on to get you first. After all that time with no one appreciating you, I get to be the one."

Emily wanted to simultaneously hug Alex, cry on her shoulder, and tear off her clothes. Her words were exactly what she needed.

"The only thing I'm worried about now is that I better be damn good considering how long you've waited."

Alex took the mug from Emily's hand and set it on the coffee table next to hers. When she turned back to Emily, she held out her hand, palm upturned.

CHAPTER EIGHTEEN

Emily's pulse whooshed in her ears, outcompeting the crackle of the fire and even Dylan's voice. She wanted Alex more than ever, but she didn't pull her into a kiss. She didn't even clasp Alex's outstretched hand. Instead, she traced lightly from Alex's wrist, over her palm, to the tip of her middle finger, and then made her way slowly back. Alex watched her, holding perfectly still.

Alex's palm was noticeably wider than hers and her slender fingers were longer. She had rough calluses from gripping something, and Emily wondered what it might be as she lightly rubbed between the smooth spots and the textured ones. As she followed the lines and the curves, she imagined how it would feel to have Alex's hand exploring her body. Would Alex be rough like she wanted, or gentle like she needed?

"You okay?"

Emily nodded, not trusting herself to speak.

In a way, the going slow was a relief—in nearly the same way that it was torture. There wouldn't be a rush to get to it, but that meant it wouldn't be over and done with either. She had to sit with every step, let her body get over the anxiety of that moment, before she got what came next.

"This is something I'd like to do more often," Emily said, moving from Alex's palm to her wrist and then inching up her forearm. When Alex had made the fire, she'd pushed up her sleeves and they were still bunched at her elbows giving Emily plenty of access to smooth skin.

"Drive somebody crazy with your fingers, you mean?" Alex closed her eyes. "You can keep that up all night if you like."

Emily's focus shifted back to Alex's fingers. She started to trace each one, but when she got to the middle, she stopped. "I don't think I can."

Alex opened her eyes. She looked up from Emily's hand and their gaze met.

"I want to be kissed." The words came out in a whisper, but she knew Alex heard. Need overwhelmed her. She hated feeling desperate, but Alex had to know that she was.

Seconds passed and neither of them spoke. Right after she'd accepted that Alex was going to make her go slow, she couldn't handle waiting. Maybe she shouldn't have picked Alex. Maybe she should have picked someone from the party who didn't know anything about her, someone she couldn't possibly have opened up to. Someone who was simply horny. That certainly wouldn't be hard. But as soon as she had that thought, she knew no one else would do. Alex was the only one she wanted.

"I don't want to beg, but I will."

"I don't want you to say anything you don't want to say. Or do anything you don't want to do. That's not what I'm about. But I also don't want to move too fast."

"I'll tell you if we need to slow down. Right now, I need you to speed up." She swallowed. Had she actually said the words aloud?

"I like that you know what you want." Alex closed the distance between them.

As much as Emily had been waiting for the kiss, knew it was coming, her breath caught when Alex's lips met hers. Alex was gentle at first, brushing against Emily's mouth with the lightest of touches, but then obvious desire made her deepen the kiss. Heat poured through Emily's body when Alex pushed into her. She opened up, not wanting to resist, and the heat turned to a fire that roared through her.

She tipped up her chin when Alex caressed her neck, giving in to another kiss as she fumbled with the buttons on Alex's shirt. As soon as she could, she slid her hand through the opening she'd made. Alex pushed against her and she gasped when she felt the warm skin of Alex's chest.

Alex took over then, making it clear she knew what she was doing—and what she wanted. She moved them off the leather couch and onto the rug, pulling off their clothing as she did. First her dress, then her bra.

Emily tried to help some, but Alex's lips were distractingly good and before she knew it, she was on her back. Alex's hands slid over her naked belly and then down past her hips.

"God, you're gorgeous," Alex said. She held her body a few inches above Emily's, not letting their skin touch. "You know that, right? Someone should tell you that every morning as soon as you wake up."

"I know I need you." Emily felt desperate with need. She was wet and could already imagine Alex's hand on the place she needed to be touched. Now she couldn't wait any longer.

"You act like you don't know how good-looking you are."

"If I say I know I'm good-looking, will you put your damn hand between my legs?"

Alex grinned. "Oh, is that what you want?"

As much as Emily appreciated Alex's gentle teasing, her need had passed anything gentle or sweet. "I want to feel you." The words came out as little more than a breath.

"You've been feeling plenty of me," Alex said. "Trying to tear my clothes off to get to me."

Emily looked at Alex then. Alex's pants were undone, and she was naked from the waist up. She'd done that.

"I like how hungry you are," Alex said, caressing Emily's cheek. "I also like those nails of yours on my back. You trying to leave marks?"

Emily hadn't meant to scratch hard, but the look on Alex's face stopped her from an outright apology. Instead, she wanted to play along. "You're too good at kissing. I wasn't paying attention to what my hands were doing."

"So you're saying it's my fault."

"Yes."

Alex lowered herself so her nipples barely brushed Emily's. "Maybe kissing's all I'm good at. Maybe I won't be any good between your legs."

"I'm worried you're going to be good everywhere." Emily moaned as Alex stroked over her nipples.

"You sure we're not going too fast?"

"Not fast enough." Emily pushed up and Alex met her lips with a deep kiss. When Alex pulled back from the kiss, Emily expected she'd move on her. She didn't, though, holding her body above Emily's and hardly letting any skin touch.

"I need you." She heard the whimper escape her throat and felt ridiculous for it, but Alex torturing her with this waiting game wasn't fair.

"Was it my hot cocoa that convinced you? Be honest. This is for research purposes. I'm hoping to get a steady girlfriend someday."

Emily laughed. Annoyed as she was, she couldn't help it. "You are too much."

"You have no idea." Alex's voice had a husky sound to it, and Emily realized then that the waiting was getting to her just as much. Alex couldn't possibly want this as desperately as she did, but there was no doubting her arousal.

"You should show me."

Alex's eyes darkened, and Emily held her breath. She gasped when Alex lowered herself onto her. A barrage of sensations hit all at once—the scent of Alex's cologne, the wool carpet pressed against her back, Alex's smooth skin pressed everywhere else, and warm breath on her neck. She rubbed against Alex, feeling like a cat wanting to be pet.

When the urge came to feel more, she didn't stop herself from nipping at Alex's sculpted shoulder. But when she tried to raise herself up for a kiss, Alex pressed her back down. The message was clear: tonight she wasn't in charge.

Emily didn't want to resist anyway. She gave in to Alex's lips and then her hands, closing her eyes as Alex caressed her. Her touch was gentle, almost soothing, but Emily could feel desire building in Alex with every inch she skimmed. Delicious desire. She loved how much Alex wanted this. Wanted *her*.

When Alex moved her attention to Emily's nipples—plying, rolling, and pinching—Emily felt a tingling buzz spread through her. Damn, Alex knew how to touch her. She dropped her head back and moaned.

"You like that?"

Emily nodded, but even as she did pleasure gave way to worry when an insistent pulse started between her legs. She didn't want to come only from the attention Alex was giving to her breasts. She shivered and tensed, trying to hold back her mounting orgasm. Alex let off, probably thinking she'd gone too far.

"I don't want to come with you only touching me there."

"Is that a real risk?"

"Mmm…Your hands might be even better than your lips."

Alex pressed a fingertip lightly on Emily's lips. "You might want to hold off making that call." Alex drew a line from Emily's lips down the center of her, then pushed her legs apart. Without any other warning, she dropped her face and suddenly her tongue was on Emily's swollen clit.

"Fuck." No other words were possible.

Alex took her with a fierceness that made her want to give over completely. She pulled up her knees, granting more access, and Alex repositioned, thrusting her tongue deeper.

"Oh. God."

Alex pulled back only long enough to look up and meet Emily's gaze. Heat seared through her. One look and Emily felt sexier than she had in her whole life. How could Alex want her this much?

Alex dropped her face again. She whipped and circled Emily's clit, then sucked, bringing her closer with every stroke of her tongue. She certainly knew how to please, but the sounds she made—low growls and long moans—left no doubt that she was enjoying every minute.

Again, Emily fought back a climax that she worried would hit too soon. But Alex felt too good between her legs and it'd been too long since someone had gone down on her. Soon there was no holding back. The orgasm came like a wave rising inside and she gave up fighting.

She screamed out, squeezing her eyes closed and clamping her knees on Alex's shoulders. A gush of release followed another shiver of pleasure. She went still and then tensed again, the climax zinging from her toes to her clenched teeth.

Alex didn't let go of her and didn't let off the pressure on her clit, only holding in place as the aftershocks ran their course. Emily heard herself say Alex's name. She breathed it out softly at first, then murmured it again, felt silly for saying it, but repeated it anyway. "I need…"

"What do you need?"

Emily wanted to answer but couldn't form any words. She needed more. Alex had given her exactly what she needed and suddenly it wasn't enough. She wanted to beg Alex not to let go, but wasn't she the one who was supposed to be taking care of Alex's needs?

Tonight was Alex's fantasy. The fire, the rug…

"I'm sorry."

"For what?" Alex moved up her body, adding soft kisses as she went from below her belly button up to her neck. She didn't move off of Emily and her weight was reassuringly heavy. "You shouldn't be sorry about anything."

Emily shook her head.

"Hey," Alex nudged. "What is it?" When Alex kissed her chin, she reluctantly opened her eyes. "What is it you need? I want to give you what you need."

"I need you." Emily closed her eyes again. She couldn't handle the way Alex looked at her. The intensity was too much. Alex wanted her, still desired her, but Emily felt the press of tears and clenched her jaw to stave them off.

The strength of her emotions caught her completely by surprise. Maybe she should have expected breaking down the first time—after all, it had been seven long years of pretending to be with someone who only pretended to want her. They were merely together on paper, sharing a house, going out together, but never kissing. Never doing anything more than cuddling in rare moments of concession. So many nights without because what she'd asked for had been too much for her wife, the person who was supposed to accept all of her, to meet her halfway, to listen to her needs—the person who was supposed to love her no matter what. Failing all that, Cass also hadn't pretended to want her. She hadn't even tried.

Now, simply being desired by someone was enough to spin her mind out of control. She willed her head to wait to process everything until tomorrow, or at least until she was alone.

Alex brushed a fingertip over Emily's forehead. "Was that not what you wanted?"

"It was perfect. Too perfect."

Alex shifted off her and Emily curled on her side, silently praying she could keep the tears at bay for a while longer. She couldn't exactly run back to Katherine's to sob alone in her bedroom.

A soft fleece blanket settled over her, and she felt Alex lie back down again. Alex rested an arm over her hip, her chest settling in against Emily's back.

"Thanks for holding me," she murmured, hoping that would be enough.

"We don't have to talk," Alex said. "But I'd like you to tell me what's wrong." A moment later she added, "If you think you can."

Emily opened her eyes. The fire blazed on but the music had stopped. She hadn't registered if the album had simply ended or if Alex had turned it off. Either way, she was thankful for the quiet. "I needed that too much."

Alex didn't say anything for a moment. She snuggled closer and kissed Emily's shoulder blade. "If it's any consolation, your needing it—not just wanting it—was hot as hell. And I'm not even a little bit tired, so if you need more…"

Emily took a steadying breath. Having Alex pressed against her, skin on skin, sent warm fuzzies all through her. She could argue that it was only the aftermath of a long overdue orgasm, but she also wanted to ask Alex to never let go.

"I don't think I realized how the first time would be."

"We went too fast, didn't we?"

Alex sounded panicked, and Emily immediately regretted what she'd said. "No. That was what I needed." She knew she owed Alex more explanation. "My wife and I separated two months ago, but...it's been a long time since I felt like someone really wanted me."

"I'm the first person you've kissed since her?"

Emily nodded.

"That's a lot of pressure. Thanks for not telling me before."

"I think you could have handled the extra pressure." That was true, of course, but Emily wondered if she'd made a mistake telling her as much as she had. Alex wasn't her counselor. And yet Alex not judging any of it tempted her to open up completely. "I love sex. That sounds silly, doesn't it?"

"Not at all. Did your wife not like it?"

"I think she liked it at first. Things were good for a while, actually. Not fireworks, but sweet, you know?" Could Alex understand sex that wasn't explosively good? Sex that was just okay but still nice to have? "Then she wasn't into it anymore. It became this thing that we couldn't even talk about."

"That's a shame." Alex kissed the nape of her neck. "If you were my wife, I'd make you happy to have this body of yours every damn day."

Alex's butterfly kisses moved down her back and then slowly up again, stopping at the curve of her shoulder. Emily ran a fingertip over Alex's forearm, the outline of her muscles visible even in the soft firelight. "Of all the women I could have broken down on, why did it have to be the sexiest one at the party?"

"I'm definitely not the sexiest. Not even close. But I'm glad you like me anyway."

"Whatever. More than half the party wanted to have sex with you, Alex." And out of everyone, Alex had picked her. Was it only because she was a party virgin? She wanted to believe it was more, especially now, wrapped in Alex's arms. But maybe that was naïve. "Before Cass and I got together, I thought sex was easy. I didn't have a lot of partners, but the ones I had made me feel like I was good."

"I'm not surprised."

"Wait, I'm not trying to brag. Especially to someone like you. What I'm trying to say is that it's been a long seven years but I'm not a total virgin."

"As soon as you kissed me, I had no doubt you knew what you were doing." Alex pulled her closer, resting her chin on Emily's shoulder. "Can I state something for the record too? It's kind of a confession."

Emily waited, wondering what Alex would possibly have to confess.

"I don't want to share you with anyone else this weekend. I don't even want to go to back to the party. I want to keep you all to myself."

Emily felt a rush go through her and was glad Alex couldn't see her face in that moment. If only she could simply admit that was exactly what she wanted too. "I bet Katherine has rules about that."

"Katherine has lots of rules. I recommend ignoring them."

"Easy for you. She's my boss, remember?" It wasn't only about Katherine's rules. The image of Madison tied up popped in Emily's mind. Even if things like that turned her on, she wasn't sure she could actually do something like that. Alex probably wouldn't be satisfied with her for long.

"I want to do more, but do you mind if we keep doing this for a while?" Emily asked. "Your holding me feels so nice."

Alex tucked the blanket around them and kissed Emily's neck again. "You know what else I haven't done—besides have sex on a rug in front of the fireplace?" She paused a beat, then said, "I've never fallen asleep in front of a fire."

"What about camping?"

"Never been."

"Seriously?" Emily looked over her shoulder to see if Alex was joking. "You've lived all over the world but you've never camped?"

"Okay, don't get all judgy, it's on my bucket list."

Emily laughed. "And here I thought you were so worldly, so experienced."

"Everybody's got something they haven't done."

"Yeah, but for most of us it's something like, oh, I don't know, being tied up in a private sex room and used for someone's pleasure."

"Is that on your bucket list?"

"Not telling." Emily smiled, enjoying that they'd fallen back into the flirting banter that had felt so easy earlier. She could joke about being tied up without having to decide if she could go through with it. "Have you ever been the one who was tied up?"

"Someone tried once, but I slipped out of their knots and ended up turning things around pretty quick."

"Why am I not surprised?"

Alex laughed, and the soft rumbling sound warmed Emily's heart. It felt entirely too good to hear Alex laugh, to be lying with her chest pressed firmly against Emily's back. The moment was perfect. She timed her breathing to Alex's and watched the flames flicker from yellow to orange to red. She was in exactly the right place, with exactly the right person.

Even as she had that thought, warning bells sounded. Perfect moments didn't last. Still, it didn't matter. Alex could move on to another woman tomorrow. In a month or two, Alex probably wouldn't remember this night, wouldn't remember their conversation, and certainly wouldn't keep the feeling of lying naked with someone simply watching a fire. Emily, however, knew she would remember all of it.

"Can I try going down on you later?" Emily felt her throat tighten as soon as the words slipped out of her mouth. It shouldn't be a big deal to ask, but it was. Alex could think she was silly for asking, but she needed to get over the hurdle sooner or later and it might as well be with someone who'd forget her after. No risk. That's exactly what Alex was, even if she felt incredibly risky. "You might have to give me pointers. It's been a long time."

"I like the sound of that. You tell me when you're ready."

"As easy as that, huh?" When Alex nodded, Emily knew that it was. She breathed out the anxiety that had welled up. They had all night, and she could feel Alex's unspoken words telling her there was no rush. It didn't make sense that someone like Alex could feel so comfortable, so easy, but she couldn't deny it. For a moment, she could just close her eyes and enjoy how perfect everything felt.

CHAPTER NINETEEN

The last smoldering ember flamed brighter for a second, pulling Alex's eyes to it, then died out. Without the fire warming the room, Alex knew the one fleece wouldn't be enough, but she hated to move and wake Emily. Her own mind hadn't let her drift off, and she knew it was more than the switch of time zones keeping her from sleep.

Carefully, she shifted up on her elbow and brushed a lock of Emily's dark brown hair back from her forehead. Emily didn't stir even when Alex lightly kissed her cheek. "I hate to wake you," she whispered.

Emily shivered. She fumbled for Alex's arm and pulled it tighter around her middle. Alex waited, expecting Emily to say something or open her eyes, but her breathing only slipped back to the measured rhythm of sleep. When Alex caressed her forearm, she still didn't wake.

The only light in the room came from the full moon and the stars brightly reflected in the snow outside. Sometime after midnight the storm had cleared and the clouds had moved on.

Alex had watched the moon appear and nearly roused Emily at the gorgeous sight of it, but with a fresh snowfall the scene out the window would be even more magical once the sun rose. The sunrise would also mean the conclusion of a night she didn't want to end. If she woke Emily, would she agree to go upstairs, or would she want to go back to Katherine's?

Minutes passed. Finally, when Emily shivered again, the worry of her getting chilled won out over the desire to not do anything given the risk of her leaving.

"Emily." Alex spoke her name aloud instead of whispering, and Emily's eyelids fluttered open. "The fire's out and you're getting cold. We have to get up."

"I'm not that cold." Emily snuggled closer, pushing her butt against Alex. Her eyes closed again.

"You've been shivering." Alex shifted to a sitting position and then stood. "Come on. Let's go upstairs."

Alex thought of offering to walk Emily back to Katherine's, but she didn't force herself to say those words. "We can still cuddle upstairs. In a bed. With nice warm blankets." She held out her hand and Emily clasped it.

"I like blankets. And beds," Emily murmured, leaning against Alex once she was standing.

Alex chuckled. "Me too. And I'd gladly carry you up to my bed, but that might be a little too caveman for your taste."

"Maybe a little." Emily smiled, eyes still closed. "Though if you planned on tying me up in your bed once we got there, I might say okay."

"I hope you remember this conversation tomorrow morning." Alex led the way upstairs, not letting go of Emily's hand. The bedroom was cool and Emily shivered, moving against Alex again. "You'll be warm once we get you under the covers."

Once Emily was finally in bed, Alex kissed her forehead. "See, that's better, right?"

"I'd be warmer if I was under you. Or if you were doing other things to me."

"I think you're too sleepy for that."

"You could wake me up the rest of the way…" Emily's voice trailed into silence, and Alex thought she was already asleep again by her even breathing.

Alex went around to the other side of the bed and climbed in. She pulled the comforter up to cover them both and then curved her body against Emily's. God, she felt perfect.

"Are you tired?" Emily asked.

"No," Alex said. "But it's late. We should sleep. I didn't want to wake you at all."

"But you did wake me. And now I'm wide awake."

"Your eyes were closed the whole way up here and now you're awake?" Alex was happy about the development even if she wanted to tease Emily for making her work so hard to get her upstairs.

"Do you want to go back to sleep?" Uncertainty slipped back into Emily's voice.

Alex took a deep breath. "I didn't fall asleep downstairs 'cause my mind wouldn't stop. I kept thinking of all the things I wanted to do with you."

"What things?"

Alex hesitated. In the dark, she couldn't see Emily's expression. "You really want to know?"

"Yes, please."

Telling Emily what she wanted to do suddenly seemed crass. Even if Emily swore this was still a night of meaningless sex for her, it wasn't for Alex. And Emily wasn't simply another woman she'd met at a sex party. She didn't want to scare her off.

"Are you thinking I can't handle it?" Emily asked.

Before Alex thought of a reply, Emily said, "I probably shouldn't say this, but when I realized what you were doing with Madison I wanted to trade places with her. For years I've had all these fantasies of things like that, but I've never had someone who wanted to do that to me. And maybe you're right. Maybe if we tried that I wouldn't be able to handle it. But I think you should let me decide."

"Maybe I should." Alex couldn't exactly bring up the fact that Madison's experience level was a little different than

Emily's, but that's exactly what crossed her mind. She trusted that Madison would tell her how far to go. With Emily, she worried they might go too far too fast before Emily realized her limits. "I don't want to mess up with you. I want to do the right thing."

Emily stroked Alex's chest lightly, then moved lower and traced the triangle of trimmed hair. "Do you always do the right thing?"

"I try."

"What if I told you that the right thing to do tonight was to stop thinking about what *you* think I need and let me decide?"

"That's fair. What do you need?"

"To go down on you."

"Okay, didn't expect that." Alex chuckled. "If that's what you need, I won't stand in your way."

"I really need it." Emily's tone was playful as her fingers trailed over Alex's belly. "You'd be helping me out."

"I like helping," Alex said, closing her eyes. She felt a surge between her legs as Emily's fingers continued to work and her body hummed to attention. "Helping definitely sounds like the right thing to do."

"And then after you're done helping me with this, I want you to tell me what you want to do with me. No holding back."

Alex didn't say yes or no. Her mind had gone to the image of Emily's wineglass flying through the air, her gasp of shock. She might say she didn't want her to hold back, but Alex didn't want to mess up what they had going. *Even if it is only for a night.*

Emily moved from her side of the bed to straddle Alex. "Okay, keep in mind it's been a long time since I've done this. I might suck."

"You know sucking's a good thing, right?" When Emily didn't play along with the joke, Alex added, "Even if you don't get me off, it's gonna feel good. And I like being part of your practice session."

Emily leaned down and kissed Alex. She rested her head for a moment in the space between Alex's neck and her shoulder. "You're exactly what I needed tonight."

"We could just lie here. Like this. You feel amazing."

"No way. I want to go down on you. More than you could possibly realize." She kissed Alex's neck. "I'm only taking a moment to psych myself up."

Alex laughed. "You're gonna be fine."

"But are you?" Emily teased.

"I think I'll probably surv—" Alex stopped mid-word. Emily had shifted between her legs and the next second her tongue dove right in. Alex's whole body went taut, nerves firing in a blinding rush. She had to remind herself to breathe when Emily started to work on her clit.

After hours of being aroused, her clit was swollen and hard. Emily could have simply pressed her thumb against her and she would have come on the spot. Instead, Emily worked her to a fever pitch with her tongue, circling and stroking relentlessly until Alex was shaking with need for a release.

Finally, Emily sucked her clit between her lips, and Alex couldn't hold back. She climaxed with a jolt, clenching Emily between her thighs. A second later, she forced her knees to part, worrying that she'd hurt Emily.

As soon as Emily shifted, Alex pulled away and turned on her side, squeezing her legs together as the orgasm continued to roll through her. She ignored Emily's protest that she wasn't finished, and only managed to shake her head when Emily asked if she could have another go. When the quivering subsided some, she looked over at Emily.

"You came too fast," Emily said.

"You're blaming me? No. That was all you. Damn, you're good with your tongue. Your ex was missing out."

Emily kissed her shoulder blade, then the nape of her neck. "You don't have to say that, but thank you."

"I'm the one who should be saying thank you."

Emily draped herself half over Alex, her fingers straying down to Alex's groin. "I forgot how good it tastes. You sure I can't lick you a little more?"

"Not now. Sorry."

Emily flopped onto her back and gave an exasperated groan.

Alex sat up and turned to her. "Poor you? Is that it?" She laughed.

"That's it exactly. I've been waiting for years for that, and you barely gave me five seconds."

"It's gotta be hard being that good. How do you handle it?"

Even in the weak moonlight, Alex caught Emily's eye roll. She laughed again. "How 'bout I let you do it again when my body's recovered a little?"

"Promise?"

"Yes." Alex met Emily's lips. One kiss blended into the next, each one more convincing that there was no reason to stop. Alex moved on top of Emily again and fresh arousal strummed through her. She knew she wouldn't actually need much time to recover.

Emily pulled away from a kiss and said, "I think I interrupted you earlier."

"You did?"

"You were going to tell me what you wanted to do with me."

Alex immediately thought of her strap-on. "I was going to ask how you felt about toys. No pressure, though. I'm quite happy doing more of what we've been doing."

"Do you mean like a dildo?"

Alex nodded.

Emily touched Alex's chest, then drew a line down to her belly button. She seemed to want to go farther but after a moment pulled her hand away. "I haven't played with anything more than a vibrator. My ex didn't think lesbians needed other things."

"Well, we don't, but it's fun." Alex couldn't tell from Emily's response if she was interested or not.

Emily bit her lip. After a moment, she said, "I think I'd like it."

"Someday? Or do you want me to grab something for us to try now?"

Emily didn't answer, and as the silence stretched, Alex wished she hadn't brought it up. She was a reentry ticket for Emily, a first step back into the world of being intimate. Suggesting something Emily had never done was a bad idea. Although, in her defense, she hadn't known it would be a new thing for Emily.

"Don't worry. We have lots of other ways to entertain ourselves." Alex hoped the innuendo gave Emily enough of a graceful out.

"Like this, for instance." Alex lowered herself until their nipples brushed. Emily parted her lips in a soft gasp. Her sounds only amped up Alex's arousal. She tried not to think about how good it would feel to slide her cock inside Emily, but as their hips bumped together her craving only increased. Knowing Emily hadn't been pleasured that way made her want to give her the experience that much more. Yet she couldn't push for it. Couldn't bring it up again.

"You feel so good under me," Alex murmured.

Emily shifted up and met Alex's lips.

CHAPTER TWENTY

As soon as Emily pulled away from Alex's lips, she knew it was the right time to ask. All she had to say was "Go get it" and Alex would. There was no doubt that she wanted her strap-on, and Emily was at least ninety-five percent sure that she wanted Alex wearing it.

Still, she held back. Partly it was old baggage from the arguments Cass had made about how lesbians didn't need cocks and shouldn't want them, and how if they did they were only copying heterosexuals—or worse, wanting to submit to the patriarchy. And partly it was embarrassment that at thirty-three she couldn't bring herself to ask for what she wanted.

Nearly all of her fantasies involved a woman wielding a cock. And yet not once had she had sex with someone in a strap-on.

Alex moved from kissing her lips to kissing her throat and then her breasts. Her leg rested between Emily's, and as she moved her thigh pressed exactly where Emily wanted her. The pressure wasn't enough to satisfy her, though. She was impossibly wet, and all she could think of was having Alex inside her. Desire thrummed through her body insistently.

Instead of admitting what she wanted, she focused on massaging Alex's back and shoulders. Alex's muscles tensed and released under her ministrations, and when she got to a pressure point and dug in her thumb, Alex broke away from kissing to moan.

"You're good at that."

"Gotta have some skills in life," Emily bantered back. She'd never been good at simply accepting praise, but the more Alex moaned, the more she trusted the compliment.

Alex's responsiveness was a drug she couldn't get enough of. It was nearly enough to make her forget her own need. Nearly. She thought of how Alex had climaxed with only her tongue—and in under two minutes. Alex had done more for her ego than years of counseling. And Alex could give her more. She wasn't Cass. Alex could give her the kind of sex she'd wanted for years. So why shouldn't she ask for it?

"You have a sexy body. I could give you a massage all night." *Although then I'd be so wet I'd probably be ready to beg.* "My ex was more feminine. All soft curves. I always thought she was pretty, but...she wasn't really my type. That sounds weird, doesn't it? Since I was married to her for ten years."

"Love's funny like that. Makes you see past looks."

"You're right." Emily wondered at how easy it was to talk to Alex about Cass. She'd undoubtedly broke ten different hookup rules bringing up her ex, but Alex made the conversation feel completely normal. She moved from Alex's shoulders to her lower back, enjoying how Alex relaxed into her touch.

"I like how I can feel all your muscles," Emily continued. "How toned you are. You have all these angles and lines." She moved from Alex's hip bones up the side of her chest before going to her backside again. "But you still have a nice ass."

"Angles and lines but an ass too? Um, thanks?"

"You're welcome." When Emily cupped her butt cheeks, Alex sank into her. She barely held in her own moan at the subtle shift. "By the way, even if you weren't lying naked on top of me, I'd still think you have a sexy butt. I probably wouldn't tell you, though. I'd be too shy, but I'd think it.

"Cass's body was a lot like mine. This probably sounds strange, but I always thought of that as a reason we would—could—figure out the sex stuff. We wore the same size bra, even. Thirty-four C." Emily stopped. "Okay, that might be TMI."

"We are naked. I think anything goes at this point. Anyway, you should keep talking. I love the way your hands move when you talk."

"Are you teasing me?" Emily nipped at Alex's arm when she laughed. The contact, and the way Alex's eyes shot to hers, made her want to bite more. Would Alex like that?

"Whatever. Massaging is only my excuse to keep touching you." She breathed in the scent of Alex. Her own musk mixed now with the cologne. She wanted to remember the smell, to let it fill her senses. There were so many things about the night she wanted to remember. What she didn't want to remember was feeling unsure. She wanted to be confident. To go for what she wanted. To enjoy how Alex felt, how she responded to everything Emily did. *Sexy* wasn't a good enough word to describe it, but her mind was too distracted to come up with something better.

"But I'd rather do other things than massage you."

"Would you?" Alex's voice sounded relaxed, like she might fall asleep if Emily let her.

"Do you want to sleep?" Emily asked, hoping the answer was no.

"Not at all. But you've got me feeling all melty."

"I don't think melty's a real word."

"Sure it is. It's in the dictionary. The spelling's tricky, but it's there. Right next to…" Alex paused, clearly trying to think of some good quip. "Melt."

"I like that sometimes you're a dork."

"You also like my backside."

"I do. And your front side. You looked especially good in those boxers you were wearing earlier. I wanted to see what you had on underneath." Emily held her breath, waiting on Alex's response.

"You noticed, huh?"

"If you're packing a dildo that big, you want to be noticed." Her heart raced. "You know, I'll probably be using that image of you standing there with that bulge as my fantasy for the next ten years."

"I could give you better material to work with." Alex pushed up on her hands. "So, if it wasn't the fact that I was packing, was it the ropes that bothered you?"

The image of the private room flashed in Emily's mind, full of high-resolution detail. "It was a lot all at once. You being there, full stop, was a shock. Then, you being there *and* half naked, Madison tied up, Katherine holding a whip…Honestly, that whip might have been the tipping point."

"Why?"

"My ex wasn't only against toys. One time, I asked her to grab my hair and she got really uncomfortable." Emily felt her cheeks heat up as Alex waited for her to go on. She was glad the room was dark. "Anyway, whatever. People like different things, right?"

"You wanted it rough, and she made you feel bad for wanting that?"

Emily swallowed. Alex had summarized it so well she couldn't do more than nod.

"What else did you want?"

"Dumb stuff. It doesn't matter now." Emily shook her head.

"Tell me. I won't judge. I've tested out all the toys. And done more things than most people can imagine. Some things that I really hope no one took pictures of."

Emily found herself smiling despite everything. "Do you always know exactly what to say at the right moment?"

"It's a talent."

Alex had too many talents. But she also felt safe. And Emily trusted she wouldn't judge. "It was more than hair pulling. Like you said, I wanted it rough. I wanted her to push me around, bite me, that sort of thing. Nothing that seemed too wild, but she didn't want to even talk about it. Once I turned my butt to her and dared her to spank me. She froze. Looked at me like she didn't want to be anywhere near me. Then she got out of bed and took a shower.

"I tried to make a joke of it after, pretended I wasn't serious. But the things I wanted didn't go away. I ordered nipple clamps in the mail and she freaked out when she opened the package. So, I threw them away. The time I asked her to pull my hair was the last time we had sex."

"Damn."

"It was all my fault. If I'd been happy with what she wanted, we'd probably still be together. Still having sex the way she wanted it. And the truth is, I was happy. But I wanted more." Emily dropped her head back against the pillows. She knew she'd messed up any chance for more with Alex. Now everything felt serious. She covered her face with her hands. "I shouldn't have told you all that."

"Hey." Alex gently pried her fingers back and kissed Emily's forehead. She kept working Emily's fingers loose and managed to free one hand, then kissed the cheek she exposed. She pinned that hand to the mattress and tugged off the other. "Thank you for telling me. And I'm sorry she freaked out on you." Another kiss. "What you wanted was okay to want. And I think you're brave for being honest."

Emily felt her chin tremble. She nodded slowly, accepting Alex's words. What she'd wanted was okay to want. She could let go of the guilt.

"If you could have anything tonight, what would it be?"

"You in a strap-on. I want you to fuck me."

"Now?"

Alex waited for her to say yes. When she whispered it, Alex kissed her once gently, then before Emily could come up for air she kissed her again hard. Emily opened for Alex, gave in when she pushed, and felt her arousal rebuild—not slowly like she would have expected, but in a dizzying rush that made her glad she was already on her back.

"Don't move." Alex pushed off of Emily and got out of bed.

Emily's heart hammered in her chest. "You want it too, right? I'm not pushing you?"

"You have no idea how much I want it."

Emily sucked in a breath. Alex's words charged through her. She reminded herself to stay calm. Freaking out now would end one of the best nights she'd had in literally years. Alex knew everything now, and her desire hadn't changed. If anything, she seemed to only want Emily more.

CHAPTER TWENTY-ONE

Emily watched as Alex went to her dresser and opened a drawer. After rummaging for a moment, she looked back at the bed. "Small or medium?"

"You're not going to offer large?"

"No."

Emily pushed up on her elbow. "I've had plenty of nights alone to entertain myself."

"This might be different."

Emily had to agree. Slipping a slim vibrator inside when she was alone and relaxed was one thing. But tonight, she wanted to be fucked, plain and simple, and she didn't want anything small. She wanted to feel everything. "Medium. But maybe you could use your hands first to get me ready?"

"I like that request." Alex chose something from the drawer and then closed it. "Medium it is."

Whatever Alex had picked, Emily couldn't see it. Alex disappeared into the bathroom, and a moment later Emily heard water running. It was no surprise Alex washed her toys. but it was comforting. She knew what she was doing. Unlike Emily.

Maybe she should have told Alex to pick the small version, but it was too late now. She reached for the covers and pulled them up to her chin. The room wasn't cold, but her nerves made her shiver.

Was she washing the same cock she'd had on earlier? The thought of Alex having sex with Madison sprang to mind. No way could she measure up to someone like Madison. Or Katherine. But it didn't matter. Any of the women Alex was used to sleeping with would have far more experience than she did. She breathed in and out, telling herself that tonight wasn't about impressing Alex. For whatever reason, Alex had agreed to help her, and she didn't need to ruin an otherwise perfect evening by overthinking things.

When the bathroom door opened, Emily closed her eyes. She didn't want to be caught staring, but more than that she worried her anxiety would only be worse if she looked right at Alex. She wanted to feel her close again, kiss her again, and have her body on hers. She wanted to be so distracted by all the sensations Alex made her feel that her mind went quiet. Then she could take Alex's cock in her hands, feel it up and down, and trust her body to make the next decision.

Alex slipped under the covers but didn't move to close the distance between their bodies. She lay still for a moment, clearly waiting for Emily to look her direction or make some move. Emily's heart pounded in her chest.

"It's okay if you're having second thoughts," Alex said.

"I'm not. It's just..." Emily hated that her voice had gone all tinny. She pressed on. "I want to feel you inside me. But you're right. This is different than me playing with a vibrator. And I know I'm not going to be as good as the other women you've been with, and—"

"Hold up." Alex put a hand on Emily's chest. She pushed up on her elbow and looked down at Emily. "You'll tell me if you want to stop, right? I need to know you'll say something."

Emily bit her lip.

"Doesn't matter why. If you want to stop, you have to promise to tell me."

"Okay."

Alex leaned down and kissed her. One simple kiss and desire flooded through Emily's body. She moved into another kiss and Alex shifted onto her. She felt the head of the dildo bump her belly, then nudge at her slit, but Alex didn't try to push inside. Instead, she kept up with the kissing.

Emily ran her hand down Alex's side, wanting to feel the harness. She couldn't feel any strap. She passed over Alex's hip and then slid around toward the front. "How are you—"

"It's a double dildo," Alex said. "When I'm in the mood, I like it better than my harness because I can feel everything. I'd turn on the lights and give you a show and tell, but…I'd rather do other things."

"Would you?"

Emily laughed when Alex whispered yes in a husky voice right against her ear. She felt a jolt of pleasure when Alex moved to straddle her and the dildo pressed on her clit. As much as she wanted Alex to push inside, she didn't think she was quite ready.

"Can you get off with it?" Emily knew it shouldn't matter, but it would make it easier to relax if this wasn't only about her. And if Alex could orgasm with it, the fantasy would be complete. Plus, Emily's ego would truly appreciate it.

"Sometimes. If the angle's right and it rubs my clit. But if I can't, or if you want a little extra, there's this." Alex reached down and pressed something, and Emily felt the vibration against her leg.

"*Oh.*"

"That's what she said." Alex chuckled. "The vibrator's my backup." She switched off the vibrations and then pushed up onto her hands and knees. "Here. Take a look if you want."

The blanket had fallen off when Alex pushed up, but Emily didn't feel cold now. She stared up at Alex, taking in the toned muscles of her arms, her gorgeous shoulders, and her chest. When she looked lower, a pulse immediately started between her legs.

The light in the room wasn't enough for her to see the color, but she could make out the shape well enough. The graceful length and the smooth curve suited Alex as if it had been personally made for her. Emily reached up and traced the tip, then lightly followed over the head and down the shaft. It was wider than her vibrator back home, yet the more she thought about how it would feel to take it in, the more she wanted that width.

"You can feel the vibrations too?"

Alex nodded. "I can feel everything. My favorite part is when I push inside."

Emily swallowed. Knowing that part of the dildo was inside Alex, and knowing she'd feel everything, made simply touching it feel intimate. As sexy as a leather harness was, she liked this more. This felt like part of Alex.

Emily gripped the shaft and Alex responded by pushing into her hand. She closed her eyes as Emily stroked. "That feels good," Alex murmured. "Really good."

Emily appreciated the compliment, though she wondered what she should do next. When Alex started subtly thrusting, anticipation gave way to mouthwatering need. She couldn't wait for Alex to push inside her, to make the same sounds she was making now, the same thrusts, when the cock was in her. Still, she wished she knew exactly how to please her. A wave of frustration rolled through her. She pictured the scene in the Katherine's private room again and wondered how Alex could possibly be enjoying this in comparison.

"Did you use this with Madison?" Emily regretted the question as soon as she'd said it, but there was no taking the words back.

Alex held her gaze for a moment, seemed about to say something, then simply shook her head.

"I shouldn't have asked that." Emily let go of the cock and dropped her hand to the mattress. In the same moment, she wanted to both disappear from the room and beg Alex to take her.

"It's fine to ask." Alex caressed her chin. "We can talk about anything. With Madison I had a strap-on, not a double. What else do you want to know?"

Emily kept her eyes closed but forced herself to ask the question that had pushed to the front of the line. "Was Madison good?"

"She was—if you're into that sort of thing."

"Are you saying you're not?"

"It's complicated. I guess part of me still likes being useful. But having sex with someone else's girlfriend gets old." Alex paused. "Is this really what you want to talk about? I'm not saying we can't, but—"

"I don't want to talk at all. But my mind won't shut off." She couldn't process everything Alex had said on top of wishing she'd kept her mouth closed in the first place. "Why'd you pick this instead?"

"Why did I pick the double tonight? Instead of the strap-on I had with Madison?"

Emily nodded. When Alex didn't immediately answer, she said, "You don't have to tell me. I shouldn't have asked. I shouldn't have walked in on all of you in the first place."

Alex kissed her forehead, then her cheek. When she brushed her lips with a light kiss, Emily hoped she hadn't ruined everything. She was still turned on, still wanting Alex. If only she could stop thinking.

"Can you open your eyes for a second?"

Emily hesitated. The whole night had been surreal. One minute she felt completely comfortable with Alex, and the next her inexperience was so obvious it pressed down on her chest like a weight she couldn't possibly shift.

Alex had to be wishing she'd stayed at Katherine's. She felt Alex move and the bed creaked as she stretched out alongside Emily.

"Okay. I'll let you get by not looking at me." Alex sighed. "I'm not saying I don't like having sex with Madison. But I'm not gonna use my favorite toy on Katherine's girlfriend."

"Why not? You like this one better, so why not use it?"

"Well, I like both—the harness and the double. But I save this for when I want something intimate."

"What you did with Madison wasn't intimate?"

"No. It was only sex."

"What are we doing?" Emily felt Alex pull away. She clenched her teeth as she waited for Alex to answer. "Can I take that question back?"

"You can if you want. I'm not sure I can answer anyway. I know this is meaningless sex to you, but it's not to me. And maybe I'm being dumb, but I don't actually care if liking you is a mistake."

"Alex…" Emily took a deep breath before pushing herself to go on. "You should stop having sex with random people if you want to find someone to love."

"Thanks. Never thought of that one before."

Alex's sarcasm didn't sting. If anything, Emily felt more drawn to her with the shield she was clearly trying to put up. "What do you want?"

"I want to spend my life with someone," Alex said without hesitation. "Fall in love, get married, maybe even have kids. I want it all. I feel like I've wasted so many years. I know I told you earlier that I'm not with Katherine, and I know you don't—"

"You sure you don't love her?"

"I like her, but love's different. She's always available. And it's easy when we're together. Plus, it's nice to be wanted."

"Plenty of women would want you."

"Maybe. Maybe not." Alex pushed at her pillow as if trying to get it fluffed in a more comfortable position, then grumbled and tossed it off the bed. "The other problem is, I like sex. I'm not going to sacrifice that simply because I'm waiting for someone. What if I never find her?"

Emily was certain it would happen. She was certain of it, like she was certain that Alex was telling her the truth about everything else. "Someone is going to come along and swoop you up. I don't know why it hasn't happened yet."

"I could give you a list of reasons. But I'd rather have sex than talk about all the ways I suck at relationships."

"'Cause you don't suck at sex?"

"Only in good ways."

Emily laughed. She reached for Alex, found her hand, and pulled it to her lips. Alex's fingers smelled like her. She kissed the knuckles and a tight feeling settled in her chest. She knew how risky it was to consider Alex for anything more than a night of sex. The chances it would work for them to date seemed laughable. Besides, she wasn't ready to jump into another relationship. Technically, she wasn't even legally divorced from Cass. But everything Alex said she wanted was what she wanted too. Could they make each other happy?

"I don't know if it matters, but the cock I used with Madison wasn't mine. I borrowed the harness and everything from Katherine's supply. She's meticulous about sanitizing and it's easier that way. Anyway. Now you know." Alex rolled onto her back. "I feel like I'm all dressed up and the party's over." She thrust her hips and the dildo boinked in the air. "Pretty ridiculous, right?"

"Actually, it's a good look on you." Emily reached over Alex's hip and circled the tip of the cock. "And who said the party's over?" She trailed her fingertip down the shaft, imagining again how it would feel to open up and take Alex in. Desire surged. "I like that you picked your favorite. For me."

Alex responded only by closing her eyes. Without thinking about it, Emily started stroking. It was obvious when Alex pushed her hips rhythmically that she liked it, but it also gave Emily space to process her thoughts. Alex had already helped her get over the first hurdle—she'd officially gotten back on the proverbial horse where sex was concerned—and now all she had to do was enjoy what Alex wanted next.

"If you're gonna give me a hand job, can I get some lube for you? It feels even better with lube."

Emily stopped stroking. She hadn't been thinking of getting Alex off. In fact, she didn't realize she could doing only that. "Would you like that? Or would you rather be inside me?"

"That's not a fair question."

Emily kissed Alex's cheek. "Then I'll decide for you. I want you inside me."

"You sure?"

She reached for Alex and a rush of nervous excitement raced through her. It felt good to go for what she wanted. Tomorrow she could process what the tangle of feelings in her chest all meant. Tonight, she only wanted one thing.

CHAPTER TWENTY-TWO

Alex told herself Emily could handle what came next. It wasn't like she was in any position to give advice on the emotions that came with sex anyway. And she was ready to stop thinking.

She spread her weight, shifting so she didn't jab Emily with the dildo, and reached for the lube on the nightstand. Knowing that this was Emily's first time, she wanted her to enjoy every minute.

"Is there anything you don't like?" Emily asked, watching Alex lube her cock. "Anything that bugs you? I'm sure you've tried everything once, and had women do all sorts of things to you."

"I haven't tried quite everything." Alex could tell by the quiver in Emily when she brushed against her that she wasn't relaxed. "For the record, anything more than a finger up my butt is too much."

"I'll try to remember that." Emily trailed her fingers up Alex's forearm. "I don't know why I'm nervous again."

"Would you let me try something?" Alex waited for her nod. "Close your eyes."

When Emily did, Alex kissed her. "Promise to keep your eyes closed until I tell you to open them?"

"No matter what? I like this game so far."

"Good."

Alex clasped first one and then the other of Emily's wrists above her head on the pillow. "And these stay here until I tell you that you can move them."

Emily made a low purring sound that sent heat through Alex's body. She could pin Emily no problem with one hand, but she wanted both hands to pleasure her and she knew now that Emily wanted to follow her orders.

When Alex let go of Emily's wrists, she leaned down and caught a nipple between her teeth. Emily gasped at the sudden bite, clutched the pillow with both hands, and then laughed.

"Damn. I wasn't expecting that." She kept her eyes closed even as she smiled. "More?"

"If you're good."

Alex circled the same nipple she bit, soothing it with her tongue and then sucking. She let it slip out of her lips. "You have nice breasts."

"Thanks. I've gotten compliments before."

"They deserve appreciation." Alex bent her head and took the other nipple into her lips. As she massaged both breasts with her hands, she pried and stroked until the nipple in her mouth was engorged and Emily was writhing under her.

When Emily's moaning gained volume, Alex broke away to bruise her lips with a hard kiss. As soon as Emily parted for her, Alex deepened the kiss. She forgot about everything else then, giving in to the kissing.

Minutes passed and Emily's lips still captivated hers. She strained her memory for the last time she'd spent so much time simply kissing. With Emily, she knew she could break a record. Then she felt Emily stroke her cock, and her body immediately decided that kissing wasn't enough.

"You moved your hand." She caught Emily's wrist and placed her hand back on the pillow. "Distracted me with kissing and I almost didn't notice. That's very sneaky."

"Gonna punish me?"

"No. I'm going to convince you how much you want to behave."

Emily groaned. "I'm so wet. I want you inside."

"So wet, huh?"

"You should check."

As much as Alex wanted to dip her fingers inside, the slow torture of foreplay felt too good. Emily's eyes were still closed and her hands were once again clasped above her head. Every breath she took made her full breasts rise and fall, the perked nipples begging for Alex to be rough.

Emily moaned when Alex slid her hand over her chest, grazing her nipples. She shifted down to Emily's center, desire rumbling through her. Had she ever been more ready to give a woman pleasure?

Alex didn't part Emily's legs or even rub down her thighs. She stopped at the triangle of neatly trimmed hair and simply rested her hand. Emily trembled with need, but Alex still didn't give in to the temptation. Her body felt as taut as a bowstring, and it took all of her control to hold back.

Emily pushed her hips up, pressing her center into Alex's hand. "Please…"

With the contact, Alex couldn't resist anymore. She dipped into Emily's wetness and was instantly rewarded with a sharp gasp. Emily bucked and slick warmth enveloped her. She pushed deeper and Emily spread her knees apart, opening for Alex.

First, she could only take two fingers, but then Alex eased in another with a gentle thrust. Emily arched her back, moaning as Alex turned her wrist. She pulled out, stroking Emily's folds, savoring the warm wetness, then pushed in again, deeper this time. Alex shifted up to kiss her lips, not pulling her hand out.

"You want this bad."

Emily nodded. Her eyes were squeezed closed but her lips parted as if hoping for a kiss. She clutched the pillow as she pumped against Alex again.

"You'd do anything I ask right now, wouldn't you?" Arousal made her feel reckless. But Emily wasn't Madison, wasn't Katherine, or any of the other women she'd been with. She couldn't push too far.

"Anything."

Emily moaned as Alex slid her fingers deeper inside. When she was easily pumping three fingers in and out, the craving between her legs got insistent. "You okay if I try something else?"

Emily licked her lips. "I want it...but part of me doesn't want you to stop with your hand. You feel so good."

"What if I promise to make it feel as good with my cock?"

Emily nodded, pushing her center toward Alex's fingers. As tempting as it was to give Emily an orgasm with her fingers, Alex only briefly stroked her clit before pulling her hand away. She shifted position, then kissed Emily again. Her hips hovered over Emily's, the tip of the cock nudging her slit. She waited, knowing Emily would open for her when she was ready.

As soon as Emily pumped up her hips, Alex thrust. Emily gasped, then parted her legs to take Alex all the way. She arched off the mattress and raked her nails down Alex's back. Alex waited for her to relax before pushing deeper.

When their hips pressed together, the feel of smooth skin and mingled wetness all threatened to push Alex over the edge. She clenched her jaw, enjoying the tremors of pleasure that raced through her, then shifted side to side, bringing more gasps to Emily's lips.

"Fuck," Emily whispered.

"Too much?"

"No." Emily's tongue slid across her upper lip. "Not too much." She shifted her grip to Alex's arms. "I like it. I thought I would."

Alex kissed her lightly. "Want me to make it feel even better?"

When Emily nodded, she got to work. The sound of Emily's need pushed Alex to give her everything. They quickly fell into a rhythm, Emily pushing up to meet her each time she thrust and moaning for more again and again. Alex forgot about being gentle, forgot about watching every cue. Sweaty skin and the smell of their sex intoxicated her, and muscle memory took over. Suddenly she couldn't stall what was coming.

As her orgasm built, she reached down to find Emily's clit, thumbing awkwardly. Her thoughts blurred as her climax took over. She kept pumping her hips but she'd lost her careful control. Her body was leading now. Right as she thought to worry about Emily, she heard her scream pierce the air and felt her thighs clench.

It was all Alex could do to keep her thumb in place as Emily tensed, shivered, and then tensed again. Knowing she'd satisfied Emily too, she breathed out and rode the waves coursing through her body, entirely sated.

Minutes passed before Emily's hold loosened. Her thighs went slack first and then her arms. Finally, she collapsed back on the pillow with a soft sigh. "Damn."

Alex eased her weight onto Emily. The aftermath of her climax left her spent, and she couldn't manage to ask if Emily needed her to pull out. She didn't want to ask anyway. All she wanted was to stop time for a moment to memorize everything. The feeling of connection. Their skin slick with sweat. The soft swell of Emily's breasts. The way their panting slowed to even, measured breaths, perfectly timed.

"Don't pull out yet," Emily murmured.

Alex kissed Emily's chin and then her lips. Did Emily feel their connection too? Feel how amazing they were together? Or was she only thinking that she'd broken a long dry spell?

Finally, Emily placed her hands on Alex's hips and gave her a push. "You want me to come out?"

A drowsy nod. Alex eased out and then got out of bed. She went to the bathroom and cleaned the dildo. By the time she got back to bed, Emily was softly snoring. She slipped under the covers, hoping not to disturb Emily, but the bounce of the mattress roused her. She reached for Alex and then curled against her.

The feeling of Emily close, along with her warm breath against Alex's neck, stirred up desires for things that made her chest ache. She could wait as long as Emily needed. She could be patient. But she couldn't imagine walking away now.

"I think I may have drifted off," Emily said. "Are you not sleepy?"

"Not yet."

"Why not?"

"I'm thinking," Alex admitted.

"Hmm. Thinking's good. But so is sleeping. Especially when you have someone nice to sleep with."

Alex chuckled softly. "I think that's part of the problem."

"Am I keeping you from sleep? Oh, are you not a cuddler? I didn't even think to ask." Emily's hold on Alex loosened. "My ex wasn't a cuddler either, but you and she are so different."

"I like cuddling."

Emily wrapped her arms tighter around Alex. "Good. Because you feel really good. Perfect, actually."

"I was thinking the same thing," Alex said, knowing the risk she was taking with the words. Emily's tone was light. Would she realize that Alex was completely serious? Would that freak her out?

"I like that toy of yours. That double dildo. It's very effective."

It had been a risk suggesting it, but it had paid off well. "I'm happy you liked it. I like it too."

"But there's one thing I can't decide."

"Uh-oh."

"Relax, you." Emily kissed Alex's cheek. "I can't decide which part was my favorite—you coming inside me or me going down on you."

"We can try everything all over again to help you make up your mind."

"You're so helpful." Even in the dark, Alex could feel Emily's smile. She continued. "As much as I'd love to say yes, I'm not sure how many more orgasms I can handle. It's been a big night for me."

"Okay. I'll let you sleep."

"I don't actually want to sleep." Emily ran her hand down Alex's chest. "I feel like a kid at the candy store." She sighed. "What if one night isn't enough?"

"Maybe we shouldn't go to sleep."

CHAPTER TWENTY-THREE

The double dildo was the second thing Emily noticed when she opened her eyes. Alex had left it on the nightstand along with her cell phone. A lamp and a little carved bear holding a crescent moon also claimed space on the nightstand. Emily guessed the bear was something from Alex's childhood. It didn't seem likely she'd buy it as an adult, and Emily wondered what story came with the little bear.

But the bear wasn't the first thing she'd noticed. That was Alex's arm—wrapped tight around her chest. Blankets were tangled about their legs and bunched at their waists, but Emily didn't reach for one. Instead, she snuggled closer to Alex.

When she shifted, she realized she was wet. Still wet, or wet all over again? How many times had Alex made her orgasm last night? She'd lost track. And she hadn't tried stretching yet, but she had a feeling she'd discover new muscles she hadn't known existed, all of which would be sore later. She wanted to tell Alex that it was all her fault, but probably everyone who slept with her bathed her in compliments. And how many women would that be?

Alex's promiscuity had seemed intimidating at first. But it was Alex's experience that had finally convinced her to open up. She thought of what she'd admitted—the hang-ups Cass had left her with and desires that had always been too much. None of it had surprised Alex. She hadn't challenged Emily on why she'd stayed with Cass, hadn't made her feel insecure about how long it had been, and she definitely hadn't made her feel bad for what she wanted.

Emily's gaze wandered back to Alex's forearm. Nothing could feel as good as what Alex had done to her last night, but being held in her strong grip was a contender for second best.

Cass didn't like cuddling even at the beginning of their relationship, and Emily had gotten used to sleeping in their king-size bed with a foot of empty space between them. She'd gotten used to it, yes, but she hadn't liked it. Now, all the mornings of waking up and feeling the cold sheets between her and Cass, knowing on some level that she was in the wrong bed, stacked themselves one on top of the other.

For the first time, instead of wondering if she could have done something to fix her marriage, she wondered why she'd stayed so long. She'd convinced herself that no relationship was perfect. They might not have had sex, but they'd had good moments. At least a few. And yet those moments weren't enough. This moment, with Alex holding her, was only added proof that what she needed wasn't too much to ask for. It simply wasn't what Cass wanted to give.

If only someone like Alex could drop into her real life. After this weekend, she'd only have morning cuddles and mind-blowing sex in her fantasies. She'd be back to sleeping on Gianna's couch while Alex would be traveling the world working her fancy job. She realized that she didn't actually know what Alex did, but if she could afford a cabin in Aspen and was planning to retire in her forties, it had to be fancy. Or at least she made more money than a chef. Not that a difference in income mattered so much, but it was one more way that Alex would never be in her reality and she'd never be in hers. Unless, Emily thought with a sigh, Alex ended up at some event that she was catering.

At the thought of food, her reliable stomach rumbled to life. Suddenly, she wanted to surprise Alex with breakfast in bed. That was a problem for more than one reason. First, she couldn't remember the last time she'd wanted to surprise anyone with a meal. Second, breakfast the morning after definitely wasn't part of the original bargain. Breakfast together meant she wanted more than sex.

Maybe it didn't matter. Breakfast with Alex could be a warm-up to a real-life date—exactly like everything they'd done last night had been a reentry into the sex world. It could be, she thought, or that could be the excuse she told herself when the truth was that she simply wanted any reason to spend as much time alone with Alex as possible.

If only Alex was someone she could actually date… She blew out a breath. Once the *if only* train had left the station there was no calling it back.

What she needed to do was slip out of bed before Alex woke, get dressed, go back to Katherine's, and start thinking about the next person she'd have sex with. But she couldn't leave without at least saying thanks. *Thanks for sleeping with me?*

Alex shifted and pulled Emily closer against her. "You awake?"

Emily nodded. She felt a warmth spread through her when Alex kissed the nape of her neck. So much for slipping out. She didn't want to think about anyone other than Alex anyway. Her light kiss was a reminder of everything those lips could do. One night and her body was sold.

"How long you been awake?"

"Not long. I'm feeling lazy and don't want to move."

"Good." Alex's kisses trailed from her neck to her shoulder blade. "I'd like to keep you here for the rest of the day."

"I'd like that, but I'd also like to make you breakfast."

"You'll stay for breakfast?" Alex gave her a squeeze. "That's the best thing I've heard all day."

Emily loved the sound of Alex's sleepy voice almost as much as her declaration. "Best thing all day, huh? You've been awake for all of two minutes."

"At this rate, I'm thinking today's gonna be a damn good day. What are we making?"

"Not we, me. I want to make you something. And it depends on what you have. Omelets maybe?"

"I love omelets. The kitchen should be fully stocked. I pay someone to buy groceries and clean for me since I'm only here for a week."

"Perfect. Then you stay right here, and I'll go check it out."

"You really don't want my help?"

"I want to cook for you."

"Hmm." Alex was quiet for a moment but didn't let up her hold on Emily. "I don't know if I like the idea of not being where you are. I could chop things. Or pretend to be helpful while I admire the view."

"Yeah, that wouldn't be distracting at all." Emily laughed when Alex nipped her shoulder. The bite turned her on as much as the murmuring sounds Alex added a moment later. But none of that was enough to distract her from the damn tap dance her heart was doing in her chest after Alex's comment about not wanting to be apart.

Alex slid her hand over Emily's thigh and then over her butt cheeks. "I like you."

"Really? Which parts?" Emily wiggled her butt against Alex's hand.

"I wasn't talking about your body. Although now that we're on the subject…your right eyebrow is damn sexy."

Emily laughed. "Is this what got me into your bed? My sexy eyebrows?"

"That and everything else. You're beautiful. But I also happen to like you as a person. *And* I really like how your body feels up against mine."

More tap dancing. Her heart was a damn traitor.

"I'm sure you don't need help, and if you like your own space, I get it, but it'd be fun to watch you do some chef magic."

Not once had Cass wanted to cook with her. Emily had decided it didn't matter since cooking was her job and she didn't need it to be something they shared. But the fact that

Alex wanted to help, or at least watch her work and keep her company, validated a desire she hadn't realized was even there.

"How about we make a deal? You let me run downstairs and check out your kitchen, and if you have the makings for omelets and French toast, I'll let you help. If we're only having oatmeal, you don't get to ogle my butt."

"Deal. Just so you know, it isn't only about your butt." Alex stroked up from Emily's thigh to her breast.

"Right. There's also the eyebrow thing."

Alex caught the tip of Emily's nipple and it perked almost instantly. When Emily pushed into Alex's hand, she wanted to forget about breakfast.

"I love what you do to my nipples, but you should stop if you want breakfast before noon."

"Is noon late for breakfast?"

"We'd have to officially call it lunch."

"You're a rule follower, huh?"

Emily shook her head. As much as she didn't want to leave the bed—or, more specifically, Alex—she knew if she stayed much longer she'd give in to Alex's hands. She was already wet, and the more Alex plied her nipples, the more she was ready to throw in the towel on the breakfast plans. But she wanted to cook for Alex. "Maybe I could convince you to come back to bed after we eat?"

Alex's hand stilled. "I don't want to give in that easy, but I think I hear your stomach growling."

"Thank you for considering my needs. Still chivalrous after you've already had me, huh?" The edge of sarcasm in her voice got a wink from Alex. Emily got out of bed and Alex flopped onto her back and closed her eyes. How the hell had she slept with someone as sexy as Alex? She still could hardly believe it had happened.

"You're almost too good-looking, you know that?"

"Look who's talking," Alex murmured. "But you're not only sexy, you cook. I think I might have died and gone to heaven."

Emily smiled. For the first time in a long time, she did feel sexy. "You haven't had my cooking yet." She scanned the room wondering where her underwear might be, then realized she'd come upstairs naked. "Could I borrow a T-shirt? And maybe a pair of shorts?"

"You don't want to make me breakfast naked?"

Emily rolled her eyes.

"Not until we know each other better, huh?" Alex climbed out of bed. She pulled out a blue UCLA T-shirt and scratched her head. Her hair was an adorable mess and she'd only managed to push it more out of place, but Emily held herself back from fixing it. "I don't have shorts...would sweatpants be okay?"

"Sure." Emily knew she'd look ridiculous wearing pants that fit Alex's long legs, but she liked the intimacy of wearing her clothes enough to roll the cuffs. The sweats matched the T-shirt. "UCLA grad?"

"Yep. Computer science. I was a big nerd. What about you?"

"I've always been cool."

Alex grinned. "That was good. Almost my level of humor, but good."

Emily congratulated herself. "Mills College."

"Oh, you weren't kidding about the cool thing. Figured out you were a lesbian early, huh?"

"I went to Mills because they gave me a scholarship, thank you very much." Emily tugged on the T-shirt. "The fact that it was a women's college was a bonus."

"What'd you study?"

"Mostly women." Emily went up on her toes and kissed Alex right as she opened her mouth to laugh. "Go back to bed, sleepyhead. I'll come get you if we're making omelets."

"I kind of like you ordering me back to bed."

"I would have guessed you like to be the one giving the orders."

"Well, yeah." Alex raised a shoulder. "But when it comes to someone making me food, I'll make an exception."

"I'll keep that in mind."

Alex caught Emily for another kiss before she made it to the door. When she pushed Alex back toward the bed, she fought the urge to follow her. Breakfast first...

CHAPTER TWENTY-FOUR

"Why is it so important that the onions be chopped in little tiny pieces?"

"Finely chopped," Emily said, leaning over the cutting board and surveying Alex's work. "And because I said so."

"That's one of my mom's favorite expressions," Alex grumbled. She pushed the pile of onions back under the knife. "You kind of remind me of her."

Emily pulled the bacon from the oven and set the pieces on a cooling rack. "Do I want to know why?"

"You both like to be in charge in the kitchen." Alex reached over and nabbed a slice of bacon. Before Emily could wrench it from her hands, she took a bite. One bite missing and a big grin on her face, she handed it back. "And you both get frustrated with me."

"I feel for your mom. Something tells me you weren't an easy kid." Emily waved the slice of bacon at Alex and then pointed to the mushrooms and the spinach. "Don't forget about chopping those too. I'll sauté everything as soon as you finish."

Alex pushed the onions into a neat pile at the edge of the cutting board and started on the spinach. "Want to critique my chopping technique again?"

"I'll wait till you've finished." In fact, Alex wasn't awful as a sous-chef. She was, however, distracting as hell in a tank top and boxers. "I'm not sure how I feel about you comparing me to your mom."

"I promise it's a good thing. My mom's a total powerhouse— she worked as a DA for a while and now she's a judge. My dad has always been one of those guys who is in awe of his wife. And he's a brain surgeon." She grinned. "They're sweet together, actually."

"Your mom's a judge and your dad's a brain surgeon? That's a lot of pressure. I hope you're not their only kid."

"Nope. I've got an older brother. He took all the pressure for me. What about you?"

"One younger sister. She's the golden child." Emily paused. "My parents didn't like that I went to Mills. And they really didn't like the fact that I brought a girl home for Christmas that first year. That was the beginning of the end."

"Are you close to your sister?"

"No…She's the only one I miss." Emily finished crumbling the bacon and went to check the muffins. Whoever had done the shopping for Alex had forgotten to buy bread but had managed to get all the ingredients necessary for blueberry muffins.

"You don't see your family at all?"

"They wrote me off when I married Cass. In retrospect, some of the things my folks said about her were true. But mostly they were upset I was marrying a woman. I thought my sister would come around, but then she went and married this pastor who convinced her I was going to hell. We exchange birthday cards. That's it."

Alex stopped chopping. "Well, that blows. I'm sorry. But it's their loss. You're amazing."

Emily looked over at her. Alex's succinct assessment repeated in her head. How did she know that was exactly what she needed to hear? All the years of Cass giving her advice on ways she should try to fix the situation, and then caveats when she tried those things and her family still didn't come round, and the only thing she needed to hear was one line: *it's their loss.*

"You know what? It is. But I've got Gi's family."

"Gi?"

"My best friend. Gianna. We met at Mills. Her family took me in as their own when my parents flipped over the whole gay thing. Their Christmases and Thanksgivings are way more fun anyway. Ready with those mushrooms?"

Alex looked as if she were about to say more, but she glanced at the pile of half-sliced mushrooms. "I was trying to go fast to impress you, but apparently I'm not fast enough."

"You should definitely not worry about being fast." Emily congratulated herself when Alex's cheeks colored.

"I'm not always that fast. Last night was entirely your fault."

"You're cute when you blush." Emily took the knife from Alex and gave her a hip bump. "I'll finish up. Maybe you can find us some juice?"

Once the vegetables were sautéed, the omelets were ready in no time. Alex made mimosas and Emily decided that if any morning deserved breaking the no-alcohol-before-lunchtime rule, this was it.

"Do you always add champagne to your orange juice?"

"Only for special occasions," Alex said, clinking her glass against Emily's.

"What's this special occasion, then?"

"A famous chef made me breakfast."

Emily shook her head. "I'm no famous chef."

"That's not what I hear. Katherine said you have a six-month waiting list."

"Well, that part's true. But only because I don't like to have more than eight clients at a time."

"She also said she went toe-to-toe with one of the Grayson heirs and some actress who both wanted to steal you."

Emily remembered the instance with the Grayson heir but only because Katherine had made a big deal telling her about it after. She'd never heard about any actress, but there was probably plenty she didn't know concerning Katherine's friends. She poked at her omelet with her fork and avoided looking at Alex as she debated bringing up something that could be a bad subject.

"Did I say the wrong thing?"

"You didn't say anything wrong." Emily took a deep breath and finally met Alex's gaze. "I want to ask why Katherine and you were talking about me, but I'm not sure I want to know the answer."

"I promise it was nothing weird. This one time I was complaining to Katherine that I hated having to make dinner every night for myself. But I also hate going out alone. I know I should be used to it with my job, but…anyway, she mentioned she had a personal chef. Told me all about you."

"You said you didn't know I was coming to the party when we met on the plane."

"That conversation I had with Katherine was months ago, and she never mentioned your name." Alex's tone was almost defensive. She blew out a breath and shifted back in her seat. "If I'd thought you were coming to the party—if I thought I'd ever see you again—I wouldn't have said yes to Madison and Katherine's threesome. I wanted to call you, but I had no idea why you were in Aspen. I thought you'd met someone online and this was the first time you were seeing them. When you didn't text me, I figured I didn't have a chance."

Emily couldn't imagine anyone having a better chance than Alex. She wished now that she'd been brave enough to text her. Not that it would have changed anything. Maybe everything had happened exactly as fate had planned. *Fate.* She'd never believed in it, and yet…

"Would you have flirted with me if you knew I was going to be at the party?" Alex asked.

"No. I would have been too embarrassed." It was the truth, but Emily hated saying it. "The only reason I flirted at all was because I figured you were a stranger I'd never see again."

"I thought so." Alex was quiet for a moment and then said, "Is that also why you decided to have sex with me last night? Because you figured you'd never see me again?"

Emily set her fork down and reached for her glass, sipping the juice slowly as she considered her answer. In a way it would have been a good plan if she'd decided on Alex purely because she was a player she'd never see again. Except Alex wasn't a player, and she'd known that all along.

"I guess it makes sense," Alex said. "You wanted a rebound. It's bad timing for a relationship and all of that."

Apparently, she'd come to her own conclusion when Emily didn't answer. "I didn't come here for a rebound."

"You sure?" Alex shook her head. "Don't answer that. You were up-front about what you wanted from the beginning. It's just...after last night I can't help wanting more. Do you blame me?"

"No. I'll probably never have a night that good again." Emily felt the heat on her cheeks but pushed on. "I'm not going to forget a moment of it."

"I don't want us to be a onetime thing."

Emily's heart skipped a beat. It was exactly what she wanted Alex to say. But she couldn't even think about dating—not even something casual. Especially not with someone who was everything she'd ever wanted.

"What can I do to convince you to take a chance on me?"

Alex's question was sincere and the expression on her face so serious that Emily couldn't bring herself to immediately shut her down.

"Silence. Okay. I get it."

"Alex, you live in Tokyo." That, of course, was only part of the problem.

"Only for the next couple months. I've got enough frequent-flier miles to go wherever I want any weekend you pick."

When she didn't argue, Alex reached across the table, palm upturned. Emily clasped her hand. She wanted to believe it could work.

Alex continued. "I haven't met anyone like you in a long time, someone I can be myself around. It feels so good I don't want it to end."

Hearing Alex put her feelings into words made her want to believe the fantasy of them together even more.

"I get that it's bad timing and I'm on the wrong continent. But is there more than that holding you back?" When Emily didn't offer any other reasons, Alex continued. "What if we spent the day together? Maybe we won't even like each other at the end of it."

"I don't think that'll happen."

Alex's face brightened. "Me neither. We can start off with something tame like hot springs…" She let go of Emily's hand and pulled out her phone. "I know you said you don't do snow, so I started thinking about other options. There's a place not far from here that we could check out. And you can totally wear a bikini to this."

She turned the phone around for Emily to see the screen. Before Emily could think of what to say, the doorbell rang. Alex glanced in the direction of the door and scrunched her eyebrows together.

"Expecting someone?"

"No…maybe it's a delivery. I'll go see." Alex handed her phone to Emily as she stood. "In the meantime, you can take a look at the hot springs. The website really doesn't do the place justice, but you'll get the idea."

Emily didn't want a break from Alex, but she didn't think it was a good idea to spend all day with her either. Not wanting a relationship was very different from saying no to someone like Alex. Already it felt like a mistake to do both—go on a date or turn her down.

With a heavy sigh, she scrolled through the webpage Alex had pulled up. Pictures of steaming pools alongside a river filled the screen. Stunning snowcapped mountains towered on either side of the river. According to the website, the hot springs were only forty minutes from Aspen. She thought of what Alex had said about the wrong timing and the wrong continent. All of that was still true. And she could add more of her own reasons for why she wasn't ready to date anyone. But she didn't want to let someone like Alex slip through her fingers.

Emily heard Alex greet someone and a woman's voice answer. The foyer was down a hallway off the kitchen and she couldn't hear either of them distinctly. As tempting as it was to try and eavesdrop, she wouldn't let herself. She finished the last bite of her omelet and then started clearing the dishes.

Alex had made short work of the omelet and polished off two muffins. Very few things she appreciated more than someone with a healthy appetite for her cooking. Why did Alex have to be so perfect for her? As much as she knew it was a bad idea, she reconsidered the idea of their dating. Maybe long distance could work for a while… She wasn't ready to jump into anything serious anyway, and with Alex in Tokyo for the next few months, they'd be forced to take things slow.

She picked up Alex's phone again, thinking of how nice it would be to relax in the hot springs with her, when a text message flashed on the screen.

Katherine: *Still enjoying the toy I gave you? Planning on keeping her all day?*

Emily stared at the words, feeling dizzy. What the hell was she thinking? It wasn't so much what Katherine said that bothered her as the fact that it was so obviously true. She was a toy for Alex to play with until she tired of her. Sure, Alex was charming. And sweet. On top of being sexy. Very nearly her perfect fit. But Emily couldn't let herself even pretend they could realistically date.

A new text bubble appeared. Katherine again. *As I'm sure you know, I do plan on collecting for this one.*

Emily set the phone facedown and took a deep, steadying breath. She couldn't decide if she was more angry at herself, or Alex, or Katherine. Nicola had warned her. Shay had, too, for that matter. Sleeping with Alex meant she'd have to deal with Katherine. *Fine.* But she was no plaything, and certainly not a pawn.

The phone vibrated with another text, but she refused to look at it. Anger made her efficient and she attacked the dishes in the sink rehearsing what she'd say to Katherine when the time was right. She'd finish cleaning up and then give Alex some excuse for why she didn't want to go to the hot springs and go directly to find Katherine.

And then what?

Emily's hand stalled with the sponge on a soapy, dripping omelet pan. She let her shoulders drop and stared out the little window above Alex's sink. There was no gorgeous view of the mountains, or even the river, like in Katherine's kitchen. The one kitchen window at Alex's looked out at a fence and a solitary pine tree. The limbs drooped under the heavy weight of the overnight snow, but the tree was still beautiful. A blue bird darted out of the tree and disappeared over the fence.

What was she going to do? She couldn't lose Katherine as a client. Not now. And she couldn't storm over to her house, chew her out, and expect things to be fine after. No, she'd have to pretend nothing had changed, that she knew nothing about the texts, and keep to the original plan. Which was not getting attached to Alex. She'd used her to get over her sex issues—exactly as they'd agreed—and now she needed to move on. If she slept with someone else tonight and carefully avoided Alex, Katherine would likely get over her jealousy and nothing would come of it.

How Alex dealt with Katherine wasn't her problem, though clearly she needed to resolve it before she tried dating anyone seriously. And she did believe that was what Alex wanted—a real relationship and a happily ever after. She deserved it.

Despite what Katherine had said, she knew Alex didn't think of her as a plaything. And maybe she did want her for more than one night. But even without Katherine in the picture, Alex was a guaranteed heartbreak for her.

Alex came back right as Emily finished washing the omelet pan. She avoided looking at her and instead focused on loading the plates and utensils into the dishwasher.

"You don't have to clean up. I can do it."

"It's no problem. I'm a whiz at this part."

Alex scratched her head, clearly aware something was wrong. "I'm sorry about the interruption. That was my property manager, Jorie. I forgot I told her I'd be free today to go over some issues with the house."

"You could still meet with her. I'll be out of your hair as soon as I finish cleaning up."

Alex picked up the mimosa glasses and brought them over to the sink. "Does that mean you don't want to go to the hot springs?"

"I can't." The truth seemed the simplest answer at the moment, but Emily felt regret wash through her. In fact, the truth was as complicated as everything else about their situation. She stepped away from the sink, carefully keeping her distance from Alex.

Alex washed the glasses and then set them on the drain rack. She rinsed and dried her hands, then leaned against the counter. "Do you want to do something else instead? We could walk around downtown Aspen. No commitment to spending the day together…"

Emily heard the uncertainty in Alex's voice and knew she should be honest with her. It wasn't fair to not offer any explanation. Yet the more she considered what to say, the more ridiculous everything felt.

"Do you have a Tupperware for the muffins?"

Alex pointed to a cabinet adjacent to where Emily stood. "Or you can leave them in the muffin tin. I'll probably polish them off in a day or two."

Emily opened the cupboard, searching for a container big enough for the remaining muffins. She spotted one under a plate of cookies. When she went to move the plate, she noticed a note taped to the cellophane wrap. Without meaning to, she read the words: *I could be free tonight if you want to meet for a drink—or more. Happy to have you back in town. ~ Jorie.*

"Jorie?" She hadn't meant to say the name aloud any more than she'd meant to read the note in the first place. Or the text from Katherine.

Alex had come over to where Emily stood. She set the plate of cookies on the counter and then pulled out the Tupperware Emily had been going for. "Jorie's the property manager. We messed around once when I was in town and she wanted to know if that was happening again. I told her no. Did you overhear some of that? Is that why you're upset?"

Emily shook her head. "You'd said her name, and then when I saw it on the note, things clicked. But I didn't hear your conversation and I don't care who you sleep with."

Alex popped the muffins out of the tin and into the container. "Then do you want to tell me why you're upset?"

"I needed what we did last night, but I'm not looking for anything more." It hurt to say it, but she had to follow through. "Plenty of women want you, Alex. And plenty of them could give you what you need."

"Why are you saying that?"

"Because it's the truth."

"It's not, but whatever. So that's why you're upset?"

"I'm not upset."

"Okay, fine." Alex held Emily's gaze. After a moment, she shook her head. "I don't believe you. You're mad at me about something."

"I'm not mad at you. I'm maybe a little mad at myself." Emily put the plate of cookies back on the shelf and closed the cabinet. She turned to face Alex, wishing that instead of arguing she could simply step forward and kiss her. Forget about Katherine, forget about how Alex wasn't hers and never would be. They could go back upstairs and tumble into bed and forget about everything...except reality would find them. "Mostly I want to be happy that I finally had sex after seven years and it was amazing and leave it at that."

"That's fair." Alex folded her arms. "You were clear that was what you wanted from the beginning. I'm sorry I pushed for more."

"You don't have to apologize. You asked me out on a date. Which was totally reasonable."

"And you're not ready, which is also reasonable."

Emily realized then that Alex was right. It didn't matter that something was still clearly going on between her and Katherine. It didn't matter that nearly all the women at the party had raised their hand for Alex or that a random property manager wanted her too. They could work all of that out if they had to, but this wasn't about Alex at all. It was about her. She wasn't ready.

"Thanks for understanding." Emily wanted to say more but couldn't. Not now.

Alex's disappointment was palpable. She ran her hand through her hair and looked around the kitchen for a moment. When she met Emily's gaze again, she'd clearly come to some sort of resolve. "Last night was nice and breakfast was perfect. Thank you."

Alex held out her hand and Emily clasped it. Her heart raced as if it hadn't been paying any attention to the conversation whatsoever. "Last night was better than nice."

Alex nodded. "I'll walk you out."

CHAPTER TWENTY-FIVE

After Emily left, Alex went back to bed. She didn't figure she'd sleep, but trying to accomplish anything else seemed like a waste of time. Not enough sleep had her mind fuzzy and she couldn't stop analyzing everything that had happened that morning. She still wasn't sure why things had gone so sideways. The fact that the night had been one of the best on record only made Emily's abrupt departure all the harder to stomach.

Four hours later, she woke from a dream about Emily. They were on a boat that was way too big for only two people to manage, and neither of them knew how to sail. Alex nearly laughed at how simple her brain was trying to make things. But even with the answer staring right at her, she still wondered why Emily wouldn't at least consider spending the day together. Her heart kept offering up helpful ideas like "maybe she's pushing you away but she wants you to call her anyway" and "maybe if you went over to see her, she'd change her mind and want to hang out."

Even after an extra-long workout, it was too early to head over to Katherine's—dinner wasn't until six—so she decided to do what she'd vowed to the night before. She went to call her dad and spotted a handful of missed texts from Katherine. The fact that she was jealous of Emily was obvious, but her suggestion that Emily was a toy bothered Alex even more. When she read Katherine's vague, almost threatening line about paying up, Alex deleted the whole thread. As soon as the messages disappeared, she had the sudden worry that Emily might have seen the texts.

Alex tried to remember what time she'd given Emily her phone and realized with a sinking feeling that there was a good chance of an overlap. *Shit.* Should she call Emily now and apologize? Or let it go?

After too long debating, she dialed her dad. Maybe Emily hadn't seen the texts. She had to hope for that. Her dad didn't answer, and she waited for the answering machine to pick up. She left a message about how she'd gotten out his old record player, and then rang her brother.

"Hey, stranger. Do you have a rash somewhere I don't want to know about?"

Alex laughed. "Nope."

"Okay, wait. Let me guess again. You ate something at a street market in some little town in India and now you have diarrhea?"

"Not this time."

"You're vomiting in Mongolia?"

Alex laughed again. "I'm fine, Doc. Promise. I don't have to be dying to call, you know."

"Technically, that's true. But what's really wrong?"

"I missed you." Alex sank down on the sofa, unable to keep the grin off her face. She had missed her brother more than she'd realized. It hit her like a rock at the sound of his voice.

"That's all? You sure you aren't at least missing a toenail after horseback riding in the outback?"

"You only get partial credit for that one. I did go horseback riding when I was in Australia, but that time I called you was because I thought my friend had heatstroke. And the busted nail wasn't mine. That was a girl I was dating who'd gone rock climbing. In Utah. And I want to state for the record that the rash was on my legs. From sharing shin pads in my intramural soccer club. *Not* an STD like you said it might be."

Rob laughed. "But you had safe sex after that, didn't you?"

"Whatever." Alex grinned into the phone. No one could argue that he didn't know what he was doing, even if his methods were questionable. And his memory wasn't bad either—even if he'd switched up a few of the events.

Ever since her big brother had gone to med school, she'd been using him as her personal advice line for any medical concern. With all her traveling, she'd had to bug him at all hours with questions he probably wished she'd never asked. But he never let her down. "How are you?"

"I'm good. Better now that I know you aren't dying. Didn't you also get some foot fungus thing when you were in Australia?"

"Thanks for remembering that one."

Rob chuckled. "It is good to hear your voice."

"Yours too. But you sound tired."

"I'm beat. Totally fucking exhausted." He sighed. "Welcome to my life. Every time I look forward to my days off, I remember I have a three-year-old *and* a four-year-old."

"No sleeping in for you?"

"Not past five a.m." He sighed again, this time heavily.

"How's Chelsea?"

"She's more tired than me. She's the one waking up in the middle of the night with Joey. He started sleepwalking and now regularly scares the shit out of us. In the middle of the night I'll wake up and he's standing at the side of our bed staring at me. It's creepy as hell."

"Do you two want a break? I'm in town for the week."

"Seriously? Damn straight I want a break. Why don't you ever give me any warning when you're gonna be here?"

Alex knew she should have given him some warning about her visit, but then he would have tried to talk her out of going to Katherine's. "I wasn't completely sure I was coming this time."

"That's what she said."

"We gotta talk, bro. Chelsea deserves better."

"Hey now," Rob grumbled good-naturedly. "I'll forgive you for that, and for not telling me you were gonna be in town, if you get your ass over here in the next ten minutes. Hold on."

Rob didn't bother putting down the phone as he hollered to Chelsea and relayed the news.

"You only get me for two hours. I have to be at a dinner party at six. But I'm in town all week so we can set something up for later."

"Wait a minute. This isn't a Katherine dinner party, is it?"

"I know what you're gonna say—"

"That you are never gonna get over her if you keep sleeping with her?"

Alex didn't talk to Rob often, but he'd heard enough about Katherine and her drama to have his own opinion of her. "Do we have to have this conversation again?"

"Apparently. 'Cause you never listen even when I'm right."

"You sound like a whiny kid."

"Well, I hang out with a lot of whiny kids."

"Maybe I could take them for a night this week? Give you and Chelsea some adult time?"

"Are you kidding? Hell, yes. Chelsea's gonna kiss you. On the lips. Be prepared. For the record, that doesn't get you out of talking to me about when you're gonna find a woman and settle down."

"You're worse than Mom. Can we agree not to talk about my getting a girlfriend if I promise you I'm looking?" In fact, she'd had the same conversation with her mom a few weeks ago. She could joke about their goals for her, pretend she didn't care when or if she found someone, but the truth was, she did care. She thought of Emily and how right everything had felt being with her. Sex aside, simply sitting together on the couch watching the fire and listening to music had made her happier than she'd been in a long time.

"You can't have a serious relationship with anyone else until you cut Katherine out of your life. You know that, right?"

"I feel like we've had this conversation before." About a dozen times. No matter how many times she argued that Katherine was only a friend with benefits, Rob refused to budge on his opinions. He was old-school when it came to relationships and needed to broaden his horizons. At least that was what she'd always told him. But had Emily pulled back because of Katherine? Maybe Emily had seen Katherine's texts. Or maybe she'd pushed too hard for a date and Emily's leaving had nothing to do with Katherine at all.

"I just think you'd be happy married, that's all."

Alex squeezed her eyes closed, exhausted by the gymnastics her brain was doing to make sense of the last twenty-four hours. "I don't know that I'm cut out for a serious relationship, let alone marriage. Women are complicated."

"Well, I can't argue with you on that one." Rob chuckled. "Get off the phone and get your butt over here. The kids are gonna go nuts when they see you."

CHAPTER TWENTY-SIX

After two hours playing auntie and wrestling with Joey and Lavender, Alex felt a little disoriented walking into Katherine's quiet foyer. She was twenty minutes late and could hear by the subdued conversation coming from the dining room that the party had already started eating, but she didn't rush to join them. As she took off her coat and boots, Rob's words ran through her head: *"You can't have a serious relationship with anyone else until you cut Katherine out of your life."*

Alex had always argued that she'd stop having sex with Katherine as soon as she had a girlfriend who wanted to be monogamous. But Katherine's texts from that morning had made her rethink even the boundaries she'd wanted to set up. It wouldn't be enough to stop sleeping with her only if she got involved with someone else. Their relationship needed to change regardless.

"Hi."

Alex looked up at the sound of Emily's voice. A rush of emotion slammed into her. Emily had soundly rebuked her that morning, but still her heart leapt to attention now. She couldn't fight it. "Hey. You look amazing."

"Thank you."

"Like, really damn hot. Smoking hot, actually."

Emily smirked. "Okay, stop. You're gonna make me blush."

"Actually, calling you 'hot' sounds crass and you definitely don't look crass." Alex held Emily's gaze. "You're absolutely stunning."

Emily didn't have a retort for that. She only narrowed her eyes, her smirk turning to a look of confident sexiness. Her brown hair fell in soft waves past her slender shoulders and a touch of makeup accentuated her eyes and full lips, but it was her silvery blue dress with a neckline that cut low and a slit up her thigh that had Alex rethinking her need for a girlfriend versus a night of fun.

"That dress is—"

"Not mine," Emily interrupted. "But it's nice, right? My friend Gianna turned me on to this website where you can rent just about any dress. I could never afford this, but I love it." She smoothed the front of the dress and then looked back at Alex. "You look good too. Nice suit. Although your hair…"

Emily walked up to Alex. She gave a little half smile when Alex sucked in a breath. "It's sticking straight up in the front and it's all wacky in the back. Can I fix it for you?"

Alex nodded. Emily was close enough to kiss but Alex didn't dare, despite the buzzing sensation on her lips. As Emily's fingers combed her hair into place, the faint smell of her perfume and the heat between their bodies made Alex dizzy with longing.

"There. That's better." Emily stepped back. Her face didn't show any evidence that the closeness had affected her. At least not as much as it had affected Alex, anyway.

"I was wrestling with my niece and nephew. That's why I'm late."

"You were wrestling in that outfit?"

"They didn't seem to mind."

"I wouldn't have minded either." Emily smiled. "You have family in town?"

"My brother and his wife live here. Along with their two kids."

Emily nodded. "Nice. Well, I won't keep you. Dinner's already started. I was going to get another bottle of wine. We're out of red."

"Katherine didn't get the wine?"

"She was chatting with Lara and I volunteered." Emily shrugged.

Alex wondered if it bothered her to be in the serving role. If it did, she hid it well. "Is everything going okay?"

"Everything's great," Emily said quickly. "Thanks for asking. How are you?"

"Good. Great."

Emily nodded, studying Alex closer now. "You sure?"

Alex hesitated. She didn't want to hold Emily in the foyer if she wanted to get back to the dinner party, but she at least needed to clear the air. "I've spent a lot of time thinking about our conversation this morning. All day, actually."

When Emily only waited for her to go on, Alex said, "It makes sense about you not wanting to jump into another relationship. In fact, if I were you, I'd be having sex with everyone here. Now's the time to experiment. Find out what you like. Not get caught by the first person who tells you you're beautiful."

Emily's expression was set and hard to read. She nodded slowly and then said, "See you in there?"

"Yeah." Alex felt her heart drop in her chest as soon as Emily headed to the kitchen. Everything she'd said had been the truth, but she'd hoped Emily would have at least argued that they could experiment together. Or even better, said she didn't need anyone else.

Alex eyed the door and considered leaving, but she couldn't make herself give up that easy. If she left now, she doubted she'd see Emily ever again. If she stayed, there was at least a chance they'd have time to talk. But she'd have to watch Emily flirt with everyone—maybe even Lara—knowing she'd encouraged her to do more than flirt.

It wasn't simply the dress that made Emily seem different tonight. Yesterday Emily had been like a deer in the headlights, but now she was completely at ease. Cool and confident. Meanwhile, Alex was the one reeling. She forced her feet to head to the dining room, bracing for what would come next.

"Fashionably late?" Lara said, raising an eyebrow.

"Time got away from me." The only seat open was one next to Lara. She sat down, wishing she'd taken longer to get her bearings in the foyer, then wondering what it was exactly that had her feeling so off. Was it only how different Emily seemed tonight?

"Do you have a girlfriend in town that you didn't tell the rest of us about?" Lara prodded.

Emily walked into the room with two bottles of wine right as Lara asked the question, and Alex felt her cheeks burn. "No girlfriend."

"Alex with a girlfriend?" Shay chuckled. "That'd be the day."

"Well, there was that property manager who couldn't keep her hands off you," Katherine said, raising an eyebrow. "She grilled me all about you when I was here last month. Apparently, you rocked her little world. I didn't give her the bad news that you've probably had that effect on half a dozen women since then."

"I stopped by my brother's house," Alex said quickly. She didn't look over at Emily despite how much she wanted to. There was nothing she could say to fix things now.

"How are Rob and Chelsea?" Katherine asked. "Still trying to convince you to get a wife and settle down and be boring like them?"

"Pretty much."

The others at the table laughed, but when Alex finally braved a look at Emily, her expression was serious. What was she thinking? She'd taken her seat next to TJ and handed one of the new bottles of wine to Madison. When Shay made a joke about Alex having a job with travel so she could leave a woman pining after her in every city, Emily's eyes lit briefly on Alex but then darted away.

Alex could take all the teasing this group wanted to throw her way—she knew that it was all in fun, with the exception maybe of anything Lara said. But what she didn't want was for

Emily to believe what they were saying. She thought back to the morning and when everything had gone awry. She'd hoped to turn things around tonight and maybe open up the conversation of a possible friendship, but now that seemed unrealistic.

As the conversation around the table turned to terrible vacations—apparently that had been what everyone was talking about earlier—Alex picked up her fork. She thought of the warmth she'd felt when she'd walked in the door at Rob's. A swell of happiness had filled her when Joey and Lavender had both attacked her with hugs. As soon as they'd let go, Chelsea had given her a kiss on the cheek and then chastised her for staying away too long. Rob had echoed the same words, pulling her into a bear hug that made tears press at her eyes. When she'd left, Rob had given his standard departing message: "Damn, do I love you, but don't get any taller." At five eight, Rob was shorter than he wanted to be, but he'd been using the same joke since she'd passed him up at fourteen. She was only an inch taller, but they both found it funny.

"Going for a full roll tonight?"

Emily's question pulled Alex back to the moment. She looked down at the dinner roll in her hand. "Tasted so good last night I thought why not go all the way."

Emily held up her own roll. "Great minds think alike."

Alex handed the butter dish across the table. "Want to go first?"

"This time I do, thanks." Emily's wink was subtle. She adeptly sliced her roll and then spread the butter on thick.

Emily was definitely different tonight. "You weren't kidding about liking butter," Alex said.

"I don't lie. Sadly, neither do my hips."

"I like your honest hips."

"Well, my hips liked yours," Emily returned.

Neither had bothered to lower their voice, and it was obvious when more than one head turned to glance between Emily and Alex that the others understood. Emily didn't seem at all concerned, and even gave Alex a coy smile as if to say that she wanted them to know.

"I think I've heard that song," Lara said. "And who doesn't appreciate hips that don't lie?"

"Are you a Shakira fan too?" Emily asked.

"Shakira, Shakira," Lara sang jokingly. "I love her. But I'm not exclusive."

As Lara and Emily chatted about favorite musicians and songs, Alex forced her attention to her meal. The soup was some sort of tomato bisque, and delicious, but she suddenly didn't have much appetite.

Normally she had no problem watching girlfriends flirt with other women, or men, for that matter. She'd had her share of threesomes as well as open relationships. So why was it so hard for her now to watch Emily smiling and laughing at Lara's jokes? She argued it was only because it was Lara. No matter what happened tonight, she didn't want Emily to get hurt.

Madison clinked her wineglass against Alex's as she raised it. "You hitting the slopes with us tomorrow?"

"Maybe. I don't have any set plans."

"Then make plans and come skiing with me. I'm dragging Shay, kicking and screaming," Madison looked over at Shay and winked. "TJ and Nicola are still weighing their options—the other option being staying in bed and having sex all day. Ava's a yes, but she's sticking to the bunny slopes."

Ava, from the other end of the table, said, "Unless I find a sexy ski instructor who wants to push me out of my comfort zone."

"Alex would be perfect for that," Katherine said. "She's an amazing skier."

"I don't know about amazing," Alex said, hoping to evade any direct answer. If Emily wanted to do something together, she wanted to keep her options open.

"Ignore her," Madison said. "Alex is the only one who can race Katherine in a blizzard."

"I remember that day," Katherine said. "And, as I recall, I won."

"Yes, you did." Alex knew by Katherine's look that, if anyone asked, she'd happily share why. She hoped the conversation wouldn't go there. Emily may have already formed her opinion of her, but she didn't need to know more of the dumb things she'd done in her past—including getting sloshed at a nightlong orgy and then agreeing to a race in a blizzard the next morning.

"Katherine's only skiing for a half day," Madison said, fortunately redirecting the conversation back to tomorrow's plans. "Unless you convince her to miss her spa appointment." She gave Alex a hopeful look. "She's already said no to me. Lara's out 'cause she's a dork and leaving us early. Meanwhile, Emily thinks the snow is going to freeze off her nipples. Apparently you told her to ski in a bikini?"

"I only said people do ski in bikinis," Alex said. "I didn't claim it was a good idea."

Shay shivered. "Kill me now."

"Right?" Emily continued. "I left Minnesota for a reason. Skiing in a bikini? No way."

"Alex just wanted to see your boobs," Shay said.

Lara chuckled. "She's not the only one."

"Is it just me, or does anyone else think it would be a total turn-on to have sex in a bikini in the snow?" Madison asked.

A chorus of "brrs" went around the table followed by laughing, but Madison clinked her glass against Emily's and said, "Here's to bikinis. And, by the way, I'm drooling over that dress of yours."

"I'm drooling too," Lara said. "Probably not for the same reasons."

"I don't know about that." Madison arched an eyebrow. She turned halfway in her seat and faced Emily. "We all know you only had eyes for Alex last night, and I don't blame you one bit, but who gets you tonight? You joining us in the teachers' lounge, or are you headed for the massage table?"

"Maybe she wants to try out the private room," Katherine said.

Alex expected Emily to blush or at least act uncomfortable when everyone turned to look her way, waiting on her answer, but she only looked back at Katherine and said, "I plan on making full use of my voyeur pass tonight."

"Ooh, I forgot that was your pick. Smart woman." Madison clinked her glass again. "I might steal that next time."

"Katherine, we're still headed back to Nice this summer, right?" Nicola asked. "Have you picked a date?"

Alex reached for her wine. She had already decided against another trip to Nice. This was her last fantasy weekend. But it wasn't only the weekends that needed to stop—she needed to put an end to all of it. No more meeting up for a weekend in Tahiti. No more spur-of-the-moment dinners in Lisbon. No Venice for twenty-four hours.

The rest of the dinner conversation was hard to keep up with. Alex's gaze, and her thoughts, kept drifting to Emily—to the delicate way she held her soup spoon, to how she dabbed the corner of her napkin against her lips, and to the smooth movement of her hand when she reached for her wine. Alex wished they were alone, but as soon as the thought crossed her mind, she was annoyed with her heart all over again. Emily was quite reasonably unavailable.

That was the hardest part—she didn't blame Emily for not wanting to date. In fact, when she thought about it logically, she wanted her to spread her wings and enjoy her freedom. She'd meant what she'd said in the foyer. Now was the time for her to experiment, not get caught in another relationship. Alex had done plenty of experimenting and she wouldn't dissuade anyone from it. How else could Emily be sure of what she wanted?

Knowing all that, when Lara leaned across the table to whisper something to Emily, Alex swallowed the bitter taste in her mouth. If only Emily could skip experimenting with Lara...

Alex noticed Katherine watching her and returned her cool stare. Katherine was good at reading people. The only thing she was better at, in fact, was reading the mood of the stock market. She probably knew exactly what Alex was thinking even now. No doubt she also had her own opinion of whether Emily would ever be ready to date, and if so, would ever consider Alex.

Katherine folded her napkin and set it on the table. "Anyone opposed to going downstairs for dessert? I had the caterer set up the fondue in the bonus room."

"Chocolate fondue?" TJ asked.

Katherine nodded, and Madison murmured her approval. "I'm picturing a blindfold, chocolate fondue, and waiting for someone to walk by and lick me."

"Any part you dip, I'll lick," Shay said, standing up.

"Me too," Lara added.

"Me three," Ava said, laughing.

Alex wished the playful mood of the others would brush off on her. Or if not playful, at least she wanted to feel some eager anticipation. She watched as everyone else paired off as they headed out of the dining room. She couldn't avert her eyes when Lara offered her hand to Emily.

"Not happy that someone else claimed your toy?" Katherine said. She'd come to Alex's side of the table but had waited until the others left before saying anything.

"She's not my toy."

As soon as Alex stood, Katherine stopped her with a hand on her chest. She leaned close, but Alex turned. Instead of getting her lips, Katherine kissed her cheek.

"I love it when you're fired up like this. I should dangle women in front of you more often." Katherine's eyes danced up and down Alex. "The problem is, you're hard to please. It's not so easy finding someone that makes the animal in you show itself." She caressed Alex's cheek with her thumb. "Don't get too caught up on her, though. She's not going to fall for you like the others. You know that, right? She's not even over her ex yet."

"I think she is, actually, but that's not the point." Alex didn't want to be arguing at all, but Katherine knew all the buttons to press to pull her into a fight.

"No. The point is, even if she was ready to date someone, she wouldn't be able to handle you. Not when you let loose."

"Katherine? You coming?"

Katherine stiffened at Madison's voice. She turned and glanced at the hallway.

"You're being summoned," Alex said.

"Our conversation's not over."

"Unless we want a fight, I think it is." Alex held Katherine's gaze. She knew Katherine hated to back down as much as she hated to lose. But it was also not the time for them to have the fight that was coming. "For the record, Emily can handle me. And if she wanted me, I'd do anything to keep her."

CHAPTER TWENTY-SEVEN

Keeping her distance from Alex was easy. In fact, Alex seemed to be avoiding her now that dinner was over. But not thinking about Alex was a different matter altogether.

Emily had tried to give herself a mental pep talk about sleeping with someone else, but she didn't want to force an attraction that wasn't there. She also couldn't pretend that she didn't still want Alex. When they'd bumped into each other in the foyer, she'd had to squelch the crazy desire to take her upstairs to her room. And then Alex had suggested she experiment with others.

How could she possibly kiss anyone else? All she could think about was having Alex's hands on her again. She didn't even care what Katherine might do in retaliation. In fact, over the course of the day, she'd gone from pissed about the texts to feeling almost sorry for Katherine. Not quite, but almost.

"I've always been a sucker for chocolate strawberries."

Emily hadn't noticed Alex come up behind her, but a zing went up her spine at the feel of her standing a foot away.

Alex continued. "But now strawberries seem kind of passé when there's kumquats and chokecherries to dip. And who came up with the idea of dipping ginger in chocolate?" She reached for a strip of candied ginger and dipped it in the chocolate. "It doesn't even sound right, but it's so good. Leave it to Katherine to get me addicted to something I'll never find anywhere else."

"Actually, you can thank Emily for that combo." Katherine was standing on the opposite side of the table and had seemed to be engrossed in a conversation with Shay and Madison, but apparently she'd been eavesdropping. She smiled at Emily and added, "But tonight's fondue isn't nearly as good as yours. There are very few things in life I like better than your chocolate. Don't tell anyone, but some nights I dream about the desserts you'll make me."

"Thank you. And your secret's safe." Emily wasn't sure what to make of Katherine jumping into the conversation, but the compliment seemed sincere.

"Which secret? The one about her dreaming about you or the one about you being an elite chef?" Lara said, coming up to the dessert table and reaching past for Alex for a strawberry. "Madison told me you can make her orgasm with one bite."

"Madison, you told me I was the only one who'd made you orgasm with one bite," Nicola said. "Did you forget Nice?" Her mock indignation made the others laugh.

"What can I say? I like to orgasm. And when I'm surrounded by the best of the best, I can't help it." Madison held up her hands. "I should have an inferiority complex being around y'all, but I don't 'cause I know you like how fast I come."

"It's true," TJ said. "You make the rest of us look good."

"Remember that orgasm contest last year?" Shay said. "How many did you get, Madison? Was it six?"

"Seven," Madison said smugly.

"And the last one was thanks to me," Lara said. "She couldn't walk after that one."

"Seven orgasms? I didn't even know that was possible." Ava looked stunned. And a little jealous.

"I want to know how she was walking after the fourth," Nicola said. "And the fifth."

"Practice." Madison laughed along with the others.

"Speaking of practice," TJ started. She raised her eyebrows at Nicola. "I'm thinking I could use some practice giving someone multiple orgasms."

"Giving?" Nicola sidled up to TJ. "I thought I was giving *you* a massage tonight."

"After you've had your hands all over me, you're gonna be all hot and bothered." TJ closed the distance between her and Nicola. They didn't kiss, but the air around them zinged with what was coming. "You'll be ready to let me do whatever I want with you."

"At this rate, we're all going to be ready to let you do what you want with us, TJ," Alex said.

"For real," Shay added.

When Nicola set her hand on TJ's chest and leaned in for a deep kiss, Emily felt her own lips tingle. Without thinking, she looked over at Alex. Alex seemed to be waiting for her, and Emily swallowed as a rush went through her. She looked away, hoping Alex didn't guess how much she wanted to kiss her. Forget going to her room. She'd let Alex take her right here.

"On that note, I think it's time for a costume change," Shay said. "If anyone didn't get the memo, the den is now the teachers' lounge."

"I'm so ready to spank you for misbehaving," Madison said, a mischievous glint in her eye. Shay only grinned.

Lara turned to Emily. "Any chance you'll be coming to the teachers' lounge?"

"I'm considering it. I want to make the most of my hall pass."

"And no one will complain if the voyeur wants to join in on the fun." Lara cocked her head. "The spanking part's totally optional. Madison and Shay like it, but I'm more about other things."

Emily knew Lara was giving her an opening to ask what she was into. And as much as she knew that she should want to have sex with Lara, the only person in the room she wanted was Alex. Still.

"Some things you don't know you like until after you try them," Shay said. "Once you get over being scared, Lara, I think you'd like getting spanked."

"I'm not scared." Lara pulled back her shoulders.

"Sure you aren't." Shay's taunting tone only got a laugh from Lara. But the energy between them made Emily guess a friendly competition was in store.

"Emily, you're definitely coming with us," Madison said. "Lara will do anything if she's got someone she wants to impress."

CHAPTER TWENTY-EIGHT

The scene in front of her should have been all she was thinking about: Lara on her hands and knees, butt bared as Madison spanked her, and Shay on the other side, holding Lara's face against their crotch. Instead, Emily was wondering what Alex was doing. Or, more specifically, whom she was doing.

She'd left Alex downstairs with the other half of the party. There was talk of Alex joining Ava and Katherine—from Katherine, of course—but Alex had been decidedly noncommittal. TJ and Nicola had tried to recruit Alex as well for a group massage. She hadn't turned them down, exactly. Instead, she'd looked right at Emily.

Alex hadn't said a word, but Emily felt as if she'd offered her the world in that moment. If she wanted anything from Alex, it was hers for the taking. Her heart had pounded in her chest as Alex held her gaze, and she'd wanted to take back everything she'd said earlier. Then before she could say anything at all, Madison had hooked her arm and insisted she was needed in the teachers' lounge. Possibly Madison wanted an audience, or maybe she was only being nice and making sure Emily didn't feel excluded. Regardless, Emily knew she had to go along with it. She needed a break from Alex even if she didn't want one.

But she'd never make it as a real voyeur. She didn't want a pass to watch; she wanted to participate. Just not with anyone in front of her. She only wanted Alex. Last night hadn't been meaningless sex, it had been the best night of her life. And now she needed a rebound from the person who should have been her rebound.

"That's enough," Madison said, her sharp voice pulling Emily back to the scene. She tugged Lara's head away from Shay, whose frustrated groan left little doubt as to how close they were to a climax, but they stopped complaining as soon as Madison pushed her breasts into their hands. Lara came up behind Madison, adjusting her harness for a cock she'd strapped on. When Madison felt it against her butt, she looked over her shoulder and smiled.

Emily swallowed. Instantly she was back in Alex's bed, reaching up to touch Alex, then tracing the curve of the dildo. She closed her eyes, imagining again how her body had opened for Alex, how much she'd wanted it. Alex had gently eased inside her, kissing her all the while. And then their hips had touched and there was nothing between them. She'd wanted to hold Alex in place, savoring the pleasure coursing through her, but then Alex had taken her to the next level. She hadn't realized how much more satisfaction she could have.

"And what exactly are you thinking of doing with that?" Madison asked.

Lara licked her lips. She pushed her hips forward and Madison's back arched as Lara's cock bumped her.

"Apparently, I didn't punish you enough," Madison said. "I should make you drop onto your knees again for another lesson."

"You want me. Bend over and I'll make this feel good for both of us."

Lara's words felt rehearsed. She was playing a role, of course, and it was what Madison wanted, but Emily couldn't help but think how much better Alex would have been in the part—her own attraction notwithstanding.

"You think you can talk to me like that?" Madison's sneer was classic. "I should suspend you."

"Go ahead," Lara said, sliding her hands over Madison's butt.

Lara was plenty sexy, as was Madison, and they were clearly having fun. Still, something was missing. As soon as Emily realized what it was, she knew it was also exactly what had drawn her to Alex and why she couldn't seem to let her go. Alex had an intensity that would have blazed through the room. Intensity that ran like an undercurrent through her making everything feel charged and ready to ignite. But the same intensity had made her gentle and patient, focused on being exactly what Emily needed that first time.

And Alex had kept her own desires on a tight leash. What would it be like when she really let go, when the leash came off?

An unbridled Alex... Demanding. Directing. In charge of everything, including her. Taking her completely, sliding in deep with forceful thrusts as she held her wrists to the bed. Emily's clit pulsed and heat spread through her. *Fuck.* Breathless, she grabbed the back of a chair to keep her knees from buckling.

The smack of Lara's hand on Madison's ass pulled her eyes back to the naked women in front of her. Madison let loose a string of cuss words and then looked over her shoulder at Lara. "You better make this worth a year of detention."

"Oh, I will."

Madison braced herself on the desk as Lara pushed the tip of the dildo into her. Emily gripped the chair tighter, knowing now how satisfying it felt to be filled and wanting Alex inside her again.

"Still want to suspend me?"

"You're definitely suspended," Madison said. "After you get me off." She grabbed the edge of the desk, fingernails digging in and curses flying from her lips as Lara pulled back and drove in again.

"Harder." Madison moaned when Lara complied, then asked again.

Lara upped her pace and Madison's moans gained volume. They were both panting now and dripping in sweat.

"More?"

"God, yes. Don't stop." Madison collapsed against the desk and Lara followed, pinning her.

Shay seemed transfixed by the whole thing, mouth open and frozen to their spot against the wall. Emily didn't blame them. As much as she hadn't felt exactly turned on at the start, she was now. Madison's nearing climax seemed to mesmerize all of them.

Lara wasn't Alex. And Emily didn't want to trade places with Madison. Yet the scene made Emily want Alex all the more, imagining the two of them together instead. Which was exactly what she hadn't wanted to happen tonight.

Madison's scream pierced the air. She shuddered with the climax and then went still. Lara held her when she tensed and shuddered again, peppering her back with kisses and murmuring soothing words.

Emily knew she was wet. She thought of reaching between her legs to satisfy her own desires. No one would mind, of course, but it wasn't what she wanted. She wanted Alex.

She heard a sound behind her and looked over her shoulder to see Katherine. At some point she'd come in, but instead of watching Madison and the others, she was looking right at Emily.

Katherine stepped forward and caressed Emily's cheek. "You're gorgeous tonight."

Instead of turning away, Emily held her ground. She could hardly breathe but wasn't about to let Katherine know that.

"Do you know how long I've wanted you?"

Katherine's words were like warm honey. As much as Emily didn't want to be charmed, the longer Katherine held her gaze the more she wondered why she fought the attraction.

"This is for you," Katherine said, handing Emily a little folded slip of paper. "I had to wait for the right moment."

It took Emily a second to realize what she was holding. Katherine's fantasy. Of everyone at the party, Katherine had picked her. She felt unsteady, still tingly from watching the scene and hot now under Katherine's unwavering gaze. Despite how uncomfortable she ought to be, arousal flushed through her.

"It's okay to say no to me. It's also okay to want it but be nervous."

Emily glanced down at the paper. As much as she wanted to know what Katherine's fantasy was, she didn't unfold the note. She wanted to give in without making any decision at all, to simply accept Katherine's desire. In a way, it would be perfect. Only meaningless sex—meaningless for real this time—exactly why she'd come to the party. Not only that, she could use some satisfaction. She was horny as hell. If Katherine considered her a plaything, she might as well get some benefits out of the deal.

"You don't have to answer yet." Katherine tilted Emily's chin up to her lips. When she leaned into the kiss, Katherine's hand slipped behind her head, pulling her closer.

Given how many women Katherine had over at her house any particular month, it should have been no surprise she knew how to kiss. But she was better than simply good. Her baiting and rewarding, the supple pressure of her lips, and the gratifying insistence of her mouth made each kiss melt into the next.

When Katherine's grip moved from the back of Emily's neck to her throat, a tremor raced through Emily. Could she really do this?

"I'll take that delicious shiver to mean you want this too." Katherine drew a line between Emily's breasts then reached for her hand. "Which makes me very pleased."

Emily didn't deny anything. She followed Katherine's lead, letting herself be pulled out of the den and into the hallway. A little release. That's all it would be. *What it should have been with Alex.*

Katherine pressed Emily against the wall with another long kiss, then pushed her dress above her hips as she stroked her legs. More kisses came as she slid her thumb under the seam of Emily's underwear. The contact immediately brought Alex to Emily's mind. She squeezed her eyes closed but the image stubbornly remained—not of Alex in bed, or even of them kissing, but Alex sitting across from her in the little café. She'd rested her hand on Alex's and her whole world had turned upside down. One touch… They'd been hardly more than strangers then and yet she'd known she'd never forget the moment. Or Alex. And so much had happened since.

Emily pushed Katherine's hand off and then turned her cheek when Katherine tried to kiss her again. "I can't."

"Why not?"

Alex. Thank god the word didn't slip out. As much as she'd thought she could give in and let Katherine do what she wanted with her, she couldn't. Emily held Katherine's folded note out to her. "I can't," she repeated.

Katherine didn't take the note back. She didn't even look at it. "It's Alex, isn't it? She won't mind, we share all the time."

Emily jerked away from Katherine's hand when she tried to caress her again. All she'd proven by kissing Katherine was that she didn't actually want meaningless sex. Despite Katherine's words, she knew what had happened between her and Alex was real and her heart wasn't going to move on without a fight. She wanted to find Alex now. She should at least tell her the truth. Nothing had been meaningless with her.

"You know, Alex is busy having her own fun at the moment. And I have plans for her later," Katherine said. "You can understand, I'm sure, how much I'm looking forward to her."

If her words weren't enough, the icy look in Katherine's blue eyes told Emily to back off. Would Alex pick Katherine if given the choice?

"She might want you," Katherine continued. "Maybe even as much as you think you want her. But we both know it wouldn't last. I'd give it two months. Maybe three. Then she'd need more than you're able to give."

Emily opened her mouth to argue, but what could she say? She'd told herself nearly the same thing that morning. Tears pressed in her eyes, but she clenched her teeth, holding them back.

"Alex needs someone as strong as she is. You'd only hurt each other trying to make it work. So do yourself a favor and sleep with someone else tonight." Katherine pressed her fingertip to Emily's lips. "Perhaps you'll change your mind about me. I'd happily give you a second chance."

Emily collapsed against the wall as Katherine strode off. She crumpled Katherine's fantasy into a tight ball. Caught between thinking everything Katherine had said was right and wanting her to be dead wrong, she tossed the note as far from her as she could manage. It didn't go far. She stared at it for a moment, feeling worse than she had all weekend. Again, Alex appeared in her mind. This time it was Alex from last night joking about hot cocoa and her taste in music. If only they could rewind to that moment.

Unfortunately, Katherine had a point. Alex did need someone strong. And even if their night together had made Emily feel like a sex goddess, it was all Alex lending her superpowers. Without her, she was back to being a mess.

Damn Alex for making her think she had a chance when it was obvious that she didn't. Emily covered her face with her hands and then instantly regretted it. Katherine's perfume had rubbed off on her skin.

"There you are." Lara's smile quickly dropped away. "What happened? Are you okay?"

Emily straightened up. "I'm fine."

"Yeah, I don't believe you. Here. Drink this."

"What is it?"

"Water."

When Emily shook her head, Lara drank the water herself. She leaned against the wall still studying Emily. "Shay's pouring shots. But it's tequila."

"You think I can't handle tequila?"

"In my experience, drinking tequila when you're angry is a bad idea." When Emily didn't respond, Lara stepped away. A moment later she was back with a shot glass. She handed it to Emily and then crossed her arms. "You gonna tell me what happened?"

"Nothing. And I'm not angry."

Alcohol wasn't going to fix anything, but she downed it anyway. As the tequila burned her throat, she wondered if

Katherine had gone right to find Alex. Was she enjoying her even now? Alex would doubtlessly enjoy Katherine—her slender body had no imperfections.

Emily didn't want to think about what they'd do together, but her mind wandered to the question. Would Alex tie Katherine up? Would she use a strap-on the way she had with Madison? Whatever Katherine wanted, Alex would be able to give it to her. Would she be rough with her? Or as gentle as the first time they'd made love last night?

Emily caught herself only after the word *love* crossed her mind. They hadn't made love last night. They'd only had sex. She doubted any of it would stay on Alex's mind for long. That she would never forget a moment of it was only one of the differences between them.

She thought again of Alex telling her to experiment. Even if it was good advice, she wished Alex hadn't said it. Instead, she wished Alex had asked her to break the rules and go back to her house. She might need more practice, but she didn't want to experiment with anyone but Alex.

"You sure you don't want to tell me what's wrong?" Lara asked again.

"Definitely sure." Emily held out the glass. "Can I have another?" Kissing Katherine had been a mistake, but at least she hadn't let it go beyond that.

Lara gestured back at the bar. "Ask Shay. I'm not gonna be the one who gets you drunk. If you're interested, I think we're moving the party out to the hot tub. Ava's convincing the others. Apparently, she and Katherine finished early."

Ava. Emily had forgotten that Katherine was supposed to be with her. How many others did Katherine plan on screwing tonight? She cussed under her breath. As much as she wanted to spend the rest of the night in her room, she knew sulking wouldn't help her stop thinking about Alex and Katherine together. "Is the hot tub still clothing optional?"

Lara grinned. "Always."

CHAPTER TWENTY-NINE

"I thought you were leaving. Did your headache get better?"

Alex glanced up at the sound of Katherine's voice close behind her. She had considered going back to her place as soon as Emily and the others had headed upstairs. Mostly that was because she didn't want to think about someone else having sex with Emily. But the excuse she'd given Katherine about a headache wasn't untrue either.

"I gave her some Advil and told her to pull up a chair," Nicola said. "No point in going home to masturbate over someone you can't have when you can masturbate with friends."

"Is that our new motto? Why masturbate alone when you can masturbate with friends?" Katherine set her hands on Alex's shoulders and started kneading. "So what happened with you and Emily anyway? One minute you're thick as TJ and Nicola, and the next…"

Alex knew she wasn't good at hiding things. Still, it stung her pride that everyone knew she was getting a cold shoulder from Emily. "Women are complicated. Maybe I should try men."

That got a laugh from everyone in the room. Alex looked up at Katherine. She wanted to say that she wasn't in the mood for a massage, but the scent of pussy on her hands caught her off guard. Ava and Katherine had disappeared into the private room together after dessert, but she hadn't kept track of them after Nicola and TJ convinced her to join them.

"How was Ava?"

"Good. You know how fun virgins can be." Katherine arched an eyebrow. "But I wanted to let her enjoy herself with the other guests as well."

"Very considerate." Alex sighed. She didn't care that everyone around her was having sex. For once, she didn't crave it at all. All she wanted was to be spending the evening with Emily. *Talking*. God, maybe she had gotten old like Lara said.

"I like you Alex," TJ said drowsily. "Always have." She was stretched out on the table, arms hanging at her side and a smile still on her face from the afterglow of Nicola's very thorough massage. "You're a good audience. Even participate at all the right times. How many people can say they have sex with their best friend watching?"

"TJ, you and I are not normal friends. We've both seen each other naked way too many times."

"Remember that first Aspen? A week solid of orgies. I saw your ass everywhere I looked."

"Were you jealous of my ass?"

TJ chuckled. "Not even a little bit. Mine got plenty of action too. Don't think I would have been able to handle more."

Alex wondered if her experience, or at least Emily's perception of it, had been the reason she'd pulled back. There was no denying she'd had a lot of sex. But she hadn't ever wanted someone the way she wanted Emily.

All day she'd thought of her. The past hour was no exception. While Nicola was rubbing massage oil over TJ's backside, Alex imagined Emily doing the same to her. And when Nicola had turned TJ over and buried her face between her legs, Alex thought of Emily's mouth on her. How good it had felt…

"Maybe, for being so good, you should get some time on that massage table too," Katherine said. She moved from Alex's shoulders to her arms.

"I think I'm good right here." As much as Alex wanted to fight it, she felt her body relaxing into Katherine's supple touch.

"We all know how good you are." Katherine leaned close and planted a kiss on Alex's neck. "That's the problem."

Alex shifted forward on the love seat and Katherine's hands fell off her shoulders. "Anyone want a drink?"

"I'd take a little of that rum Katherine was passing around last night," Nicola said.

"Mmm, me too," TJ said.

Alex turned to Katherine. "Want the same?"

"Sure. But the bottle's upstairs in the den."

"No problem. Oh. The den." Otherwise known as the teachers' lounge. Alex didn't want to walk in on that scene, particularly if there was any chance Emily was part of it, although she couldn't imagine her participating in anything as wild as what Lara and Madison would come up with. Maybe she'd hang out with Shay... Shay could be good for her. Build her confidence. Despite being sometimes clueless, Shay was never unkind. If Alex could choose, which of course she couldn't, she almost wished Emily was with them. Anyone but Lara.

"In case you're worried, I don't think you'll get recruited," Katherine said. "Last I heard the party was moving to the hot tub."

Alex considered asking if Emily was part of the hot tub group but then thought better of it. She could find out for herself. And if Emily wasn't with the others, maybe she'd want to talk.

"I'll be right back."

Clothes were strewn all over the den, but as far as Alex could tell Emily's silver dress wasn't among them. She only let herself take the briefest of glances, however, before picking her way between the rearranged furniture over to the liquor cabinet.

Once she'd found the bottle of rum and gathered four tumblers, she considered whether or not she should look for Emily. Had the whole evening been too much and she'd gone up to her room? On one hand, Alex wanted Emily to enjoy herself. On the other, she wouldn't be heartbroken if Emily had opted out. Maybe she'd even realized she could experiment with Alex instead of someone else.

She started back to the stairwell still debating whether to look for her or not when the lights on the patio caught her attention. She paused by the French doors leading to the courtyard and squinted to see the hot tub. The yellow-orange glow of the lights gave everything a muted look save for the crystal-white snow that covered all the surfaces. A narrow path of exposed flagstone led from the door to the steps of the hot tub.

Alex recognized Madison's profile first, then Shay sitting next to her. They were both naked and steam from the hot tub rose up around them. Lara was directly opposite Madison, sitting on the edge with her feet in the water. Her knees were parted, and someone was between her legs. Alex's stomach clenched when she noticed the tousled dark hair. *Emily.* She didn't want to see what was happening, but she couldn't make herself look away.

Lara combed her fingers through Emily's hair. She braced her hand at the back of Emily's head and pushed her hips forward. Water splashed up and Emily pulled back, clearly needing air, but Lara only moved with her. Alex closed her eyes and slowly counted to five. When she looked out at the hot tub again, Emily had moved her arms from under Lara's legs to around her waist. Her face was pressed against Lara's center. Alex could still only see the back of her head, but there was no doubt now that she was going for Lara of her own volition. Knowing no one was forcing her didn't make watching the scene any more pleasant, but it stopped Alex from storming outside and yanking Lara's hands off Emily.

When Lara arched her back, her mouth opening in a gasp, Alex couldn't stand it anymore. She quickly turned and nearly walked right into Katherine.

"Sorry. I didn't hear you come up the stairs."

"You were distracted." Katherine motioned with her chin to the patio. "I don't blame you. She's putting on quite a show. Looks like Lara's enjoying it too."

Alex unclenched her death grip on the bottle of rum. She could hear her pulse roaring in her ears and knew she had to talk herself down. And quick. Katherine was only trying to get under her skin. She loved to rile her.

"All this time I had it in my head that you were one of those people who doesn't get jealous. Now I'm thinking maybe those people don't really exist. They just haven't found something they want bad enough to be jealous when someone else claims it."

"Fuck you."

"Would you?"

"Don't." Alex could hear the anger in her voice and wondered how Katherine could keep smiling at her like a damn Cheshire cat. She set the bottle of rum and the tumblers on the little hall table. The thought of having a drink with everyone now was too much. She needed to go home. "I'm happy you're enjoying this, but I'm not."

"Want me to help you?" Katherine reached forward and fingered the button at Alex's neck. "I don't often get a rise out of you. This is the most fun I've had in a while." She undid the button her finger had been circling and then dropped to the next. "My jealous streak has never been in question. Yours, however, is something fun and new. You know, you can close your eyes and pretend I'm her. I wouldn't mind being used. You're unbelievably sexy tonight. It's taking every bit of control I have to not beg you to fuck me right here."

Alex pushed Katherine's hand off her shirt. "I'm done. I told you that. I don't want any more games. And I'm not jealous. I want Emily to be enjoying herself. With anyone who isn't Lara. You know how she is."

"So you're being protective."

"Yeah. Is that a horrible thing?"

"Course not." Katherine's silky voice didn't hide anything. She wasn't buying Alex's line.

"You know Lara can go too far. I don't want what happened with Annette to ever happen again. It won't when I'm around."

"So chivalrous."

"Screw you. We both know it bordered on abuse. I can't believe you'd take her side."

"I'm not denying that she took things too far. She was drunk. We both saw that too. It's not an excuse, but it is an explanation. You, on the other hand, were completely sober when you left Madison tied up and walked away, so don't stand there and act like you're any different."

"What happened with Madison was entirely different—"

"Entirely?" Katherine shook her head. "Leaving her was irresponsible and dangerous. And for what? A pretty girl who caught you with your pants down?"

"I apologized to Madison already. And she wasn't in any danger. She wasn't alone."

"No, she wasn't alone."

Katherine held her gaze and Alex felt the walls pressing in. She'd walked out on Katherine too. Why hadn't she seen that before? And her apology to Madison had been little more than a side remark over dinner. God, what a selfish ass she'd been. "I'm sorry. I didn't think—"

"You often don't think, Alex. I've gotten used to it. My point is, you and Lara are the same and you aren't gaining anything staying mad at her. Lara apologized, Annette forgave her, and we all moved on. At least most of us." She inclined her head. "And that was two years ago. She learned her lesson."

"She hasn't changed."

"Well, you and I see her differently. She's been sober for over a year now and she's made a lot of other changes—I doubt you noticed since you're too busy hating her." Katherine paused. "I gave her a second chance and she hasn't made me regret it yet. The way I see it, she'd be good for Emily. Push her limits a little. Don't get me wrong, Emily's a good kisser, but she has a lot to learn. Lara could help her there."

"How do you know Emily's a good kisser?" The question was answered with a little tilt of Katherine's head, and Alex caught herself before a cuss slipped out. She felt a wave of dizziness. "When?"

"Tonight. I've been wanting to for a while now, and I can't say I was disappointed. At least not with that."

Alex clenched her jaw. Katherine's tone made it clear that kissing wasn't all they'd done. *Dammit*. She should have seen it coming.

"You look surprised." Katherine's tone had changed, almost as if she were gloating.

"You did this to get back at me."

"Of course not. I love a sex party virgin as much as you do. Always so eager. And, God, do I love a woman who moans. Those sounds she made…mmm. But you already know all about those sounds."

Alex swallowed. "Why? If it wasn't because you were pissed at me, what was the reason?"

Katherine raised a shoulder. "I told you why. I've wanted her for a while now. And she's wanted me. You should have seen the way she looked at me when she came for her interview. That whole first month she couldn't keep her eyes off me."

"I don't believe you." Alex charged ahead, too angry now to keep her voice in check. "It drives you crazy that she's someone I actually like. You can't handle the idea of me finding someone and falling in love."

"You falling in love with Emily?" Katherine snorted. "For how long? Three weeks?"

Katherine's sarcasm only pushed Alex further. "Every time I try to date someone, as soon as it gets serious, some shit comes up in your world and I drop everything to come to you. You know exactly what you're doing. The question is why I keep falling for the same damn trick. Why do I keep coming to rescue you?"

"Chivalry, I'm sure."

"I'm not joking."

"Oh, I can tell." Katherine drew a line down Alex's chest. She stopped at Alex's belt and traced the buckle. "I love how fired up you are over this."

"Stop."

"Pretty words, but you're not pushing my hand away this time. Do you really mean it?"

Alex didn't know if she meant it or not. Did it matter if she had sex again with Katherine? Now that she knew Emily had let Katherine have her, everything had shifted. Suddenly she wondered if maybe that was what Emily had wanted all along. Was the reason Emily had pushed her away that morning because she'd wanted Katherine instead? Was she only Emily's warm-up?

"I'll take that as a no."

Katherine stepped forward and pressed into Alex's lips. As much as Alex didn't want Katherine to even be near her, she moved into the kiss. She wished she were kissing Emily, even knowing all that Emily was doing to Lara and had done with Katherine. It didn't matter. She wanted Emily anyway, so much that instead of stepping back as her brain screamed for her to do, she moved into Katherine's lips. Anger blended with desire and her lips set the pace as her appetite begged to have Katherine right there. In the hallway.

She pushed Katherine back a step when she parted her lips, then back another step until she was against the wall as she deepened the kiss. When Alex pulled back, they were both breathless. "I need to stop kissing you. I need to be done."

"So you've said. But we both know that's not happening tonight. Tomorrow you can break up with me. Except we're not actually dating."

Katherine tried to pull Alex against her and then growled when Alex didn't budge. She slid her finger under Alex's collar, then stepped away from the wall and kissed Alex's neck. "Want to go outside and give them all a show? We could do better than Lara and Emily and you know it."

Alex shook her head. "I'm leaving. I'm done, Katherine. No more."

"So, see you tomorrow?"

"I'm not playing a game." Alex was done with all of it. With Katherine, with her sex parties, and with women who only wanted one night. By the forced flirty tone in Katherine's voice, she knew it too. "You know where to find me if you need something, but I can't do this anymore. No more sex parties, no more anything. You and I aren't good for each other."

"Anything else? Or is that the end of your prepared remarks?" Katherine's words carried a real bite now. "Why don't we cut to the chase and say what's actually going on? You're used to getting what you want, and you don't like it when you don't. Go ahead and make it about something else. But sex parties aren't the problem. Neither am I." Katherine paused for a fraction of a second. "And fuck you."

Alex considered all the arguments against what Katherine said, but part of her wondered if some of it was true. She exhaled. "Fuck."

"Finally, we're on the same page." Katherine slipped her hand behind Alex's neck and pulled her into a kiss.

The French doors next to where they stood opened suddenly. As Alex pulled back from Katherine's lips, she registered Emily, dripping wet and naked, staring open-mouthed back at her. Seconds passed. Alex couldn't think of what to say. She half expected Emily or Katherine to break the silence, but no one spoke.

Then Emily turned and walked toward the staircase. It wasn't until Alex was aware that she was staring at Emily's butt that she realized any chance she thought she had was truly gone.

CHAPTER THIRTY

No matter which way Emily turned her head, the piercing sensation in her left ear wouldn't go away. The rest of her wasn't much better off. Tequila always gave her a headache, but she was nauseous, too, and every time she tried to sit up the room swirled around her.

She knew at least some of the others were awake. She'd heard doors opening and closing and voices in the hallway. But she wasn't sure what time it was, and she didn't want to brave looking at her phone for fear she'd lose the half glass of water she'd managed to drink. Fortunately, she'd left the glass on the bedside table the night before—she'd anticipated some of this, at least. Just not the stabbing ear pain. That couldn't be from the tequila.

"This weekend's full of fun new things," she mumbled, eyes still closed. Maybe if she could fall back asleep, she'd wake up and her ear would be back to normal.

A knock sounded at her door. She forced her eyes open but didn't raise her head from the pillow. "Yeah?"

The door opened a moment later and Lara peeked in. "You okay in there?"

"I can't move."

"Shit. You sound terrible." Lara crossed over to the window opposite the bed and pulled the drapes closed.

As soon as the room darkened, the throbbing in Emily's head let up. Unfortunately, her ear still screamed in pain. "That's better. Thanks."

"Too much tequila." Lara's assessment was quick and decisive. "Did you drink some water before you went to sleep?"

Emily shook her head and then immediately regretted it. She tried to brace herself as the room went into a spin. "Something else is wrong with me, though."

Even through her hazy eyes, Emily could see that Lara's look bordered on panic. "I'm getting TJ."

Before Emily could stop her, Lara had gone. Emily closed her eyes, trying to stop the swirling.

The door opened again a moment later and TJ's voice seemed to come from far away. "Hey, Emily, is it okay if I come in?"

Emily sighed. "Yeah."

"Shay and Lara are with me too."

Great. Emily hoped no one else was on their way. Especially not Katherine. Or Alex.

"I hear you had too much tequila?"

Emily murmured, "Maybe."

TJ sat down on the bed and touched Emily's forehead. "You don't feel feverish. That's good."

"Do you think tequila could make my ear hurt?" Emily hoped TJ would say that was a rare symptom of overindulging in blue agave, but it sounded ridiculous to her too. When Emily opened her eyes, TJ and Lara seemed to be in some kind of silent communication.

"You slipped getting out of the hot tub," Shay said. "Remember? You grabbed the railing and missed. You went under and Lara grabbed you. But I didn't see you hit your head."

Emily felt even more sick that she had no memory of that. She looked over at Lara. "Thanks for catching me."

"It was nothing. I wish I'd stopped you from drinking that tequila."

"I think you tried. I didn't want to listen to any advice last night." She touched her head, wishing the throbbing would stop. "How bad do I look?"

"Well…"

Emily groaned as a fresh stab pierced her ear. "It feels like someone skewered my head. Through my left ear. Now I feel bad for tomatoes when they get made into kebabs. And bell peppers."

TJ chuckled, and Shay said, "You're funny when you're drunk."

"I'm definitely no longer drunk. Unfortunately." When she was drunk, she hadn't cared so much that Alex and Katherine were making out. Or that she'd caught them in the same damn hallway where Katherine had kissed her. Now that she was sober, she couldn't stop thinking about all of it.

"I think I have an ear infection, but there is no way I'm getting out of this bed. Everything spins as soon as I try to move."

"We should call Alex," TJ said. "She'll know what to do."

Shay agreed. Emily heard Lara suggest instead that they take her to urgent care. She didn't like either option.

"Why would you call Alex?"

TJ already had her phone out. "Her brother's a doctor. She calls him all the time about medical stuff whenever anyone comes down with something."

"Can you please not call her?"

TJ's thumb hovered over the screen. "She won't mind."

"What happened with you and Alex anyway?" Shay asked.

"Nothing."

Lara said something about Alex being a waste of oxygen, but TJ muttered something that made her drop it. Under other circumstances, Emily would have asked why Alex and Lara didn't get along, but now she only wanted everyone to stop talking.

TJ drummed her fingers on the edge of the phone. "Emily, the thing is, Alex knows a lot about medical stuff herself. She might not even need to call her brother."

"Aren't both of her parents doctors?" Shay asked.

"Only one's a doctor," Emily answered. She knew the question was directed at TJ, but she didn't care. "The other's a judge. Shit." She squeezed her eyes shut as the nausea swelled again. "Can you please not do that tapping thing, TJ?"

TJ stopped drumming on the phone. "I think we should call Alex. There aren't a lot of options if we can't move you."

Emily breathed in through her nose and out through her mouth several times, desperately hoping she wouldn't vomit. With three of the most attractive people she'd met in ages staring at her, that was the last thing she needed.

"Are you embarrassed about her seeing you like this?" TJ asked. "You don't have to worry about that. She's seen all of us in embarrassing situations. Literally all of us."

Shay nodded their agreement. "All of us."

"They're right. And she's helped all of us." Lara sighed. "We probably should call her."

Emily closed her eyes again. She knew they were all still staring at her, waiting for her to agree to ask Alex for help. But the image of Alex lip-locked with Katherine wouldn't leave her mind. She didn't want to see her after everything that had happened. "Can you come back and check on me in two hours? If I'm not better, then we can call Alex."

After a moment of the three of them all deliberating, Lara said, "I'll grab her some Advil and we'll let her sleep. But only two hours."

Emily heard the shuffle of feet and the door opening and closing. She drifted back to sleep only to be awakened a moment later by Lara's hand on her shoulder. She'd returned with two pills, which Emily swallowed and then closed her eyes again.

The door closed behind Lara and the room was blissfully quiet. She didn't know if she'd fall asleep again, but she didn't want to do anything else.

"Hey, sleepyhead."

Emily opened her eyes at the sound of Alex's voice. It took a moment to focus, and in the dim light she couldn't make out details, but it was definitely Alex sitting at the edge of her bed. She covered her face with her hand. "Ugh."

"I get that you don't want me to be here right now, but everyone was worried. Lara never calls me, and I've had four phone calls from her today. The last one she sounded a little panicked." Alex paused. "Want a sip of water? Your glass was empty, so I got you a refill."

Emily nodded. Her throat was parched and she could hardly swallow her own spit. She knew she must look awful, but at the mention of water, that was all she could think about. At least the drapes were closed so Alex couldn't see her that well. Before she thought better of it, she sat up and took the water glass. This time, fortunately, the room didn't spin. Unfortunately, the ache in her ear turned to a pounding. She took a small sip of the water, worrying that the nausea would return if she pushed it, then handed the glass back to Alex. "Thank you."

She dropped back on the pillows and closed her eyes. "I don't think I'm going to vomit. But I think I need a doctor. There's something wrong with my ear."

"Want me to give you a ride to urgent care, or do you want me to call my brother?"

"Can you decide for me? I don't feel as awful as I did earlier, but it hurts when I try and think. What time is it?"

"Two."

"In the afternoon?" Emily couldn't believe it was that late. "What day is it?"

"Monday…I'm calling my brother. It's a holiday anyway. He'll be home."

"Okay." Emily didn't open her eyes as Alex chatted with her brother. She answered all the questions Alex asked, wishing that Alex didn't sound as sexy as she looked. When Alex lightly pressed her palm against Emily's forehead to check for a fever, her gentle touch triggered a whole cascade of emotions. Emily clenched her teeth to keep the tears back. God, she was a mess. As soon as Alex lifted her hand, saying to her brother that she didn't think there was any fever, Emily wanted to beg Alex to put her hand back on her head. Alex's touch had made everything stop hurting.

"You up for a drive?"

Emily opened her eyes. The concern on Alex's face made her emotions all the more unbearable. "Does he think I need to go to urgent care?"

"He said we can swing by his house first and he can take a quick look at you. It'll be way less painful than us sitting around for hours in a waiting room."

"Do we have time for me to brush my teeth?" Emily could handle looking like a mess considering how she felt, but bad breath was over the line.

"Definitely. He doesn't live far, and my car's right out front. You can even shower if you want."

"As long as the room stays put."

"I can't promise that. Here, take my hand." Alex held out her arm. "I'll help you up. My brother said it's probably vertigo from an ear infection. Or a sinus issue. Either way, he didn't seem to think you were gonna die. Maybe tomorrow, but not today."

Despite everything, Emily couldn't help smiling. "Thanks for that." She took Alex's hand, telling her mind to be quiet as it immediately noted how nice the strong, steady grip felt.

Once she'd sat up, Alex waited for her to slowly stand, then slipped an arm around her waist. "This okay?"

"Yeah." Better than okay, actually. As nice as being wrapped up in a warm blanket fresh out of the dryer. All Emily wanted to do was melt into Alex's arms. Except for the fact that she couldn't stop thinking about her possible bad breath.

She took a tentative step, then another. "So far, so good."

"Yeah, at this rate you're gonna break out dancing by the time we reach the shower."

Emily grunted but Alex only chuckled. They reached the bathroom and Alex paused in the doorway. "Want me to keep the lights off?"

"Yes, please."

"You probably want privacy, too, but can I turn on the water for you?"

Emily nodded. She braced herself, one hand on the sink and the other on the wall, when Alex let go of her to start the shower. She thought of the few times she'd been sick and Cass's response. Or lack thereof. Cass didn't want anything to do with sick people. Partly it was because she was paranoid about catching anything, but the other half of it was that Cass couldn't handle weakness of any kind. In herself or in anyone else.

"Okay, it's warm now. Want help with your clothes?"

"Not even a little bit." The idea of Alex undressing her for this reason was too much.

Alex held up her hands. "Totally understand. I'm gonna wait for you on the other side of this door. If you need me, call out and I'm coming in. Even if you're naked."

"You don't have to do that."

"I want to," Alex said. "And, honestly, I think I should. You're standing there swaying and I think a feather would take you out. Besides, I've got nothing else to do."

Emily waited until Alex had stepped out of the bathroom and closed the door before flipping on the lights. She grimaced when she caught sight of her reflection and quickly looked away from the mirror.

After the shower, she almost felt normal. Almost. Except for the earache and the vertigo. She wrapped herself in a towel and brushed her teeth, wondering if Alex was playing on her phone while she waited. Was she the type to be on social media? Emily wanted to look her up online, but she didn't even know her last name. She considered all the ways she could find that out, then finally cracked the bathroom door and squinted down at Alex. "What's your last name?"

"Murphy."

"Okay. Alex Murphy, can you grab clothes for me? I'm doing pretty amazing here—not dizzy unless I move—but I don't think I should lean over and dig through my suitcase."

"I got your back, rock star." Alex hopped up from the spot on the floor adjacent to the bathroom door where she'd taken up residence. "Why'd you want to know my last name?"

Emily hesitated answering. She could come up with a lie, but she didn't see the point in trying to save face, and she was stuck on the fact that Alex was genuinely sweet on top of everything else. Knowing what to say at exactly the right time was probably only a skill she'd learned to get women, but sitting on the floor as close to the bathroom as possible in case Emily needed help? That was different. That felt real. What also had been real, Emily reminded herself, was the fact that Alex had made out with Katherine last night even though she'd said she was over her. "There's probably a dozen Alex Murphys on Instagram. And Facebook."

"Probably." Alex held up the light gray sweater Emily had packed and a pair of black leggings. "This okay?"

"That's perfect. Underwear and a bra, too, please."

"Got it." Alex leaned over the suitcase, searching for the other items. "Maybe I shouldn't say this, but it makes me happy to know you'd want to look me up. After last night I wasn't so sure."

"I'm so not ready to talk about last night."

"Fair enough." Alex crossed the room and held out the bundle of clothes. "Honestly, I'm not ready to talk about it either. You do have my number, you know. You can text me anytime. I could also give you my address in Tokyo. Then you wouldn't have to hire a private investigator to find me." She winked. "I'd give you my email, but I'm not online much unless I have to be for work."

"Course you're not." Emily realized that she should have guessed that Alex would be too cool for social media and saved herself from asking. She sighed. Today she couldn't even pretend to be in the same league. "Give me a minute to get these on, and I'll be ready to leave."

CHAPTER THIRTY-ONE

Alex and her brother looked nothing alike. Where Alex had a lean swimmer's build, her brother looked more like a studious teddy bear. He had a mop of brown hair, a full beard, a pudgy belly, and little round glasses that matched his round face. When he greeted Alex with a hug and a hearty laugh, he only seemed to confirm the teddy bear image.

"I'd hug you as well, but if you're still feeling dizzy, you'd probably rather I don't." He stuck out his hand. "I'm Rob. The handsome, smart one in the family."

Alex elbowed her brother and then admitted he was right. They both laughed. If at first the siblings didn't look alike, their full smile was identical. Emily thought of the first time Alex had flashed that same smile at her and how her heart had danced. *Stupid heart.*

Emily shook Rob's hand, but before she could thank him for offering to see her at his home, a loud pattering of feet and a woman's voice interrupted. "I said, don't run with a popsicle in your mouth!"

"You're about to meet the whole family," Rob said. "Brace yourself."

A little girl with a red popsicle sticking halfway out of her mouth and a tangle of blond curls came racing toward them. On her heels was a toddler dragging a blanket, also with a popsicle. A few feet behind him, an attractive woman in a tank top and sweatpants brought up the rear.

"Lavender." Rob pointed to the older of the two kids first, then to the toddler. "And Joey."

"And I'm Chelsea. Welcome to chaos. We gave them popsicles hoping you wouldn't be greeted with ear-piercing screams." She smiled at Emily. "I got an ear infection last spring. Loud noises only made it worse. Especially at the octaves these two can reach."

"I appreciate that." Emily smiled at the two kids with red popsicle juice already dripping down their chins. "You two have extra-nice parents. Popsicles are the best. What flavor?"

"Strawberry," Lavender said, plucking the popsicle out of her mouth and grinning.

"Not strawberry." Joey bunched his brow. "Cherry."

"Strawberry," Lavender argued.

Joey's scowl deepened. "Cherry!"

"I know where this is going," Alex said. She scooped up Joey, blanket, popsicle, and all. "You promised to show me your dinosaurs yesterday. Where are they?"

The scowl disappeared instantly. He pointed at the stairs. "Up. You carry."

"Watch your step in Joey's room," Rob said. "And if you think it looks like a tornado touched down, you should have seen it before we cleaned."

"Thanks for the warning."

Rob nodded. "It'll only take a minute for me to peek at Emily's ears, but you'll be stuck up there with dinosaurs until dinnertime."

"I want to show Aunt Alex my toys too," Lavender said.

"That's only fair, right?" Alex shifted Joey to one hip and held out her free hand to Lavender. "First dinosaurs, then you get to show me your favorite toy."

"Horses! I have so-oh many. You have to meet all of them."

Alex chuckled. "Somebody better rescue me."

As Alex headed up the stairs, Rob turned to Emily. "So. Dizzy, headache, nausea, and your left ear aches? Anything else?"

"The headache and the nausea are mostly gone...I took something," Emily paused, trying to remember what Lara had given her. "I think it was Advil, but I was a little groggy at the time. Anyway, I think most of those signs were from too many tequila shots."

"Been there." Rob chuckled. "But your ear still hurts?"

Emily nodded. "And I'm still dizzy if I move too fast."

"I so remember that feeling," Chelsea said. "Sorry, hon. Betcha a dollar you got an ear infection. The good news is that I made Rob get a whole bag of extra doctor stuff to keep at home after the kids were born. If I have to deal with a doctor, I want some benefits."

"Hey, I'm not that bad."

"Mmm, depends on the day." Chelsea laughed and poked Rob's side. "Actually, you're amazing, and we both know it."

"Most days." Rob grinned. "Let me get my otoscope."

"We'll be in the family room," Chelsea called. Rob had already disappeared down the hall, but Chelsea pointed the opposite direction. "Can I get you some tea or anything?"

"I don't think my tummy's ready for that, but thank you."

"Right. Nausea...Sorry about that." Chelsea led the way over to the sofa. "So, other than getting sick, how was your weekend? Alex mentioned this was your first time. She keeps saying she's done with Katherine's parties and then signing up for another one. Can't really blame her—they sound amazing. Sometimes I even wish I were into women just so I could go. How do you get invited to something like that anyway?"

Emily couldn't think of what to say. Chelsea was sitting across from her on the sofa, smiling and relaxed, openly asking her for a recap on a sex weekend. What threw her even more was that Alex had mentioned her.

"Katherine is one of my clients. I'm a personal chef. Anyway, that's how I got the invite."

"And you've been enjoying it?"

Emily hesitated. "I'd say it's been good for me."

Chelsea tilted her head. "Hmm. Not a resounding yes."

"Parts of it have been good." Emily immediately recalled the moment Alex had kissed her. She could still feel the sensation of Alex's lips pressing against hers. God, that kiss had undone her. A warmth swept through her as she thought of everything Alex had done to her after that kiss.

"And Alex?"

Emily opened and closed her mouth. She let out a deep breath. "Yeah. Those were the good parts. I like her a lot, but it's complicated."

"She had that same look in her eyes when she talked about you yesterday."

"I kind of want to ask what she said, but…"

"She said a lot." Chelsea smiled. "Couldn't stop talking about you. You're the first person she's told us about from one of these parties. Except Katherine, of course. I know you work for her, but I'm not a big fan of hers."

Rob appeared before Chelsea had time to say more. Emily wished they could talk for a few more minutes, but Rob jumped right in with the exam.

After he'd taken her temperature, he listened to her chest and looked down her throat. Then he checked both ears and confirmed she had an ear infection.

"Can you be my doctor from now on?" Emily said. "That was more of an exam than I've ever had."

"Sure. But Alex said you lived in San Francisco, right? That's a long drive for a physical."

"You're worth it, sweetie," Chelsea said. "Besides, Alex will thank you for giving Emily a reason to come back to Aspen."

"She would." Rob chuckled. "Speaking of, when do you fly home?"

"Tomorrow morning." Emily had been happy about the early morning flight when she'd first seen the tickets because she wouldn't have to reschedule any of her Tuesday clients, but now getting up for a six o'clock flight sounded awful.

"Any chance you can push that back a day or two? I'm not keen on you flying until the swelling goes down in that ear."

Emily shook her head. "I can't stay an extra day at Katherine's." In fact, she probably could ask, but the truth was she didn't want to. "And I can't afford to change my flight. Can I try taking more Advil?"

"You could stay with me."

Emily hadn't heard Alex come into the room. She looked up at the sound of her voice and saw Alex with Lavender in one arm, Joey in the other, and an Easter bonnet on her head complete with fake flowers.

"Nice hat," Chelsea said. "Is that a pterodactyl hiding in those bluebells?"

"I think it might be." Alex continued, "Seriously, though, Emily. You staying with me is no problem at all. And I've got about a billion frequent-flier miles. I could get you a free flight whenever you want it."

"I can't." She couldn't accept Alex's generosity. How could she pay it back? "But I agree with Chelsea. That hat is perfect for you."

Alex winked. "Sexy and I know it."

Alex was right, even if she was joking. Emily stopped herself from saying as much. Even in a ridiculous bonnet Alex looked hot, and the fact that she could swing two kids in her arms without looking out of breath only added to her appeal.

"You should consider the offer," Rob said, looking at Emily. "No one wants a ruptured eardrum."

"Except maybe Lavender." Alex bounced her arm and Lavender giggled. "See? Lavender wants one."

"I want one too," Joey said.

"You don't even know what you want. All you want is to be wrestled. And maybe tickled," Alex said, bouncing Joey as well.

The next minute, both Alex and the kids were on the floor. She gave them each a horsey ride and then tossed them in the air. It wasn't long before they were both simultaneously laughing and screeching.

Despite the noise, Emily couldn't stop smiling. She loved watching Alex romp with the kids and the big smiles on everyone's faces. Again, the thought that Alex was exactly the type of person she'd always hoped to find crossed her mind, but this time it was promptly followed by the image of Alex kissing Katherine. *Not exactly.*

Chelsea touched her knee, and Emily looked over at her.

"I know you're worried, but you don't have to be. She really means it when she says it's no problem to have you stay. And to get you a flight."

Emily started to nod, but at the same moment the stabbing pain in her left ear came back. She clapped her hand over her ear and squeezed her eyes closed. Chelsea called to Alex and the kids, and the noise stopped abruptly. A second later, the stabbing ebbed and Emily took a slow, deep breath.

"Sorry about that," Alex said quietly. "My fault entirely. I rile up the kids."

"You do," Chelsea said. "And then leave them to us. But they love it."

"Auntie privileges are the best." Alex stood up. The kids clamored for more attention, but she calmed them down whispering something to each one, then walked over to the couch. She met Emily's gaze. "Sorry."

"It's fine. Really. The pain goes away as fast as it comes."

"So, what does the doc say? Ear infection?"

Emily nodded.

"I'm gonna call in an antibiotic," Rob said. "I'll need your info when you're ready, Emily."

Alex reached into her pocket and pulled out a pen. "Is this enough? Brookstone's her last name, and her phone number's on there. You can't keep the pen."

"You've been carrying that around in your pocket?"

"You gave it to me," Alex returned.

"Sort of. And sort of you stole it." Emily wasn't mad. She was, however, a little taken aback. All this time Alex had her pen in her pocket?

"You can have it back if you really want it."

Emily wanted Alex to keep it, even if her reasons for wanting that were problematic. "It's sweet you kept it."

"You didn't know that Alex is ridiculously sentimental?" Rob set his hand on Alex's shoulder. "I gave her a little carved bear that I made in camp when I was twelve, and last I checked, she still has it somewhere."

"On her nightstand," Emily said. She felt a blush hit her cheeks as soon as the words left her lips. It was no secret, of course, to Rob or Chelsea that she and Alex had slept together, but she worried that her noticing the bear might cross some line.

"And I love that bear," Alex said. "I also love this pen. It writes very nicely."

"Don't let her fool you. It's nothing about the pen and all about you. You've seen that bear," Rob said, taking the pen from Alex. "But she'll never lose this now. Takes her a while to find something she likes, but then she holds on." He tapped his phone to life and started copying the info off the pen.

Emily looked up at Alex. As soon as she'd thought she'd figured out Alex, she realized she was completely wrong. Again.

"Date of birth?"

Emily answered the rest of Rob's questions as he passed the pen back to Alex.

"We can stop and pick up meds on our way back," Alex said. "Am I taking you to Katherine's, or do you want to come home with me? I know my little cabin isn't as swanky, and the food will probably be takeout…"

Emily felt the others waiting on her answer. She wanted to say yes, but there was so much she and Alex hadn't talked about. The palpable tension between them, as well as the warm tingling sensation she got every time Alex looked at her for too long, weren't going away. But neither was the fact that Alex was someone her heart had no business getting attached to. She'd been so angry last night—at Katherine, at Alex, and at herself—but now she didn't know how to feel. And she couldn't simply ignore everything they'd done.

Maybe none of that mattered. Staying a few nights at Alex's didn't mean she was agreeing to sleeping with her. It also didn't mean she planned on seeing her again after. The only definite was that if she stayed with Alex, she wouldn't have to face Katherine until the next time she had to prepare her dinner.

"You sure it's okay?"

"I'm sure." Alex held out her hand. "And now I'm gonna pretend I'm not super excited 'cause I don't want you to think I'm a big dork."

"After that Easter bonnet? I think it's a little late."

Rob and Chelsea both laughed. Alex only held Emily's gaze with a playful smirk on her lips. It didn't make any sense, but they were back to flirting. Emily wanted to hold on to the way Alex was looking at her. She also wanted to hold on to the bubbly happy feeling that rose in response. What she didn't want to think about was how spending any more time with Alex was a terrible idea.

CHAPTER THIRTY-TWO

"You're awake." Alex set Emily's suitcase next to her boots and then shrugged off her coat. She'd tried to hurry as she grabbed Emily's things from Katherine's, but TJ and Shay had bumped into her and both wanted an update. All she'd said was that Emily had an ear infection and would be staying with her because she couldn't fly out in the morning. That was really all there was to the story, as much as she wished Emily's decision to stay with her had been about more than that.

"I don't know how I keep drifting off." Emily rubbed her eyes. "Probably won't be able to sleep at all tonight. Although this sofa is possibly the most comfortable thing ever. I feel like I've sunk into a cloud."

"You should be in an ad selling sofas. Looking exactly like that. You already got your lines down. They'd sell those things like hotcakes."

Emily rolled her eyes.

"Glad to see your spunk's come back."

"You think this is spunk? You clearly don't know me well." Emily picked up one of the throw pillows and raised it up like she was going to chuck it at Alex. When Alex laughed and put up her hands to block it, Emily laughed too. "Put your hands down. I wouldn't throw a pillow at you."

"Why not?"

Emily dropped the pillow and sighed. "Because. You're you and I'm me."

"I might need more of an explanation."

Alex waited, but Emily didn't say more. Emily had napped while she started a fire, and then, since Emily was still sleeping, she decided to run over to Katherine's to grab her suitcase. She hadn't moved from her spot on the sofa, and the blanket was wrapped around her shoulders exactly the way Alex had left it. At least she sounded a little stronger and wasn't quite as pale.

"I'm making you ramen unless you want something else," Alex said.

"Ramen sounds amazing."

"Don't get too excited, it's the packaged stuff that comes with the little flavor packet. Although, it is way better ramen than what you can get in the States. I started hunting for the best ramen on my first trip to Tokyo. It's kind of become an obsession."

"You're about to make me the best packaged ramen Tokyo has to offer?"

"I am." Alex grinned. "After years of careful research and way too many dinners alone."

"I'm not sure if that's sad or sweet."

Alex lifted a shoulder. "Me neither." She headed to the kitchen, fighting a magnetic pull to the sofa. As much as her body might want to wrap her arms around Emily, her head wasn't ready. She couldn't shake the image of Emily between Lara's legs, and although she tried to pretend it was a protectiveness that had made her ready to bolt through the glass door, she wondered if it wasn't plain and simple jealousy—exactly as Katherine had said. But thinking of Katherine and Emily together didn't make her angry so much as discouraged. She'd been in a funk all morning, feeling sorry for herself and annoyed that she'd let someone she'd only known for a weekend get that much under her skin. Exactly when she'd convinced herself to skip the final evening of the long weekend and not even bother going back to Katherine's to say goodbye to Emily, Lara had called.

Although the conversation had been mostly about Emily's being sick, Alex had finally apologized to Lara. She'd admitted that she'd jumped to conclusions about what had happened when Lara had walked away from her sub. Then she'd admitted that she'd done nearly the same thing with Madison. What she hadn't expected was for Lara to start crying. Two years later and Lara still felt horrible about everything with Annette. Alex meant it when she told her it was time to let it go. She'd also meant it when she'd said she wanted to work on them being friends again. Lara had even eagerly proposed a visit to Tokyo, and Alex wondered then exactly how much she'd misjudged things between them. And misjudged Lara.

She got out a pot and filled it with water, then switched on the gas and waited for the burner to light. The kitchen was open to the family room, but Alex could only see the back of Emily's head from where she stood. After everything, she had to admit Katherine was right. Lara could be good for Emily. They'd clearly connected, they were both single, and they both lived in San Francisco. But Alex felt sick at the thought of suggesting a future date for the two of them. Maybe she didn't have to be the one to do it. Maybe they'd figure it out on their own.

"I love the sounds you're making in there," Emily said. "Nothing says sexy like a woman who can make me soup when I feel like crap."

"Nice to know you're easy."

"I have my moments," Emily bantered back. "I'm not used to people cooking for me."

"Does heating up ramen actually count as cooking? I could throw in some veggies and grilled chicken if your stomach's up for it. That's my bachelor standby meal."

"Go ahead and wow me. My stomach's ready." Emily looked over her shoulder at Alex and said, "I thought you said you only made hot cocoa. Now ramen. What else you got up your sleeve?"

"A pretty decent scrambled egg? It's amazing I've lived this long, actually, considering I can hardly cook for myself." Alex opened the fridge and poked around through the veggie drawer. "Anything you don't like?"

"Raisins."

"I meant, are there any veggies you don't like? But I'm with you on the raisins...Wait. Wasn't 'raisins' your safe word?"

"It was a last-minute decision. And I was under a lot of pressure."

Alex chuckled.

"Why's your safe word 'kiwi?'"

Alex closed the fridge. She went to the sink to rinse the carrot and a handful of spinach leaves, and considered her answer. "It's not 'cause I don't like them."

"An ex from New Zealand?"

Alex laughed. "No. I love New Zealand. And every New Zealander I've met so far."

Emily had turned around on the sofa so she faced Alex, her elbows on the back cushion and her chin in her hands. Now that they were looking right at each other, Alex knew she had to tell her the truth.

"It's kind of a dumb story."

"I want to hear it anyway."

"I threw a kiwi at my brother." She started peeling the carrot. "We were fighting over who could push the grocery cart. He always got to push it because he was bigger." A familiar knot of anxiety made her want to stop there. She hadn't told anyone the full story; not even her mom knew the details. It was silly to be holding on to guilt from something that had happened when she was eight years old, but she knew that the emotion that had made her throw the kiwi would always be in her.

"All of a sudden I got so mad. Nothing seemed fair. I'd never be as big or as strong as he was. And I knew I'd never be as smart. I couldn't ever measure up. Not in my parents' eyes for sure, but not in anyone's eyes. Not even in mine. So, I grabbed the closest thing I could find—we were in the produce section and I happened to grab a kiwi. I chucked it right at his face. Hard as I could."

"What happened?"

"Well, there was a lot of blood." Alex tried for a light tone, but the knot in her stomach only tightened. She finished with the carrot and started rinsing the spinach, focusing on cleaning each leaf instead of looking over at Emily. "I broke his glasses. The wire rim cut his eyebrow, but his nose was bleeding too. He dropped to his knees and started bawling. I froze—didn't go to him, didn't call for my mom. But she heard him crying and rushed over. She hadn't seen what I'd done. But she knew whatever had happened was because of me…She shoved me out of the way and told me she'd deal with me later.

"She kept asking Rob what had happened. Didn't believe him when he said that he'd slipped and fell, so she turned to me and said, 'What'd you do?' I looked at Rob and he shook his head, so I said, 'He fell.' To this day I don't know why he lied. It was only a kiwi. I didn't even think it would hurt him all that much."

She pulled out a cutting board and started chopping the veggies. The water on the stove came to a boil as soon as she finished, and she quickly tossed everything in and turned down the heat. "Most people don't ask."

"Probably they assume you don't like kiwis."

"Probably." Alex held Emily's gaze. "I don't want to hurt anyone. I know people are into it, and I've been asked to do stuff I regretted later. I'm always afraid I'll go too far. That I'll lose control."

"Bet you never threw another kiwi at your brother."

"Well, no." Alex smiled. "That was actually the last time we really fought. After that, we'd start to get into it and then one of us would stop. I also got taller than him."

"I don't think you have anything to worry about."

Alex wanted to argue that Emily didn't know her that well, but she stopped herself from saying as much. She opened the package of noodles and tossed that into the pot with the veggies. After adding a clove of garlic, a teaspoon of her favorite spice blend, and a splash of sesame oil, she went back to the fridge to find the leftover grilled chicken she'd made for lunch.

Emily touched the low of her back, and Alex straightened. Her heart raced with the sensation of Emily's hand on her, but she didn't let on as she closed the fridge and turned. "Look at you, up and walking around like it's nothing. You worried about my cooking after all?"

"No. I know you got this. It smells heavenly in here already. But I need to tell you something."

"Should I be worried?" Alex tried to joke, but Emily's face was serious.

"I didn't mean to suggest that you shouldn't be careful. Or that the fear of going too far is silly. It's not. But I barely know you and I feel completely safe with you. I trust you wouldn't hurt me. I don't think you'd hurt anyone. Not intentionally, anyway." Emily stepped forward and lightly kissed Alex's cheek. "Can I set the table?"

When Emily pulled back, Alex had to remind herself to breathe. She pointed to where the soup bowls were and then went to fuss with the ramen, grateful for something else to think about other than how much she'd wanted Emily to kiss her lips instead of her cheek. After adding the chicken, she let the pot simmer for a minute.

Emily came over to the stove and fanned her hand over the soup pot, inhaling the steam. "I might need this recipe."

"You haven't tasted it yet."

"I do have skills." Emily tilted her head. "Sometimes you don't need to taste something to know you'll like it."

"Can't argue there." Alex smirked. "Could you grab the bowls? This is ready."

As she dished out the soup, the smell of the steaming broth made Alex's stomach rumble. Lunch seemed like a distant memory, but ramen was also her favorite winter meal. She only hoped it would be up to Emily's standards. Probably offering to cook for a chef hadn't been a smart move.

They settled in at the table, and Alex felt happier than the moment deserved. She knew part of it was that Emily was letting her take care of her. Despite everything that had happened. The other part of it was simply having someone over to share a meal in her little cabin. She loved the cabin, but it was nothing like Katherine's mansion. Not a lot of updating had happened since the late eighties, and although there was nothing functionally wrong with the space, it wasn't fancy. Kind of like the kitchen table. Not only was it scratched and stained, she'd had to put a wedge under one leg to keep it from rocking. Still, it worked as a table. If she was there more often, she'd replace it and have other things fixed too. But in her head, she'd always thought of doing those things with someone else. Taking in their input, their wants. Making the cabin a perfect love nest instead of only a landing pad.

"Oh my god. This is either the best soup I've ever had, or I'm starving."

Alex smiled. "I doubt the first option is true, but thank you."

"Seriously." Emily brought the bowl up to her lips, abandoning the spoon. "You can make me this ramen any day of the week."

Alex couldn't help watching Emily. She made little moans between sips, closing her eyes as she did, and by the time she finished, Alex wasn't even halfway through her bowl. "I can make more if you'd like. I didn't think about it, but this is probably all you've eaten today."

"As much as I'd like seconds, I want to keep this down. But I might beg for more tomorrow. You really sure you're okay with me staying here?" Emily didn't pause long enough for Alex to answer before saying, "I think your brother's right and I shouldn't fly tomorrow morning, but I feel so much better. I can go back to Katherine's. And you don't need to get me a ticket."

"Would you rather stay at Katherine's?"

"No. I'd rather stay with you."

Alex's heart seemed to murmur "I told you so" to her wary brain. Still, everything felt shaky between them. "I have so many free miles it's ridiculous. Let me get you a flight. It's nothing to me."

Emily shook her head. "I'd need to pay you back somehow."

"You wouldn't need to because I'd be happy that I could help. It'd make me feel chivalrous." That was a good excuse anyway. Alex tipped the bowl to her lips and finished off the last of the broth with a moan. "No matter how many times I eat this ramen, it doesn't get less good."

"And you were teasing me about selling sofas."

"You saying I could sell you on ramen?"

"You could sell me buckets of ramen. You could sell me on a lot more than ramen, actually, but yes." Emily yawned. "Sorry. Suddenly I'm sleepy again."

"I'll go set up the guest room," Alex said, standing up.

"You don't have to. I'm fine on your couch. I'm used to couches, and yours is a huge upgrade from Gianna's."

"You wouldn't prefer a bed?" Alex picked up their bowls and carried them to the sink.

"Truthfully, I'd rather sleep in your bed. With you. But I know that's probably not a good idea. And if this the start of a cold or something you might catch—"

"I'm not worried," Alex interrupted. "I don't think you have something infectious. I think it's the combination of too many tequila shots and getting dunked in the hot tub. The altitude probably didn't help either."

"I didn't get dunked." Emily caught Alex's gaze. "Shay said I slipped getting out of the hot tub, but I don't remember that part. Wait, did you see Ava go under?"

"Ava?"

"When I came in and saw you standing there—with Katherine—I wondered how much of that show you'd seen... Ava and Lara were going to town. Ava wanted Lara to be rough. She asked Lara to choke her, but she wouldn't do it. How I remember that part but not falling into the hot tub is a good question. Shay said I was reaching for the railing to get out and I slipped and went under. But I can't remember it. I don't ever want to drink tequila again."

"Wait, that was Ava with Lara? Not you? But I thought you and Lara were hitting it off."

"Lara's attractive for sure, but..." Emily's voice trailed. "You thought I had sex with Lara."

It was more of a statement than a question, but Alex nodded. She felt like an idiot. Now that she thought of it, from the back Ava and Emily did look similar. And with wet hair, their long brown locks would have been hard to tell apart. She'd seen someone else in the hot tub across from Shay and Madison, but in the dark she hadn't been able to tell who it was. And she hadn't stopped to think.

Emily continued. "And then you had sex with Katherine. Because of what you thought you saw, or because you wanted her?"

"I didn't have sex with Katherine." Alex stopped herself from calling Emily out on what *she* had done with Katherine. It didn't matter. But it was annoying that Emily's tone seemed to suggest she'd done something wrong when she knew she wasn't the only one who'd kissed Katherine last night. And Alex had stopped at the kissing. "We broke up last night. Not that we were dating, but I ended whatever it was that we had."

"Why'd you end it?"

"It's been a long time coming. But then you made me realize what I wanted. Katherine's not it."

Emily didn't press Alex for more explanation. She also didn't say anything about what she'd done with Katherine or if she wanted her. The question spun round and round in Alex's head. She turned on the sink, waiting for the hot water, then rinsed the bowls and pot, avoiding Emily's gaze.

"Is it okay if I don't help you clean up? I'm feeling a little lightheaded again."

"No problem at all. Besides, you cleaned up last time." That breakfast had started out fine but ended with them worse off as well. Maybe they needed to stop eating together.

Alex finished with the dishes and dried her hands. She went upstairs to find clean sheets and an extra blanket, and when she came back downstairs, Emily was curled up on the sofa again.

"Thanks for going to get my suitcase and my things," Emily said. "Did you see Katherine? I was sitting here thinking I probably should tell her where I am."

"She wasn't there when I stopped in. Shay said she went out with Madison first thing and hadn't come home. She'll be back for the evening activities, I'm sure, but I told Shay we wouldn't be there." Alex wondered if, despite being sick, Emily wished that she could make it to the last night of the sex weekend. She, for one, was glad her part in it was over, but maybe Emily didn't feel the same. Did she long for Katherine?

"Was Shay home alone?"

"No. There was a poker game going with Shay, Ava, Nicola, and TJ. Nicola was winning. And singing. She's got a gorgeous voice. Like you." Alex set the clean sheets and blanket on the coffee table. She wanted to add how glad she was Katherine hadn't been there, but she kept that to herself. "Lara flew back to San Francisco tonight."

"Shay said that Lara caught me when I went under the water. Pulled me up."

"Lara has her moments."

"But you don't like each other?"

Alex hesitated. "We used to be friends. Then some things happened and we were both dumbasses. I think we decided this morning to give each other a second chance." Which would be easier now that Alex knew Emily wasn't interested in hooking up with Lara. She didn't need to admit that part, however. "Lara was really worried about you. Called me a bunch of times. You sure you want to sleep down here?"

Emily nodded.

"Well, if you change your mind, these sheets are for the guest room." Alex wanted some excuse to stay longer, to continue the conversation they'd nearly started, but she didn't know if there was any point. Emily would only stay for a couple of nights, and when she left, the chances of her looking back were slim to none.

"I'm going to bed. Holler if you need anything—or if you get up and you get dizzy again. My door'll be open and the cabin's not that big. I'll hear you."

"Thanks."

Alex glanced at the fire. The logs still had a lot to burn, but she knew the temperature in the room would drop when the fire went out. "If you get cold, there's more blankets in the closet by the door. I'll turn up the heat, but it still gets chilly in this room. It's fine by me if you decide to join me upstairs."

Emily seemed about to say something and then bit her lip.

"Not for any other reason than to sleep," Alex quickly added. "I know you think the sofa's comfortable, but my bed's nicer."

"I know I suggested it earlier, but...sleeping with you now would be hard for me."

"Okay." Alex couldn't argue despite how much her body wanted her to. "Offer still stands. And there's the guest room too."

"I'll stay here for now. Thanks for everything."

CHAPTER THIRTY-THREE

The wind seemed to be playing with the snow, scooping up handfuls and tossing it high in the air. In the bright morning light, each flake sparkled like a sugar crystal. Emily watched the shimmering crystals, seemingly suspended in air as if gravity had taken the day off. Flakes slowly drifted downward only to be caught up in a fresh gust and sent skyward all over again. The scene was transfixing, but Emily's thoughts wandered far from the snow.

Sometime in the middle of the night, the fire had burned out. She woke chilled and pulled on the extra blanket Alex had left for her. Minutes passed, and she couldn't fall back asleep. She thought back on the night she'd slept with Alex and how perfect everything about it had been. How Alex had held her close and she'd felt warm from the inside out.

Knowing Alex was only upstairs, it had been hard to ignore the lure of going to her, of snuggling against her. She didn't want to wake her—Alex had seemed exhausted last night— but she needed to feel someone close, and her warmth was so tempting. Her shivering had finally pushed her off the sofa, and she'd crept quietly upstairs.

Alex had left the door open as promised. When she slipped under the covers, Alex had rolled toward her. She was naked, but that didn't stop her from wrapping her arm around Emily. A moment later, her breathing went back to a slow, even pattern, and Emily knew she was asleep. As impossible as it seemed that she'd relax with Alex lying next to her, Emily had drifted off moments later.

Now Alex's hold loosened, and Emily held her breath. She wondered if she should pretend to be asleep still. As much as she'd been enjoying the press of Alex's chest against her back and Alex's warm hand resting on her belly, she worried that she should have snuck out already.

"You awake?" Alex whispered.

Emily nodded.

"You're nice waking up to." Alex brushed her lips against Emily's shoulder. "It's beautiful out there, isn't it?"

"It is."

"Did you get cold when the fire burned out?"

Emily nodded again.

"And here I was thinking maybe you were in my bed because you couldn't resist me." Alex's tone was light, making it clear she was joking. She kissed Emily's shoulder again. "How do you feel? Does your ear still hurt?"

"Only if I lie on that side. But it's way better overall."

"Good." Alex rolled over and stretched. After a moment, she got out of bed and went to the bathroom.

Emily lay on her back, counting the wood beams that crossed the ceiling. She wanted to tell Alex the truth: that despite everything, she was drawn to Alex like a damn moth to a flame. The cold was only an excuse. But what then?

Alex came out of the bathroom and went over to her dresser. She pulled on a pair of boxers, then picked out a shirt and a pair of jeans. "I was thinking I'd go downstairs and try to drum us up some breakfast. Then maybe we can talk about plans for the day? We don't have to do anything, of course, if you're not up for it. But it's a sunny day, and it could be nice for a walk downtown. I can show you around. Or we can take the gondola up to the lodge. Even if we don't ski, it's a gorgeous view."

"Can you come back to bed for a minute?"

Alex hesitated. She had one foot in the leg of her pants and was balancing with the other off the ground. She set her foot back down and cocked her head. Emily waited for her to ask the question that seemed to be on her lips, but she didn't say anything. Instead, she dropped the jeans and the shirt on the floor and sat down on the edge of the bed.

Emily braced herself before starting. "I wanted to go with you to the hot springs. When you asked, I should have said yes."

"Why didn't you?"

"Katherine." Emily pushed the pillows against the headboard and sat up. "I didn't believe that you didn't want her. And we both know Katherine wants you. The way she looks at you...it's nothing like how she looks at Madison."

"I don't want Katherine."

"I know. And you said you broke up with her. But when you kissed her..." Emily shook her head. "I'm nothing like Katherine."

"You turned me down before you saw me kiss her. And I know what it looked like, but—"

"That's not the only reason. When I saw that note from your property manager, I knew she'd stopped by because she wanted you too." Emily took a deep breath. No matter how many times she told herself Alex wasn't the player everyone said she was, she couldn't help thinking of Katherine's words: *Two months, maybe three.*"

"Look, I appreciate you letting me stay here, but I don't want to make things harder for either of us. I can't get close to you. This has to be only a good time."

Emily didn't want to say the rest. That how she felt around Alex scared her. That how Alex looked at her made her feel something she hadn't felt in years, and that she stopped thinking when she was close to her. Because when she started thinking again, she knew falling for someone like Alex was a huge mistake.

Alex reached for Emily's hand. She entwined their fingers and then brought Emily's hand up to her lips, kissing her knuckles. "I like you. How I feel when I'm with you is different than what I've ever felt with someone—and I know you're thinking that I probably say that to everyone, but I don't. You're different."

Emily wanted to believe Alex, but she shook her head.

Alex continued. "When you saw Katherine kiss me, that's all that happened. You walked into the middle of it. But I'd been telling her I was done all weekend. She wouldn't listen. I tried pushing her away, but a lot was going on in my head at that moment. I was mad because I thought you were with Lara, and then because Katherine told me she'd had sex with you too. And obviously it doesn't matter, and I wasn't going to bring it up because you were at a sex party and that's what you're supposed to do. But I've never felt jealousy like that. I couldn't think, and—"

"Wait." Emily's mind was spinning. Katherine had told Alex *what*? "I didn't have sex with Katherine."

"You didn't? She said you were a good kisser."

Emily cocked her head. "Are you going to argue that point?"

Alex opened and closed her mouth. "No, but—"

"I stopped her at the kissing. She wanted more, but I stopped her. Apparently, you and I had that in common." Emily raised an eyebrow. "Then she basically told me to keep my hands off you."

"But you're attracted to her?"

"Was. Yes." Emily sighed. "Now? Definitely no."

"Why'd you stop her?"

"I can't believe Katherine made you think I had sex with her," Emily said. She didn't want to answer Alex's question and hoped she'd let it slide. What was she going to do about Katherine? She couldn't keep her as a client. And she'd gotten several of her other clients on Katherine's recommendation. "She's so damn manipulative."

"Can we go back to the other part? The part about you stopping her and why?"

Emily wasn't going to lie, but admitting that she wanted Alex, after everything she'd said earlier and still knowing it couldn't possibly work, didn't seem fair. "It's complicated."

"I'm too complicated for you?"

Emily felt momentarily stunned. Alex hadn't given her a pass. In fact, she seemed to know exactly what Emily wasn't saying. "Alex, you're sweet. And smart. And charming. And definitely the sexiest woman I've ever been with. All the things I could ever want. But that doesn't mean you're good for me."

Alex breathed out, her gaze dropping from Emily's. The bed creaked as she got up. She walked over to where she'd left her jeans and pulled them on, then reached for her shirt. Emily watched her finish dressing, her heart stuck in her throat. She knew her last sentence had stung, and she wanted to take it back, but pretending they could somehow work together wouldn't make it true.

"I can try to make us French toast. You mentioned that before, so I picked up a loaf of sourdough. Or, scrambled eggs and bacon?"

"You don't have to cook for me," Emily said.

"I know I don't have to, but I want to. You'd probably make better food, but you're my guest."

Emily got up and walked over to where Alex was waiting. She stopped a foot in front of her. "I want you to be good for me. Almost as much as I want to be good for you."

"All I was asking is for you to take a chance on us. I think we could be exactly who we both need. And want."

Emily shook her head. "I haven't even signed divorce papers yet. Cass only agreed to a trial separation. She said I needed time to think and I didn't know what I was doing. That's when she froze all of our bank accounts. Then she called everyone we know and told them all I was having a nervous breakdown."

"Shit."

"Yeah." Emily breathed out. "The thing is, I didn't need time to think—I've known Cass and I weren't right for each other for years now. But I'm nowhere near ready to jump into another relationship. Ten years is a long time to be with someone. I'm still trying to figure out who I am now without trying to make her happy anymore. And maybe you and I would have something amazing, but part of me thinks you don't know me well enough to be as sure as you seem."

Alex didn't argue. She only held Emily's gaze, making it all the harder to resist her.

"For the record, I'm dying to kiss you anyway," Emily said.

She hoped Alex would take the cue and simply kiss her. But she didn't. She only nodded.

When Alex reached for her hand, Emily fought back a wave of disappointment. Now that they'd ironed out that a relationship was off the table and this couldn't be anything more than sex, Alex was out. The lingering question of whether or not Alex was a player disappeared in that one moment.

"Whoever gets you is going to be one lucky woman."

"I could say the same to you," Alex said. "Your ex didn't know what she had." She gave Emily's hand a gentle squeeze and then let go. "Mediocre French toast, or eggs and bacon?"

Emily dropped her shoulders. "French toast. But I'll make it if you give me a minute to get dressed."

"Take your time. I'll start some coffee."

Alex closed the door carefully behind her and Emily sank back down on the bed. She knew she'd hurt Alex's feelings, and even if she knew it'd been the right thing to say—to make it clear that Alex shouldn't hold out any hope—she wanted to take it all back. How could they spend the rest of the day together?

The door opened and Alex wheeled in her suitcase. "Figured you probably wouldn't want to go downstairs to get dressed. The heater hasn't kicked in yet down there."

Emily got up to take the case. As she reached for the handle, she brushed Alex's arm. She noticed Alex take a subtle step back and her chest tightened. Alex didn't even want her close.

"Thank you."

"I got the coffee started but I'm waiting for you on the French toast. Maybe I can learn a thing or two from watching a professional chef." Alex's smile seemed forced. "Anything else you need up here?"

"Would you mind if I took a shower?"

"Go right ahead. There's shampoo and everything, but I'll bring up some warm towels too." She started out and then paused in the doorway. "Oh, I was thinking I should probably call the airline and set up your flight. When do you think you'll want to head out?"

"As soon as possible. I feel so much better than I did yesterday. Tonight, if there's anything available."

Alex nodded. "I'll see what I can do."

Instead of coming up with some excuse to keep her upstairs, Emily only watched Alex go, carefully closing the door behind her. Alex being nice and helpful smarted more than if she'd kicked her out. With a sigh, she pulled her suitcase over to the bed. When she got back home, what was she going to tell Gianna about this part?

CHAPTER THIRTY-FOUR

Alex caught her breath as Emily stepped into the kitchen. Still damp from the shower, her brown locks fell past her shoulders like smooth dark silk. Her eyes shone brighter than ever, outlined by her long lashes, and her cheeks held a pink flush from the hot water. She was dressed simply in a pair of jeans and a green plaid flannel. A second passed before Alex recognized that the flannel was hers. It certainly looked better on Emily, especially with the top two buttons undone. A white tank top peeked out from underneath.

Maybe it wasn't polite to stare, but Alex couldn't seem to do anything else. Despite how stunning Emily had been Sunday night in the silver dress and perfect flowing hair and makeup, Alex found her even more attractive now. Of course, she couldn't admit that, and she was more than a little annoyed that her libido could be kicked into overdrive even after Emily had unceremoniously declared that she wasn't good for her.

"Is it okay that I borrowed this?" Emily tugged at the bottom hem of the flannel. "I didn't bring enough warm layers."

"Definitely. My cabin's a lot draftier than Katherine's place. And you're sick."

"I know it seems too fast, but I think I might be all better. Or at least mostly better. My ear isn't hurting at all." She tapped her ear with her finger and shrugged. "Do you think the antibiotic could have worked that quick?"

"I could ask my brother."

"No, don't bother him. I'm just happy I'm better. Between sleeping in and that hot shower, I feel like a million bucks."

"You look like a million bucks." At this point, Alex decided, it didn't matter if she was honest. But when Emily met her gaze and tentatively smiled, she wondered if attraction did more harm than good. "Coffee?"

"I'd love some. It smells heavenly in here."

"Nothing smells quite as good as coffee first thing in the morning," Alex said. "This one's yours." She handed Emily a mug. "I left room for cream. Sugar's on the counter."

"Mmm. You clearly know how to make a woman happy."

After their earlier conversation, casual flirting felt jarring, but before Alex could decide what to say in response, Emily turned her back to pour cream into her coffee. Alex's gaze fell to Emily's butt. She had perfect curves for snug jeans. The longer she stared, the more she wanted to step forward and run her hands over Emily's round backside. She quickly averted her eyes when Emily spun around.

"That was the wrong thing to say, wasn't it? It's not easy for me to be around you and not flirt." Emily shook her head. "Maybe it'd be better if I left now."

"You don't have to leave. I can handle a little flirting. Even if it isn't going anywhere."

Emily's brow furrowed. "Then why'd you look upset?"

Alex swept her mind for something she could say instead of the truth—*I was admiring your ass and you turned around before I was done staring.* "You caught me thinking." Mostly that was the truth. "Before I forget, I called United. The soonest they can get you to San Francisco is tomorrow morning. Flight leaves here at six. Will that work?"

"That works. And it'll give me time to decide what I'm going to say to Katherine."

"What do you mean?"

"I'm not going to work for her anymore. I'd like to tell her why in person."

Alex recalled what Emily had said before they'd spent the night together—that she couldn't do anything that would jeopardize her job. They'd done exactly that. "I thought you needed her as a client."

"I do." Emily sighed. "But I'll figure it out. I'm also thinking maybe I should get a hotel room tonight."

"That's up to you, but it's not a problem for me if you stay. You could stay here all week if you wanted."

"Aside from the fact that I have to work, I think me staying that long would be hard on both of us, don't you?"

Alex didn't answer. Emily's *"You're not good for me"* comment ran through her mind again. She went over to the cabinet where she stored the bread and set that out on the counter with the eggs and the jar of ground cinnamon. "I'll confirm tomorrow's flight, then. It's been a while since I've made French toast. Is there anything else you need?"

"Alex."

"Yeah?" Alex didn't look at Emily. She opened the next cabinet and found a bottle of vanilla extract.

Emily tapped her shoulder. "Alex."

Alex turned around and Emily didn't step back. They were close enough to kiss, and the question of whether or not Emily was about to do exactly that blocked out all other thoughts.

"If I learned anything from my ex, it's how to avoid hard conversations and play the everything's-fine-when-it's-not game. I can get us both through the day if we want to pretend nothing's wrong. But I'd rather you tell me why you're mad."

Alex looked from the vanilla extract in her hand down to the floor and noticed the fuzzy green Kermit slippers on Emily's feet. *The lucky Kermit slippers.* Between trying not to stare at Emily's cleavage peeking out from the edge of her tank top and ogling her butt in the jeans, she'd entirely missed the slippers.

"I'm not sure if it's karma or maybe just ironic," Emily said. "I go to a sex weekend to get over the baggage Cass left me with, only to be drawn to the one woman who doesn't want casual sex and is a poor communicator."

Alex set the vanilla extract on the counter. "First off, I'm a very good communicator—when I want to be. Second, I'm not mad, or upset, but you caught me staring at your ass earlier and I didn't want to say that was what I was doing. Third, you're wearing my lucky Kermit slippers."

Emily's lips curved, hinting at a smile. "Why are they lucky?"

"You sure you want to ask?"

Emily shook her head. She started to step out of the slippers, but Alex stopped her.

"You're going to be cold down here only in socks. Besides, Kermit is sexy."

"You could've lied and told me they were lucky 'cause you'd won them in a raffle."

Alex grinned. "If you want, we can say that's the reason."

Emily gave the slippers another look. "Oh well. They're on now." She glanced back at Alex. "You sure there wasn't something else on your mind?"

"Oh, there was. But I don't feel like being a good communicator at the moment. I'd rather make French toast. I'm starving."

Emily put her hands on her hips and gave Alex a long look.

"You're really sexy when you do that. But I don't want you to be sexy right now."

"I think you can handle it," Emily returned.

Alex looked over the ingredients lined up on the counter. Anything to avoid being turned on by Emily right this second. "What else do we need for French toast?"

Emily walked past her and picked up the loaf of bread. "I'm glad you got sourdough. It makes the best French toast."

"I went to the store for Lucky Charms. Then I saw the sourdough and thought of you."

"You see bread and think of me? Don't know how I feel about that," Emily joked.

"It was more about making French toast."

"So you weren't thinking of me?" Emily teased. "I don't buy it."

Alex couldn't help smiling. She also couldn't argue.

After a moment, Emily added, "Are you going to stay mad at me all through breakfast just because I'm sexy and you can't handle it?"

"No." Alex wasn't actually mad, and she could tell Emily knew it. "But you in those Kermit slippers is a lot to take in."

"Ahem, we're focusing on French toast now." Emily sniffed the bread and pursed her lips. "Not bad. But it is all about the bread."

"Here I figured it'd be all about the butter with you." Alex added the butter dish to the growing pile. "Cream?"

"That'll do. You know that first night of the party when I asked you if you didn't like rolls?"

Alex nodded.

"I had this image of you in my head." Emily paused. "I was all wrong. I'd sized you up as a cocky player. Basically, like the first impression I had of Lara. And I felt intimidated by everything I thought you were about. Unfortunately, I was still drawn to you."

"What does that have to do with rolls?"

Emily smiled. "Look at you being snarky."

Alex chuckled. "Okay, maybe I deserve that, but I'm serious."

"I couldn't not talk to you. Rolls were the only thing I could think of, and I had to say something."

"Even though I was a player?"

"You're not. But yes. And honestly, if that's what you were, things would be a whole lot simpler right now. Where's your whisk?"

"Top drawer." Alex pointed to the cabinet behind Emily. "Lara's not actually like that either. The truth is, she's got a lot of insecurities." Alex leaned against the counter, watching Emily tap the whisk against her palm. "What part would be simpler?"

"What part about us, you mean?" Emily hesitated. "If you were a conceited player, it'd be easier to walk away and not wonder what could have been." Turning back to the cabinet on her left, she cleared her throat and said, "Remind me again where you keep mixing bowls?"

Alex pulled a bowl from the shelf next to where she was standing and waited for Emily's nod of approval before setting it on the counter. "So you know who I am and you still want to walk away?"

"Do I know you? I asked myself that when I was showering. I have no idea what you do. I don't know what your life goals are, or who your friends are—unless Katherine counts."

"TJ counts. We've been friends since we met working at Cisco back in the day. I don't have many other friends. Lots of acquaintances, but not a lot of people I'd call if I needed to talk, you know? My brother is my closest friend and you met him. And you know the type of person I am."

"I know you're sweet and charming and..." Emily eyed the egg she'd selected from the carton and then sighed. "And perfect." She cracked the egg into the bowl. Then another, but separated the yolk from the white. At Alex's raised eyebrow, she said, "Makes it taste a little lighter. Not too eggy. At least I think so, anyway."

"I'm not perfect."

"Well, you seem like it." Emily added in vanilla and cream. She reached for the whisk. "Just because I want to have sex with you and leave and not look back, doesn't mean I'd be able to." She added a pinch of cinnamon, whisked for a moment, and then added another pinch.

Emily set a pan on the stove and lit the burner. She added a pat of butter to the pan and watched it sizzle. "I don't know how long it'll take before I get you out of my mind, Alex. What I do know is that I'm going to compare everyone else I meet to you. And no one else is gonna come close." She motioned to the loaf of bread. "Can you get out two slices?"

"I don't know your life goals either. Or your friends. But I want to." Alex handed over the bread.

"Gianna would like you," Emily said. "She's my best friend."

"The one whose couch you sleep on."

Emily nodded. "And at the moment, my big life goal is getting off her couch and into my own apartment. I've never lived alone. Your turn."

"Life goal?"

"Or what you do for work." Emily dunked the bread in the egg mixture. "You've gotta have an elevator pitch. Or is it a big secret? My guess is foreign investor."

"Tech consultant. I worked for a bunch of the big guys for a while—Apple, Amazon, eBay—and made a ton of money. Enough that I felt like I could start out on my own. So that's what I've been doing for the past eight years. Companies hire me when they have an idea that they want to take to market."

"And you like it?"

"Parts of it I love. But I'm tired of all the travel."

Emily nodded. "That's what you said on the plane. I thought you were so cool then."

Alex grinned. "Now you know better."

"Now I know you're better than cool." Emily used tongs to lift the first piece of bread onto the frying pan and then adjusted the heat. "And your life goal?"

"I've had plenty of life goals. But each time I reach one, I wonder if it was the wrong goal. At the moment, I'm tired of being alone. I want to share life with someone. I want a family."

"Wife and a couple kids?"

"Cheesy, right?"

Emily shook her head.

"I feel like I've been wasting time. I look around and I have things, but they're only things. I want to find someone who wants to build a life with me. Wow, that sounds even cheesier out loud than in my head."

Emily looked up from the frying pan and held Alex's gaze. "Yeah, it's cheesy, but I know what you mean. The thing is, being married isn't all that."

"I think that depends on who you marry."

"Maybe." Emily turned back to the stove. "I don't want to get married again. Been there, done that. And it sucked. But I do want kids. I think that was the last straw with me and Cass.

We hadn't had sex for years and all of that, but I kept thinking we had a pretty good life together otherwise. We were at a point where I wanted to have the kid conversation. I thought she wanted them too—she always said someday she did. Turns out, somewhere along the way she changed her mind."

"I'm sorry."

Emily shrugged. "I could make a long list of things we should have talked about. Anyway, finally I realized that if I wanted to have kids, I could make it happen alone."

"You want to have kids alone?"

"Why not?"

"Kids are a lot of work."

"So are relationships," Emily said. "I'm not saying I wouldn't like to have someone to love, someone who wanted to share life like you said. But it's not what I'm looking for at the moment."

"First you're getting off your friend's couch?"

"Exactly," Emily agreed. "Life's been full of baby steps lately."

When Emily turned away from the burner to dip the next slice of bread, Alex occupied herself getting plates and utensils. The kitchen filled with the smell of the French toast cooking—butter, cinnamon, and sugar—and Alex's stomach rumbled. As hungry as she was, though, she'd trade eating for watching Emily in the kitchen all day. She breezed from one thing to the next, slicing oranges, flipping French toast, and whipping away the items they'd taken out of the cupboard, all while looking as sexy as could be.

When she finished dusting the French toast with powdered sugar and the bag puffed in her face as she closed it, sending little flecks of white into her dark hair, it was all Alex could do to keep her hands to herself. Emily was the best and worst kind of temptation. She wanted sex and nothing more. Their different life goals seemed to prove how incompatible they were. And yet Alex had to make certain she didn't step too close. If she did, the desire to pull her into a deep kiss and satisfy her desires would win out. But more sex would only leave them both worse off.

Wouldn't it?

CHAPTER THIRTY-FIVE

Alex was easy company in the kitchen, which meant that she stayed out of Emily's way but knew when to step in to help. As much as Emily usually liked that, in this case Alex being helpful and perceptive only made everything harder. More than once, Alex quickly stepped out of the way to avoid any chance they'd brush against each other. On the third time it happened, as Emily was hanging up a towel and Alex sidestepped around her with one of the plates laden with powdered-sugar-dusted French toast, Emily caught the other opposite edge of the plate Alex held.

"Careful."

Alex cocked her head. "Trust me, I won't drop this. I can't wait to eat every last bite. I might even lick my plate."

"That'd be a good way to make me jealous," Emily said. She didn't let go of the plate, and Alex glanced down at her hand. When Alex looked up, Emily nearly leaned over the French toast to plant a kiss on her lips. She imagined doing it, imagined how much she'd enjoy it, but she couldn't bring herself to move.

As much as she wanted to prove to Alex that they both wanted the same thing, at least in this moment, she couldn't cross the line Alex had drawn.

"I was thinking maybe of going with you when you talk to Katherine. Maybe you'd like backup?"

"I can handle Katherine." As much as she wasn't looking forward to it, she knew she could tell her what she needed to say.

"Yeah, but I feel responsible for you losing Katherine as a client. Maybe I should have never invited you over. Maybe I messed everything up."

"Everything that happened this weekend was my choice, Alex." Finally, Emily let go of the plate. "Except this not touching you part."

"You touching me would make it a lot harder for me to not want to do more." Alex glanced from the plate, to the table, and then back to Emily. "Do you want to sit down and eat?"

"Not really." Emily folded her arms. "I think I should go."

"Why?"

"Because I've pretended I didn't want sex before and I don't want to do it again. Not with you. With you it's too damn hard. And I get that you want more than sex. Part of me likes you better because you're being so stubborn about it. But all I want is to kiss you right now and it's driving me—"

Alex stepped forward and met Emily's lips. The plate clattered as Alex dropped it on the counter. Then her hands were on Emily, unfolding her arms and wrapping her in an embrace. Emily's knees felt weak. Alex's kiss was everything she wanted.

"I might regret this later, but you have no idea how much I want you," Alex murmured. She only let Emily have a quick gasp of air before sealing her lips again. Alex pushed her back a step, then another, until Emily's butt was against the edge of the kitchen table.

"I don't want you to do something you'll regret," Emily said, her body humming with anticipation despite her words.

"I can take care of myself, don't worry."

Alex shifted deftly between Emily's legs. Her next kiss had none of the gentleness she'd had the first night, and her hands felt greedy, wanting to be everywhere on Emily's body all at once. Alex moved against her, kissing her throat then yanking off the flannel and kissing the skin she'd exposed.

Emily flushed with desire when Alex unzipped her jeans. *Thank god she's not stopping at kissing.* Her clit pulsed with need and she nearly pushed herself onto Alex's hand. She wanted Alex inside her. The sooner the better. Instead of being embarrassed by her need, she suddenly wanted to admit it. To claim the truth. "I want you inside."

Alex hitched Emily's jeans down past her hips as she kissed her again. Before Emily could even get Alex's shirt unbuttoned, Alex had shoved aside her panties. Emily arched into Alex's hand. She soaked Alex's palm as she rode her fingers, moaning out her pleasure.

Alex slid in and out, her thumb pressing roughly on her clit as she shifted and then dropped to her knees. She tugged Emily's jeans all the way down and ripped her underwear off as well. The next moment Alex's tongue coursed between Emily's folds.

Emily combed her fingers through Alex's hair until she gave in to the temptation to grab hold. Alex's tongue didn't slow down at all when Emily pulled her hard against her. If anything, she worked harder.

Emily felt the climax rising as Alex worked in circles and strokes. Every time she pushed her hips forward Alex met her, and suddenly she couldn't hold back. She held Alex against her and came with a scream. Alex moved with her as the orgasm rolled through her body. A long minute passed before she worried that she was hurting Alex. She let off the pressure on the back of Alex's head, and a shiver went through her as Alex's tongue whipped over her clit one more time.

When Alex stood up, Emily kissed her. "Damn, that felt good." She licked her lips, trying to regain herself against the wave rushing through her. "I don't think I deserved that, but thank you."

"Oh, we're not done." Alex narrowed her eyes. "We're just getting started."

Emily gasped when Alex's hand snaked between her thighs. She didn't think she wanted more, but when Alex slid into her, her muscles clenched eagerly. "Fuck. That feels good."

"You feel good. Good enough to have all day long." Alex lifted Emily up onto the table. She pushed her back a few inches and then slid two fingers inside.

"Fuck. Again." Emily moaned as Alex pumped harder.

Alex added another finger and Emily didn't think she could take more, but when Alex said, "You want more, don't you?" she nodded. Her body begged her to say yes. The way Alex handled her, no loving tenderness, only a mind-numbing appetite to have her, made Emily want to do anything to please her.

Every time Alex rocked into her, she moved with her, following her lead and hoping she'd be able to give enough. She wanted to give her body over completely to Alex's desires. If there was nothing left after, she wouldn't complain. *This* was what she'd needed all along. Alex was way too much and exactly the right amount all at the same time.

"You like it hard," Alex said.

Emily nodded. She couldn't manage words and was thankful that Alex didn't push for that. If she'd asked her to beg, she would have, but one look at Alex and Emily knew she was over the edge too. At least they were both in deep.

"After I get you off, I'm taking you upstairs and making you come all over again. All day...over and over. You'd like that, wouldn't you?"

Another nod. Emily didn't know how much she could take, but she wanted it all the same. Her breath came in quick pants and she was coated in sweat. So much for thinking Alex's cabin felt chilly. No part of her was cold.

She loved how Alex had her pinned, how the table slapped her backside every time Alex rocked into her, how rough and raw everything felt. Wetness dripped down her butt cheeks and her center buzzed. She didn't know if she'd come again, but she didn't want Alex to stop.

"Is it messed up if I tell you that I want you to know what you're missing?" Alex said, her words clipped with her own heavy breathing. "All the things I could do to you..." Before

Emily could even nod, Alex continued. "I know you like this. And I know you like me. Even if you don't want to admit it. But this is only us getting started."

God, she wanted everything Alex could offer. But wanting someone like Alex wasn't sane. Surrendering to her was walking a line between pleasure and an abyss. One misstep and she'd be gone. Knowing all that didn't change what her body wanted, however.

"Say you want it."

Emily looked up and met Alex's gaze. The intensity she saw reflected took all words, all thoughts, from her. She tried to rise up, but Alex's palm pressed against her chest, holding her in place on the table. Her throat went dry as arousal drummed through her. She felt claimed by Alex's firm grip, in her possession to do with as she liked, and more turned on than ever.

"Do you want this or not?"

Emily couldn't believe Alex expected her to speak. Clearly, she had no idea how far she'd pushed her, how near an orgasm she was. "I want you."

Alex swallowed. Something passed in her eyes, then the next moment she moved her hand lower and spread Emily's folds. Alex's other hand was still pumping deep inside and Emily was powerless to resist. No part of her wanted to anyway. When Alex's tongue slid over her swollen clit, she moaned louder than ever.

Alex didn't let up with her hand, but the whipping on her clit increased as well and Emily felt a storm building inside her. In seconds, she couldn't hold back. Cum squirted out of her. She tried to pull her legs back, cringing with embarrassment, but Alex only moved with her.

"Now that's what I like," Alex said. She kissed up and down Emily's thighs, murmuring more praises.

When Alex pulled out, Emily clenched her legs together, the lingering orgasm sending fresh shockwaves. She accepted Alex's kisses, but her lips felt as weak as the rest of her and she wondered what to say. Ignoring that she'd ejaculated wouldn't make it go away, but nothing like that had ever happened to her.

"I'm sorry for—"

"Don't even think of apologizing. That was amazing. You're amazing. You needed someone to take you there. All the way."

"I needed you," Emily murmured. She was thrown by the rush of emotions swirling in her chest, by how her body responded to Alex, and by how her heart was ready to throw every caution to the wind. She tried to relax back on the table but was aware now how uncomfortable the rough wood planks were. "Next time I want a pillow."

"Is that so?" Alex kissed her again, then grazed her neck with her teeth, sending a tremor of fresh desire through Emily despite the fact that she was completely spent.

"Yes." A moment later, she added, "Please."

Alex smiled. "You can have a pillow. I want you in my bed anyway."

"So considerate." Emily was still out of breath, but she wanted more all the same. "But I don't think I can move at the moment."

Alex encircled her waist and lifted her off the table. She set her on the ground. "I'd carry you up, but..."

"I love that you could carry me," Emily said. "But know better than to try."

Alex tilted Emily's chin up to her lips. Her deep kiss made Emily tremble all over again. She wrapped her arms around Alex and leaned against her. God, she felt good. So strong, so solid...and so turned on. Emily loved how hungry Alex was for her. She wanted to do everything to pleasure her in return.

"You were holding back the first time with me. I didn't know how much until now." Emily relaxed in Alex's arms, knowing she was letting Alex hold her up and not caring. She could still feel aftershocks between her legs. "I like it when you let go."

"I'm not feeling done yet."

"I know. Which makes me very lucky." In that moment, impossible as it seemed after two orgasms, Emily was ready for more. Every part of her wanted Alex back inside her. "I think you're going to have to let me eat something first, though. You're a lot to keep up with."

"One bite now. We'll take the plates upstairs."

"That eager, huh?"

"Do you have to ask?" Alex let go of Emily and went over to the counter where she'd left the plates. She cut a bite of French toast and held the fork out to Emily.

"Oh, that's good." Emily let the powdered sugar and butter fill her senses. She opened her mouth for another bite, and Alex complied. After she swallowed, she nodded at the plate. "You're not going to try any?"

"I don't want anything to ruin my appetite." Alex picked up both plates. "Besides, we have all day."

"You really planning on keeping me in bed all day?"

"Depends entirely on how good you are." Alex had already started up the stairs but looked back at Emily and added a wink.

Emily scooped up her pants and her underwear and followed. She'd never been issued a challenge quite like that before, but she knew that's exactly what Alex's words were. And she wanted nothing more than to be good enough to be kept all day under Alex's lock and key.

CHAPTER THIRTY-SIX

"I know we'll have to leave this room eventually, but I don't want to. I want to stay here forever." Emily played with Alex's hair, running a fingertip up the shaved section at the back and then combing through the longer tousled strands.

Alex didn't look up at Emily's words. She'd collapsed after the orgasm took her, and now that she was finally spent, she couldn't manage even lifting her head. Between Emily playing with her hair and the delicious stirrings in her lower half, she felt close to perfect. And Emily's words threatened to push her all the way. If only she meant it.

"I like you this way," Emily said.

"Exhausted?" Alex's lips curved into a smile, but she didn't open her eyes.

"Relaxed."

"I am." Alex shifted, and she felt Emily clamp her thighs. "Should I not come out?"

"I want you to stay inside me a little longer," Emily said. "Even if I'm going to be sore later." She pushed her hips up, wiggled her butt under Alex, and then dropped back to the mattress. When Alex moved again, Emily's arms wrapped around her. She held tight but let her knees splay further. "My muscles keep clenching. They want to pull you deeper inside."

"I like the sound of that."

Alex gave a subtle thrust. Emily purred, her nails digging into Alex's back.

"I can't take more, but then you do things like that and I want you to try."

"Not sure I can give you much more at the moment," Alex admitted. "That last time was over-the-top good."

"Even by your standards?"

"In the running for best orgasm ever." Emily's smug look made Alex want to add more compliments.

"Better than the sort of orgasms you get in Katherine's private room?"

"Way better."

"Can we call her up now and ask if she heard you scream? As messed up as it is, I'd like Katherine to know what I can do to you."

Alex chuckled. "Go right ahead."

Emily went back to playing with Alex's hair. "And I thought I was loud. When you came inside me like that…mmm. So hot."

"What's hotter is that you're letting me stay right here. Inside you." Alex breathed out. "I like this part the best."

"My first impression of you did not include that you'd be a snuggler."

"Yes, but you also thought I was a cocky player."

"Are you saying I'm a bad judge of character?" Emily arched an eyebrow.

"Maybe."

"Well, I like being wrong about the snuggling even more than those other things." She hugged Alex tighter against her. "This I could get used to."

Alex turned her head to the other side so Emily wouldn't see the emotion that rolled through her. Why couldn't Emily see that they had something worth taking a chance on? She clenched her teeth, wishing she could go back to the euphoria of only minutes ago.

She wondered what time it was. Hours must have passed since they'd made breakfast, and her stomach picked that moment to remind her about the uneaten French toast. As hungry as she'd thought she'd been, what she'd needed hadn't been food. She'd needed Emily.

And Emily had let her have her fill. Over and over. First against the door—they'd hardly made it up the stairs before Alex had needed to have her hands on Emily again. Then on the bathroom counter with Emily pressed against the mirror, on the rug next to the bed, and finally on the bed itself. That's where she'd lost control, climaxing so hard she collapsed, unable to think and hardly able to breathe. Only now was she coming down from that impossible high.

"Did I hurt you that last time? I kept telling myself to be careful with you and then..."

"And then you let go. I loved it. You make me feel so damn sexy. Like you can't get enough of me."

"There's a reason for that."

Emily shifted. "As much as I don't want you to, I need you to come out now."

Alex kissed Emily's neck, then her collarbone, then her breast as she slowly eased out. Once she was all the way out, she rolled onto her side and put her hand over Emily's center. "I want this to be mine all the time."

Emily laughed. "A little possessive, are you?"

Alex had intended the comment mostly as a joke and was glad Emily went along with it, but the truth in her words settled on the sheets between them. "I'm not usually possessive. Or jealous."

"But you were jealous thinking I was with Lara."

"And Katherine."

"I only wanted you that night." Emily curled on her side, facing Alex. "Katherine told me that you'd get tired of me before long. I hated her for saying it, but I think it's true. There's only so many places we can have sex in this cabin."

"But it's a big world."

"And you could show me it all, I'm sure." Emily caressed Alex's cheek. "I'd enjoy every minute. And then what?"

"I wouldn't get tired of you. Katherine's wrong about that. She doesn't actually know me that well, she only thinks she does. I want more than sex."

Emily ignored Alex's words and rolled on her back. "I don't know what I did to deserve today, to deserve you, but getting on that plane tomorrow is going to suck."

"Then don't get on. Stay here with me. Spend the week." Alex knew Emily wouldn't agree, but she had to ask. When the silence stretched, Alex had her answer. Even if expected, the letdown stung. "You hungry?"

"Starved."

Alex sat up and rubbed her face, scanning the room. She spotted the plates of French toast on the dresser. *Right. Breakfast.*

She took off the harness and tossed it on the nightstand, then climbed out of bed. Her legs were shaky, but her stomach drove every step. "I think I have orange juice in the fridge."

"Water's fine."

As Alex set the plates on the bed, Emily's brow furrowed. "What's wrong?"

"I'm not going to impress you with cold French toast. Could I make you dinner? I'd like to make something fancy for you."

"You can definitely make me dinner. But I plan on enjoying this French toast first." Alex forked a bite into her mouth and moaned. It was more room temperature than cold, and several hours old, but still by far the best French toast she'd ever had. She took another bite and moaned again. She'd played up the first moan, but there was no need pretending. "This is delicious. Seriously. You've ruined me for French toast now. I never want to eat anyone else's again. Only yours."

"Well, that's fair," Emily said. "You've ruined me for sex."

"Ruined, huh? That seems like a problem. I mean, avoiding French toast so you don't get disappointed is one thing—there's always pancakes—but avoiding sex?"

"Yeah, I'm sure one day I'll curse you. Maybe tomorrow. Not today. Today, I'm too drunk on you."

"Drunk?"

Emily nodded but didn't explain. She took a bite of the French toast and chewed. "You're right. This isn't bad. But I'm so hungry even raisins might taste good. You made me work up an appetite."

Alex tried to focus on the food, but her thoughts had circled back to Emily leaving. "Is there anything I could say to convince you to stay the rest of the week with me?"

Emily swallowed the bite she'd been chewing. She reached for the water glass on the nightstand and took a sip. "I don't get sick days, Alex. Or vacation days. When I don't work, I don't get paid. I explained things to the family I usually cook for on Mondays, and it was a holiday anyway, but my Tuesday and Wednesday clients aren't happy. I'll make it up to them, but I can't get any further behind."

"What if I came to you? I could be in San Francisco next weekend." A week seemed too long to wait, but it would be something. Some plan.

"I already agreed to help Gianna. She's got a catering business, too, and next weekend is a big gig for her." Emily pushed her empty plate aside and leaned back on the pillows. "We're scheduled for a wedding—rehearsal dinner on Saturday and banquet brunch on Sunday. I can't get out of it."

"Then in a couple weeks, maybe. You could come to Tokyo. I can show you around. It's a beautiful city. I can get your ticket, obviously. You'd only have to get the time off. Or we could meet up in Hawaii. My brother and I have a condo in Maui that we share."

"You don't get it. I'm broke. I can't take time off. And since there's no way I'm going back to work for Katherine, I need to make sure I keep my other clients happy. My job might not be as important as yours, but it's the one I've got."

"I never said your job wasn't important."

Emily waved off Alex's words and continued. "I've worked hard to get the reputation I have, and I don't want to screw it up. I can't flake on my clients, or on Gianna. I can't drop everything and fly around the world because I want to have sex."

Emily's tone carried a warning, but Alex pressed on anyway. "I could come to you. You wouldn't have to go anywhere. Tell me which weekend. I'll get us a place in the city."

"Alex, you're not hearing what I'm saying. Our lives are completely different, and you have no idea what mine's like. I don't have a condo in Maui or a cabin in Aspen. I'm living on my friend's couch because I have nowhere else to go.

"My world has been a total disaster for the past two months. When Cass froze all of our accounts, I literally showed up on Gianna's doorstep with a suitcase and nothing else. I'm barely keeping my head above water now. I can't drop everything because I met someone who knows how to fuck me into next Tuesday."

Alex felt the last sentence like a punch to the stomach. Was that all this was for Emily? Was it still only about sex? She picked up their plates and got out of bed. Emily didn't stop her when she left the room.

Downstairs, she pulled on a sweatshirt. The sun shone through the windows, but without a fire in the living room, the kitchen felt like an icebox. She started washing the dishes, avoiding any glances at the kitchen table. How long would it take before she could sit down to eat without thinking of Emily spread across it?

"Here." Emily held out her hand. "I'll dry."

"You don't have to."

"I know I don't have to. I also don't have to say sorry, but I am. And I want to say it. Now give me the bowl."

Alex passed the dripping mixing bowl to her. "I'm sorry too."

Emily tilted her chin. "I didn't actually say sorry yet. Just that I wanted to say it."

Alex chuckled. "Fine. Should I take back my apology then?"

"No." Emily's look was clearly apologetic. "I'm a little bit of a mess at the moment." She finished drying the bowl and reached for the coffee mug Alex had finished rinsing.

Alex held it up out of her reach. "Around here, if you want something, you gotta go for it."

"So I've noticed." Emily's smile barely lifted the corners of her mouth. After a moment, she dropped her hand. "I keep screwing things up with us. Your offer to come to San Francisco was sweet, and so was flying me to Tokyo or Maui. I should have said that instead of starting a fight. But this is all a lot."

"I know."

"Now things are going to be awkward all over again, aren't they? Like Sunday. I'm sorry."

"You don't need to apologize. I keep pushing even when you show me where your line is." Alex passed the mug to Emily finally. "So what happens next?"

Emily lifted a shoulder. "I was thinking maybe we could go for a walk? Then you could build another fire and make us some hot cocoa. I'm still scheming what I'm going to make you for dinner."

"I meant, what happens when you go back home? What happens with us?" Alex finished cleaning the last pan and passed it to Emily to dry. "You really don't have to make dinner. We could order delivery."

"I want to cook for you."

"Naked?"

Emily smiled. "How big a fire are you gonna build?"

"I can promise to make it hot as a sauna in here."

Emily leaned over the pan and kissed Alex's cheek. She went back to drying the pan, but after a moment, her hand stilled. When she spoke again, the light tone was gone from her voice. "I haven't been able to tell you exactly why it can't work with us because I hadn't really put my finger on it until just now. Honestly, I kept wishing there was a way. And going back and forth in my mind between thinking it would work and knowing it wouldn't."

"I don't know if I want to hear this."

"Yeah, well, you don't have a choice. You fell for someone who wants to be a good communicator." Emily winked. She set the pan on the counter and then took a deep breath. "I don't have my own pans, Alex."

"Not sure I'm following."

"I'm a chef and I don't have my own pans. After I moved out, Cass took a bunch of my stuff and put it in storage. Storage that I can't get to. It's not really a big deal because I cook in other people's kitchens, and Gianna and I share things when one of us has a big job to cater."

"So you need pans? And pots, I'm assuming, too."

Emily touched Alex's arm—a light touch but it sent a thrill through Alex all the same. "Stop those wheels from turning right now. I don't need you to buy me anything, and you better promise not to."

"But I could."

"I know, and pots and pans aren't my point." Emily didn't move her hand from Alex's forearm. "I need to be on my own two feet before I can be in a relationship with anyone. Especially you."

"Why especially me?"

"Because you'd be happy to take care of me, and I know you could, but that's not what I want from you. We wouldn't last that way, and we'd both get hurt in the end."

Alex couldn't argue with anything Emily had said. She took a deep breath and let it out slowly. "I'm gonna wait for you. And don't tell me not to because I won't listen anyway. I know you'll be on your own two feet in no time." She reached for the pan Emily had set on the counter. "Until then, early Christmas present?"

Emily swatted at her shoulder. "You're a punk."

Alex smiled, but her chest ached when Emily smiled right back at her. There was nothing she could fix, nothing she could do to help, and no way she could fight to make Emily change her mind. All she could do was make the most of the rest of the time they had together. "We don't have much daylight left. We better head out soon if we want that walk."

CHAPTER THIRTY-SEVEN

Emily had never wanted to miss a flight as much as she did now. The long weekend had turned into five amazing days—only one of which she wished she could get a redo on. But in less than one hour she'd be headed back to California. Colorado had been almost too good to be true. Even the snow didn't seem so bad when she was wrapped up in Alex's jacket. Or in her bed.

"You can drop me off at the curb."

Alex cocked her head. "Do you actually think I'd do that? After everything?"

"Well, no."

Alex pulled the rental SUV into a parking place and turned off the ignition. She went around to the back and grabbed Emily's bag. Emily took one last look around, making sure she wasn't leaving anything behind. She had a moment of déjà vu and thought of the last time Alex had dropped her off at the airport. How different she felt now...

After a moment's hesitation, she picked up Alex's phone still plugged into the car's USB port. She quickly set the next song to be played and then hopped out.

Alex was waiting for her. She caught Emily's hand and gave it a squeeze, then started across the parking lot. Emily's heart suddenly felt heavy in her chest. She didn't want to say goodbye. Neither spoke as they crossed the line of cars waiting to pick up passengers, and Alex didn't suggest they say goodbye there.

Travelers and a few airport workers hurried past them as the glass doors slid open. Emily didn't want to hurry even though she knew they'd pushed it timewise. She hadn't wanted to get out of Alex's warm bed that morning and had snoozed the alarm twice before accepting reality.

She made her way over to the check-in counter, and Alex didn't leave her side when she stepped in the short line to drop off her luggage. Since she couldn't bring herself to say goodbye there either, she didn't try. Once her luggage was tagged, the finality of her return to SFO stared at her in black-and-white bold type. But still she didn't let go of Alex's hand as she headed for security.

"I don't want you to wait for me to be ready for you," Emily said quietly. There were only half a dozen people ahead of her, and she knew she couldn't wait any longer to say the truth. "I have no idea how long it will take."

Alex didn't say anything, but her grip tightened.

"It was only supposed to be a long weekend, but it was so much more." In so many ways. Emily wondered how much of it Alex would remember. Which part was her favorite? She stopped herself from asking.

"I know you don't want to have this conversation, but I'm serious, Alex. Waiting's a mistake. I like you a lot, but I don't want you to put anything on pause because of me." The line inched forward. Only three people were now between them and the uniformed TSA agent. "If someone else comes along who you like—"

"I don't want anyone else. And I want to respect what you're saying, but I can't not wait for you."

"What if it's two years, Alex? You can't put your life on hold for that long." When Alex only shook her head, Emily pressed on. "We might be amazing in Aspen when we're both on vacation, but how long would we last in the real world? It doesn't make sense to put your life on hold for an unknown."

"We're not an unknown. And do you honestly think I wouldn't put in the work to make us last?"

Emily opened her mouth to argue that wasn't what she meant, but one look at the sincerity in Alex's eyes and she couldn't manage even breathing.

"I'm not going to let you slip through my fingers, Emily. You're the best thing that's come along in my life in I don't know how long. I'm going to wait as long as you need."

The TSA agent cleared her throat. "Ticket and identification please?"

Emily took a shaky breath. She reached into her purse, fumbling for her wallet. "Usually I'm more organized. I'm sorry." Once she'd handed the agent her license and the ticket printout, she turned to Alex. "I don't want to say goodbye."

"This isn't goodbye."

Alex wrapped her arms around Emily. The embrace was quick, almost as if Alex couldn't handle too long of a goodbye either. They'd had their goodbye kiss in bed that morning anyway. When Alex let go, she brushed her lips against Emily's cheek. "I can text you, right? That's not part of giving you space to get on your own two feet, is it?"

"I'd love to get texts from you."

"Good. I'm going to text you all sorts of inappropriate things."

Emily laughed. "You wouldn't."

"Oh, I would." Alex stepped back. "I'll see you when you've got your own pots and pans. In San Francisco maybe."

"There'll be less snow," Emily said. She took her ticket and license back from the agent and Alex stepped to the side. "If you change your mind on the waiting for me thing, it's okay. I'll understand."

"I'm not changing my mind." Alex raised her hand.

Tears brimmed in Emily's eyes. She returned the wave and then quickly stepped into the queue to have her carry-on scanned. When she looked back at the TSA agent's counter, Alex was gone.

* * *

Alex turned on the car and then turned it off again. She stared at the handful of planes waiting on the tarmac and wondered which one Emily would board. If only there was one more seat on the plane... She knew she needed to let Emily go—at least for now—but all the unknowns and the what-ifs made her question if they truly had a chance.

The pen was still in her pocket. She took it out and read the imprint, thanking her former self for being ballsy enough to steal it. But all she had from the past five days was a damn pen. She hadn't thought to take any pictures, though Emily had snapped some on their walk through downtown. Alex smiled, remembering how Emily had said that the town might actually be pretty without all the snow. She'd been joking at the time, taking picture after picture and oohing and ahhing about the snow-covered mountains with the crystal-blue sky above and the foreground of pines. The scene had been gorgeous, enough to make Alex's chest ache. But it was Emily she'd been staring at the entire time.

She took a deep breath and reached for her phone. It might be ridiculous to text Emily now, but she didn't care.

Alex: *Want to come back when there's no snow?*

Emily: *Yes. And you're silly for texting me twenty minutes after saying goodbye.*

Alex: *We didn't say goodbye. Miss you already.*

Emily: *Check your phone. What's the next song up?*

Alex squinted at Emily's text, wondering what she could possibly mean. She hit the button to bring up her music and laughed out loud when she saw the song waiting to be played. Bob Dylan: "Lay, Lady, Lay."

Alex sent a laughing emoji, followed by: *Didn't even know I had any Dylan on my phone.*

Emily: *Turns out you have better taste than you realize. Play it. I'm going to play it too and pretend I'm still in your arms.*

Alex clenched her jaw to stop a rush of emotion. She leaned back in the seat and hit the Play button. Dylan's voice rolled through the car. When she closed her eyes, she saw Emily sitting on the rug in front of the fire with the old albums scattered all around her.

When the song ended, her phone buzzed with a new text. Emily: *Thank you. For everything.*

Alex: *That sounded kind of final. Did you mean it to be?*

Emily: *No, but I'm boarding. You can keep texting me if you want. I'm going to be sad when I land and I'll need something to make me feel better.*

CHAPTER THIRTY-EIGHT

Four months later...

The buzzer rang, and Emily dropped her phone on the coffee table. She went to open the door, scooting between boxes and the furniture she had yet to find a place for.

"You know, they got apartments on the first floor too." Gianna huffed as she walked into the apartment. "But you gotta go all the way up to the third floor."

"Bet the first floor doesn't have a killer view of the dumpsters like I do." Emily gave Gianna a hug. "Missed you."

"It's been three days since you moved out. You couldn't have missed me that much."

"It's boring watching Netflix without someone who throws popcorn at the screen."

"I should add that to my profile. Wonder if I'd get any hot dates." Gianna dropped her purse in the midst of the chaos of moving boxes and then plunked down on one of said boxes, fanning herself as she caught her breath. "So. When they putting in the elevator?"

"Right after they add a parking garage." Meaning never. "Did you have any trouble finding a spot?"

"You know I got the parking gods on my side." Once she'd caught her breath, Gianna straightened up and flashed a wide smile. "All right. I'm ready for the tour."

"You don't have to go far. In fact, you can see it all from here. This of course is the foyer, or if you prefer, the front room. It also doubles as the living room, family room, and dining room."

"Convenient." Gianna nodded her head as she scanned the small space. "What's next?"

"Next, we move on to the kitchen." Emily pointed to the other side of the room where a counter divided the carpeted space from linoleum and a hallway kitchen. "The best part is that if I had to play 'floor is lava,' I'm pretty sure I could jump from the kitchen counter onto the sofa and in one more leap, be on my bed."

"You never know when you'll need to leap into bed," Gianna said.

"Did I mention that the bathroom doubles as a closet?"

"Tiny houses are all the rage. And it's gonna be easy to clean."

Plus, it was all her space. Small, and probably temporary, but a landing pad that was all hers. Gianna walked from the living room to the kitchen and then to the bedroom, making little *mm-hmm* sounds the way she always did. After she'd poked her head in the bedroom, she circled back to the living room.

"It might look a little bigger without all the boxes. I mean, not much bigger, but..." Emily glanced again at the pile littering the front room. "I like it."

"And it's a step up from my saggy couch for sure."

"You know how much I love your couch." It was nice to have a bed, however, and her own room. "And you took me in when I had nothing." At least now with the divorce settled, she had her things out of storage—including all her pots and pans. She'd sent a picture to Alex when she'd unpacked that particular box. "I owe you so much, Gianna. I don't think I'd be where I am today without you. And six months was longer than either of us planned."

"Stop before I start crying. You know you'd have done the same for me," Gianna cleared her throat. "So. How's it feel to be finally living in your own space?"

"A little lonely, but I'll get used to it. Kind of ridiculous that at thirty-three I've never lived by myself." The first night had been nice. The next she'd been lonely and stayed up late chatting with Alex, who was still in Tokyo. The third night was the worst. Alex had to cancel their usual video chat date, and for the first time since leaving Aspen, she'd gone to sleep without their saying goodnight. Realizing how attached she'd gotten, she'd spent the morning trying to talk herself down from a freak-out about the whole thing.

But what she couldn't ignore was that she felt closer to Alex than she'd ever felt to Cass. Four months of talking nearly every night went a long way toward knowing someone—and officially falling for them. More than that, the closer she'd gotten to Alex, the more she felt herself growing into her own, as if opening up to someone else had allowed her to get to know herself again.

Probably guessing the direction of her thoughts, Gianna said, "You won't be lonely for long. You'll have Alex soon. One more week before Aspen, right?"

"Yep." Although a week seemed too long to wait. "Do you think it's a problem that I talk to her every day?"

"Why would it be?"

"I don't know. I keep thinking maybe I let myself get in too deep."

"You're worried you love her?"

Emily sighed. "I'm not worried. I know it. And she's…well… her."

"Your gorgeous fantasy woman who everyone else drools over but who's only in love with you?" Gianna paused long enough to make her point clear. "Poor you."

Emily laughed. "Thanks, Gi. But I don't know if she is in love with me. She hasn't said it, anyway. And maybe it's too soon for me to be in love again. How do you know for sure if something isn't a rebound?"

"Are you serious right now? I've seen the two of you on those video chats. You're both in love. Now stop worrying and be happy. Those of us who aren't in love are about to lose our patience with you."

Emily wanted to believe that Gianna was right. In her heart she thought she was, but they hadn't said the love word yet. Twice Alex had slipped up and nearly said it, then covered with "I love-like you, goodnight," to which Emily could only laugh because it was dorky enough that she could imagine Alex saying it on purpose. They both seemed to be waiting for the right moment, but until she heard Alex say the words, she wasn't certain.

"You're going to have so much fun in Aspen," Gianna said.

"I hope so."

Alex had invited Emily to Aspen, insisting she ought to see the place in the summer before completely discounting the town. Emily didn't admit that since she'd fallen in love in Aspen, it would forever have a place in her heart, snow or no snow. She'd fretted about taking time off, but after going four months without Alex she needed to see her. Needed to wrap her arms around her. And she most definitely needed to kiss her.

"What if she gets tired of me?"

"Stop." Gianna gave Emily her I-mean-business look and then added, "I've heard her say goodnight to you. She's in deep. And after four months she's still texting you how many times a day?"

Emily's phone beeped with a text and they both laughed.

"Five bucks says that's her."

Emily went over to the counter where she'd left her phone and flipped it face up. "I owe you five bucks." She cleared her throat and read: "*Don't think I can wait a whole week to see you.*"

"Mm-hmm."

Emily smiled. Her chest felt tight. Alex didn't need to say the words. She knew the truth. She also knew Alex wasn't a rebound. Alex was more real than anything she'd ever had.

"As much as I want to see her, it's going to be even harder coming home alone this time. I won't have her, and I won't have your shoulder to cry on about it. I'll have an empty apartment."

"You make the popcorn and I'll be here."

"Thanks, Gi." Emily sniffed. She straightened up. "Okay, I'm not letting myself get all sad and mushy before I even get to Aspen." She sent a quick note back to Alex with a sad emoji and then a promise to make the wait worth it. Turning back to Gianna, she said, "Let's talk about tonight and your hot date. Where are we meeting Lara?"

"Miss Chavelle's. She said she liked Caribbean food." Gianna shook her head. "Still can't believe you talked me into doing this. I'm too old for blind dates."

"You're thirty-three. That's not too old for anything. And you and Lara are going to hit it off. I'm sure of it. Even Alex agrees."

In fact, Alex was the one to suggest it. They'd apparently repaired their friendship over the past several months, and Lara had even visited Alex in Tokyo. She was still sober and working through all of that, but Alex felt confident she was in a good place—which was enough recommendation for Emily.

"Besides, she's gorgeous. And I've heard from Nicola that she's very good in bed. So even if it's only for a night, it'll be a good one."

"Only you would include references about her abilities in bed." Gianna rolled her eyes. "I guess if I don't get to go to a sex party myself, the next best thing is a graduate of the program."

Emily laughed. "I love you, Gi. Have I told you that lately?"

"But what if there's no chemistry?"

"Then we'll all hang out and have dinner and that'll be the end of it." Emily doubted that would happen. Regardless, she was excited to see Lara again. Lara felt like a link to Alex and a reminder of the good parts of the sex party. And it was because of Lara that she'd gone to Alex's house after the tequila incident. If they hadn't reconnected then, they might never have resolved all the misunderstandings. "I won't leave unless I can tell you're ready to jump her bones."

"Stop waggling your eyebrows at me," Gianna said, her eyebrows dancing in return. "Okay, tell me everything you know about her again."

* * *

"Why are you smiling like that?"

Alex held up her phone. "Emily sent me a picture of her new place."

Lara squinted at the screen. "Is that her bathroom?"

"Well, yeah, but look." Alex pointed to the snapshot of Aspen stuck on the bottom corner of the bathroom mirror.

Lara shook her head. "I can't believe it. You found someone as cheesy as you."

"Being sentimental isn't a bad thing."

"You still carrying around her pen?"

Alex reached into her pocket and whipped it out. "Gonna tease me for it? Go ahead."

Lara laughed. "No way, man. You're the one with the girlfriend."

"I don't know if we're technically there yet."

"Whatever. You two text nonstop. The only reason you haven't asked her to marry you is because you've been stuck in Tokyo."

Alex started to argue, but Lara shot her a look that made her realize there was no point trying to hide anything. "I keep wanting to say 'I love you' but I want to do it in person the first time. And maybe it's too soon? It's only been four months."

Lara dropped onto the couch next to Alex. "Okay, first things first. You need to tell her about the interview."

Alex set her phone down. "I've never been so nervous about an interview in my life."

"Because this is about more than a job. It's a big step."

"I know, and I'm not completely qualified to—"

"Bullshit. You're plenty qualified. When I was helping you with that cover letter, more than once I had to stop myself from feeling jealous about all the damn things you've done."

"Whatever. You're a lawyer."

"As of last week." Lara exhaled. "I still have trouble thinking of myself as anything more than a bartender who can't handle her booze."

"But you are more now. A lot more." Not only had Lara finished law school, she'd passed the bar exam and gotten a good job. Her life had completely turned around from even a year ago, and Alex was proud of her for how hard she'd worked. The one piece of advice that Katherine had given her about giving Lara a second chance had paid off. "You're a different person now that you don't drink. I actually like you."

"Well, you're still an asshole and way too good-looking, but I like you too." Lara laughed. "I'm serious about the job interview. You're completely qualified. But if they don't want you, someone else will. You know that. The big step is you moving here for Emily."

Alex breathed out. Her stomach had been a hard knot since she'd gotten off the plane that morning and it had nothing to do with the long flight. Even though she talked to Emily all the time, she wasn't certain that Emily was ready for more. And she'd made a promise not to push her. Moving to San Francisco might feel like a push, but Alex couldn't handle staying away any longer.

Despite sharing everything from mundane snags she ran into on her job to what she thought of when she slipped her hand between her legs at night, she'd stopped short of telling Emily about tomorrow's interview. She also hadn't said that instead of a video chat tonight, they'd be seeing each other in person.

When she'd planned it all out, she'd been certain the surprise was a good idea. At first it was only about setting Lara up with Gianna, but then the interview came up and the timing worked. She managed to get in touch with Gianna privately and ran everything past her first. Instead of a blind date with Lara and Gianna alone, Alex had suggested that Emily go—to make it feel more casual. Emily had been game to see Lara again and had quickly agreed, wanting to ease the awkwardness of a blind date. Hopefully, she'd also be happy that Lara wasn't going to be alone.

"What if she doesn't want to see me?"

Lara's eyebrows bunched together. "Seriously?"

"Well, she told me she needed time, and maybe this is going to feel like I'm pressuring her. Moving here and everything. Dammit, I should have asked her first."

"You haven't moved here officially yet. I'm not going to argue that you need to talk to her, but maybe nothing needs to change in your relationship. At this point, she's basically your online girlfriend, right? All this means is that instead of being twenty-four hours away, you'll be in the same state. You can date in person. It's not like you're TJ showing up in London unannounced asking Nicola to marry her."

"Yeah, but they were dating for years." One month after Aspen, TJ had flown to London. Alex never thought it would be possible, but TJ had convinced her dad to move. She'd changed jobs, moved in with Nicola, and set her dad up in a flat next door. So far, it was working. "Emily and I haven't even agreed to the girlfriend thing—"

Lara held up her hand. "I get it. We won't use the girlfriend word. You're kinky online friends who show each other their titties, probably with clamps on them."

Alex bust up laughing. Lara knew her too well.

"Do you honestly think she isn't going to be over the moon to see you?"

"I don't know." Even yesterday, Alex had been convinced that Emily would be happy to see her, but now she was too nervous to think straight. She wanted Emily more than she'd ever wanted anyone. It wasn't only how amazing the sex had been in Aspen. It was everything that had happened in between. All the conversations that neither had wanted to end. All the little things they had in common. Even longing for kids and wanting a family. "I really hope she's happy to see me, but…what if she isn't? What if I think this is a whole lot more important of a relationship than she does?"

"That's why love bites. There's no way to know."

"You kind of suck at relationship advice."

Lara nodded. "I totally do. Which is why I'm single at thirty-seven and going on my first blind date."

"You're gonna rock this blind date." Lara didn't seem completely sure and Alex knew she needed more to convince her.

"Think about it. You're a lawyer, you're good-looking, you're a smart-ass—I mean funny—and you genuinely care about the people you love. You're gonna knock Gianna's socks off."

"This is my first real, sober date."

"Oh."

"Yeah." Lara exhaled. "I kind of stopped dating after I stopped drinking. Aside from Katherine's parties and random hookups, I couldn't do it. I tried a couple times, but turns out I'm not as brave when I'm not drinking. If it's only sex, I'm good to go. But talking to a woman and trying to make a real connection?"

"You can do this," Alex said. "I know you can."

"I still can't believe I let you talk me into a blind date."

"You're gonna be fine. Turn on your charm. You still got it, even if you're old enough to be going gray."

Lara jabbed Alex's arm and then furrowed her brow. "Can you see gray hairs on my head?"

"No, I was teasing you, goofball. Besides, you bleach your damn hair. And we're not that old."

"We? You're thirty-nine. I'm not *that* old."

Alex shook her head. "I swear, sometimes you're like the little sister I never wanted."

"Do you mean it?"

Lara's question was endearing. Even if mostly sarcasm, Alex knew there was a hint of truth to it. "Actually, I do." Neither had said as much aloud, but there was no doubt rekindling their friendship had been good for both of them.

Alex gave Lara a halfhearted sideways shove, and Lara laughed as she almost lost her balance. She looked back at Alex, still grinning, and stuck up her middle finger.

"Gianna's gonna love you," Alex said. "Emily keeps saying how you two would be perfect together. She's good at reading people."

"Then why'd she pick you?" Lara winked.

Definitely more like an annoying little sister. "Remind me again why we're friends?"

"'Cause TJ moved to London and no one else will put up with either of us."

"Oh. Right." Alex wished TJ was still in California and the three of them could all hang out like old times. "I miss TJ."

"Me too. I miss Katherine's sex parties too."

"I don't." It was the truth. As fun as it had been, and while she missed friends, Alex didn't long for the rest of what came with Katherine's parties. Besides, nearly all of the old crew—Lara, TJ, Nicola, and Alex—had decided to stop going. Katherine would find a new group. Or not. Alex didn't care anymore. "I also don't miss Katherine."

"We could have our own parties someday," Lara continued. "I bet Emily would be into it. We could convince TJ and Nicola to come to San Francisco…"

"I'm not saying no to a sex party, but you're gonna have to give me some time. Right now I don't want to think about sharing Emily. I want her all to myself for a while. If she'll have me."

"If she'll have you? Damn, you really are in love."

"Hopelessly." Alex wasn't even going to pretend it wasn't the truth. "Maybe Gianna will be exactly who you were meant to find. Maybe it'll be fate, just like with me and Emily."

"You realize that wasn't fate who put you two on the airplane together, right? That was Katherine. By the way, how many more of these cheesy lines do you have up your sleeve?"

"Lots. And Katherine may have set up the flight, but she didn't make a snowstorm." Or anything that happened after.

CHAPTER THIRTY-NINE

"You sure you want to bring that whole bag of ramen?" Lara kept eyeing the brown grocery bag full of packaged noodles like she was uncomfortable walking next to it.

"I'm telling you, Emily's gonna love it." Alex hefted the bag higher. "It's a long story."

"It might be a long story, but it's also weird."

Admittedly, Alex had stressed about the decision of what to bring Emily. She'd thought of jewelry or simply flowers, but that seemed too cliché. A practical housewarming present didn't feel right either. "I'm weird. Is bringing a girl ramen weirder than any of my other crazy ideas?"

Lara chuckled. "Actually, no."

"Besides, this isn't just any packaged ramen. It's the world's best ramen. I made it for Emily when she was sick, and she loved it." Alex took a deep breath. The sign for the restaurant had come into view and with it a nervous excitement. "I know you're the one going on a blind date but, man, my hands are sweating."

"You're bringing your girlfriend, who you haven't seen in four months, a bag of ramen. I'd be nervous too. We're a few minutes early. Maybe we could swing into that corner shop and you could throw in a pack of gum."

Alex laughed. "You're an asshole."

Lara eyed the bag again and shook her head. "I got an idea. What if you slip a ring in that bag?"

"I'm working up the courage to ask how she feels about me moving to the same damn state. She's not ready for a ring."

"But you are."

Alex didn't answer. She'd been ready to jump in with both feet months ago. Getting to know Emily better had only made her more certain of everything. Her fingers were crossed that Emily wouldn't pull back now.

"Where are you going to put that bag when we get to the restaurant?"

"This ramen is really bothering you, isn't it?"

"Think about it for a minute. We're going out to eat with a grocery bag full of ramen. And Emily's a chef. You think she wants your packaged ramen?"

Alex stopped walking. "Okay, listen, the bag's not completely full of ramen."

"What else is in there?"

"Rope."

Lara's confused look turned to a knowing smile. "*Oh*. She wants to be tied up."

"Close, but not exactly. She said she's always had a fantasy of tying someone up. And having her way with them."

Lara's mouth opened as she put two and two together. "Damn. You're braver than I thought. Ever been tied up before?"

"One time, but I got out of the knots. This time I'm not going to try. Gonna let it happen. Let her do what she wants."

"No wonder you're nervous about this." Lara slapped Alex's shoulder and laughed.

"Mostly I'm excited."

"All right. I take back everything I said about your ramen. You're one crazy dude, you know that?" Lara stopped talking and leaned to the right, squinting at someone across the street. "Is that Emily over there?"

Alex followed Lara's gaze. She spotted Emily standing on the opposite side of the street, waiting to cross at the light. In a yellow sundress with her long brown hair pulled back, she was so beautiful Alex didn't have words. Her heart settled in her throat and she wondered again if surprising her was a good idea. Emily was talking to her friend and not looking their direction.

"That is her, isn't it?" Lara asked again.

Alex managed a nod.

"Then that must be Gianna. She's hot. Like, really hot." Lara caught Alex's arm. "How do I look?"

"Like you're ready for a hot date." Alex looked down at the grocery bag in her arms. "Maybe I shouldn't have brought ramen."

* * *

"Remind me again how I let you talk me into a blind date?"

"You're gonna love Lara. Promise." Even if seeing Lara again brought back memories of Aspen and made her miss Alex more, it'd be worth it. Getting Gianna a date was the least she could do.

The light changed, and Gianna looked like she was having second thoughts. Emily caught her hand and pulled her into the intersection. "If you aren't into Lara, we'll stuff ourselves with jerk shrimp and fried plantains. My treat. Either way, it's a win."

They crossed the street and joined a short line that had formed outside the restaurant. Emily turned back to Gianna. "Maybe we should get some of those Creole doughnuts too. I'm so hungry. Smelling all these yummy spices makes me want to eat someone."

Gianna held up a finger, making an *O* shape with her mouth. "What?"

"Behind you."

Emily turned around. Her heart skipped a beat. It couldn't be. *Alex.*

"Hi. I, uh, was in the neighborhood and—"

Emily leapt off the ground. Alex caught her, laughing, and spun in a circle before setting her feet down. Emily ignored the press of tears. She didn't care if they fell or not. Alex was here.

"So, it's okay that I'm here?" Alex said.

"Yes." Emily met Alex's lips for a long kiss. God, she'd missed her. She didn't want the kiss to end, but then Gianna—or maybe it was Lara—cleared her throat and Alex pulled back. She didn't loosen her hold on Emily, though, and her face broke in a wide smile.

"Hi," Alex said again.

"Hi."

"I was nervous that maybe you wouldn't be happy that I'd show up without warning—"

Emily pressed her finger to Alex's lips. "I am completely going to make you pay for this stunt. All night long."

"All night, huh?"

"Unless you had other plans."

"You are my plans," Alex said. "And you know it."

Emily did. She didn't know how she could be so sure of something that felt too good to be true, but there was no doubt in her mind. "I love that you came a week early to hang out with me, but I am going to have to work some of that time."

"I kind of have this work thing too…"

"What do you mean? I thought all of your clients were in Asia."

"This would be a different work thing." Alex took a deep breath. "Tonight, my only plans are you. Tomorrow, I have a job interview for a company based in San Francisco."

Emily's mouth fell open. "You're thinking of moving here?"

"If I get the job, commuting from Tokyo would be a huge pain in the ass, so, yeah." Alex's smile seemed tentative. "Nothing's for sure yet, and I wouldn't take the job if you didn't think me moving here was a good idea, but it's a great company and I'm ready to move up. I'd get my own place, of course, and even if it doesn't work out with us I won't regret moving here. I want the job and—"

"Stop talking." Emily leaned close and whispered, "No pressure, but you better nail that fucking interview."

Alex laughed. "I like a little pressure."

"Good. Because I can't wait for you to move here." Emily wanted to jump into Alex's arms again and give her an even bigger kiss. She wanted more than kissing, so much more, but they could take their time now. Soon they'd have all the time in the world. "I want to hear about the job. And all of your plans. But first, I'm hungry."

"Can I buy you dinner?" Alex asked.

"You may."

Alex bumped against Emily's hip and grinned. "It's going to be hard to eat when all I want is you."

"Hmm. You'll work it out I'm sure." Emily kissed Alex— only a quick peck this time, but she hoped Alex knew it carried a promise for more to come. She suddenly remembered Gianna and Lara and felt a pang of guilt for ignoring them. When she looked at Gianna, however, she got a reassuring wink.

Lara and Gianna were introducing themselves and laughing as if they already had some private joke going. Emily looked at Alex again and then at the line of people around them. None of it felt real. She was so happy she was floating, and everyone seemed to be smiling at her as if they knew it. Of course, they'd all seen her jump Alex, and they'd seen the kiss.

"I can't believe you're here," Emily said, touching Alex's arm and shifting closer. She wanted to rub her hands up and down Alex's body to convince her own body that she was real. As much as she'd loved their nightly chats and all that they did besides talk, she wanted more. Much more. And now, Alex was here.

A grocery bag heaped with packaged ramen caught her eye. "Is that your bag?"

Alex looked down at her feet. "Oh. Yeah. That's for you." She picked up the bag and handed it to Emily with a sheepish smile. "It's a little silly."

"You brought me a whole bag of the world's best ramen? That's not silly. That's amazing." Emily's mind jumped to what she'd pair with Alex's ramen. There'd be time for meal planning later, of course, but she was already looking forward to it. And to cooking with Alex. "You're the best."

"There's another surprise under all the noodles. Something you might like even more."

Emily had no idea what it could be, but the look on Alex's face made her think it would be best opened later. "Maybe I'll save that surprise for when we're alone?"

"Probably a good idea. Does that mean you're taking me home?"

"I might take you home and keep you."

"I'd like that." Alex smiled. "But first I have to tell you something."

Emily waited, suddenly nervous.

"I know we haven't gone on an official date yet or anything, and I know I promised I wouldn't pressure you, so please don't feel like you have to respond. It's okay if you're not ready. But I have to tell you because I can't keep it inside any—"

"I love you," Emily said. The words sprang to her lips and she couldn't hold them back. "I think maybe you were getting to that part, but I couldn't wait."

Alex laughed. "I was getting to it, but clearly I was taking too damn long."

"It's okay. You're fast at other things."

"I love you too," Alex said. "It's not too soon to say it?"

"Not too soon." Emily smiled.

"Then I'm gonna say it again. I love you. So damn much."

Emily didn't think she'd stop smiling for the rest of the night. "You know how I said you weren't good for me? I was wrong."

"It's okay. I knew it all along."

"And you were right." Emily caught the front of Alex's shirt and pulled her close again for one more kiss. "That smug look on your face is driving me crazy. I might have to take you home right now."

"And tie me up?"

Emily opened her mouth and then glanced down at the bag. "Tell me that's my surprise."

"Maybe we should order our food to go and you can find out."

"Yes, please." When Alex reached for her hand, Emily entwined their fingers. She didn't ever want to let go.

Bella Books, Inc.

Women. Books. Even Better Together.

P.O. Box 10543
Tallahassee, FL 32302

Phone: 800-729-4992
www.bellabooks.com

Printed in the USA
CPSIA information can be obtained
at www.ICGtesting.com
LVHW090355200824
788694LV00004B/63